When the Roses Bloom

Joanne R. Roche

Riverhaven Books

www.RiverhavenBooks.com

When the Roses Bloom is a work of fiction. While some of the settings are actual, any similarity regarding names, characters, or incidents is entirely coincidental.

Published in the United States by Riverhaven Books,
www.RiverhavenBooks.com

ISBN : 978-1-937588-55-7

Printed in the United States of America

Ellen Goldsberry, Developmental Editor
Cover artwork by John Mulcahy
Designed by Stephanie Lynn Blackman
Whitman, MA

"So whatever you do, do all for the glory of God"
1 Corinthians 10:31

Part I

Chapter One

September, 1945

Screech! Screech!

The wheels of the trolley pitched forward with painstaking motion. The conductor poked his head out the window, looked around, and waved heartily at Elizabeth. Wind tugged at her skirt and pulled at the collar of her jacket, loosening tendrils of hair from the neat bun arranged in the back of her head. There was no time to stop and fix it, however, or she would miss the trolley.

"Evenin', Elizabeth," the conductor hailed her, as she reached the train's platform. "Didn't know if you were gonna make it or not."

"I wasn't too sure myself, Harry," she called back as she struggled to catch her breath.

She climbed the steps of the streetcar and pulled herself up.

"Tell your grandfather I'll pick the two of you up in an hour."

Harry Snyder and her grandfather, John Burke, had met almost half a century ago, part of the wave of Irish immigrants that had come to the Boston area in search of housing, jobs, and food. They had moved into the same neighborhood within months of each other and had been the best of friends ever since.

"I will. Thanks." She tossed a smile over her shoulder as she jostled her way into the car. She grabbed onto the nearest rung and held on tightly as the door squeezed shut and the trolley rolled forward then backward before lurching onward towards its next stop.

The trolley was always crowded, especially on Friday afternoons. It was even more packed than usual today, the start of Labor Day weekend. Everyone, it seemed, was in a hurry to begin the holiday. The country was still jubilant about the end of WWII, and the mood of the commuters was lively. It had been a six-year war, whose victory was dampened by the fact that their beloved president and leader, Franklin Delano Roosevelt, had died only weeks before the war ended.

Elizabeth knew she'd have to hurry. After she met her grandfather at home, they'd be traveling up to York, Maine, a quaint seaside town nestled on the rocky shores of the Atlantic Ocean.

She always looked forward to visiting Grandpa's younger sister Mary, or Aunt May as she was affectionately called, but she was especially looking forward to seeing the Sullivan sisters who lived next door to her aunt. She had known the sisters since she was a young girl when she stayed with the Sullivan family days while Aunt May worked, and they were as close to her as if they were her own siblings. Mary Francis, at twenty-four, was a year older than Elizabeth, and Dolly was a year younger. While Mary Francis and Elizabeth often saw eye to eye on things, it was Dolly who loved to be contrary. Elizabeth loved her all the more for that.

While Dolly, dramatically, had declared that she was setting her sights on being a movie star, Mary Francis and Elizabeth shared the more traditional dream of being happily married with children. Elizabeth, though, wondered if that day would ever arrive, considering that the few boys she had gone out with held little appeal for her beyond the first date or two. For Mary Francis, though, things might be different. Apparently, since Elizabeth's last visit, one of Mary Francis's 'friends' had become a steady beau. Elizabeth couldn't wait to hear the details.

Elizabeth was lost in her thoughts when the trolley careened to a stop and the doors jerked open. She heard Harry call out, "Last stop, Lower Mills!"

Elizabeth followed the remaining passengers off and nodded to some familiar faces before hurrying down the street towards home. Elizabeth knew that Grandpa, consistently punctual, would be packed and ready to go the moment she walked in the door, and Harry, who would be driving them to Maine, would be, as he had indicated, there to pick them up in less than an hour.

She scanned the houses of her neighborhood. Dorchester, Lower Mills, had been home to Elizabeth Keene her entire life. It was a close-knit, thriving community of working-class immigrants situated in a corner of Boston near the banks of the Neponset River. She and her grandfather shared a handsome, although somewhat weather-beaten, six-bedroom colonial on busy Adams Street at the edge of the Boston-Milton line. John Burke would often comment on how providential it had been that he and his young wife, Rose, had bought such a large house in the fall of 1900, shortly after they arrived by boat from the shores of Ireland, for, in their wake, numerous relatives and friends had followed them, most with only the change in their pockets and gratitude for having survived the journey.

John and Rose began offering people a place to stay, and it became commonplace for their five extra bedrooms to be in a continual rotation of occupancy. Even the parlor couch often supported a friend, neighbor, or cousin, and the guests showed their gratitude in whatever way they could. A few gave money, but most, lacking cash, shared time and skills: the women cooked and did household chores and the men helped with whatever repair or maintenance work needed to be done.

As Elizabeth rounded the curve in the road, she saw the familiar iron fence that surrounded the small front yard, the roses gracing the doorway. As she hurried through the gate, her grandfather appeared.

He ambled over to greet her with a sound hug and a kiss.

"Well, if it tisn't the prettiest lass I ever did see this side of the Atlantic!" he exclaimed, with a hint of glee.

"Grandpa!" Elizabeth looked up lovingly at him as she giggled. "If I'm the prettiest lass this side of the Atlantic, what did you used to tell Grandma?"

"Why, that she was the prettiest lass on the other side of the Atlantic, of course! You can't have a whole ocean to yourself, you know."

Elizabeth shook her head and laughed. Grandpa was seventy years old, with an occasional fleck of black among his snow-white hair and beard. The deep blue of his eyes had faded somewhat, and he moved more slowly now than he had in earlier years, but his attitude was as upbeat and optimistic as ever.

~

Elizabeth hurried to collect her things and grab a bite to eat before Harry's arrival. At the last minute she remembered to run to the backyard to cut pink roses from the trellis that Grandpa had constructed years ago and which now boasted roses in a potpourri of colors. When her grandparents had settled in Boston, one of the first things her grandpa had done was to plant rosebushes in honor of his wife. Grandma Rose had established the tradition of collecting a bouquet of roses for special occasions and holidays. Elizabeth's mother, and now Elizabeth, kept up the custom. Today she was bringing a bouquet in honor of Aunt May's birthday that they would celebrate this weekend.

Harry drove up, honking his horn. They stowed their bags in the back and the three sat in front, Elizabeth in the middle. It was a rare treat for Elizabeth to travel by automobile, for cars were still scarce from the war effort. The only people who used them as a daily mode of transportation were the well-to-do, who could afford the expensive price tag and the cost of maintenance, or a lucky person who was able to find a cheap, used vehicle. Elizabeth knew that Harry had been fortunate to get a good deal from a friend who was in the car business, and he was more than generous when it came to offering rides.

It was after eight o'clock when Harry dropped them off on his way to his son's house in Kennebunkport, north of York. Aunt May was waiting for them in the gathering darkness, and she hugged and kissed them both when they reached the top of the steps.

Auntie May's home was intimately familiar to Elizabeth. From the time she was school age, Elizabeth had stayed with her grandfather's sister in the summer while Grandpa worked in Boston. Auntie May had been one of the first to follow John and Rose across the Atlantic to Dorchester and had stayed with her brother and sister-in-law for a few months when she had arrived in the States. Unlike her older brother, however, Mary Burke did not take to living in the city, and the coast of Maine attracted her because it reminded her of the rocky shores of Ireland. She had never married, but she had found employment in York as a maid at a rooming house; she saved enough money to buy her small home next to the Sullivans.

Elizabeth had enjoyed her summers with Auntie May almost as much as she treasured living with Grandpa. She had loved listening to the roar of the sea when she was in bed, the curtains gently billowing with the salty sea breeze. She thrilled to the refreshing chill of swimming in the cold Atlantic and lying lazily in the sand with the warm sun shining on her. Summers would have been perfect if Grandpa had been there as well, and Elizabeth often thought, with regret, that he was in Boston coming home to an empty house. She knew during that time that he missed her as much as she missed him.

"Land sakes!" Auntie May now exclaimed, giving Elizabeth an especially long hug. "What took so long? I was beginning to get worried!"

"Oh, you started worrying before we've even left," Grandpa scolded lightly. "If you came to Boston to live with us, then you wouldn't have to wonder where we are."

John Burke was always after his sister to come live with the two of them, just as May was always after the two of them to come live with her. Although each knew the other was happy and content right where they were, they never stopped trying to convince the other to move.

"Now, don't get me started on that just yet," May chided as her blue eyes twinkled impishly. "At least sit down and have some supper, and then you can continue."

To Elizabeth food always tasted better in Maine, and not just because Aunt May was known for her culinary skills, but because it was prepared by someone who was the closest thing to a mother she had ever known. There were cold chicken salad sandwiches, greens from Aunt May's garden, and her renowned lemon meringue pie for dessert. After finishing and washing the dishes, Aunt May asked if they wanted to walk next door to see the Sullivans. "I don't know who is home over there, but I saw Dolly take something off the clothesline a little while ago, and she's always lively company, Elizabeth."

"That's an understatement," Grandpa replied laughingly.

Dolly, or Dorothy Ann as she was officially called, was the third child in the Sullivan family. Dolly's grandiose visions of becoming a glamorous movie star or model were not completely unfounded, as she had long ringlets of hair that curled enticingly around her face when they managed to escape from the various bows and ribbons she applied, and her china blue eyes shone out from her soft, creamy skin. Like Mary Francis, she had a tall, slender frame, and when she moved or walked there was a grace and carriage about her that reminded one of a ballerina. Unlike her sister, though, there was not one coquettish smile or come-hither gaze in her eyes that had not been practiced a thousand times in front of the mirror before using it on whomever happened to be her current fancy.

There was, Elizabeth recalled, only one facet which had previously clouded Dorothy's exuberant outlook on life: her name. Dorothy thought her name was a particularly dreary, commonplace one that smacked of plainness and sensibility – all unfamiliar qualities to her. Why couldn't she have a sophisticated and elegant name, like Eleanor, or Estelle, or even Amanda?

Dorothy had wailed against the injustice of such a misfortune; it was more than any girl should have to bear. Then one day in school she learned about former President James Madison and his wife Dorothy, or Dolly, as she was called. Dorothy Ann was exalted. She had not had any idea that the name Dolly was a nickname for Dorothy and that it was used not only by a woman who had been a trendsetter, but a president's wife no less! Dorothy immediately announced that she would no longer answer to the name Dorothy, but Dolly. Her family was more than happy to put up with this variation of her actual name in order to put an end to her pleas to adopt another one.

The sun had set and stars now sprinkled the evening sky when they strolled over to see the Sullivans. Charles and Margaret Sullivan and their infant son Joseph had moved into the two-story Cape next door to the house that Aunt May now owned. The two houses were nearly identical. A well-beaten dirt path between the two houses was a physical sign of the close relationship the two families had.

As Elizabeth led the way up the front steps, she saw a pitcher of lemonade and a plate of cookies on the porch table. She also noticed Charlie Jr. sitting suspiciously close to the table, cookie crumbs on his lips.

"Charlie," she asked laughingly, "did your mother really leave you in charge of a plate of cookies?"

"No," he answered matter-of-factly. "She doesn't know I'm out here."

Grandpa chuckled. "I'm sure that's the gospel truth."

Eight-year old Charlie was the youngest Sullivan child, fourteen years junior to Dolly. Although he was as dear to his parents' hearts as the others, he was indeed a handful. Margaret Sullivan liked to say that their first-born had been fashioned in the very likeness of Christ. From there, the succeeding children had followed in varying degrees of holiness and sanctity all the way down to Charlie, who was the very incarnation of the devil. Margaret Sullivan was often – even daily – found offering up thanks that the Lord had spared them the knowledge of discovering what a fifth child would have been like.

Margaret Sullivan appeared at the screen door. "For goodness sake! I thought you'd never get over here. We saw Harry drop you off over an hour ago. What have you been doing?"

"Talking and eating," Aunt May replied.

"I guess you'll be doin' some more of both those things with us, if you care to sit a while." Margaret motioned to the table. "I just put out some lemonade and cookies."

At the mention of the word "cookies" Charlie slipped by his mother and disappeared inside. Elizabeth surmised that the youngster had decided not to be at the scene of the crime if cookies were detected missing.

After everyone was seated, Aunt May inquired where the rest of the family was. Margaret explained that Dolly was home, having been grounded for missing curfew the previous weekend, and Mary Francis was hemming a dress she was making. As if on cue, Mary Francis appeared at the screen door, and, after dutifully greeting Grandpa and Aunt May, pulled Elizabeth inside.

Before Mary Francis could speak Elizabeth said, "How is everything going with Robert?" She lowered her voice in case they could hear her on the porch. "Do you still think he's 'The One'?"

"Oh, yes. I can't even think of anyone else. Never mind that right now. You won't believe what I'm going to tell you." Without waiting for a response, she blurted, "Dolly is out on a date!"

"But your mother said that she's grounded."

"I know. That's why I can't believe she snuck out. Only Dolly would break a curfew while she's still being punished. She climbed out the bedroom window after making me swear I wouldn't rat her out to Mama and Papa. But I just had to tell you!"

A look of worry creased Elizabeth's brow. "I can't believe Dolly would try sneaking out, even though I know she doesn't mind taking risks."

"I know. If Mama and Papa find out, I can't even imagine how angry they'll be, although sometimes I wish I had the kind of nerve she has. She always seems to have so much more fun."

"Well, I'm afraid she won't be having any fun for a very, very long time if your mother catches her."

Margaret Sullivan was a loving, devoted mother, but she had a reputation for being a strong disciplinarian when it came to her children.

"That's true. Just the same, I can't wait to find out how tonight went!"

Mary Francis cocked her head towards the front porch and whispered, "Listen, there's Mama calling us. Come over as soon as you can in the morning, Elizabeth, so we can find out every detail about tonight from Dolly. Just remember, mum's the word." Mary Francis pressed her fingers over her lips as the two young women returned to the group on the porch. Margaret Sullivan handed them each a glass of lemonade.

As Elizabeth sipped her drink, she couldn't help but feel disappointed that Dolly wasn't home. She couldn't wait to see her in the morning; she did not need prompting from Mary Francis.

Although Mary Francis was dear to her heart, it was Dolly who kept the two of them laughing. In contrast, Mary Francis was shy and modest. She worked at the dressmaker's shop in town and loved seeing fabric made into beautiful dresses, skirts, and blouses. She was tall, with long limbs and a slender body that showed off the lengthy, straight pencil-A skirts that were all the rage. Although Mary Francis would never have entertained the idea of becoming a model, like Dolly did, she was the picture of one with her up-to-the-minute clothing styles, her lanky body, her soft brown eyes, and her chestnut-colored hair that she often fashioned in a French braid.

Numerous young men had noticed her features, and she had dated several, but one young man in particular, Robert Perry, seemed to have captured her heart. He was not only friendly and outgoing, with a great sense of humor, but he was ruggedly handsome, with deep blue eyes and a ruddy countenance from working at his father's lumber mill. His firm jawline matched the confidence and self-assurance that emanated from him.

Elizabeth liked Robert immensely and was truly happy for Mary Francis. However, she couldn't help but wonder if she would ever be lucky enough to find someone who would capture her heart in the same way.

The next morning Elizabeth was helping Aunt May wash the breakfast dishes when Mary Francis rang up on the telephone. Elizabeth took the call.

"Can you come over right now?" Mary Francis rushed. "I haven't had a single chance to ask Dolly about last night, but she's just finishing her chores, and then she'll finally be free. Now hurry over or I'll die if I have to wait a moment longer to find out about last night!"

"Was that Mary Francis?" Aunt May asked after Elizabeth hung up. "If she's looking for you, why don't you run along?"

Elizabeth tried to protest but her great-aunt motioned her along. "Go along now and I'll finish up these dishes while I have a good old-fashioned chat with your grandfather."

Grandpa was leafing through the Portsmouth Herald and looked up. He also motioned that she should scoot out the door.

Elizabeth departed but not before promising to help with dinner that evening. When she arrived at the Sullivan's, Mary Francis was waiting in the doorway. Without another word, she grabbed Elizabeth's arm and pulled her upstairs and into the bedroom she shared with her sister.

Dolly was seated at the dressing table, feverishly removing bright red nail polish from her fingernails. She held up her hands every few seconds for inspection. A small amount of makeup was acceptable in Margaret Sullivan's household, but colorful nail polish – especially red – would never be tolerated. Dolly was apparently trying to erase all evidence of her night out.

"Well?" Mary Francis asked, as soon as she could get her breath to speak.

There was no response from her younger sister.

"*Well?*" Mary Francis repeated.

"Well what?" Dolly asked absent-mindedly.

"Aren't you going to tell us what happened last night?" Mary Francis demanded, growing more impatient by the second. "Or are we going to grow old standing here while you tend to your fingernails?"

"Who's 'we'?" Dolly asked, as she glanced up. "Oh, Elizabeth, you're here!" Dolly jumped up and ran across the room to hug Elizabeth, knocking cosmetics off the dressing table in her rush.

"How are you?" Dolly asked, embracing Elizabeth tightly. "I've missed you so! You must bring me up to date." She stepped back but continued to hold Elizabeth's shoulders. "How's everything at home? How's your grandpa? And have you met anyone new?" Dolly drew out the word 'new,' making it clear that she only wanted to hear about possible love interests.

Elizabeth shrugged her shoulders. "Oh, Dolly, let's talk about you! Tell us everything about last night!"

Dolly clapped her hands in excitement. "We had the most wonderful time! We went to the Littlefield Dance Hall!"

As soon as Elizabeth heard the name of the hall, she couldn't help but feel a twinge of jealousy. It was an extremely popular place, about forty-five minutes inland from York, and was popular with couples. She had always wondered what it was like.

"The Littlefield Dance Hall!" squealed Mary Francis. "You must tell us everything!"

"Harry James was playing..." Dolly paused, letting the name hang in the air.

"Harry James!" both girls cried in unison. Harry James was one of the biggest names in the area.

"Did he play *You Made Me Love You*?" Elizabeth asked.

"Of course he did," Dolly replied, with the air of one who was an expert on such matters.

"What else? What *else*?" Mary Francis pressed.

"We danced the *Bop* and the *Boogie Woogie*, and we had fruit punch and all kinds of little cakes and cookies. They weren't homemade ones, you know," she stated with authority. "They were from a real bakery, and the hall was decorated with crepe paper and balloons with pink and white streamers. It was just one of THE most heavenly nights I think I've ever had!"

"But, Dolly," Elizabeth pressed, "you haven't told us who you were *with*!"

Mary Francis demanded, "Well, go on! What else happened? Did they play the *Anniversary Waltz* at the end and throw confetti in the air, just like at weddings, and have everyone dance real slow?"

Dolly replied with a defiant expression on her face. "I'm not really sure."

"What do you mean 'you're not sure'?" Mary Francis asked. "They always play the *Anniversary Waltz* at the end. It's tradition."

"Oh, how do I know?" Dolly replied rather crossly, now looking directly at Mary Francis. "I can't remember every little thing, especially whether they played one silly song or not."

"Yes, you're right," Mary Francis agreed with a gleam in her eye. "I'm sure she can't remember, especially when she wasn't there to hear it because she was out behind the barn necking!"

"Is that true?" Elizabeth asked Dolly. In her heart she felt it was the truth by the expression on Dolly's face, and she wished that she had a boy who would like to kiss her.

"Oh, all right, it is," Dolly blurted.

Mary Francis shrieked and buried her face in her hands.

"Oh, don't be such a prude, Mary Francis! All the girls do it and, if I do say so myself, it's thoroughly enjoyable!"

"Not ALL the girls do it, Dolly. I happen to know plenty who don't, although you obviously cannot be included in that group," Mary Francis retorted with a withering glance, which seemed to have no effect on her sister. "On the other hand, I have no intention of ever being part of such a degrading and embarrassing scene. The only man that will be allowed to kiss me will be my future husband."

"Oh, what's the fun in that?" Dolly argued. "Someday when you're an old married woman, don't you want to be able to remember all the toads you kissed before you found Prince Charming?"

"With your usual way with words, you make that sound so appealing, Dolly," Mary Francis said.

Elizabeth broke into the conversation. "Is that who you're waiting for, Dolly? Prince Charming?"

"Yes, I am," she replied confidently, with her chin set firmly and a look of determination in her eyes. "And he'll come someday. I know it."

She placed one arm across her chest and began to speak eloquently. "For lo, he is coming over hill and dale, stopping not but for a morsel of food here and there to sustain him as he rides. And when he comes, he will gather me up with one sweep of his mighty arms and carry me off into the setting sun." Then she crossed her other arm over the first one and, bowing her head, sighed deeply.

Mary Francis rolled her eyes.

Dolly paid no heed to her, however, for she was still caught up in her theatrics. Deciding to end it on an appropriate note, she passed the back of her hand across her brow and sank to the bed in a make-believe swoon.

Suddenly, a muffled yelp was heard. "Ouch!"

All three girls stared for a moment at each other, confused. Then Dolly leaped up from the bed and, bending underneath, pulled out a squirming Charlie, who tried desperately to escape her vice-like grip.

"Why, you little sneak!" Dolly shrieked, shaking him angrily. "Not only have you been hiding under there this whole time listening to our conversation, you're supposed to be washing the kitchen floor for me!"

"It didn't need washin'. It wusn't dirty," Charlie replied calmly. The fact that Dolly looked fit to be tied appeared not to disturb him one little bit.

"As if you knew clean from dirty." Dolly retorted, her eyes looking at Charlie's red-stained hands clutching a crumpled-up bag of licorice.

"Now, you listen to me and you listen good, you hear? You march right downstairs and start scrubbing that floor before Momma finds out it hasn't been done, but not before you promise not to repeat one single word of what you heard in here."

"And what if I don't promise?" Charlie asked.

"Then I'll tell Momma that the reason the cat was sick last week was because you put laxative in his milk bowl, that you've skipped Sunday School for the last three weeks straight, and that you've traded your lunch for firecrackers more times than I can count on two hands."

"All right, all right, I won't tattle!"

"Good. Now put your hands in front of you," Dolly demanded. "Knowing you, you'd cross your fingers behind your back."

A pair of sticky hands was held up inches from Dolly's face.

"Are you sure that's good enough?" Elizabeth tentatively asked. She hated to question Charlie's ethics, but she was well aware of his reputation for being underhanded.

"If nothing else, a Sullivan's word of honor is always upheld, as long as no loopholes are left open," Dolly replied as Charlie headed towards the door. As he passed by, however, Elizabeth noticed something crème-colored and filmy-looking protruding from the pocket of his overalls.

Elizabeth cleared her throat. "Charlie, what's that sticking out of your pocket?"

Everyone looked at Charlie's overalls.

Dolly shrieked, "My nylon stockings I just bought yesterday!"

"What on earth are you doing with Dolly's stockings?" Mary Francis asked.

"My friends and I use them for Cops and Robbers," he replied defensively. "What else is the bad guy supposed to use to mask his face and still be able to see?"

Dolly was enraged. "It took me weeks to save up for them! Charles Matthew Sullivan, I told you before if I ever caught you stealing my stockings again, you wouldn't live to see third grade."

Dolly reached out to grab him, but Charlie was too nimble. He brushed by her outstretched fingers and rushed down the stairs with Dolly fast on his heels, threatening him with all sorts of punishment.

Mary Francis and Elizabeth stayed behind, leaning against the hall banister and watching the comical scene below. Elizabeth knew that Charlie aggravated his sisters, especially Dolly, but having a brother – or a sister – still would have been nice. Maybe that's why she spent so much time thinking of getting married and having a family. She would never have any siblings, but having children, she imagined, would be wonderful.

The next morning both families piled into Charles's pickup. Aunt May and Margaret sat in the front seat, and the girls, Grandpa, and Charlie climbed into the open bed in back. Dolly, as usual, complained about having to keep her skirt covering her knees as she sat with her legs tucked underneath her.

Joe, the Sullivan's oldest child, had recently been ordained at St. John's Seminary in Brookline, Massachusetts. His first assignment, much to his mother's delight, had been in the picturesque town of Ogunquit, which was only a fifteen minute ride from York, and the Sullivan family made a point of traveling up at least once a month to see him celebrate Mass. They were going to do that this morning, then attend a church picnic.

Elizabeth was delighted to see Father Joe; she was as proud of him as his own family. Everyone loved Father Joe, and Elizabeth understood why. He even joined in the square dancing following the picnic, pulling parishioners from their chairs to join in. Even Dolly was in good spirits again after seeing her older brother. It didn't hurt, she confided to Elizabeth, that she'd also retrieved her precious stockings and bestowed a couple of sound whacks on Charlie's behind.

On Sunday evening they celebrated Auntie May's birthday.

Elizabeth studied her aunt. At 5'3", she was almost a foot shorter than Grandpa. She was thin and wiry from her years of manual labor and her continual work in the garden. Elizabeth couldn't help but notice that she was much more spry and energetic than Grandpa. Being seven years younger than her brother probably accounted for the difference.

Margaret Sullivan had the birthday dinner at her house. Elizabeth had presented Aunt May with the roses from Dorchester on Friday evening and decided to find more for the Monday celebration. She cut a dozen bright pink roses from May's garden for a centerpiece at the Sullivans'.

When May had first arrived in York, there were already wild roses that rambled among the shore's embankments. She had decided she would grow her own and, true to her word, the backyard of her house was now sprawling with rose bushes of many varieties and colors.

Margaret served lobster salad made from lobsters Charles had pulled from his crates. Lobster was a favorite meal for all, and whenever Charles brought lobsters in on his fishing boat, *Ladies Three*, named after his wife and two daughters, the large pot at the Sullivan house was put to use.

The next morning when Elizabeth got up, Grandpa and Aunt May were listening to the radio. The Japanese had surrendered to the Allies the day before. The war was truly over.

"Finally, the rest of the soldiers can come home and be reunited with their families," Grandpa said while rising to pull out a seat for Elizabeth.

Aunt Mary nodded. "And hopefully we'll be able to store enough sugar in the cupboard again without relying on the ration books."

Harry picked them up in the afternoon to return home. Elizabeth would have loved to stay longer, but they both had to work in the morning, and Grandpa had been overly tired lately. He was too old to be working, but when she tried to bring the subject up, he just laughed it off.

"What in the world would I do with myself at home all day?" was his routine response.

She couldn't help worrying, however. After promising they would be back up for the Armistice Day weekend, they piled into Harry's car to head home.

While Grandpa dozed in the front seat, Harry plied Elizabeth with questions. She never had much opportunity to talk to him directly; usually Grandpa kept up the conversation. Now, it seemed, Harry wanted to hear all about Elizabeth's life. She was surprised at his interest but happy to fill the time talking.

Harry brought up the subject of Grandpa's garden. "Of course," he said, "we all know how much he loves his rose bushes."

"Yes," Elizabeth nodded. "They bring him such happiness."

"And comfort, I'm sure."

Elizabeth looked questioningly at Harry, and he explained. "I remember when I first met John. He and your grandma had just bought your house. He said he was planting rose bushes because it gave him something to take care of."

"I never knew that," Elizabeth said.

"Us men folk don't talk too much about stuff, you know, but I think he was a little bit lonely not knowing hardly anyone when they arrived here from Ireland. But he had Rose, and the two of them were very happy together, especially after your mother was born. He didn't say too much when your parents died, or later when your grandmother died but he was sure glad he still had you."

Elizabeth nodded. Her mother, Claire, had died giving birth to her, and her father, Richard, whether through carelessness due to the grief over losing his beloved wife or perhaps an unconscious inability to go on without her, had been struck down by a horse and buggy after leaving his departed wife's side.

Harry was deeply sympathetic. "I remember when I found out what happened. It's still one of the saddest stories I've ever heard."

"Yes, I know most people think that when they hear it, but I've always taken comfort in the fact that my parents were so deeply in love with each other. One of my most fervent wishes is to someday have the same kind of marriage that they enjoyed, and that Grandpa and Grandma Rose had."

"I'm sure you will," Harry replied comfortingly. "I'm sure some lucky lad will scoop you up before you know it."

Elizabeth didn't say it, but she doubted Harry's prediction would come true. After all, she met few eligible men living as she did with her grandfather. The men she worked with were either married or twice her age. Part of her didn't mind, though, as she couldn't imagine leaving Grandpa. For the moment she had to be – and she was, she told herself – content to live with her grandfather in the rambling old house they called home.

Chapter Two

It was late on the Friday afternoon of Labor Day weekend, and most of the staff at Hodge's Investments had left, eager to begin the three-day holiday. Alan Bates, newly appointed Junior Vice-President of Operations, was one of the few employees left on the eighth floor. He was not averse to getting his own weekend started, but he had only been employed at Hodge's for a week, and he wanted to make sure that his spacious, finely-appointed corner office was organized and ready to go on Tuesday.

He gazed around appreciatively at the accouterments of his success. He felt justified in occupying this type of office with the accessories that accompanied it. Built-in mahogany shelves, holding his ledgers and investment manuals, lined the walls on either side of the door. A leather chair was stationed behind the glass-topped table upon which lay a matching leather desk pad and note tablet. A fountain pen embossed in gold with *"Hodge's Investments"* lay on top of the pad.

Alan reflected on how far he had come. He had grown up in a small town in Connecticut with his parents and an older brother. His father had been president of the town bank. From a young age, Alan had enjoyed working with numbers, and he had excelled in math. He apprenticed under his father throughout high school and during his college summers. He might have succeeded his father as president of the bank, but he had chafed at the smallness of the town. His family – even his brother – was seemingly content with the easy-going, laid-back style that it offered. Fortunately, his brother had joined his father in the business, leaving Alan free to pursue bigger dreams.

Alan had mentored under an accountant at a small, prestigious firm on Manhattan's Upper East Side, and he had acclimated quickly to the fast-paced business world. Alan had felt fortunate to escape the draft. His birthday – December 18th – had not come up. At the time many men were volunteering, including many of Alan's friends and co-workers, and Alan considered signing up, more from peer pressure than a sense of patriotic duty. However, when he heard that all the slots for officers had been filled and any new draftees would be delegated to the rank of private, his decision was made. He had no intention of trading in his new job at a distinguished firm in New York, along with a comfortable lifestyle, for the hardships of war. He fabricated a story just before the medical exam that his bad back had flared up from an old tennis injury, thereby giving him the rank of 4-F – physically unfit for service. Alan had made it a point to walk stiffly whenever he was at work or at social events, despite the raised eyebrows of several people who questioned the timing of his back problem. Alan hadn't minded enduring their suspicions. He had his life just the way he wanted it and that was all that mattered.

He would have been content to stay in New York, but the opportunity to work at the junior vice-president level at the illustrious firm of Hodge's was more than he could pass up. Hodge's was a name of great distinction in the Boston area, surpassed only by the name Kennedy in business and social worlds.

Becoming a junior vice-president at the age of twenty-nine was no small feat, even by his own ambitious standards. It gave him great hope that eventually he would rise to the position of president, if not in the firm of Hodge's Investments, then in some other equally prestigious company in another city.

Because his secretary, Janine, had already left for the day, he strode down the hall to return a manual to the conference room. As he turned back towards his office, three other secretaries were heading towards the elevator. They noticed Alan walking by, and one of the girls – a buxom redhead – approached him.

"I'm Betty Higgins. I work down the hall." She gave Alan a sultry look. The other girls giggled.

"A pleasure to meet you," Alan replied coolly.

"It's definitely a pleasure for me." She leaned close to Alan. "A group of us are meeting down the street after work. We go every Friday afternoon. Care to join us today?"

Alan smiled slightly. He was well aware that single young men were quickly noticed by single women in an office complex and his status as an eligible male had apparently been noted.

"As lovely as you ladies seem, alas, I have plans for this evening."

Betty pouted slightly as she replied, "Too bad, we can always use an extra male to add to our crew."

"I'm sure there are many other eligible bachelors at the local watering hole to suffice."

"Maybe, maybe not." Betty glanced back at her friends, who snickered.

Alan sought the haven of his office. He closed the door behind him to discourage further conversation. He was not adverse to female company - on the contrary, pursuing the opposite sex was one of his favorite pastimes and the redhead was very appealing. However his career was first and foremost, and he would not allow himself to be distracted at work. Alan had no intention of being in a committed relationship – at least not until the right kind of girl came along. And that 'right girl'? She would be not only rich and beautiful but would also come from a notable family that was socially connected. That would be a rare find, but he only had to find one, and he was more than willing to wait. He had also told the truth when he had said that he had other plans. He was meeting a potential client for drinks and dinner, mixing business with pleasure. It was one of the ways he planned to jump ahead of his competition when it came to advancing his interests.

Snapping his briefcase shut, he double-checked that his office was in order. Closing the door behind him, he turned his key in the lock and proceeded down the hall. Henry Hodge's suite was at the end of the corridor, and as he passed the closed door he noticed the president's name emblazoned on the nameplate in bold, black letters. Alan paused to envision his own name on that door. "Not bad," he said to himself. "Not bad at all."

Chapter Three

The day after Labor Day, Grandpa and Elizabeth resumed their usual routine. Grandpa went back to work at the paper mill and Elizabeth returned to her secretarial job at Hodge's Investments. Elizabeth had gotten the job eight months ago after responding to a posting in the local newspaper. Her grandfather did not normally support the idea of women working outside the home; however, unlike her grandmother and mother, Elizabeth did not have a husband or child to care for, so Elizabeth could make Grandpa see the sense of it. Also, Grandpa knew that Elizabeth was lonely being home all day.

Hodge's Investments was on Milk Street, in the heart of Boston's financial district. The bustle of the city thrilled Elizabeth, and she counted herself lucky to have employment in such a thriving place. Elizabeth was secretary to Mr. Neil Summersby, one of several accountants who worked under Mr. Hodge, the president of the company. The office supervisor, who was Mr. Hodge's secretary, was Lillian Graham, a tall, thin woman in her early fifties who had worked there for over ten years. She was an outspoken person, almost abrasive in her demeanor, although Elizabeth had experienced that she was also generous and good-hearted. Elizabeth immensely enjoyed working at Hodge's. When she first started, she had felt nervous regarding her typing and shorthand skills, fearing they would not be up to par, but Mr. Summersby had quickly put her at ease by praising the quality of her work.

Initially she had hoped to become friendly with Janine, another one of the executive secretaries, but they had not hit it off very well during their brief conversations. Janine had asked her which boutiques and clubs she liked to frequent, and Elizabeth had been embarrassed to reply that she had no familiarity with either. After that, Janine was polite to her, but she never asked her to go to lunch or to go out after work.

Another co-worker, Betty, was often pulled from the typing pool to work with Elizabeth because of Mr. Summersby's heavy workload. Betty had introduced her to several of her friends from the typing pool, and that group had seemed much friendlier.

Betty was completely opposite to Elizabeth. She was a free spirit – she hated to be tied to a schedule, and her priority was usually focused on how to attract members of the opposite sex. Elizabeth remembered the first day she and Betty had met. Elizabeth had been putting some files away when she'd heard the rapid clicking of heels. She turned to see a girl with curly red hair come careening around the corner and fly into a nearby desk. The girl glanced quickly at the clock on the wall, which read quarter of nine, and then leaned out into the aisle to see if anyone was around. She clearly hadn't noticed Elizabeth seated in the other direction. Then the young woman threw her pocketbook down and began rummaging through it, then dumped the entire contents on the desktop.

Pulling a small compact towards her, she flipped the lid back and began quickly applying mascara, eyeliner, eye shadow, lipstick, and blush, looking in the tiny mirror of the compact to assess the results. Then she threw everything back in her pocketbook save for the comb, which she had just enough time to flick through her hair before Lillian Graham rounded the corner.

Pulling out a handwritten page from the haphazard stack of material on the corner of her desk, she snapped it onto her typing stand and began rapidly typing.

Lillian Graham stopped at Betty's desk.

"Good morning Betty. Had a good weekend?"

"Hi, Lillian. Yes, fine. How about you?"

"I'm fine, but I do have a suggestion for you. You might want to put a piece of paper in your typewriter in case anybody wants to read whatever it is you're typing."

Betty peered at her typewriter and a small smile broke out. Lillian started laughing out loud and Betty's response was to toss her head as if she didn't care one little bit. Elizabeth tried very hard to pretend that she hadn't noticed what had just transpired. Lillian turned to Elizabeth and introduced Betty. Betty seemed unperturbed by the fact that someone had been an audience to her early morning performance.

While Elizabeth counted Betty and a few others as female friends at Hodge's, she had also hoped that a job in the heart of Boston would allow her to meet single young men. Nothing, so far, had materialized on that front. Elizabeth knew that ten months was a short amount of time, so she was still hopeful. And, she surmised, she was more likely to meet someone while working in Boston than if she had been home alone all day doing chores.

Sometimes she felt as if she spent too much time thinking about getting married and having children. Maybe it was because she had never had siblings or because she had never known her parents, or maybe it was just her nature to have marriage and children at the top of her list. She often brought this up with her Aunt May.

"Don't you worry," Aunt May would say. "You'll meet someone when you least expect it."

To Elizabeth, however, this seemed like shaky advice, as Aunt May herself had never met anyone special enough to marry. Once Elizabeth had asked Grandpa if Aunt May minded not being married or having children. Grandpa had replied, "Your great-aunt has always been content with whatever her lot in life was. It's a great virtue to have."

Elizabeth hoped it wouldn't be a virtue she would have to shoulder when she was older.

In spite of her yearnings, Elizabeth was fond of her routine with Grandpa. During the week Elizabeth and Grandpa ate supper together each evening, and after supper Grandpa would help her do the dishes. In the winter he would fill the kitchen stove with coal he carried up from the bin in the cellar and the two of them would settle down for the evening. Grandpa often returned to the cellar to work on his latest woodworking project. Woodworking was a skill he had acquired from his own father. Grandpa was both talented and generous, and consequently there was hardly a neighbor or friend who did not have a plant stand, bookshelf, or a footstool fashioned from his hands.

Elizabeth also took advantage of that quiet time to engage in her favorite hobby, reading. It was difficult to go anywhere in the house without encountering an assortment of books. They were sure to be found stuffed between seat cushions, teetering on the hallway steps, or stacked on the table in the parlor. She also enjoyed writing stories, but unlike the books she read, they were not to be found scattered throughout the house. Her most ambitious project was a manuscript for a novel, which she kept tucked away in a drawer of her bureau. She wanted to keep it a secret, as she didn't feel ready to share it with anyone until it was complete. She did hope to finish it within the coming year and, maybe then and only then, would she be brave enough to share her work. One of her most fervent wishes and secret desires was that someday it might be published. Of course Elizabeth hadn't a clue how such an thing would ever become reality,

Weekends were also full of routine for Elizabeth and her grandpa. Fridays were Grandpa's poker night, and Elizabeth often had the house to herself. On Saturdays, Elizabeth did the ironing and baking for the coming week. There was not much to do in the way of dusting and polishing, for most of their time was spent between the kitchen and the front parlor. The furniture had lost its luster over the years, and the carpets were worn and bare in spots, but they were clean and homey and served their purpose well enough for the two of them.

Each Sunday they attended early morning Mass, followed by a hearty breakfast of bacon, eggs, and hash. Afterwards they often visited friends or friends stopped by. Elizabeth appreciated their routine, and she knew Grandpa thrived on it. But she also felt she was on the edge, waiting for something – anything – to shake up her life a bit.

Chapter Four

Alan looked up from the report he was reading and saw Neil Summersby standing in the doorway. They had met during Alan's initial staff meeting; Neil, graciously, had offered Alan a hand if he ever needed it. Such a time was now, for Alan was frustrated by the complexity of one of the investments he was reviewing.

After Neil walked him through some of the documents, Alan looked at his watch. It was well past the official end of the workday. Alan stood and stretched. "I feel like I've been bent over for hours."

"That's because you have been. Come on. I'll buy you a couple of drinks and dinner down the street somewhere, and then you'll feel much more loosened up."

Alan narrowed his eyes. He had learned not to be too trusting when it came to business associates. "Don't you have to get home to a wife and kids?"

"Both my sons are now part of the working class and this is the night my lovely wife, Eleanor, has her knitting club over, so it is well known at Hodge's Investments that any employee is welcome to dine with me on Tuesday evenings. Otherwise I will be at the local diner by myself. That's preferable to listening to the clack of knitting needles and tidbits of gossip."

"I interpret your offer as both candid and desperate."

"You are correct. I'll grab my jacket."

"Great. And wherever we go to dinner, just make sure there are some pretty girls hanging about."

"Looking for a girlfriend?" Neil eyed him curiously.

"Not necessarily, just a few I can rest my eyes on – maybe someone who's up for drinks."

"Just drinks? Nothing serious? No marriage in Alan Bates's future?" Neil gave him a sly smile.

"I didn't say that. I just have no intention of marrying the 'neighborhood girl' from the local diner. When I marry, she'll be all class."

Neil wagged his finger at Alan. "You never know what hidden gems there are in the world."

"Well, I'm not much of a scavenger. If there's a bright diamond in the room, she'll be the one I'll go after. Let's go."

Alan and Neil walked a few blocks to a neighborhood bar that was known for its burgers. After they ordered a drink, Alan decided to throw out a question regarding a fellow employee. He still didn't know Neil very well, but he was very interested in sizing up his competition at work and he sensed that Neil would be candid.

"What do you know about Phil Lawrence?"

"Phil's a great guy. He's one of our finest finance managers. Very knowledgeable in his job and has a lot of potential – like you. Why?"

"I'm supposed to be working on a project with him. I just thought you might have a feel for him."

"As I said, one of the best. Cheers!"

Alan raised his glass, but inwardly his mind was turning. So far, none of the other men on Mr. Hodge's staff had seemed any threat to Alan. Just from an initial meeting with Phil, however, Alan felt that Phil could be a real shining star. If they were going to present a project together, Alan had to make sure that he came out looking like the brighter of the two. The first part of the question was how to make that happen. The second part of the question was when.

Chapter Five

During the remainder of September, Elizabeth heard nothing from Mary Francis or Dolly. Grandpa spoke to Aunt May regularly, but none of the news that Elizabeth was anxious to hear about was conveyed: What were Mary Francis and Dolly *really* up to?

On the last Friday of the month Harry, off-duty from the trolley service, was over for dinner before he and Grandpa headed to their poker game. They had finished eating and were clearing the table when they were startled by the ringing of the telephone, causing both Elizabeth and Grandpa to jump. They received few phone calls, and Grandpa picked it up gingerly. After listening for a minute, he lowered the receiver and turned towards them. He spoke carefully to Elizabeth. "That was Fred. Your grandmother has been feeling poorly and the doctor was called in. Your presence has been requested."

Fred was her paternal grandparents' butler and chauffeur. Fred and Grandpa had always had a certain alliance, having become acquainted when Fred had first begun working for the Keenes, and they were steadfast friends now. Fred was also part of the Friday night poker crew, along with Harry, Grandpa, and several other men in the local area.

"Is it really so serious that the doctor needed to be summoned?" Elizabeth asked. Her grandmother had always sought attention with a multitude of trivial maladies, but the fact that she was under a doctor's supervision gave her cause to be concerned.

"I'm sure having a doctor means she's getting whatever care she needs. It's too late to go tonight, but Fred thought tomorrow afternoon would be a good time to visit."

"Of course I'll go," Elizabeth replied. She bit her lower lip, and Grandpa reached across the table to place his weathered hand on top of hers.

That evening Elizabeth worked on her novel, but she couldn't stop worrying about her grandmother. Grandpa had told her that when she visited her Grandmother Keene the next day she should expect that Paul Keene, Elizabeth's uncle and Virginia and George Keenes' only living child, would be there. Grandfather Keene was away on business, but Paul was staying by his mother's side.

At age forty Paul was still a bachelor and worked for his father, George, out of his Cambridge office. He was deferential towards his mother, seeming to rise above her frequent complaints. More often than not, however, Paul was traveling for business, and Elizabeth felt that he always seemed happiest when he was preparing to leave on a trip. She couldn't blame him. It was such an eerie, formal house to live in.

Elizabeth found Paul aloof, which made her uncomfortable around him. She knew she wasn't the only one who felt that way. Paul often visited various Boston financial firms in his work for his father and Elizabeth had heard rumblings from time to time at Hodge's that Paul Keene was 'standoffish' and 'arrogant.' No one, yet, had made the connection that Elizabeth and Paul were related, and Elizabeth remained silent, wanting to be assessed on her own qualities and not her uncle's reputation.

On Saturday morning Elizabeth hurried to leave for the walk to her grandmother's home. As she was about to leave, the phone rang. It was Fred, calling to inform them that Mrs. Keene had just passed away.

Elizabeth burst into tears. This was the first family member she had ever lost that she was old enough to mourn. As a child, she had viewed Grandmother Keene with some trepidation. With her stern countenance, her silvery hair elaborately piled on top of her head, and the multi-layered gowns she insisted on wearing despite the current fashions, she presented a regal and imposing figure. Grandmother Keene had also been the only grandmother Elizabeth had ever known, always showing interest in her grades at school and her visits to Maine. When she gave Elizabeth a kiss on the cheek to say hello and goodbye, there was a softness in her eyes that told Elizabeth that her Grandmother loved her.

Grandpa did his best to comfort her. "I think you were always one of the greatest joys in her life. I know she enjoyed your visits immensely, and you brought a good deal of cheer into her life."

Elizabeth nodded in reply, too choked up to say anything. After a moment she said, "I'll still need to go over, I suppose, to see Uncle Paul."

Grandpa was ascending the stairs slowly, his hand gripping the rail. Although his arthritis had worsened in recent years, Elizabeth had not noticed him in this much pain before.

"Are you uncomfortable?" Elizabeth asked in concern. "Do you want me to call Dr. Tinsdale?"

"No, no, no." He smiled warmly at her. "I think it's the cold weather. Pretty chilly for the end of September! It makes me stiff. I was planning to go over with you, but how would you feel about walking up alone?"

"Of course." Elizabeth tried to sound as if it was fine, but inwardly she quailed. It was always a somber atmosphere at her grandparents', even without the added aura of death in the air.

She set out as soon as her chores were done, rounding the corner past Walter Baker's chocolate factory on Adams Street, a landmark that Grandpa always bragged about. It was the oldest chocolate company in the United States.. The lingering aroma of chocolate assailed her nostrils. The sky, filled with ominous clouds, began to release large drops of rain. By the time she reached the top of Adams Street, the drops became a downpour. Elizabeth started to run. When she rang the bell, Fred answered and gave her a big hug.

"I'm so sorry, Elizabeth. I know this is a tremendous loss for you." He escorted her to the drawing room where Paul was standing at the far end, gazing absent-mindedly out the window.

It was not unusual to find him there. Paul seemed to prefer solitude to people although, whenever Elizabeth visited, he was always courteous and she noticed he even had a dry sense of humor whenever she was fortunate to hear him interact with others.

Elizabeth knew she must speak to him, but for a moment, an almost overwhelming desire came over her to tiptoe past and retreat to the front door. However, she was too well-disciplined to do anything so rude.

"Excuse me, Uncle Paul. I just wanted to tell you how sorry I am about your mother." She paused a moment, waiting for Paul to interject a word or two, but he did not even turn to acknowledge her presence. Elizabeth began again. "If you need me for anything, just call me…"

Paul's voice suddenly cut across hers, surprising her.

"You're just like her, you know. Your mother, that is," he stated, speaking with apparent difficulty. "I saw the similarity from the time you were just a little girl. You have that wide, innocent gaze just like your mother used to have, as though everyone and everything in the world is good and sweet and kind."

He spoke slowly and methodically. "You're not really alike in looks. Actually, you resemble my brother much more. No, it's in your mannerisms, your facial expressions. It's the way you move your hands when you're trying to explain something, the sound of your voice, and your laughter." He nodded his head. "Yes, especially your laughter. It reminds me so much of your mother. When I'm around you, it's like seeing your mother come back to life again, so much so… "

He stopped short.

Elizabeth could see his jaw tighten up as he swallowed visibly. Finally he spoke again. "We were all devastated, but Mother seemed to take it the hardest. She couldn't cope with it. She was never much of an optimist before, but after your parents died, she began snapping at people, finding fault with everyone and everything. I'm afraid I wasn't very good at dealing with it myself. I missed your father terribly. We'd always been each other's favorite companion.

"We also missed your mother. She was so special. The spring before you were born, your mother came over for a visit to see how the rose bushes were doing that she had planted for my mother. We were strolling in the garden, and your mother turned to me and said, 'An April rose – that's you.' I remember I laughed and said to her, 'I can't say I've ever been called any kind of flower before, but why an April rose? Why not a March rose? Or a June rose?'

"I remember she looked straight at me and replied, "In April a rose has grown enough so you can see its long stem and its colorful petals, but it is still too early for it to bloom, so you can't yet see how beautiful it is inside."

Paul looked away for a moment, and Elizabeth watched the pain that traveled over his face. She found her own heart aching for the mother she had never known, and it was a few moments before she was able to speak.

"I think that's the nicest thing I've ever heard anyone say to someone, Uncle Paul," Elizabeth whispered gently.

"Yes, I think so, too," he replied. He glanced at Elizabeth and held her gaze for a moment.

They were both silent then, but it was a comfortable silence. For Elizabeth's part, she wondered how different things might have been if Claire and Richard Keene had lived. How different her life would have been. How different Paul's, and Grandpa's, and Grandmother Keene's would have been as well. Her parents' deaths had undoubtedly drastically altered all of their lives.

"Uncle Paul," she began uncertainly, "I'm so grateful that you talked to me, because I feel as though I've gotten to know you a little better. I'd like that to continue. Perhaps we could get together again soon and talk some more."

"I'm usually very busy," he said, almost as if the prior conversation had not taken place. He proceeded to walk by Elizabeth as he spoke.

Almost without realizing what she was doing, Elizabeth threw her hand out to grasp his arm.

"Uncle Paul," she pleaded, speaking more boldly than she had ever dared to speak to someone almost twice her age. "I know this isn't the proper time to bring this up, but when this is all over, come and stay with my grandpa and me for a while. You wouldn't be intruding at all! Grandpa used to have so many people stay over when they first came over from Ireland; one person wouldn't be any bother."

The hallway clock chimed, signaling that it was noon. Elizabeth had to go.

"Please think over what I've said. Remember, you're always welcome." As she finished speaking, she reached up and kissed him on the cheek.

A startled look came into her uncle's eyes, which made Elizabeth smile. Turning, she crossed the front hall, flew out the front door, and raced down Adams Street as if the very ghosts of yesteryear were nipping at her feet.

When Elizabeth arrived home, Grandpa had leftover ham and fresh brown bread waiting for lunch. While they ate, Elizabeth reported everything that had happened with Paul.

As she finished her story, Grandpa shook his head and clucked his tongue. "Poor lad! I'm afraid he's had rather a rough time of it growing up there. I'm sure your grandparents did the best they could, Elizabeth, but I don't think it was an easy home to grow up in. Your father seemed to cope with things a lot better than your uncle did, and I think he was your uncle's only support. When your parents died, your uncle lost the only two people who had taken any special interest in him, and he withdrew because he just didn't know what else to do.

"I'm very proud of you," Grandpa continued, giving Elizabeth an affectionate hug around her shoulders. "That was very good of you to invite Paul to stay with us. You were right. He needs to get away from all those old memories and get back into the mainstream of life."

Elizabeth sighed. "I'm afraid my offer didn't do much good. As I said, when I left I felt as if he'd already returned to his old self."

~

Grandfather Keene had not been able to get back to the States before his wife's passing. The Trans-Atlantic ships from Europe were often delayed, and once in the States he had trouble getting a train from New York to Boston. That evening, they received another phone call from Fred. Mr. Keene had arrived and it had been decided that Mrs. Keene would be waked on Tuesday and then buried on Wednesday morning at Old Calvary Cemetery.

On Tuesday evening they walked up the steep hill to the Keene's house. They were escorted into the drawing room by Fred, where George and Paul Keene stood by the deceased. George Keene came forward to greet them both, kissing Elizabeth formally on the cheek and shaking Grandpa's hand.

"John, Elizabeth. Glad you could come. Appreciate it."

"Of course we'd come," Grandpa returned. "We're very sorry about Virginia's passing."

"Oh, yes, yes, yes. We'll miss her terribly," George Keene uttered, but the words lacked emotion. He proceeded to go over the funeral details, and he spoke quickly and efficiently, as if it were just another business problem to be handled and solved.

Paul briefly nodded to them, but he was talking with several visitors and did not approach.

Elizabeth debated over whether or not to talk with him, but her courage failed her. Besides, he looked troubled, and Elizabeth did not want to add to his sorrows. She finally decided that if he had wanted to talk, he would approach them.

She walked over to her grandmother's casket, and knelt down to say a prayer. When she rose, she realized that Grandfather Keene was behind her. She turned to see him talking with a tall, young man with deep brown eyes. He was one of the most handsome young men she had ever encountered, and she felt shy as she looked across at him.

"Elizabeth, this is a business associate of mine – Stephen Wright," her grandfather said.

Stephen reached out to grasp her hand in a warm handshake. "If I had known what a beautiful granddaughter you had, I would have insisted that we do some of our transactions here."

Elizabeth blushed at his compliment, not sure how to reply. Just then she heard a commotion behind her and turned to see Charles Sullivan walk through the parlor door, his entire family and Aunt May behind him. With a cry, she excused herself and ran across the room to embrace them.

"You're all here! Uncle Charles, you gave up fishing today just to come?"

"For something as important as this, I can make time." He gave her an affectionate hug. "Besides, I was able to get out early this morning to fish."

"I had to leave school early," Charlie piped up.

"Such a sacrifice," Aunt May said, smiling.

As the adults turned towards Grandpa, Dolly squeezed Elizabeth's arm. "Who's *that*? Over *there*?!"

Mary Francis and Elizabeth both turned to see where Dolly was looking, but Elizabeth only saw her Uncle Paul standing near his mother's casket.

"Dolly, who are you looking at?" asked Mary Francis.

"Prince Charming, that's who! He's standing at the end of the casket."

Elizabeth laughed. "Dolly, that's my Uncle Paul. I think you must need glasses if you think he's Prince Charming."

"That's your uncle?" Dolly cried. "You've got to introduce me!"

Mary Francis reprimanded her sister. "For goodness sake, Dolly! He must be twice your age and, even if he wasn't, his mother just passed away, and he's certainly not interested in finding a date at her wake."

"I just want to offer my condolences. After all, isn't that what we're here for?" Linking her arm in Elizabeth's, she pulled her along. Elizabeth had no choice but to comply. Mary Francis quickly followed, speaking in a low tone.

"Elizabeth can introduce you, but that's all," Mary Francis warned.

Dolly tossed her head, smoothed her dress, and tucked some loose stands of hair behind her ears.

Paul turned towards the trio. His eyes narrowed and his brow furrowed. His expression reminded Elizabeth of one his mother used to wear when something was not to her liking.

"Uncle Paul," she began, "these are my dear friends from Maine, Dolly and Mary Francis Sullivan."

Dolly immediately curtsied before rising to say in a breathless voice, "Please accept our deepest sympathies for this terrible tragedy that has befallen your family. Our most fervent thoughts and prayers are with you during your darkest hours."

Mary Francis, looking at Paul's slightly bemused face, gently corrected her sister. "Sister, dear, I don't think it's considered a 'terrible tragedy' when someone dies of natural causes at the age of eighty-two."

Paul nodded his head first toward Mary Francis, then toward Dolly. "Thank you for your kind words." He then returned to his rigid manner. "Now, if you'll excuse me, I have some details to attend to."

Dolly stood watching him depart, her hands on her hips. "Of all the rude behaviors I have ever seen! Can you believe he just walked away with barely a word to us?"

Mary Francis angrily turned to Dolly. "Talk about bad behavior. Do you always have to turn every conversation into a romantic opportunity? He's probably thinking that we're the most self-centered women he's ever met, and rightly so."

"You're right, Mary Francis," Dolly agreed. "I'll go apologize."

Mary Francis grabbed her arm. "I don't think that's happening. Just leave him alone, and let him bury his mother in peace without any more distractions from you."

Dolly crossed her arms defiantly but stayed in her spot. Elizabeth, meanwhile, was keeping an eye on Paul. He remained apart from the small groups of people who came to pay their respects. As the evening progressed, Paul avoided contact with Elizabeth and Grandpa. Elizabeth felt sure that she had gone too far with her words to him on Saturday, and Dolly's over-the-top condolences hadn't helped bridge the gap.

Chapter Six

 Alan knocked on the half-open door of Neil Summersby's office. He saw Neil leaning back in his chair reading the newspaper. Neil looked up at the sound of the knock.

"Alan, come on in," he said, waving him to the chair opposite his desk.

"What's going on?" Alan asked with a smile. "No secretary out front; your door is open so any Tom, Dick, or Harry can wander in, and you're reading the newspaper? I don't think you're going to win the 'Most Professional' award today."

Neil laughed and sat upright. "I didn't know I was in the running, but if I had to defend myself, I would state that technically I still have one minute left on my lunch hour, my door is open because I knew you would be here for our 1:00 meeting, and my secretary wouldn't be able to announce you because she's at her grandmother's funeral today." Neil folded the paper in front of him. "You might know of her grandmother – or at least of her grandfather – George Keene, the business tycoon."

"THE George Keene?" Alan's eyes widened.

"See for yourself." Neil pushed the newspaper across the table, his finger on the obituary.

"Wow! Why is an heiress earning her keep working for a bum like you?"

"Actually, she never mentioned her family connection, so I haven't a clue. I didn't even connect the names. I just happened to see it in the newspaper. I can tell you, however, that she's the hardest working and most efficient secretary I've ever had. No sense of entitlement that I can see."

"Is she single?"

"She is indeed. Why? Suddenly interested?"

"I'm always interested in rich, young, single heiresses." Alan gave a low whistle. "Once or twice I've exchanged conversation with her when

I stopped by here. I think I'll have to put in more serious effort to get acquainted."

"If you do plan on 'getting acquainted,' as you say, don't expect a stuffy socialite. She's pleasantly unassuming."

'Unassuming,' Alan thought, was not an adjective that he had ever used when describing a desirable girl. However, Neil was impressed by her, so perhaps she was promising. He certainly wasn't going to bypass the opportunity to pursue an heiress to a vast family fortune.

Alan began to formulate a plan. He asked Neil if he wanted to meet for lunch the following day. Alan had shied away from socializing at work, except with Neil, because Neil was the one coworker Alan felt he could trust. This was probably, Alan surmised, because Neil seemed unperturbed by Alan's ambitions. Perhaps this was because Neil was in his late fifties and was not focused on getting ahead, or maybe it was because of Neil's laid-back personality.

Alan knew he had already ruffled a few feathers with many of his coworkers, but it didn't faze him. He had expected as much when he started working at Hodge's. As Junior VP of Operations, he had introduced ideas that were on the cutting-edge of business practices – all gleaned from his work experience in New York. He also knew that his presentations at weekly staff meetings were forceful and to the point, and his success sometimes came at the cost of some of his fellow employees. If his actions resulted in resentment or bitterness on their part, though, that was their problem, not his.

Neil happily accepted Alan's invitation. "As long as you're paying," he said with a grin.

Alan was more than happy to pay. If he timed it right, it would be the perfect opportunity to talk with Elizabeth Keene.

The next morning, while Alan walked to work from his downtown apartment, he reviewed his plan. He wanted to speak to Elizabeth Keene alone, if possible. He didn't know if she came in early, but if she did, he might be able to catch her before the day began. Alan decided to wait near the 8th floor elevator and speak to her if she emerged.

Alan bought a newspaper from the stand on the corner and carried it with him to the 8th floor. He positioned himself against a far wall and opened the paper. Several fellow staffers came in, each nodded curtly in greeting. The elevator doors opened again and, to his relief, Elizabeth Keene emerged alone. She was wearing a simple navy blue dress and worn-looking blue flats. Apparently her wealthy grandfather was not showering her with a clothing allowance. As she turned towards her office area, he noticed her poise. She carried her head high, not in an arrogant way, but in a way which reflected etiquette and refinement.

As Elizabeth passed in front of him, he greeted her. She politely offered a 'good morning' and kept walking. Alan considered following her, but just then Phil Lawrence rounded the corner. Phil gave him a questioning look, as if he sensed that Alan had something up his sleeve. Alan rolled up the paper, picked up his briefcase and, without a word, strode to his office. He would ask Janine to buzz Neil's office to say that he would swing by to pick him up for lunch at twelve o'clock, then he would arrive a few minutes early to talk with Elizabeth.

~

At ten-minutes-to twelve, Alan strode toward Neil's office. Elizabeth was seated at her desk, typing.

She looked up at him with a tentative smile.

Up close, Alan could see warm, hazel eyes, full red lips, and a smooth, ivory-tinted complexion. Clearly, she was a beauty.

"Elizabeth Keene," he said, as a statement. He touched the nameplate on her desk.

Elizabeth paused in her typing and looked at him questioningly.

Alan leaned toward her. "I heard through the office grapevine of your grandmother's passing. I'm so sorry. Was it sudden?" Alan asked gently.

Elizabeth paused. "She'd been ill on and off for quite some time, so it wasn't a complete surprise. We just didn't realize it was as serious this time."

"I offer my most sincere condolences. Obviously, I've heard of your grandfather. I'm sure you realize the name recognition he has. I've admired him greatly for his skill and expertise in business. Most can't say they've accomplished as much in their career as he has."

"Yes, he does very well," Elizabeth murmured and picked up a file from the corner of her desk.

Alan hoped he hadn't been too forward. He figured that her whole life may have been under public scrutiny, and she had probably learned to put up boundaries.

The phone rang and Alan waited while Elizabeth took a message. After she hung up, he said, "Well, I shouldn't keep you. It looks like you have work to do and Neil will be out any minute for our lunch. Say…" he added, as if it had just occurred to him, "would you be interested in getting together some time after work for a drink? Or dinner?"

Elizabeth looked at him, flustered. "Oh – oh, yes. That would be nice," she stammered.

"Great! How about next Friday – a week from tomorrow - after work? That is, if you're free."

"Yes, I am free." She offered him a shy smile.

"Good. I'll meet you right here at five o'clock."

"Okay then." Elizabeth pushed papers aside on her desk and fumbled for the intercom button. "Let me buzz Mr. Summersby for you."

Just then the office door opened and Neil appeared in the doorway. "I thought I heard voices out here."

"You heard correctly," Alan replied. "Ready to go?"

Alan and Neil walked toward the elevator, then Alan turned back toward Elizabeth. "Don't forget about our date next week," he called. Out of the corner of his eye, Alan saw Neil's eyebrows arch upwards.

"Apparently, you've been very proactive in making inroads with Miss Keene."

Alan slapped Neil on the back. "You just don't know me very well yet, Neil. But if you stick around, maybe you can pick up a few tips on how to get ahead."

"With women? You forget, Alan, that I'm married. So I'll watch from the sidelines. It promises to be quite a show."

Chapter Seven

 The following Thursday evening Elizabeth stood in front of her closet, pondering clothing options. She wished she could afford to buy something new, but she would have to make do with what she had.

After selecting and then discarding various items of clothing, she decided on a navy tweed suit in wool that she normally did not wear until it was colder. It had been chilly all week, even for early October, so she thought it would be suitable. Besides, her light blue frilled blouse was washed and pressed, and she only had to shine her navy blue shoes to complete her outfit.

She had avoided telling her grandfather about her date, not wanting him to stew. But now she'd have to let him know where she'd be tomorrow night. She carried her shoes downstairs in order to shine them and found him at the kitchen table. "Grandpa, I've been invited to dinner tomorrow night by a young man from work."

"So, you caught someone's eye now, did ye? He must have a good eye for a pretty lass!"

"Oh, Grandpa," Elizabeth scolded, her cheeks turning red.

"What time is he picking you up?"

"He's not. We're going out right after work."

Grandpa's expression immediately sobered. "In my day – and your mother's day for that matter – a man picked up a girl at her house and met her parents. I'm sure that same practice still continues today."

"I know, Grandpa. But I'm sure we're going out someplace in Boston, and it's just easier than coming all the way home and then going back into town again." She kissed his cheek reassuringly. "Don't worry. The next time we go out – if there is a next time – he'll pick me up at the door. Okay?"

"Well, okay." His expression softened a little as he gazed fondly at his granddaughter.

~

On Friday morning, Elizabeth dressed with care. She fastened a brilliantly laid, gold-leafed brooch with two diamonds on her lapel. It had been her mother's engagement gift from her father. She stood back from the mirror to look. Not bad, she had to admit.

When she arrived at work, Betty was the first one she ran into. She immediately noticed her dressy outfit. "Do you have a date tonight?"

"Yes, Alan Bates asked me out."

"Alan Bates! Aren't you lucky? I would die to go out with him. In fact, I'm surprised he's never asked me out. I seem much more his type," Betty giggled.

"Oh, are you? Well, apparently I must be his type since he asked me instead of you." Elizabeth gave her a playful nudge on the arm.

"Well, don't forget to tell me next week how the date went." Betty turned on her heel to walk to her desk, leaving Elizabeth shaking her head. She certainly was a character.

~

At promptly five o'clock, Alan and Elizabeth took the elevator to the lobby and walked through the revolving doors. Alan hailed a cab and, as they got in, he told her they were going to The Parker House for dinner and drinks, and he asked if that sounded appealing to her. Elizabeth had never been to The Parker House; she merely smiled.

When they arrived, the maître d' greeted Alan by name and showed them to their table.

"Would you like something to drink before ordering?" Alan asked as the waiter hovered. "Martini? Tom Collins? Bloody Mary?"

"I'm not sure. I'm afraid I haven't had any of those combinations."

"How about something non-alcoholic? A ginger ale?"

"That would be fine." Elizabeth breathed an inward sigh of relief. Elizabeth had little opportunity or desire to imbibe. Alan ordered her ginger ale and a gin and tonic for himself.

"Now, then," Alan began. "Why don't you tell me a little about yourself? Parents? Any brothers or sisters?"

"No. My parents both died when I was born, and I was their only child."

Alan looked stricken, and Elizabeth hastened to add, "I know; that's how everybody reacts when they hear that, but it was a long time ago, and I've been so fortunate in so many other ways."

"Well, I'm sure that's certainly true, considering the success of your grandfather. You must be on your own quite a bit, however. I know your grandfather travels extensively."

Elizabeth looked confused for a moment and then she understood. "Oh, I live with my other grandfather – Grandpa – my mother's father. George Keene is my paternal grandfather."

"So," Alan continued, "what else can you tell me? Do you come into town a lot? Are there any special clubs you like to go to? Any special hangouts you like?"

"No." Elizabeth blushed. Alan was making her acutely aware of her unsophisticated life. "I guess I don't have what you'd call a very exciting lifestyle. I do go to Maine quite a bit though. My great aunt lives there." Elizabeth considered telling Alan about her novel but decided against it. Instead, she said, "I do like writing quite a bit. I spend a lot of time on it."

Alan shrugged, and she was disappointed that her hobby registered such little interest. Elizabeth decided to ask a few questions of her own.

"What about yourself? I'm sure you have a much more interesting lifestyle than I do. Does your family live around here?"

"No. I'm from Connecticut originally. My parents still live there and I have an older brother who's married and lives near them."

"You must miss not living near them."

"Not really. I've basically been on my own since I left for college. I call them occasionally and go home for the holidays. That's good enough for me."

Elizabeth found it surprising that one could be so casual about one's family, but she was, she surmised, probably more sentimental than most because she had such a small one.

"Where did you go to school?"

"Brown University. Graduated Magna Cum Laude – 4th in my class, I'll immodestly add."

"That's impressive. Is that your class ring?" Elizabeth asked, noticing the massive gold band with emblazoned emblem on his right hand. "It's quite handsome."

Alan quickly twisted the ring so that the emblem was face down. "It is, but let's not talk about old college days."

"Okay then, why did you come to Boston?"

Alan told her about his days in New York and his career jump to Hodge's. "If I become a big enough fish around here," he concluded, "like your grandfather, I'm sure I'd consider making a move back to New York. I do always like to have a challenge ahead of me."

"You sound very ambitious," Elizabeth said. She saw a gleam of intense determination in his eyes such as she had never seen on anyone's face before. It almost frightened her. He smiled so charmingly, however, that she was disarmed.

Alan leaned toward her. "How about you? Are you ambitious? What's your goal in life?"

"I want to get married someday and have children."

To her surprise, Alan scoffed. "Surely you must have more goals than that. Maybe you just don't realize it yet."

"Oh, no. Really I don't. Maybe it's because I never had a traditional family life with parents and siblings, but that's truly what I desire more than anything."

"Maybe you have a point about not having had a family to grow up with," Alan conceded, leaning his chin against the tips of his fingers as he spoke. "But I still think that you will eventually want more than that."

"Like what?"

"A beautiful house, nice furniture, expensive jewelry, fancy clothes."

Elizabeth paused. "Some women do yearn for those things, but I usually don't spend much time thinking like that, especially when the odds of getting them are slim – at least on my salary."

"But not out of the realm of reality someday," Alan interjected. "I'm sure you stand to inherit quite a bit when your grandfather passes on."

"I've never given a thought to it. Besides, I'm sure my uncle – my father's brother – would inherit everything, which is fine with me."

Their food was served, and for the rest of the evening it seemed to Elizabeth that Alan's attention drifted. She felt as if somehow the evening had gone sour. After the meal he called a cab to take her home and he did not bring up the topic of getting together again. Nor did he try to kiss her.

~

During the next week, Elizabeth saw Alan only from a distance. She tried to casually catch his eye several times, but he was either too preoccupied or too far away to notice. When she reported to Betty about her date, Betty boosted her spirits. "It's only been a few days. When you do see him, try to act cool – like it's no big deal that he hasn't contacted you again."

"But wouldn't he think that I'm not interested?"

"Trust me: if he's interested, he'll ask you out again; if he doesn't, then you've got your pride intact."

She was still puzzling over Betty's words as she sat toying with the food on her dinner plate that evening. Betty clearly had more experience with men, but Elizabeth still wasn't very optimistic about Alan asking her out again.

At that moment there was a knock at the back door. Grandpa rose to answer it. Paul Keene stood there. If Grandpa's face registered surprise, his voice didn't, for he boomed in his hearty voice, "Come in! Come in! No need to stand there hovering on the doorstep, especially with this brisk wind tonight!"

He drew Paul inside, taking his suitcase from his hand. He ushered him towards the table, saying, "Elizabeth, set another plate and heat up some more of that stew."

Elizabeth ladled out the warm stew and cut some fresh slices of bread. While Paul ate, her grandfather carried the conversation. He talked of local happenings around town and what was going on at the paper mill. Paul only interjected a word or two as he ate, but at least that forbidding look he usually wore was absent from his face.

When they had finished supper, Grandpa stood and said, "Elizabeth, we'll be in the parlor. Would you mind putting on some tea?"

Elizabeth heard the parlor door shut and she knew from prior experience that a private discussion was to take place and they were not to be disturbed.

Elizabeth put the water on, washed and dried the dishes, and began preparing a tray. Finally she heard the parlor door open. Bearing the tray with steaming hot mugs of tea and a plate of hermit cookies, she entered.

She was surprised, however, to find only her grandfather present.

"Where's Uncle Paul?" she asked nervously. She was afraid he had departed as suddenly as he had arrived.

"I sent him up to the spare bedroom so he could put his things away," Grandpa replied. "We just had a small talk. I think he's going to be fine. He just needs to sort some things out and pull himself together. I made him promise he'd stay with us for a little while, although I don't think he needed much convincing. He said he plans on finding a place of his own, probably in town, but there's no need for him to think about that right at the moment."

They heard footsteps on the stairs and Paul entered the room.

"Thanks for supper. I think that was the best beef stew I've ever had." Then his sober face lightened up. "But don't tell Mother's cook I said that if you ever run in to her."

"I wouldn't dare," Elizabeth giggled. "What's going to happen to your cook, and to Fred?"

"My father released both. He gave them good allowances, though; I saw to that. Our cook will retire, and Fred's already lined up another job. The house is going to be closed up for now. Father's never there, and I prefer not to stay."

The thought of that enormous house dark and empty saddened her. And what bothered her even more was that no one would be there to tend the roses.

~

The next day when Elizabeth came home from work, she saw the shed door open and the light on. Paul was there, and it appeared as if he had been working hard, for the floor was neatly swept and many of the old harnesses, tools, and paraphernalia that had collected over the years had been organized in an orderly fashion.

"What do you think?" Paul asked, with a hopeful look on his face.

"It looks wonderful. But you really didn't have to do this, Paul. We're more than happy to have you. Besides, this must have taken hours."

"I want to earn my keep somehow, and I've actually enjoyed it. It's kept me busy, while giving my mind a chance to clear. I also chopped up all the crates out back for the woodstove."

For years, Grandpa had brought discarded wooden crates home from the paper mill. The crates made excellent kindling.

"Grandpa will be thrilled. But don't feel as if you've got to find things to do. You should be relaxing. Grandpa says you haven't taken a vacation in years." Elizabeth stopped short. She didn't want it to seem as if they had been talking about Paul behind his back.

"Yes, he's right. I haven't. That's why I've decided to take a short trip, to Europe. I plan on leaving the weekend before Thanksgiving."

"But you just got here. Surely you can wait until after the holidays."

"I'd like to, but I have business to attend to and, besides, Father wants me there for the holiday. I'm not sure why exactly. Holidays never seemed to matter a great deal to him before. Perhaps because Mother's gone now, he feels more sentimental. Don't worry, though. I'll be back before the Christmas bells finish chiming."

"Will you come back here to stay with us?"

"I don't see how I could refuse such an invitation. So maybe for a while, but I'll have to get out on my own eventually. Father's offered me full control of the Boston offices if I want them. I'm not sure that's what I want long-term, but I've decided to give it a chance."

"What will your father do?"

"He's going to expand the international side of the business, and I'm almost positive he'll make his residency in Switzerland. He might as well. After all, many of his business ties are there, and that's also where his mistress lives."

Elizabeth's jaw dropped. She had always known that her grandparents' marriage had been difficult and trying, but she had never imagined that her grandfather had sought other companionship, and, according to what Paul was implying, for so long. She had not even heard of anyone having a mistress, except in novels.

"Apparently this is quite a surprise to you. I guess I'm so used to it that I've forgotten to be appalled by it."

Paul leaned against an old sled, its runners rusty and slats cracked and Elizabeth perched herself on a low wooden crate, listening. "I'm sure you knew that Mother and Father never really had a good marriage. Their marriage came about as an ideal financial partnership between two very wealthy families."

"Oh, Paul," cried Elizabeth. "I'm sorry."

For the second time in as many weeks, Elizabeth reached up to kiss her uncle on the cheek, only this time she did not fear what his reaction would be. And indeed, Paul gave her a smile.

As Elizabeth walked towards the house, she could hear Paul whistling. He seemed happier than she'd ever seen him, and the fact that she'd contributed in a small way to his current frame of mind made her start whistling too. Paul was going to be just fine. At least she hoped so.

Chapter Eight

Alan was working late in order to finish a presentation for the following day. They had a new account with a major client, partially, Alan was sure, because of his presentation skills. He was determined to fully prepare his materials before leaving for the day. He looked up to see Neil standing in the doorway.

"I saw your light on and thought I'd stop by," Neil said. "Got much more work to do?"

Alan sighed. "Actually, I think I'm done, but it's certainly been a long day."

"Catch a bite to eat?" Neil asked.

"What, an extra knitting club night at the Summersby house?"

"You got it. It's my wife's social outlet. By the way, how was your date with my secretary last week?"

"Not bad," Alan replied as he began to pack up his belongings.

"That doesn't sound very promising," Neil pressed.

"Don't get me wrong. She's a very nice girl. I just don't think she's my type."

Neil shrugged his shoulders. "Hey, you gave it a shot. By the way, I just read in the paper that her grandfather is going to expand his international operations. As if he doesn't already have the lion's share in the U.S. He certainly seems to have the 'Midas Touch'."

International operations. Alan made no reply to Neil's information but, inwardly, his brain was racing. Maybe he had been too rash in dismissing Elizabeth Keene. After all, just because he had no intentions of a serious relationship with her didn't mean that he couldn't keep it on a casual level. If he did, he was bound to meet her grandfather sooner or later, and such a connection could benefit his career. Besides, he had enjoyed her company well enough. He had nothing to lose, at least until someone better came along.

Alan slapped Neil on the back and smiled. "That's the second good piece of information that you've given me in less than a fortnight. When I make my fortune someday, Neil, I think I'm going to have to cut you a share of it."

Neil laughed. "That's very generous of you. Nobody will ever be able to say you don't have a good heart."

Alan smiled. "Clearly, you must be asleep at the staff meetings or you wouldn't be saying that."

Neil laughed again. "So you noticed?"

Alan gave Neil a self-satisfied grin. There was nothing worse in business – at least in his mind – than being known as a soft touch. He had no intention of letting anyone think that of him.

~

"That was an excellent presentation, Alan, just excellent." Mr. Hodge extended his hand. "Those were some wonderful new ideas for investing. Did you come up with them on your own or did someone help you?"

Alan glanced toward the end of the conference room where two secretaries were gathering coffee cups. "One of the managers in the finance group had some input."

"Well, make sure you tell him it was a great presentation."

"I will sir. Thank you."

Phil Lawrence had been the chief architect of the presentation. Phil's father had passed away over the weekend, and he had called Alan on Monday to see if Alan could arrange to have the meeting postponed. Alan had told him he couldn't promise anything. And since he hadn't made a promise, he was not obligated to do anything, and the meeting went on as scheduled, with Alan confidently presenting Phil's material. If Phil had wanted to be part of the presentation, Alan thought, he should have delayed his father's funeral. After all, if you're dead, then waiting one more day to be buried in the ground for eternity shouldn't matter.

A few days later, an invitation came from Mr. Hodge's office. It requested that Alan meet with him and his vice-presidents for lunch in the conference room on Friday. It was routine for Mr. Hodge to meet with his upper level employees to enjoy a catered lunch while discussing weekly updates and upcoming events. It was obviously a nod to Alan, and his presence at the luncheon did not go unnoticed by fellow workers.

Alan had only been in his office for a few minutes after the lunch when Neil knocked on his door. He entered without waiting for permission.

"On the fast track, pal?" Neil smiled.

"They're probably just letting me get my feet wet," Alan replied guardedly. As much as he liked Neil, he didn't know him well enough to risk him spreading comments around the office. He didn't want to alert the others that he really was on the fast track until he was too far ahead for them to catch up.

"Believe me, you're being pegged as a potential executive staff member – oh, not for quite some time, but Mr. Hodge always likes to have someone in the wings, and he makes up his mind very quickly about people. I believe you have passed the first round."

Alan shrugged his shoulders. "Aren't you ever interested in throwing your hat in the ring?"

"Naw, I was too late in the game. The service was my career – and my vocation. When I retired five years ago, I was grateful enough to get this job. I enjoy it here, but I'm too old to climb the ladder, so to speak. I do, however, get a kick out of watching others ascend."

"What else can you tell me about Mr. Hodge?" Alan asked.

"Oh, a lot. Henry Edward Hodge was born into wealth and privilege as the son of a distinguished surgeon, but he firmly believes in a man making his own living and not living off the family silver. He went to Harvard, earned a business degree, and decided to open an investment firm. The rest, as they say, is history. He lives on Beacon Hill, is married to his college sweetheart, and they have one daughter who graduated from college last spring and who is the pride and joy of their lives. That about sums it up."

Alan laughed. "You should write social columns for your next career."

"No thanks. Tracking down the maître d' at the Ritz in order to find out if Jimmy Stewart had the haddock or filet mignon for dinner while he was in Boston is not my idea of fun. Thanks for the compliment though." Neil turned towards the door. "I've gotta get back to work, and I'm sure you do too."

Alan closed the door behind Neil. It was a real boon to have Mr.

Hodge take a liking to him, but it wouldn't do him any good if he didn't get his work done. He could savor his accomplishment later on at Joe & Nemo's. He planned to have a drink in one hand and the prettiest girl at the bar in the other.

Chapter Nine

The next morning Elizabeth was working at her desk when she looked up to see Alan Bates walking towards her boss's office. Alan briefly nodded in her direction as he passed and then, pausing, he turned around. He stared at her for a moment and then asked, "What are you doing tonight?"

"Nothing," she replied quickly, causing Alan to laugh outright. "What's so funny?"

"Well, when most women are asked if they're busy or not for a particular night, they don't usually just say 'nothing'."

"Well, I was going to do some writing."

"Then you are definitely free." Alan smiled at her winningly and her heart skipped a beat. "You know," he said, leaning down on the stack of documents on the corner of her desk, "I must admit, I didn't expect to be asking you out again. You see, I'm usually not interested in your type. However, I find your personality rather refreshing."

Elizabeth wasn't sure if that was a compliment or not, but he was gazing at her with such a warm, lazy smile that she quickly decided it must be.

"I'll meet you right here after work, okay?"

Elizabeth immediately thought of her Grandpa's disapproval of going out directly from work. But she didn't want to challenge Alan. "Okay," she agreed.

Elizabeth called home at the end of the workday to let Grandpa know that she was going out with Alan that night. She hoped he would be home and she breathed a sigh of relief when he heard his cheery voice on the line. However, his tone changed upon hearing her plan.

"I thought he was going to pick you up here the next time you went out," he said sharply.

"I know, Grandpa. It's just that it came up unexpectedly and it's so much more convenient to go out straight from work."

"That's not the point, whether it's convenient or not. A proper gentleman would make a point of meeting a girl's family and not go out gallivanting with her any time he wishes. Am I right?"

"Yes, Grandpa."

"Then I'm to assume that the next time you go out, he will pick you up at home. Understood?"

"Yes." Elizabeth felt the blood come to her cheeks. She knew Grandpa was right. It would have been preferable to have Alan come to their home and meet Grandpa face to face. She had just been too timid to ask.

~

After work they once again took a cab to The Parker House. As they were seated, Elizabeth's recollection of her grandpa's concern brought a troubled expression to her face. She also wondered about Alan's comment earlier.

"Alan?"

"Yes?" he drawled in a lazy tone.

"Earlier at the office, when you mentioned that you usually don't date my type – what type did you mean, exactly?"

"Are you asking what type do I usually date, or what type are you?" He flicked his hand at her. "Never mind. If you're a normal, full-blooded female, you'll want the answer to both." He leaned back and let his eyes roam the room. "Now, let's see. The girls I usually date are much more independent. They've been on their own for a while, and they know what they're looking for in life. They also know what to expect on a date from men, whereas your type – "

"Yes?" Elizabeth prompted.

Alan smiled. "As I said before, I've never dated a girl like you before. Let's just say you're a refreshing change."

Elizabeth didn't know if that was good or bad. Then she remembered what Grandpa had always said about her grandma. He said he had never known anyone like her before and that she had caught his fancy right from the start. Perhaps that was what Alan was trying to say. That just seemed so perfect. Elizabeth turned a broad smile towards Alan. Tonight was proving to be lovely.

~

The following week Alan asked Elizabeth out again, for Friday. Elizabeth immediately accepted. Encouraged by the fact that Alan seemed to have taken an interest in her, she summoned up the nerve to ask him if he would mind picking her up at her house. "My grandpa would like to meet you," she stated rather shyly. She hoped Alan did not think her too old-fashioned.

Alan hesitated before nodding his head. "Why yes, I'm sure he would. Why don't I pick you up a little later? That will give you enough time to go home and change. Would seven o'clock work?"

"That will be fine."

When Betty dropped off some typing later that day, Elizabeth told her the exciting news.

"That's great. Of course, I still have a grudge against him for not asking me out, especially seeing as how I met him before you did, but that's not your problem. Anyways, good luck, and don't forget to keep me updated."

~

On Friday night, at precisely seven o'clock, the doorbell rang. Elizabeth had been ready and waiting for fifteen minutes, but she forced herself to stay upstairs and let her grandfather answer the door.

Elizabeth could hear Alan and her grandpa exchange greetings, and then their voices became inaudible as they walked into the parlor. In a few minutes, she heard her grandpa walk out to the hallway and call up the stairs for her.

After counting to ten she descended, trying to calm her pounding heart. She could hardly believe that Alan Bates, with his mesmerizing blue eyes and wavy blond hair, was standing in her very own parlor.

Alan turned to greet her politely. He seemed tense.

Elizabeth decided that he must be nervous about meeting her grandfather for the first time.

~

For the next three weeks Alan consistently asked her out for Friday nights and, at Elizabeth's request, picked her up at home. Elizabeth sensed that Grandpa was not happy about her seeing him. She wasn't sure why. Alan would pick her up at home as Grandpa had insisted and he would exchange polite conversation with Grandpa, but both men seemed ill at ease with each other. Only once had Grandpa tried to speak to her about Alan. It was on a night when Alan had brought her home later than usual. As she ascended the stairs for bed, Grandpa appeared at the door to his bedroom, his robe wrapped tightly around him. "Perhaps we could have a little talk –"

"Yes, Grandpa," Elizabeth agreed, although her tone said otherwise.

"Would you want to think about perhaps dating some other men?"

"I don't want to see anyone else right now. I like Alan."

"It wouldn't hurt to just try a date or two – "

Elizabeth cut in before he had a chance to continue. "It's very late, Grandpa, and I'd just like to go to bed. Goodnight."

She hurried up the stairs before he was able to stop her. She had never in her life interrupted her grandfather without apologizing, but she had no desire to discuss the topic. She knew her grandfather meant well, but she had every intention of continuing to see Alan, and nothing that Grandpa said would change her mind.

Chapter Ten

On Friday afternoon Alan checked that he had all his needed papers in his briefcase before he locked the door behind him. *You can't be too careful*, he thought. Alan knew that more than a few of his coworkers would be only too happy to take credit for ideas he had. He was already one of Mr. Hodge's favorite employees, and Alan was happy to make sure everyone was aware of this. He had overheard one manager call him 'territorial' and 'pushy' and Alan couldn't be happier. He wanted a reputation that made others feel intimidated.

He wasn't picking up Elizabeth at her house until seven, so he decided to stop for a drink with Neil at Joe & Nemo's beforehand. The bar was already crowded with businessmen and working girls. They settled themselves on barstools and Alan brought his martini to his lips. Neil toyed with his beer.

"I've been meaning to ask you about Elizabeth, Alan," Neil began. "I thought my secretary wasn't your type."

"She actually isn't, but I enjoy her company and, to be honest, she is a refreshing change from the more worldly type of girl, if you know what I mean."

"No, I get it." Neil paused a moment to take a swig of his beer. "Elizabeth is not only one of the nicest girls I've ever known, she's as pure as they come. Doesn't smoke, drink, and, from my personal opinion – and not that I'm prying – she's probably like a schoolgirl on her first date."

Alan grinned. "You got that right. For all those reasons, I shouldn't have bothered with her beyond the first date, but somehow she holds my interest." Alan downed his martini. "How about one more drink before I have to get going? I'll buy."

~

When he arrived at Elizabeth's doorstep, he was greeted by John

Burke, who was talking with an unfamiliar man. Elizabeth's grandpa introduced him as Charles Sullivan, a fisherman from Maine. As soon as he mentioned the name, Alan put two and two together. Elizabeth had mentioned the Sullivans from time to time, and he remembered that she and her grandpa were close to this family. Mr. Sullivan, John Burke said, had come to Boston in order to attend the wake of an old friend. As John Burke introduced Alan, he added that Alan was an investment manager at the firm where Elizabeth worked.

"That's interesting," Mr. Sullivan commented. "Over the past few years, I've put some money aside and I've been thinking for a while of investing it, but I don't have any experience in how to go about it."

Alan peered at Mr. Sullivan. He noted the dress jacket, shiny from use, which hung from Mr. Sullivan's sloping shoulders. His rumpled shirt was tucked into trousers held up by an oversized belt. His face had a weathered, eager look. Alan cleared his throat.

"I'm sorry, but our firm only handles large sums of money." The moment he spoke, he could tell that he had insulted Mr. Sullivan.

A wave of red spread across Charles Sullivan's face. He sputtered, "Seems like a good amount of money to me!"

"I'm sure it is, Mr. Sullivan. I'm sure it is."

Mr. Sullivan stayed silent, looking embarrassed.

Alan looked toward the stairs, hoping Elizabeth would come down so that he could escape her grandpa and family friend.

John Burke looked visibly angry as he turned to call for Elizabeth.

As she descended, the three men were completely silent. Elizabeth looked at each of them in turn. "Is everything okay?"

"Of course. We just have to get going. We're running late." Alan put his hand on top of hers and pulled her toward the car.

He had no intention of discussing what had happened. If John Burke related to his granddaughter what had transpired and Elizabeth became upset, then so be it. The worst that could happen was that she would refuse to date him anymore, and that, Alan thought, might be an appropriate end to a relationship that was probably never meant to be.

Chapter Eleven

Armistice Day fell on the second Sunday in November, and the following day, Monday, was to be a day of observance. Elizabeth and her grandfather had planned on spending the weekend in Maine so that they could take part in Father Joe's birthday. They also wanted to attend the town parade in York.

When Alan asked her out for the next Friday, Elizabeth told him about their plans. She suggested going out Thursday night instead.

"Sorry," Alan promptly answered, "I have plans for then."

Elizabeth couldn't help feeling disappointed. "Perhaps we could get together on Sunday when I get back?" she asked.

"I'm afraid not," Alan replied firmly. "I'm booked the rest of the weekend. But don't worry about it if you can't make it. We'll just go out the following Friday. Okay?"

"Okay," Elizabeth replied, trying not to show her disappointment. She was rather peeved that Alan did not appear to be too upset about not being able to see her, and that he had not offered to elaborate on his other plans.

Alan seemed to sense her unhappiness. Reaching over her shoulder, he wound a strand of her wavy, dark hair around his finger as he murmured, "I think I'm really going to miss you all next week until the next Friday."

Elizabeth whispered in return, "I'm going to miss you, too."

Alan leaned forward to casually brush his mouth against hers. When they at last parted, her heart ached at the thought of having to wait two weeks to see him outside of work. Even the thought of having extra time to work on her novel did not assuage the heartache she felt.

~

The following weekend Elizabeth was still feeling down. She missed Alan and was silent on the way up to York. On Saturday night, after the birthday cake had been cut and everyone had drifted out onto the front porch, she trudged upstairs with Mary Francis to the girls' room. She had hardly sat down at the foot of Mary Francis's bed when Charlie wandered in.

"Why does Lizabeth look so sad?" he asked Mary Francis. He hopped onto the bed next to her.

"She's sad because she misses her boyfriend," Mary Francis explained.

"Elizabeth has a boyfriend?"

"He's really not my boyfriend," Elizabeth said.

"Of course he is," Dolly declared. She had just entered the room, a second slice of cake in hand. "How long have you been going out?"

"Well, we first went out the week after Grandmother died, so that would be about," Elizabeth counted on her fingers, "four, five, almost six weeks."

"Six weeks," Dolly echoed. "Why, you're not only going out, you're going steady!"

"Dolly," Mary Francis interjected, "much as I hate to admit that I agree with you on anything, I do think you're right, that Alan is most definitely her boyfriend. But I think that's different than going steady." Mary Francis directed her question towards Elizabeth. "He hasn't asked you to go steady, has he?"

"No."

"You see," Mary Francis said. "Case closed."

"Oh, pooh!" Dolly snorted. "No one *asks* someone to go steady anymore. That's so old-fashioned!"

"Then how do you know you're going steady?" Elizabeth asked.

"It's just understood, that's all," Dolly answered, with the confidence of a person who knows about such matters. "Trust me. You're going steady."

Elizabeth doubted very much that such was the case. Somehow she had the feeling that if they were, Alan would have stated so in no uncertain terms. She was willing to conclude, though, that Alan was her boyfriend. Perhaps one day they would go steady, and she even found herself fantasizing about one day walking down the aisle on her grandpa's arm, with Alan at the end of the aisle waiting for her.

Chapter Twelve

Alan was looking forward to the coming three day weekend, all the more so since Elizabeth would be in Maine, giving him an extra degree of freedom. He stuffed papers from his desk into his briefcase. As usual, he would spend part of the weekend working, but he was also looking forward to a date he had lined up. He wouldn't have minded spending some time with Betty, the buxom redhead at work. She had clearly been interested in him until he began dating Elizabeth. She had cooled her interest though, probably due to the girls' friendship. It didn't matter. He hadn't far to look to find a companion for the weekend.

On Friday night his date with Deedee turned out to be quite enjoyable. She was a waitress at one of the area bars and they had exchanged glances enough for Alan to know she was interested. Her generous assets were what he was more interested in at the moment. It was too bad she was just a waitress. If she had come from a wealthy prestigious family, he would have been content with seeing much more of her. However he didn't have to worry about her reading too much into their get-together. She had been very upfront about her independence; therefore, she was exactly the kind of girl it was fun to spend time with, no strings attached.

After a casual dinner, they went to Alan's apartment in order to relax. Sliding next to her, he tipped her head back for a long kiss which was well received. As his lips roamed her throat, pushing her sweater off her shoulder, Deedee giggled.

"Am I your nightcap?"

"Yes, and I'll take a double shot."

"Be my guest. Oh, Alan," she struggled to a sitting position, which by no means slowed Alan down, "I keep forgetting to ask you, do you work with a girl named Betty Higgins?"

Alan stiffened but kept his tone casual. He didn't want Betty telling

Elizabeth that he had been out on a date. "The name sounds familiar. Why?"

"She just comes in the bar sometimes and I think she said she worked in the same office as you."

"She might, but I prefer not to discuss my personal life at work, so there's no need to mention to a fellow coworker that we've gone out, understand?" Alan hardened his voice as he spoke so that Deedee would understand very clearly what he was trying to tell her.

"Sure, doesn't matter to me."

"Good. Now I have other things on my mind." He pulled Deedee close to him again and ran his hand up and down her leg. Whatever happened on this leather couch, it would be far more than he would probably ever get from Elizabeth Keene.

Chapter Thirteen

The Friday following the Armistice Day weekend brought November's full chill. Through the tall windows of the Parker House Elizabeth watched leaves swirl on the sidewalk. She had become very familiar with the restaurant, as it was where she and Alan went on each of their dates. Besides being a distinguished restaurant - which Elizabeth learned was very important to Alan - it was a popular watering-hole for his fellow associates and clients because it was so near the financial district. It was not uncommon for their meal to be interrupted by a friend or colleague who stopped by to say hello, or for Alan to excuse himself when he saw a familiar person arrive.

Elizabeth began feeling slightly resentful that the only night he was ever available was Friday night. Of course she didn't know what other obligations he might have and, as Grandpa always said, you could never understand a person until you had walked a mile in his shoes. With that thought in mind, Elizabeth kept her complaints to herself. After all, Alan was smart and funny, and he always had a comical story about something that had happened during the week. Elizabeth, in turn, decided to tell Alan about her novel.

Alan replied, sardonically, that he didn't know too many secretaries who became famous authors. "Besides," he'd said, "why spend time writing when you can spend it having fun?"

That evening they sat waiting for their check to arrive. Alan suggested, "I thought perhaps we could go to my place for a while after this and relax."

Elizabeth stared at Alan with a startled look and stammered, "Oh, I don't think – I mean, it's not that I wouldn't want to– "

Alan finished the thought for her. "Are you trying to say that you don't think it would be proper? Never mind. I think I already know the answer."

Alan pulled a cigarette case out of his breast pocket before he continued talking. "Elizabeth, have you ever thought about moving out from your grandpa's house? You know, finding a place of your own?"

"Why, no, I haven't," Elizabeth confessed. Such a thought had never once flitted through her mind. "We're very content living together, and I think that if I were to move out, my grandpa would be very lonely."

"Surely your grandfather expects that someday you'll move on. He can't expect you to live at home your whole life, and I'm sure his card buddies would keep him company. If you were worried about expenses, you could always move in with a couple of girlfriends. Then you could go where you want and do what you want, whenever you felt like it. You could also have eligible, young men over to visit." Alan smiled and laid his hand on top of hers.

The waiter appeared with the check and Elizabeth slid her hand out from under his. She tried to collect her thoughts. The fact that Alan wanted to spend more time with her sent a flush to her cheeks, although why he would think she would want other eligible, young men to visit her when she was seeing him, she could not fathom. She also could not understand why it should matter to Alan whether or not she had a place of her own. After all, wouldn't it be just as improper for him to visit her at her apartment as it would be for her to visit him at his?

She forgot these questions, however, as soon as they pulled up in front of her house, for Alan started kissing her more passionately and intensely than he ever had before. He only stopped when Elizabeth managed to wiggle out of his close embrace, whispering a hurried goodnight before escaping to the warmth – and safety – of home.

Chapter Fourteen

The only appointment Alan had left on his agenda before taking leave for Thanksgiving week was his 'new employee' review with Mr. Hodge. Mr. Hodge had repeatedly praised his work, so he was looking forward to it. He was escorted into Mr. Hodge's office by Lillian Graham, and Mr. Hodge waved him to the seat in front of his desk, rising briefly to shake hands.

"Come in, come in! I'm sure you're not too concerned about this meeting, Alan. You've achieved a lot in a very short amount of time. In fact, I've hardly seen such productivity and ingenious ideas from such a young employee."

"Thank you, sir. Your words are indeed a high compliment coming from such a successful businessman."

Mr. Hodge nodded in acknowledgement. "By the way, I know you and Phil Lawrence teamed up for a project recently. At least I thought you had. I don't recall you two presenting it."

"To be honest, sir, he was capable enough, but –" Alan paused to clear his throat. "Phil rather left me holding the bag the day of the presentation. It was some personal reason, but in my opinion it could have waited."

"I'm surprised. I've heard very good things about Phil otherwise."

"As I said, sir, he's qualified enough. Hopefully he'll be more dependable in the future."

"Thank you for your input, Alan. And one more thing. I figured I'll 'let the cat out of the bag' by telling you that at our staff meeting on Monday my daughter, Priscilla, is going to begin working here."

Alan's brain began contemplating the dynamics of such a scenario. "That's wonderful, sir. I'm sure she'll be an excellent asset to the company."

"Obviously I'm very biased, but I do think she's well qualified. She graduated from Wellesley College in the spring with a BSA in business, so I think she will do just fine. Hopefully the next time her picture is in the paper it will be in the business section, not the art section."

Alan looked at Mr. Hodge quizzically. "Excuse me, sir. I'm afraid I don't quite follow your reference to the arts."

"My wife and daughter are very involved in the city's museums and galleries, so there's always some fundraiser or gallery showing where they're getting their picture taken."

"If her picture does show up in the art business section in the future, I'll be sure to notice her."

"If her picture is in the paper, don't worry, she'll make sure everyone notices. But thank you for your interest, Alan. I'm sure I can count on you and the rest of the staff to give her a warm welcome."

~

Alan returned to his office contemplating the possibilities created by having the president's daughter as a fellow employee. She would definitely be close to him in age as she had just graduated college. Obviously she came from a wealthy and privileged family. Alan wondered whether or not she was beautiful. And, if she was, would it be wise to pursue the president's daughter? Probably not. If the relationship didn't work out, things could get messy at work, and he didn't want anything to compromise his career. No matter, she was probably heavy-set and dim-witted, which meant he wouldn't have a dilemma at all.

Chapter Fifteen

Three days before Thanksgiving, Paul, Elizabeth, and John Burke gathered for supper. Paul was planning to leave for Europe the next day. Elizabeth again implored him to delay his trip until after Thanksgiving. "Surely a few days won't make much of a difference," she pleaded.

"Believe me when I say I'm very flattered by the notion of being missed while I'm gone. As I told you before, I have business to take care of in Europe, but that's not the only reason I'm leaving. You see, Father is getting married on Thanksgiving Day."

With a clatter, Elizabeth's knife and fork tumbled to her plate before somersaulting over the edge onto the floor. Elizabeth was stunned. Her grandfather was remarrying less than two months after her grandmother had passed away? This was unconscionable. And why was Paul just now telling them this? Or had Grandpa known all along?

Grandpa reached to pick up Elizabeth's utensils and Paul calmly reached behind him to take a clean set of cutlery out of the drawer. He handed them to Elizabeth.

"It's going to be a simple ceremony with just a few friends of theirs. Besides, as you know, Thanksgiving isn't a holiday in England, but their reception is going to include a turkey dinner with all the trimmings. Afterwards, they're leaving for their honeymoon during which time I'll cover the business for my father. I'm also going to take advantage of that time to transfer all the international operations of the Boston office over to his offices in England. As you know, I've been running the Boston office for quite a while, but now that my father's remarrying and starting a new life in England, he's asked me to officially take over here. I think it will not only be a wise business move, but it will also be better on a personal level."

Elizabeth's head was still swimming. When she managed to speak, all she could murmur was, "Will you be back in time for Christmas or New Years?"

"I should be. They're going to Switzerland for Christmas. Until they leave, I'll work with my father on all the business details. After I get back here, I'd like to find an apartment, but if it's not too much trouble, I'd like to stay here until I do. If that's all right, that is."

"Of course it's all right," Grandpa said, reaching over to give Paul a friendly slap on the back. "You know you don't even have to ask. You're family. And I don't think you have to ask how Elizabeth feels."

Elizabeth cleared her throat. "There might be someone else who will be sorry to see you go overseas."

Paul paused in his eating. A flush of color came to his cheeks.

"I couldn't help but notice," Elizabeth continued, "the letters that have come addressed to you from Dolly." Elizabeth gave Grandpa a knowing smile, then rose from the table.

Paul gave a forced laugh. "Dolly? She has some sort of school girl crush. I'm merely polite to her. I doubt she'll give me a second thought while I'm gone." Paul pushed back from the table and Elizabeth's eyes followed him out of the room.

"I suspect," she said to her grandpa, "that Dolly will give Paul plenty of second thoughts."

~

The following morning Paul left for Europe and Elizabeth and Grandpa left for York, catching a ride with Harry. Elizabeth felt assured that Alan would be missing her this weekend. After his advances on the last date, wasn't it clear that he was getting serious about her?

For once it was nice to know what Alan was doing when he wasn't with her. He'd told her he'd be in Connecticut with his family. Perhaps this was a good sign that he would begin confiding in her more and more. Elizabeth was anxious to talk to Mary Francis and Dolly about Alan. She knew they would be excited for her.

On the way to Maine, Grandpa surprised her by bringing up the subject of her novel. She had finally told him a bit about what she had been working on, as he was always teasing her about hiding it in her room. Now, Grandpa shared that news with Harry.

"Why don't you try getting it published?" Harry asked.

"I've thought of it from time to time, but I really don't have a clue how to go about it."

"The paper mill sells their paper to several publishing companies," Grandpa said. "One of my friends at work has the names of editors he can give me. Why don't you give it a try?"

Elizabeth's eyes lit up. "Oh, Grandpa, that would be wonderful! I only have the climax to write. I'll start working on it when we get home. Grandpa, you're the best!"

"And I," said Harry, "will be the first to buy your book when it gets published."

~

Harry dropped them off at Aunt May's, promising to pick them up Sunday afternoon. Aunt May was waiting for them with some refreshments. While they ate, Aunt May pestered Elizabeth with questions about Alan. "How is your boyfriend? Do you think he is 'the one' for you?"

Elizabeth blushed. "I don't think we're too serious yet, but he's so much fun to be with, and we go out most every Friday night."

Aunt May nodded her head. "Sounds like he's smitten with you. Do you think so, John?"

"I suppose so."

Elizabeth noted Grandpa's lack of enthusiasm. Alan had been picking her up at home every Friday, which she thought would have satisfied Grandpa, but it seemed that Alan could never rise in Grandpa's estimation. Alan also seemed to be noncommittal whenever she mentioned her grandpa. She hoped time would help the two men have more comradery.

At least when she saw the girls, they would be excited to hear about her dating status. When the three of them rang the Sullivan's doorbell, Dolly opened the door, looking over their heads as the rest of the family crowded around to wish them a happy Thanksgiving.

"Where's Paul? Isn't he coming?" Dolly looked almost panicky.

"I'm sorry," Elizabeth replied. "He left for Europe yesterday in order to spend the holiday with his father."

A shriek escaped from Dolly, to which Mary Francis reprimanded her. "For goodness sake! Do you have to take everything so hard? He barely even knows us and you expect him to spend Thanksgiving with us. Why don't you ask Elizabeth about Alan? At least she has a real boyfriend, instead of one she just fantasizes about."

Dolly turned to her friend. "Elizabeth, I am sincerely striving to be interested in your dating status, but I just need a few moments to compose myself after this tragic turn of events. If you'll excuse me, I'll be upstairs in recluse." Dolly turned and climbed the stairs, her head held high while everyone watched her ascent.

As she disappeared, Margaret Sullivan shook her head. "Heaven help the man who marries her."

"Prayers, my dear mother! Lots of prayers!" Father Joe teased.

"Who do you think I'm praying for at every Mass? Now, come on into the parlor."

As everyone followed Margaret, Mary Francis pulled Elizabeth into a corner. "Elizabeth, you must tell me everything that's new with you and Alan. Does he still take you out every Friday night? Has he given you any little presents? Do you think you're in love?"

"I'm not sure I'm *in* love, but I'm falling fast. However Alan hasn't said anything like that to me yet, so I'm not sure what he's thinking."

"Well, clearly he's interested in you if you see him every Friday. Why don't you invite him to Sunday dinner or go to a movie on a Saturday night?"

"Actually, I did suggest both those things, but he always seems to have plans."

"What does he do the rest of the weekend?"

"I do know he does office work at home, so it must take up a lot of his time."

"He certainly can't spend all weekend just doing work. Are you sure he's not dating anyone else?"

Elizabeth looked so aghast that Mary Francis hastened to reassure her. "I'm sorry, Elizabeth. I don't even know why I said that. I'm sure he's just so busy with work, just like you said."

They were interrupted by Father Joe who, having just learned about her manuscript from Grandpa, asked how it was coming along. Elizabeth told Mary Francis and him about Grandpa's offer to provide her publishers' names through his job at the mill. She was appreciative of their interest; however, Mary Francis's comments had rattled Elizabeth and she found it hard to discuss her writing. She had always taken Alan at his word, but it did seem rather implausible that anyone could spend almost their whole weekend doing office work. Was there something that Alan was hiding from her – or rather, someone?

Chapter Sixteen

On the Monday morning after the Thanksgiving weekend, Alan hurried down the hall for the weekly staff meeting. He hadn't seen Elizabeth yet that morning. He wondered if she was going to avoid him since she'd clearly tried to escape his advances the last time they'd gone out. No matter. He had bigger fish to fry at the moment.

He stopped outside the board room door to adjust his tie and took a brief moment to appear calm and relaxed before he entered. It was a small thing, but he always strived to look as if his day was going smoothly in front of his boss.

Most of the fellow managers had taken their seats. As Alan made his way halfway down the table from Mr. Hodge, Alan spotted the young woman who was seated to the right of his boss – clearly his daughter. What he saw took his breath away. She was beautiful, with golden blond hair that was pinned up in the back of her head and sapphire blue eyes fringed by golden lashes. Her black tailored linen suit was complimented by a matching set of opal earrings and necklace that glimmered against her creamy skin. Her makeup looked professionally done, and she had an aura about her that reflected higher education and polished etiquette.

Mr. Hodge stood up and cleared his throat. "Gentlemen, before we start our meeting, I would like to introduce my daughter – Priscilla Hodge."

Immediately there was a unanimous clapping of hands.

"Priscilla will be joining our company as a consultant. She graduated from Wellesley College in May with a B.A. in Business Management and, when she submitted her resume to me," and at this Mr. Hodge gave Priscilla a comical smile, "I suddenly realized the candidate I was looking for was right under my nose."

Everyone laughed.

"All kidding aside, even though she is my daughter, I know she is well-qualified for the job. I am certain you will enjoy working with her; she is certainly looking forward to working with all of you. "

There was another smattering of applause while Priscilla stood up to acknowledge her father's introduction.

After the meeting Alan maneuvered his way towards Priscilla, barely hiding his impatience to introduce himself. Many of the staff milled around her, offering congratulations and wishes of goodwill. One of them was Phil Lawrence. Phil had been icy to Alan ever since he had presented Phil's ideas at that staff meeting, but Alan didn't care. He approached Phil and Priscilla, standing to his full height. Phil, a full head shorter than Alan, gave Alan a darted look, made a small bow to Priscilla, and walked away. Alan was pleased. He had subtly exerted his power, and he was sure Priscilla had noticed. As he stood face-to-face with her, she rested her blue eyes on him, a half-smile flitting about her lips.

"It is indeed an honor and a pleasure to meet you, Miss Hodge."

"Why, thank you." She reached out to grasp his extended hand. When she went to withdraw her grasp, he held onto it, his usual method for getting a girl's attention.

Priscilla gave him a slightly flirtatious look. "I'm sorry, I didn't catch the name," she whispered huskily.

"Alan Bates. I won't keep you, but if you should need any assistance at all, I am more than willing to be of aid."

That afternoon he could do little else but think of Priscilla. He was completely transfixed by her. She was not only extremely beautiful, she had style, class, and obviously came from a prestigious family. She was, he knew in his gut, the girl he had been waiting for, the girl he wanted. He didn't know if she had a boyfriend. That was highly likely considering what a prize she was for any man she came into contact with. But even if she did, he was willing to compete for her, and there was no time to be lost. He suddenly dismissed the principle of not dating the boss's daughter.

Should he ask her for a date immediately, or would that be rushing it? Should he act only mildly interested in order not to appear too eager? He finally decided he would find opportunities to interact with her, and then he would ask her out. One thing he was sure of, he would not be dating Elizabeth Keene anymore. He genuinely liked her; she had a natural beauty, she was easy-going and had a good heart. And of course she had a wealthy grandfather with potential connections. But she did not have the finesse and social expertise he was looking for.

He did not want Priscilla to think that he was seeing anyone, so he needed to stop interaction with Elizabeth immediately. He never liked to verbally end relationships; he had discovered from previous experience that such a strategy was messy and drawn out. Avoidance was much easier. He could quietly move on, and she would be out of his life. After all, it wasn't as if he had made her any promises or asked her to go steady. She would be able to work on that silly book she was always talking about, and eventually she would find someone else more suited to her Pollyanna view of the world. He could already tell that Priscilla Hodge had a view of the world he could appreciate. She was exactly the type of girl he had been looking for.

Chapter Seventeen

The Monday after Thanksgiving, Elizabeth was filing material for Mr. Summersby when she noticed someone moving into the vacant office at the other end of the hall. Elizabeth had heard that the company would be bringing on a new financial consultant; perhaps this was her.

The woman was pretty – beautiful in fact – with ash-blond hair that was styled in a French twist at the back of her head. It made her look very mature and sophisticated, although Elizabeth guessed she was no older than she was. The newcomer's office, where several boxes were piled outside, was located near Janine's desk, who no doubt would divide her secretarial duties between the newcomer and Alan. Elizabeth hoped, for the new employee's sake, that she would have better luck befriending Janine than she had.

Lillian Graham came around the corner with a stack of documents. Following Elizabeth's gaze she commented, "So, she's finally arrived."

"Is that the new financial consultant?" Elizabeth asked.

"Yes. She's Mr. Hodge's daughter. Frankly, I can't understand why she's coming to work here. Henry Hodge has more money than he knows what to do with, and I'm sure she's well taken care of. I guess you have to give her credit for wanting to pull her own weight. I just hope that she doesn't start bossing everyone around."

"Why would she do that?"

Lillian laughed. "I can see that you haven't been in the working world very long. Let's just say that when a family member of the boss starts working for the company, before you can say *Jiminy Cricket*, they're acting like they own the company too. But there – I shouldn't go judging her before even giving her a chance." Lillian deposited several file folders on Elizabeth's desk. Then she leaned forward. "Just don't look too surprised," she said as she winked at Elizabeth, "when I say I told you so."

Elizabeth did not have to wait long to meet Miss Hodge. That afternoon Mr. Summersby gave her a document to deliver to the new employee. She walked up to the office and saw that Priscilla Hodge was talking with Janine. The women turned to look at her. Elizabeth was suddenly conscious of her attire, everything from her worn loafers to the metal barrettes she had shoved into her hair that morning.

Elizabeth smiled nervously. "Hi, I'm Elizabeth Keene," she said to Priscilla. "I work for Mr. Summersby at the other end of the hall."

Priscilla stared back at her, her lips slightly parted as if she could not believe what was standing before her.

Janine spoke up, but not before exchanging a private glance with Priscilla. "Elizabeth, this is Priscilla Hodge, Mr. Hodge's daughter. She's going to be working here as a financial consultant."

"I hope you like it here." Elizabeth smiled weakly, but there was no response, only a cold stare from Miss Hodge's ice-blue eyes. "Uh, Mr. Summersby asked me to bring this down for you to review and sign."

Elizabeth extended the document to Priscilla, but she did not take it. "Just put it on the desk please." Then she turned back to Janine.

Elizabeth felt the blood rise to her cheeks. She knew she had been dismissed, and she walked away feeling the brunt of their rudeness and a little embarrassed. She wondered if she should have approached Miss Hodge differently. Perhaps she should have complimented her on her new position or thought of something more interesting to say. Then she recalled the look the two women had given each other, as if there had been a private secret between them. Maybe because Janine had never cared for her she had already pitted Priscilla against her.

At the same time Elizabeth had a different concern. All week she had waited for Alan to stop by to invite her out for Friday night, but he had never appeared. The nearest she had been to him was when she spotted him down the hall talking to Priscilla. She hated to admit it, but a wave of jealousy had washed over her. Why did Alan have time to chat with Priscilla and yet couldn't find sixty seconds to walk down the hall to say hello to her? Undoubtedly he had noticed that Priscilla was very pretty, and that she wore beautiful, expensive clothes. Elizabeth was no match for Miss Hodge regarding beauty and fashion. She tried to keep her hopes up, however. If Alan really cared for her, as she did for him, then another woman wouldn't change the way he felt.

On Friday afternoon, after other employees were getting ready to go home, she loitered at her desk, hoping against hope that Alan would stop by to invite her out. If he did, she would be ready to go at a moment's notice. At quarter past five, however, he still had not appeared, and when she walked by his office, she found it in darkness.

~

That night Grandpa, Harry, and Fred ribbed each other while they ate Grandpa's homemade Irish stew. They then turned their ribbing to Elizabeth.

"What, no fancy dinner tonight?" Harry asked.

"She'd rather spend time with the three of us, of course!" Fred added.

Grandpa laughed but looked at her questioningly.

"I'd like to catch up on some writing," Elizabeth offered, not meeting their eyes. She went upstairs and closed the door to her room.

~

It had been two weeks since their last, amorous date. She replayed their last time together again and again in her mind. Resolutely, she picked up her manuscript but found that she had no interest in writing. After crossing out several sentences, she tossed the manuscript on the floor and buried her head in her pillow, trying to stem the flood of tears. Had she done or said something wrong? When she had escaped from his physical advances, had she put him off permanently? She considered confronting him, but she remembered Mary Francis saying that a man should always pursue a woman. Mary Francis was probably right. Elizabeth thought about consulting Betty, but she was not sure she could trust Betty to give her advice befitting a lady. Elizabeth decided, reluctantly, that she could only hope for the best.

Chapter Eighteen

In the week following Thanksgiving Alan had the good fortune to run into Priscilla several times. When he saw her in the hall, he made a point of giving her a broad smile. On Thursday he stumbled upon her working in the conference room alone. He took in the sweep of blond hair, the finely sculpted cheekbones, and the creamy, slender neck.

"Mind if I impose?" he asked.

Looking up, Priscilla tossed the report she had been reading on the table. "Not at all."

He grabbed the chair opposite her and sat down. He noticed the name of the client on the top of the report. "I see you're taking over the Mortell account. How much time have you blocked off for your meeting with them?"

"From three to four-thirty tomorrow afternoon. Why do you ask?"

"I'll just give you a tip and suggest that you take your time with them. They're a loyal client of ours, but they do like to be catered to, so taking extra time will definitely be worth your while."

"Thank you. I appreciate your advice." Priscilla's eyes appraised Alan, then she pushed the report to the side with a manicured finger. "I must tell you that my father is very impressed with your business expertise."

"I appreciate such a high compliment." Alan leaned close to her. "I would appreciate it even more if his daughter were also impressed by me."

Priscilla arched her eyebrows and examined Alan's face. "I don't think his daughter knows Mr. Bates well enough to decide whether she's impressed or not."

"Perhaps Miss Hodge would like to go to dinner with Mr. Bates tomorrow night after her meeting with the Mortells and she can have an opportunity to assess him." Alan held his breath. Had he gone too far?

Priscilla raised her chin and gave Alan a deliberate look. "Miss Hodge would be pleased to dine with Mr. Bates. Miss Hodge accepts his invitation."

"Excellent! Would the Parker House be an acceptable place to dine?"

"It's one of my favorite places. Shall we say five-thirty? I just need a little time to get my belongings together after the meeting."

"Perfect. I'll let you get back to work now." Alan turned to go, then looked back over his shoulder and gave her a wink. "If you need any more help with your report, you know where to find me."

~

On Friday Alan found it hard to concentrate on his work, something that rarely happened to him. At four-thirty, when he passed the conference room, he saw it was vacant. At least the meeting hadn't run late. A few minutes after five he packed up his briefcase and ducked into the men's room to check his appearance. He pulled a small flask of cologne from his case and splashed a bit on his cheeks. He ran a comb through his hair and straightened his tie. Making a good impression was going to be important. When he left the men's room fifteen minutes later, he felt very confident that Elizabeth would be gone for the day. He would certainly prefer to leave work without running into her.

~

Alan and Priscilla chatted companionably as they walked to the restaurant. Alan learned that Priscilla had been tutored at home by private teachers until high school. She had attended the prestigious Winsor School for Girls in Boston before attending Wellesley.

When it was his turn to talk about his upbringing, Alan mentioned growing up in Connecticut and then going to Brown. "How interesting," Priscilla chirped. "Then you must have had Professor Steinbeck for Economics. He and my father have been friends since their own college days."

Alan paused. "I may have. Much of my college days are a blur. You know how it is." He gave her a conspiratorial smile.

Priscilla clucked her tongue at him. "Oh, you bad boy!"

Alan laughed and took her elbow to guide her to their table.

When they were seated, Priscilla said, "You seemed very surprised when I said I would go out with you."

"I didn't know if there was a boyfriend in the picture or not."

Priscilla shrugged. "There have been some. If I wanted to date a man solely based on wealth and fame, I'd probably have a ring on my finger by now, but there's been no one who's held my interest for long. And now it's my turn to ask you. Janine is under the impression that you are seeing Neil Summersby's secretary, Elizabeth Keene. Is that right?"

Alan felt his face flush. He was embarrassed and at the same time angry with Janine. She had a reputation for being the office gossip. He answered dryly, "We had a few dates – nothing steady."

Priscilla was not going to drop the subject. "Pickings must have been slim. She seems so pathetic – that horrible hairstyle and those hand-me-down clothes! She's tried to befriend me, but I can't imagine what we would have in common."

As ambitious as he was for the finer things in life, Alan felt obliged to defend Elizabeth. "She's a decent person. I'm sure she was sincere in her efforts at friendship."

Priscilla conceded slightly. "You're probably right. But I don't think she runs in my circles."

In spite of his overwhelming attraction to Priscilla, Alan felt slightly repulsed by her condemnation of Elizabeth. It seemed uncalled for, but he had learned that women could be very competitive.

Aside from this brief exchange, Alan immensely enjoyed the evening. They had similar interests and goals. They both enjoyed the Boston night life and all it had to offer.

Alan hailed a cab to take them to the Hodge's home in Louisburg Square, where he would drop her off. He had already decided he would ask her out again and felt comfortably sure that she would accept.

At her doorstep he asked, "How would you feel about going out tomorrow night?"

"Miss Hodge accepts again," Priscilla said, slowly lowering and then raising her eyes.

Alan stepped close to her. "I was hoping you would say that," he whispered. He had planned on playing it cool on their first date, maybe ending the evening with a kiss on the cheek, but the moment was unfolding before him, and he wasn't going to lose the opportunity. Lightly pushing her back against the door, his lips landed hard on hers and he wrapped his hands around her waist. She responded to his affections, arching her neck as his lips roved along her cheekbone and along the hairline at her temple.

She laughed lightly as he sought her lips again. "I think I will have to go in before this gets out of control."

Alan's eyes blazed with lust. His passion for her could not be hidden. He fought to keep his voice steady as he reluctantly let her go. "Until tomorrow."

"Goodnight," Priscilla whispered, opening the door with her key and slowly closing it behind her.

She certainly seemed proficient in the art of romance, Alan thought as he entered the waiting cab. They had both dated others and she, like Alan, had probably been intimate enough with others to know what to expect. She was no innocent – not like Elizabeth Keene – and he enjoyed dating a girl who not only welcomed, but enjoyed his advances.

On every level they were compatible. The only thing that marred her character was what Alan sensed as an air of superiority that she had towards others beneath her station in life. That was probably to be expected, considering the exclusive lifestyle she had led. Well, thought Alan, no one was perfect. It certainly wasn't going to stop him from pursuing her.

Chapter Nineteen

In the weeks after Thanksgiving, many of Elizabeth's co-workers were in a giddy holiday mood, but Elizabeth couldn't summon the heart for it. By Friday of that second full week back to work, Alan still had made no effort to contact her, and Elizabeth came home that night exhausted and dispirited. She made excuses to Grandpa and went to bed early. In her room she lay looking at the ceiling, wondering if Alan was just not interested in her anymore. But if that was the case, why?

The following morning Grandpa, getting into the spirit of the season, hauled the box of Christmas decorations up from the cellar. In spite of her melancholy mood, the decorations lifted her spirits. Many of the ones they had used for years had been made by her mother. In addition there were beautiful, expensive ornaments that Paul had given to them that had belonged to her grandmother. This would be her first Christmas without Grandmother Keene. She hoped her grandmother was truly at peace. Elizabeth wondered what would become of her grandparent's house. Grandfather Keene would probably sell it now that he was living in Europe, and Paul would probably not want it.

On Saturday night, while Grandpa was at Harry's for poker, Elizabeth worked on her manuscript. Her heart was heavy, but she found herself able to write, and she was getting excited that she would be finished soon. Then she would think about sending it to one of the publishers Grandpa had offered to find for her. It probably stood little chance of being published, but if she never tried, it would certainly never happen.

By Monday she was still despondent over Alan. She confided her worries to Betty at lunch. "Believe me," Betty said. "I completely understand how you feel when you're around him. One gaze from those dreamy eyes and I also fell for him big time. But I can tell he's the type who's got a wandering eye."

Elizabeth stared at Betty as tears welled up in her eyes. "Are you saying that he's interested in other girls?"

"I don't want you to get too upset about it. Just because a man is attracted to other women doesn't mean that he isn't interested in you."

"I don't understand how any man could be interested in more than one woman at a time." Elizabeth shoved the remainder of her sandwich back in its bag. "I know I couldn't be interested in two men at once – especially if the man is Alan."

Betty looked at Elizabeth gently. "A woman whose heart is for only one guy – you certainly are a rare breed in my world, Elizabeth."

The next morning Elizabeth was taking the elevator from the lobby to the eighth floor when the elevator stopped at the second floor. When the door opened, Alan was waiting to get on, and her heart leapt. He nodded briefly to her as he removed his fedora. She was excited that she had such an unexpected opportunity to see him.

"Hello, Alan. I'm so glad I ran into you. I haven't seen you for so long." She hoped she did not sound as if she were gushing. What would Mary Francis say about that?

He returned her greeting politely. "Hello, Elizabeth. It's nice to see you too."

"You must be so busy at work," she continued, a bit more hesitantly. The elevator doors closed and they jolted upward.

"Yes, extremely so."

"I figured that's why I haven't seen you at all," Elizabeth ventured, hoping he would pick up on her words and mention something about being sorry they hadn't gotten together.

"Yes, exactly." Alan looked away as he spoke, intent on watching the floor numbers as they passed by.

"Perhaps if you're free sometime, we could get together," Elizabeth suggested, practically cringing at her own words. She knew Mary Francis would be appalled at her audacity. Only Betty, and perhaps Dolly, would approve. She had never in her life dreamed that she would speak so boldly, but the words had spilled out before she had even realized, and she found her heart was beating even faster in the hope that he would take her up on it.

"I'm afraid I'm going to be very busy for an indefinite period of time, what with my workload and all. You understand."

"Oh, yes, of course." She tried to smile as if she completely understood, but in truth she didn't. Did that mean that they weren't going out anymore? Was it all over between them? They had enjoyed such good times together. She felt as if the person standing next to her was a stranger. She had overheard several of the men in the office criticizing Alan's overbearing and superior attitude when dealing with them, yet Elizabeth knew the other side of him, and she knew that if others at work could only see this side of him, they too would realize what a wonderful person he really was.

The elevator stopped on the sixth floor to let some people on. After the doors had closed again, Elizabeth dared to ask one more question. She tried to keep her tone light. "Are you going to the company Christmas party next week? I'm really looking forward to it."

"I believe so," Alan replied off-handedly.

"Maybe I'll run into you there." Elizabeth realized she was probably making a fool of herself, but she couldn't help it. Maybe it was just as he said. He was simply too busy to make any definite plans right now. After all, he had always spent a lot of time at work, even evenings and weekends. Perhaps if she saw him at the party he would loosen up and their dating life would be back on track.

Chapter Twenty

He'd had successful back-to-back dates with Miss Priscilla Hodge, and Alan was more than ready for the next one. At promptly six o'clock on Saturday of the following weekend he stood on the door stoop of the Hodge residence and rang the bell. He hoped that Mr. Hodge would be the one to open the door. He knew Priscilla's father was impressed with him. If Mr. Hodge should ask him, even jokingly, what his intentions were towards his daughter, Alan would be more than ready to declare his desire to someday call Priscilla his wife. He realized his rush of feelings would be considered overly precipitous in the eyes of others, but for him there was no hesitancy. Priscilla possessed every qualification he was looking for in a wife – beauty, style, class, and social connections.

It was not Mr. Hodge, but a butler, who let him in, offering to hold his hat while escorting him through a large entryway with a polished marble floor. As they entered an ornately decorated sitting room, Mr. Hodge rose from a wing-backed chair to greet him.

The servant immediately disappeared as Mr. Hodge encouraged Alan to take the seat opposite him. "Priscilla told me you were taking her to The Ritz, so I hope you don't mind that I took the liberty of calling the maître d'. I have a private table there, and I asked him to set it aside for the two of you."

"Thank you, sir. That's very thoughtful of you."

"No problem at all. I'm glad to be able to add to an evening for my beloved daughter and one of my finest employees. Ah, here she is!"

Alan quickly stood. Priscilla was as captivating as ever in a black silk dress that fell to the top of her calves. Satiny black high heels showed her lovely curved legs to their best advantage. Around her neck was a double string of pearls.

"Hello, Daddy. Hello, Alan." She kissed each of them lightly on the cheek.

"You look lovely, dear," Mr. Hodge stated. "Don't you think so, Alan?"

"Absolutely. In fact, I have never seen a more beautiful woman."

Priscilla peered at Alan from underneath her lashes.

"Alan, Mrs. Hodge was hoping to be here to meet you, but she's getting ready for a gallery showing at the Museum of Fine Arts. Priscilla here is also heavily involved in the Art Society. At any rate, I'm sure you'll meet Mrs. Hodge in the near future. Now, off with the two of you," Mr. Hodge urged them. "I don't want to make you late."

After they were ensconced in his car, Alan said, "I hope you take my words as a compliment, but I don't know many young women who are so interested in museum art."

"I know. I'm always a little surprised at it myself. I'm sure it seems stuffy and boring to a lot of people, but I've always been attracted to the beauty of art. I probably like it because my mother has been involved with museums all my life, so I've grown up around it." Priscilla arranged her dress around her legs and turned her body toward Alan. "How about you? Besides work, what's your passion?"

Alan glanced sideways at Priscilla. He caught the sexual innuendo in the way she stressed the word 'passion.'

He spoke slowly, not bothering to hide his smirk. "My *passion* is beautiful women – or maybe just one beautiful woman – and I think I have just hit the jackpot."

"You certainly know how to charm a woman." Priscilla edged her body a little closer to Alan and leaned her head on his shoulder. Her nearness aroused him, and he knew that she knew it.

They stopped for a drink at the Ritz's bar before heading to their table. Priscilla was apparently well known at the Ritz and several men stopped to talk with her. Alan was glad when they finally reached the privacy of their table. During dinner Alan could not keep his eyes off Priscilla and he gleaned that Priscilla felt the same. She often leaned forward to talk to him in a husky voice and batted her golden eyelashes flirtatiously.

Afterwards they drove to Faneuil Hall, the three-and-a-half story brick structure looking majestic with its arched windows and domed cupola on top. Snow fell lightly, adding to the holiday atmosphere. As they walked along the cobblestones, Alan saw Betty Higgins walking towards them with a group of friends. Alan quickly turned aside, engaging Priscilla in conversation in the hope that she and Betty would not notice each other. Just as they rounded the corner of the Market, however, Alan heard his name. He pretended not to hear and strode quickly along with Priscilla. Hopefully Betty would not pursue them. After a few moments, he breathed a sigh of relief. Then he realized his efforts to avoid Betty probably wouldn't matter. Elizabeth would know soon enough that he was seeing Priscilla.

They hurried back to Alan's car, glad to escape the frigid air. When they arrived at Priscilla's house, he parked at the curb. Before Priscilla had a chance to open the door, Alan reached for her, pulling her close as his lips sought hers. "I've been waiting all night for this," he said.

They spent more than a little while wrapped in each other's arms. Alan pulled away only because he was not keen on having Mr. or Mrs. Hodge peer out the window and bear witness to their intimate moments.

As Priscilla prepared to leave, Alan asked, "What are you doing next weekend?"

"Going to the office Christmas party, just like you, remember?"

"That's right, I forgot." Alan grimaced to himself. How could he forget when Elizabeth had also mentioned it? He changed the subject. "I just want you to know, the only reason I'm not taking one more goodnight kiss is because I wouldn't want to lose your father's respect."

"I wouldn't worry about that. My father thinks very highly of you, and so do I. In fact, I think I may have met my match." Priscilla smiled coyly.

Alan's eyes darkened in intensity. Those were exactly the words he wanted to hear. "And I mine."

Chapter Twenty - One

The office Christmas party was to be that night and Elizabeth was a bundle of excitement. She wanted to look stunning in hopes of catching Alan's eye. She regretted that she'd have to wear her party clothes to work, but she'd have no time to come home between the end of the workday and the gathering. Hopefully others would also be going directly and would be dressed up at work.

Elizabeth had bought an emerald green silk dress to wear for Christmas, and she thought the office Christmas party a worthy enough occasion to wear it. Her black suede, ankle-strap shoes complimented it nicely, and she had even gone to the trouble of putting her hair up in rags the night before, something she normally never did during the week due to lack of time and energy. The resulting curls bounced lightly around her head and she couldn't help but smile at the effect. Maybe Alan would regret his indifference toward her.

At work several of the managers, including Mr. Summersby, commented on how nice she looked. Elizabeth felt almost giddy with excitement at the thought of the party that evening.

Lillian had kindly offered to drive her and Betty over to the luxurious Longwood Towers in Brighton, where Mr. Hodge had rented out the Tudor-style vintage ballroom for the office party. They left the office shortly after five o'clock.

When they arrived at the function room, Mr. Summersby introduced Elizabeth to a group of clients and he bought a round of drinks for everyone. Eventually talk turned to business and Elizabeth was glad when she saw Betty and Lillian talking with a group of secretaries from the typing pool. She politely excused herself and went over to talk with them.

Soon the room was noisy and crowded. Elizabeth kept an eye on the entrance, watching for Alan. She couldn't help but stare when she saw

Priscilla arrive with Janine. Priscilla had clearly gone home before coming, for she wore a black satin dress that literally glittered with sequins and a pearl gray fur was draped around her shoulders.

"Well, well, well," commented Lillian as they all eyed Priscilla. "I guess we know who the 'Belle of the Ball' is tonight."

Elizabeth made no comment, but she glanced at Betty and couldn't help feeling a twinge of satisfaction that Betty obviously felt the same way she did. The girls exchanged smirks and then began talking about the coming holiday. Lillian asked Elizabeth about her plans and she was in the process of telling them that she'd be spending Christmas in Maine when she saw Alan walk by. He appeared to be looking for someone but never rested his eyes on her. She saw him make his way towards the bar. Quickly turning to Betty, she whispered in her ear, "Can you walk over to the bar with me? I want to see if Alan will talk to me."

"Of course, but don't get your hopes up too much."

The two girls walked quickly until Alan was standing directly in front of them, waiting in the drink line. Betty prodded Elizabeth forward to stand next to Alan. When she reached him, Elizabeth cleared her throat. Alan turned in her direction and Elizabeth feigned surprise.

"Hi, Alan."

"Hello, Elizabeth." Alan grimaced, as if annoyed by her presence.

She wished they hadn't followed him now, but she wanted some sign from him. "I was hoping I'd see you here."

He didn't respond, turning instead to speak to the bartender. "One Scotch straight up, please." After a moment's hesitation, he glanced at her. "Did you want anything to drink?"

Elizabeth shook her head.

Alan handed over a crisp bill in return for his drink and walked away.

Elizabeth mumbled, "Have a good night."

Elizabeth walked dejectedly away and Betty hurried to catch up with her. "Elizabeth, just forget him. He's not worth your effort, and if you run into him later tonight, just pretend as though you're having a great time and you haven't even noticed him."

They reached the girls from the typing pool, who were discussing hem lengths, but Elizabeth barely paid attention. She had her eye on Alan, who appeared to be looking for someone. Elizabeth hoped it was not

Priscilla Hodge. Even though she'd seen Alan at Priscilla's desk during the past two weeks, she'd wanted to believe that it was related to business. She watched him now, and she could barely breathe. Alan made his way to where Priscilla was standing and slipped his arm around her waist. He then bent to kiss her caressingly on the cheek.

In one single moment, Elizabeth's world turned upside down and she found herself reeling. Could this be happening? Could this be a terrible hallucination? Had Alan, dear sweet Alan, just kissed Priscilla Hodge? If there had been any mistake in what she saw, it was verified by a second kiss, this time bestowed on Priscilla's lips. It was obvious that such affections were not new to Priscilla, for she seemed to welcome them as she bent her head back for more.

"My, my, my," tisked Betty. "Will you look at that? Alan Bates is making a beeline for the boss's daughter. I always said he had a wandering eye."

"I guess he was never going to bother with us typing pool girls," sighed one of the girls in the group. "But look at them now – making a spectacle of themselves."

Priscilla Hodge! Elizabeth's eyes begin to swim with tears. What a fool she had been! What a stupid, little fool! Betty had tried to tell her not to put much faith in him, yet she had chosen to. Now she could see that all the telltale signs had been staring her in the face. Elizabeth blinked hard and brushed her eyes to try to stem the oncoming flood. This was no time to give in to a fit of tears.

Elizabeth blinked rapidly and tried valiantly to look as if Alan's actions were nothing to her.

Betty, however, could see through her façade. She leaned close. "Are you okay? Believe me, I'd be a wreck if I found out my 'boyfriend' was seeing someone else."

"I'm fine. You know what they say, *Easy come, easy go*! I think this is going to be a short evening for me, though. There's somewhere else I need to be."

"How are you getting home?" Betty whispered.

Of course, Elizabeth thought, Betty fully realized that 'somewhere else' only meant home.

"I'm all set. I can call a friend for a ride."

Actually, she had no idea how she was to get home, but that mattered little at the moment. All she knew was that she had to get out of the place immediately.

At the coat room she turned in her ticket and waited with her back to the crowd. The coatroom attendant had trouble finding her garment and Elizabeth had to point it out to her. It was ironically right next to the gray fur that sparkled like glitter. She shoved her arms into her cloak and quickly left through a side exit.

As she slowly walked along, taxis sped by, some already loaded with passengers, others waiting for new customers. A taxi! Elizabeth had never taken one alone in her entire life, but it seemed her only option. She signaled to the closest cab and told the driver to take her to Dorchester, Lower Mills. "How much?" she asked hesitantly, after seating herself in the back.

"Four-fifty."

"Fine," she returned, although inwardly she quailed at the thought of spending that amount of money, plus a tip, just to get home.

When the taxi pulled up to the curb in Dorchester, Elizabeth handed over her carefully hoarded money. She ran up the walk, praying that Grandpa would be home. She rushed through the front door and there he was, coming up the hall. Elizabeth hurled herself into his arms.

"Well, well, well. What's all this?" He pulled far enough away to be able to see her face streaming with tears. "I take it you didn't have a very good time at the party, although I'm curious to know why. You were so looking forward to it."

"Oh, Grandpa!" Elizabeth sobbed. "I've been such a fool!"

"Does this have anything to do with Alan?"

"Yes," she cried between gulps.

He led her into the parlor and helped her sit, handing her his handkerchief before positioning himself next to her. Elizabeth blew her nose and wiped her eyes.

"Grandpa, I've been such an idiot. I can see now that Alan never had any serious intentions towards me. In fact, I think he only went out with me when he didn't have anything better to do."

"How did you find all this out? Did he tell you so?"

"No, but Alan was at the party with a new employee, who is also the founder's daughter. It appears this woman is his new girlfriend. After hearing some of the girls at the party talking tonight, I realize how naïve I've been."

Elizabeth sat back and looked at her grandpa beseechingly. "You know what the worst of all this is? It was affecting my relationship with you. I knew you were unhappy about my dating Alan. I knew you wanted to talk to me about it, but I didn't want to listen to what you had to say. I should have realized that if caring for someone is making someone you dearly love unhappy, something is very wrong."

He smiled lovingly at her. "Well, it's hard sometimes to see things clearly when you're right in the middle of it."

She gave him a long hug and continued, "I want you to know that this will never happen again. No one will ever make me be at odds with you. In fact, I've decided that if you don't give your full approval of someone I date, then I won't have anything more to do with them."

"Now, don't start screening dates according to who I like and don't like," Grandpa gently chided. "You'll be the one making a life for yourself with that special person, not me. I just want to make sure that, whoever it is, they'll love and cherish you as much as you deserve. If you have that, then everything else will work out. Understand?"

She gave him a weak smile. "Yes, Grandpa."

"Good. Now how about some hot chocolate before we turn in?"

Elizabeth nodded. There would be no more talk of Alan that night. Grandpa was known to settle something and then move on, putting it behind him for good, and Elizabeth knew that she would be expected to do the same. It would be hard, though. Without warning, another tear started to fall. Elizabeth wiped it away quickly. She could not let Grandpa see her crying. She was just going to have to learn to get over Alan. Although right now she had no idea how.

Chapter Twenty - Two

The band was playing a jazzy version of 'Jingle Bells' and twinkling lights festooned the ceiling. Alan wove his way through the crowded room, jostling coworkers. His goal was to find Priscilla while at the same time avoiding Elizabeth.

Alan knew that Priscilla had gone home after work in order to change, but she should have been there by now. He finally saw her near the entrance. She looked as beautiful as ever. As Alan reached her side, he slid his arm around her waist and kissed her on the cheek.

Priscilla smiled, and, aware that others had noticed his embrace, he bestowed another kiss on her neck. It was a perfect opportunity for everyone to know not only that he was dating Priscilla Hodge but that she was off limits to other potential suitors.

Mr. Hodge approached them, kissing his daughter and shaking Alan's hand. As they chatted, Alan noticed Elizabeth looking at him from across the room. The hurt look on her face was unmistakable. Alan quickly glanced away. He felt a twinge of guilt but just as quickly dismissed it. After all, he had only dated her for a couple of months.

When Priscilla excused herself to visit the ladies' room, Alan joined a group of men. Neil was there, as was Phil.

"This building is quite elegant," Phil was saying. "The waitress was telling me that it was built in 1924."

"Yes," said Neil, "it's the stone towers that they're known for. Longwood Towers is very well-known in the Boston area."

Phil glanced in Alan's direction. "Just like the Hodge name that Alan seems very interested in being part of."

Alan glared at Phil. "Meaning what?"

"Meaning dating the boss's daughter in order to get ahead at work."

An awkward silence overcame the group. Alan had no intention of being cowed, however.

"Priscilla and I have a mutual attraction to each other that is completely separate from our jobs, and I suggest you keep your opinions to yourself, Phil."

Neil intervened. "People date coworkers all the time, Phil. After all, that's where we spend most of our time." He put an arm around Phil's shoulder. "Let me buy you a drink."

Alan was grateful that Neil had defused the situation, but he knew it was only temporary. He would have to keep an eye on Phil. Clearly, he was going to be trouble.

As the crowd began to thin, Alan asked Priscilla if he could drive her home.

Priscilla eyed Alan suspiciously. "I would say yes, but I need to get up early for an art exhibit, and I have the feeling that you'd be expecting a very romantic 'thank you' before I go inside."

Alan leaned close to her ear. "I could promise you it wouldn't happen but, unfortunately, that's not a promise I would be able to keep."

Priscilla leaned back and laughed. "I appreciate your honesty. But I need to go home with Daddy. He likes the company."

Alan wrapped Priscilla in her fur stole and made his way to the parking lot. After a bad start with Elizabeth, Priscilla had made the party quite enjoyable. She was very social but had given him her undivided attention this evening. She certainly seemed to welcome his advances. It crossed his mind that Priscilla even seemed aggressive on a romantic level. He didn't mind in the least; he was used to it with girls he met in local bars. She was as ambitious and competitive as he was, so maybe it came with their personality type. He felt that he knew what made Priscilla tick. And, because of that, he knew he'd have to play his best game to make sure she kept her eyes only on him.

Chapter Twenty - Three

 On Monday morning Elizabeth arrived at the office with some apprehension. She was afraid that everyone at the office would know not only that she had left the Christmas party early, but why. Her fears proved groundless, however.

Betty was waiting for her when Elizabeth got to her desk. "Don't worry about a thing," she consoled her. "A couple of the girls asked where you went and I told them you hadn't planned on staying long. They didn't really put two and two together, that you used to date Alan. They don't really know you well, and you never really made it public knowledge."

"Thanks, Betty. You're a real peach."

"What kind of a friend would I be if I didn't look out for you? It's just too bad that someone so good looking on the outside could be such a rotten apple on the inside."

Elizabeth also feared bumping into Alan. How quickly things changed, she thought to herself. Only a week ago, she would have been overjoyed to run into him. Now she prayed that she would be spared the embarrassment of it.

But, as the week passed, Elizabeth found it relatively easy to avoid Alan. He was either in meetings or ensconced in his office. Even though she couldn't help her heart from beating a little faster when she occasionally caught sight of his blond head from a distance, she was relieved when she was able to avoid meeting up with him.

She had not been as fortunate with Priscilla. She seemed to run into her everywhere, and Priscilla was haughtier toward her than ever. It was clear that Priscilla knew she had been the victorious winner of Alan's heart.

Priscilla smiled triumphantly at Elizabeth when she saw her and often gave a derisive laugh, making Elizabeth feel even more like the fool she felt herself to be.

~

That weekend Elizabeth tried to show enthusiasm when Fred came over to help Grandpa put up a Christmas tree. She was showing Fred some of the ornaments that had come from Grandmother Keene when they heard a loud crash in the next room.

"Grandpa!" Elizabeth rushed into the kitchen and saw Grandpa struggling to get up from the floor.

Fred, close behind her, grabbed one of Grandpa's arms to help him into a nearby chair.

"Are you all right?" asked Elizabeth, alarmed. "What happened?"

"I'm fine, I just slipped." Grandpa smiled but rubbed his cheek where a welt was starting to form.

"It's not the first time you've slipped, though." Fred put in.

Elizabeth looked in alarm at her grandfather. "Why didn't you tell me?"

"You know I don't want to worry you. My legs aren't as young as they used to be, but it's nothing I can't work around."

Elizabeth wet a cloth in cold water and held it against the side of his face. She looked at Fred, who shrugged, is if to say, 'What can you do?'

Elizabeth gave her grandpa a kiss on the cheek. She was worried, no matter what he said.

Later Fred and Grandpa left to play cards at Harry's and Elizabeth dialed up Aunt May.

"Have you noticed him struggling physically?" Elizabeth asked.

"He's been fine whenever I've seen him. I know you're concerned, and it's good to keep an eye on him. I'll see if I can talk him into moving up his retirement date next time I talk to him."

"Thanks, Aunt May. Maybe he'll listen to you."

Elizabeth felt a little better when she hung up. At least Aunt May hadn't noticed anything, although of course she didn't see him on a regular basis. Maybe it was for the best that Alan had not had any serious intentions towards her. She'd need to focus on Grandpa for the foreseeable future, and she wouldn't have it any other way. As usual, Grandpa was right. There was a silver lining in every cloud.

Chapter Twenty - Four

"Alan, it's beautiful!" Priscilla gazed at Alan with shining eyes then looked back down at the Christmas gift. It was a brooch - a pair of silver bells whose two clappers were tiny diamonds. She fastened it to the left lapel of her coat. "You really didn't have to get me anything this extravagant."

"It's no big deal," Alan replied. He would have given her a diamond ring if they had been dating longer, but they hadn't even been going out a month, and he didn't want to scare her away. He kissed her lightly on the lips. "I would have given it to you before last night's company Christmas party, but I wanted some privacy."

They were sitting in the Hodge's parlor waiting for Priscilla's parents. The Hodges had tickets for the Boston Symphony that night and they had invited Alan. Master pianist Alex Borovsky was headlining and, although classical piano was not one of his interests, if the Hodges invited him somewhere, he was going.

Mr. and Mrs. Hodge walked into the sitting room together and Pricilla pivoted to show off her brooch.

"It's just lovely, Alan," Mrs. Hodge gushed. "You certainly have good taste."

"I think I detect a Long's Jewelers piece, eh?" Mr. Hodge put in.

"That's right, sir. Nothing but the best for our Priscilla!"

The Hodges' chauffeur drove them to the symphony. Alan grasped Priscilla's hand during the ride from Beacon Hill to Massachusetts Avenue. There, throngs of people were arriving at Symphony Hall. Mr. Hodge asked Alan if he had attended concerts here in the past.

"Of course," Alan replied. He hoped Mr. Hodge would not ask him specifics. Once inside Alan memorized the features of the hall: the Renaissance style, the polished maple floors, the high-backed leather chairs. He closely watched Serge Koussevitzky as the conductor and

Alex Borovsky's classical piano performance. If the Hodges wanted to talk about the evening, he wanted to be ready.

Afterwards they descended the stone steps and several young men from work passed by. They tipped their hats to the Hodges and Alan. Alan placed his arm possessively around Priscilla's shoulders. Everyone at work was welcome to know that she was his.

When they pulled up to the Hodge's home, Mr. and Mrs. Hodge politely left Priscilla outside with Alan while they went inside.

Priscilla lifted her chin and gave him a coy look. "I meant to ask you. We're having a family party next Saturday night. It's nothing too elaborate – just some relatives we see every holiday. Can you come?"

"I'm there." Alan surmised it was probably going to be a dreary get-together of aunts, uncles, and other relatives, but it would be worth it in order to be able to spend time with Priscilla. It would also be a chance to make a good impression on her relatives. How quickly things had changed. Only a month or so ago he'd been with Deedee at a local bar while Elizabeth Keene had been away. Now he was being invited to the boss's home for a family Christmas party.

Chapter Twenty - Five

Late on Christmas Eve, Elizabeth and Grandpa traveled to Maine. This time they were joined by Paul, who had just returned from Europe. Paul drove his car, a brand new 1945 Ford Studebaker. In spite of her heartache, Elizabeth was looking forward to the holiday.

Around noon on Christmas day they trod the well-worn path to the Sullivan house, their arms laden with presents and food to share. The door was opened by Charles Sullivan, and the whole family, minus Dolly, stood behind him. Elizabeth was surprised that Dolly was not at the front of the group, for Elizabeth had told Dolly that Paul would be coming.

Then Elizabeth spotted her. She was standing in the parlor entrance underneath a large spray of mistletoe. Elizabeth didn't know whether to laugh or cringe.

Everyone moved through and Dolly tilted her head up just as Paul was about to reach her side. At the same time Charlie barreled past, Christmas presents in hand. His quick movement caught Dolly off balance and she stumbled, falling into Paul's arms.

Dolly's expression of dismay at Charlie quickly changed to delight once she realized the new – and more advantageous – situation she was in. As Paul sought to steady her, Dolly clung to him, pleading helplessness.

"Put your feet on the ground," Father Joe ordered with a grin. "You're not drowning."

Dolly repositioned herself and once again held her face towards Paul. With a smile, Paul kissed her gently on the cheek, causing everyone to laugh.

Dolly looked at Paul with an enraptured look.

Paul, thought Elizabeth, seemed quite tolerant of the situation. Perhaps, Elizabeth mused, Paul was more interested in Dolly than he let on.

Later that day Dolly gave Paul a most peculiar-looking gift. Paul courteously thanked her for the handmade gloves. In response, Dolly jumped up from her seat crying, "They're not gloves! They're woolen socks!" She rushed up the stairs and locked herself in her room. Paul, with Elizabeth in tow, had offered repeated assurances through the closed door that he had known that they were socks all along and that he had just been teasing. Dolly finally emerged with a weak smile.

Elizabeth watched the two of them for the rest of the day. Despite all the presents Dolly received, she looked as if she had already received the greatest one of all. And Paul, she noticed, seemed to always have Dolly in his line of sight.

~

That evening Elizabeth finally got a chance to be alone with Dolly and Mary Francis to tell them about the details of Alan's defection to Priscilla Hodge. As she had hoped, they were completely sympathetic.

Dolly gave Elizabeth a big hug. "I know you're upset, Elizabeth, and I would be too, but honestly, you're better off without him. Look at the way he treated Papa…"

"Dolly!" Mary Francis cried, although it was too late.

Elizabeth looked questioningly at the two girls, wondering what they could be talking about. What could Uncle Charles have to do with Alan? Suddenly, with a pit in her stomach, she knew. She remembered the day that Charles Sullivan had met Alan at their house.

"Tell me what happened," she whispered, as she pressed her hands to her cheeks. "I have to know."

Mary Francis glared at Dolly before turning towards Elizabeth. "Papa knew that Alan was an investor, so when he met him that day, Papa asked him if he could help him invest some money. Alan told him that whatever savings he had was not enough to be worth Alan's time."

"He said that?" Elizabeth whispered.

"Not in those exact words, but Papa knew that's what he meant."

"Papa may not have a lot of money, but he's got something that Alan Bates doesn't have – CLASS!" Dolly raged. "I'd give him a good piece of my mind if I were you!"

"Now, you know Elizabeth's not like that," Mary Francis argued.

"She could never do that to someone, no matter how deserving they are of a good telling off."

"Maybe his new girlfriend will treat him the same way he's treated Elizabeth and she'll break up with him. Then he'll realize not only how awful he's been, but how much he really loves Elizabeth." Dolly became more and more excited as she spun her scenario. "He'll come crawling back for forgiveness, and after disdainfully refusing all his desperate pleas, Elizabeth will toss him aside, leaving him to weep in his own misery."

"Oh, I – I don't think that's likely to happen." Elizabeth had to smile at Dolly's dramatic scenario, but she also wanted to cry. "I don't think he'd ever come crawling back. Besides, he…he never treated me half as nice as he's treating Priscilla. He's taken her to plays and movies and dancing, and even given her presents. I know because she brags about it to Janine, who tells Betty, who of course tells me. The only place Alan ever took me was the Parker House, and that was just so he could close more business deals." With that, Elizabeth broke down in sobs. Mary Francis rushed over to place an arm around her.

Elizabeth cried wholeheartedly for a few more minutes, then lifted her tear-stained face and whispered, "I guess I just have to keep remembering what Auntie May always says – that things will get better even though it may not seem so right now."

"Those are very wise words from Auntie May," Mary Francis agreed. "You just keep thinking that. And here's a bright spot: you'll have more time now to work on your writing. Then you will definitely start feeling better. You'll see."

Chapter Twenty - Six

Alan barely remembered how much he had been looking forward to the New Year's party he was now impatient to leave. One of Priscilla's college friends was throwing the party, and Alan had been anxious to spend time with Priscilla after a week visiting his parents and brother. The party had seemed like a good idea, as he'd known the party-goers would be graduates from many of the prestigious Boston colleges – including Harvard and MIT – and he determined many of the attendees would hail from elite families in town. He had anticipated making a few connections.

Unfortunately the evening had not turned out as he had hoped. There were many young men and women whose last names he immediately recognized, and they were friendly enough, but they had an immaturity that Alan found unappealing. Everyone at the party seemed intent on drinking as much as he or she could hold. He was also surprised – and slightly concerned - at the number of drinks Priscilla had imbibed. He now saw her reaching for yet another martini. Alan decided it was time to intervene.

Grabbing the drink just before Priscilla's hands closed around it, he said, "I think it's time to go, darling."

"Why, is the sun coming up?" asked one of the party goers.

Everyone around them laughed, but Alan focused on Priscilla.

"I can certainly sleep in late," Priscilla slurred, "if we stay up for the rest of the night."

"I don't think that your parents would approve of that."

"I'll just tell them that you dropped me off at my girlfriend's house after the party." Priscilla sweetened her voice and ran her tongue over her lips. "Wouldn't that be nice, Alan? We could spend the rest of the evening together."

Hoots went up from those around them. Alan was shocked. He had never thought that Priscilla would be so public in her desires, and he was embarrassed.

"I think it would best if we get going." He grasped Priscilla's hand and pulled her along behind him to the door. There, a young man that Priscilla had been chatting with earlier blocked their way. "Hey, look! The prettiest girl at the party is leaving!" Pulling Priscilla close to him, he gave her a long hug. Priscilla laughed as he tipped her face towards his and kissed her firmly on the lips.

Alan was livid. It was bad enough that Priscilla had made a fool of herself, but to be allowing another man to kiss her was intolerable. Alan tore her from the man's embrace and yanked her through the door.

Once in the passenger's seat of his car, Priscilla offered effusive apologies. "Alan, don't be mad! I didn't even know he was going to do that!"

"You certainly didn't try to stop him!"

"We're old friends. It was just a friendly kiss. You're making a big deal out of nothing."

"A friendly kiss is a kiss on the cheek or maybe – maybe – a quick kiss on the lips. I think strangers would have a hard time believing that you're dating me and not that guy."

"Well, I certainly didn't ask him to stay for the night, did I?"

"Maybe it's not too late!" Alan regretted his words as soon as they were spoken.

"Are you accusing me of being looth?"

Alan realized that her speech might not be the only thing impaired; she might not even remember this conversation tomorrow.

"Look, I'm sorry. I didn't mean to imply that and I shouldn't have said it. You should know I get upset when I see someone else coming on to you."

"He wasn't 'coming on to me.' Everyone gives each other hugs and kisses – especially on New Year's Eve."

"Okay, okay, although I still don't think it's a very good idea. Guys are different from girls, you know. Physical contact just makes a guy want more."

"Is that how you feel when you're close to me?" Priscilla whispered as she slid next to Alan so that her body pressed against his.

"That's exactly how I feel," Alan replied softly. He began to slowly kiss Priscilla, and his anger was diffused. He didn't particularly care for the side of Priscilla he had just seen, but now that they were alone again, she seemed like her true – albeit intoxicated – self.

He had to wonder, though, how well he really knew this girl. They got along well, but she seemed overly interested in being the life of the party. He probably wouldn't mind so much if he didn't feel nervous that someone richer and more successful would steal her away. Of course, if they got married, that wouldn't be a worry anymore.

Marriage was something that he had been thinking. It seemed crazy, since they had only dated for a little over a month, but aside from her propensity to seek the limelight, Priscilla seemed everything he wanted in a wife. If she became his, she would not be available, and that would cut off competition and probably most of her antics. Then, Alan thought, being in the limelight would be something they could share. He smiled to himself. Having his picture in the paper as part of the Hodge family would be something he wouldn't mind in the least.

Chapter Twenty - Seven

The day after New Year's Elizabeth was working through lunch in order to keep up with the accelerated workload associated with the upcoming acquisition. She was filing correspondence when Mr. Summersby came out of his office, handed her a stack of documents, and asked her to have Alan Bates sign them right away. After a moment's hesitation Elizabeth walked toward Alan's office. Just as she dreaded, Janine was away at lunch. She would have to enter Alan's office.

She could see him working at his desk through the partially open door and she knocked tentatively. Alan barked, "Come in," without looking up.

Elizabeth entered tentatively. When Alan finally looked up, his face instantly turned to a frown.

"If you need something," he said in a frost-tipped voice, "you can ask my secretary."

"I – I'm sorry," Elizabeth stammered. "But Janine is at lunch and Mr. Summersby needs these signed immediately." She handed him the folders and he took them without saying anything. He scratched his signature on the sheets, handed them back to her without comment, and then bent over his work again.

Elizabeth looked down at the golden sweep of his hair. Her heart leaped to her throat, and, in spite of the feelings of anger she felt towards him, she still could not help caring for him. She continued to stare and Alan, noting her continued presence, looked up with an annoyed expression on his face.

"Is there something else you wanted? If not, you're excused. As you can see, I'm very busy."

Elizabeth turned to leave, but before she was even aware of what she was doing, she turned back again and asked quietly, "Why didn't you tell me you weren't interested in seeing me anymore?"

Alan's pen halted and he momentarily hovered it over the sheet of paper on his desk before he continued writing. Without looking up he said, "I really don't think that's an appropriate question for the workplace, do you?"

"No – no it isn't," Elizabeth had to admit. In fact, she was very well aware that it wasn't, and she would never have asked him at work if there had been any other opportunity to do so.

"Then I think we can consider this matter closed. Please close the door behind you as you leave." He turned again to his work, but Elizabeth just couldn't let it drop.

"I just want to talk to you for a few minutes, Alan." For the moment she did not care if it appeared as if she was begging.

He finally looked up and, with a loud sigh of exasperation, he threw his pen down and glared at her.

Elizabeth swallowed nervously. "I just don't understand. Was it something I said, or did, or maybe didn't do?"

Alan groaned loudly. "We had some good times together, a few laughs, okay? That's all it was. Now I've found someone else to spend my time with. I think that's simple enough for you to understand."

Elizabeth bit her lower lip. "How can you treat it like it was nothing? The whole time we went out, I was under the impression that you cared for me, that you enjoyed my company – "

"Look! I never told you anything that was misleading, nothing that I haven't told a hundred other girls I've gone out with. I never told you I wanted a steady relationship, and I certainly never said anything remotely suggesting anything permanent. I'm afraid you misinterpreted a few flirtatious comments for something that they most definitely did not mean!"

Elizabeth stared back at him, her face burning with embarrassment. Alan was telling her in no uncertain terms that not only was he not the least bit interested in continuing any kind of relationship with her, but that it had never been important to him.

She spoke in a low voice. "Yes, you're right. I'm afraid I did misinterpret you. I was very much mistaken in thinking that you were also looking for someone to love and care for – "

Elizabeth got no farther before Alan leaned back in his chair and laughed uproariously. "That's one of the funniest things I've heard in ages. You know, I think if any other girl had walked into my office and told me that they loved and cared for me, I would have given her a standing ovation for a superb acting performance. But not you. No, you're different, Elizabeth. I think that's what I found appealing about you. I must admit at times I couldn't figure out what it was, but I think you have just given me the answer."

"Which is?" Elizabeth pressed, feeling both angry and humiliated.

"It's that perpetual idealism of yours. This eternal belief that the world is this sweet, sunshiny place where everyone loves each other and there's a multi-colored rainbow behind every stormy cloud. It's a totally absurd way to view life, but it's quite amusing."

"I don't consider it amusing!"

"Well, no offense, my dear, but I'm afraid that's about all your idealism is good for. It might sound nice that everyone magically falls in love, gets married, and lives happily ever after, but I'm afraid it's not very realistic."

"Are you actually saying that you don't believe a man and a woman really marry for love?"

"Perhaps your problem is you get a little confused when people use the term love when they mean something entirely different."

"What do you think they mean, then?"

"I think what they're really referring to is personal satisfaction. Each person is looking for whatever opportunities or goals in life the other person can fulfill for them."

"Such as?" Elizabeth prompted.

"Oh, wealth, power, status, prestige. We all have our price you know, as difficult as it may be for you to accept it."

Elizabeth looked at him stonily. "Perhaps there are a few cases where people marry for those things, but I think that's only a small fraction of people. All the married couples I know got married because they genuinely loved and cared for each other, and they were willing to stick by each other no matter what hardships came upon them."

"Well then, my dear, I'm afraid you have a lot to learn about living in the real world. Only a fool marries for love, and I suggest that you remember those words of wisdom. You may regret later in life that you ignored them."

"I can hardly imagine regretting marrying someone that cared for and loved me deeply no matter what his bank account and status in life."

Alan shrugged his shoulders as if to say that it was of no interest to him what she did or didn't do with her life.

There seemed nothing else to say then, and Elizabeth turned once again to go. Her hand was on the doorknob when she half-turned around to ask, a catch in her throat, "And I suppose Priscilla gives you all of those things that you seem to value so highly?"

Alan looked down at the papers on his desk and picked up his pen as he replied, "Perhaps. Again, please close the door behind you."

So it was over. She knew, now, how little the relationship had meant to him. She felt a stab in her heart. She had never taken it casually, even from the start, and instinctively she knew that she never could, not with Alan, and not with anyone else. Commitment and loyalty were qualities she had automatically assumed were present in every relationship, and if things didn't work out, she thought the person would at least be able to tell the other one face to face that it was over.

Suddenly thoughts of Grandfather Keene entered her head. Did he have Alan's attitude toward marriage? Had he strung her grandmother along all those years? Perhaps the world of relationships was not as she had always assumed it to be. Elizabeth realized that, as Alan had said, her view might be naïve. Just the same, she would never go into a relationship seeking status or wealth. Like Mary Francis, like Dolly, like Grandpa John and Grandma Rose, and like her parents, she would seek love.

Chapter Twenty - Eight

 As soon as Alan heard the door click shut, he looked up from his papers and threw down his pen. He rose from his desk and walked over to the side table to pour a cup of coffee. He could use something a lot stronger, but unfortunately a drink was not an option.

He sipped his coffee, giving himself a few minutes to calm down. At least that episode in his life was behind him. He should have surmised that Elizabeth Keene wouldn't just disappear without making a foolish declaration of love.

Spontaneously he reached for the phone to dial Priscilla. He hoped she was back from lunch. If she was and he could spend just a minute talking to her, he could steady himself and be able to refocus on his work. He was afraid she was still at lunch, so he was relieved to hear Priscilla's voice on the other end of the line.

"Good afternoon, Miss Hodge speaking."

"Good afternoon, Miss Hodge. This is Mr. Bates, who considers himself deeply fortunate to be able to hear your beautiful voice in the middle of a workday."

"It certainly doesn't take much to make you excited."

"Believe me, Miss Hodge, everything about you makes me excited, but that's not why I called. What are you doing Saturday night?"

"Nothing yet. Why? Are you planning on changing that status?"

"Absolutely. How about seeing a movie or dinner – something with just the two of us?"

"I guess you're not keen on any group events after our last time together, is that what you're saying?"

Alan could hear a tinge of resentment in her voice and he hurried to assuage her suspicions. "Not at all. In fact, the only reason I wouldn't be open to getting together with a crowd is that when I want to be romantic with a woman, three or more people cramps my style."

"In that case, Saturday night sounds wonderful."

Alan felt calm and happy as he hung up the receiver. Distress over his interaction with Elizabeth had dissipated the moment that he began talking to Priscilla. Thank goodness the stunningly beautiful and sophisticated Priscilla Hodge had entered his life.

~

"Alan, you're right," Priscilla whispered. "This is very romantic."

Alan couldn't agree more with Priscilla, although she was undoubtedly referring to the movie and he most assuredly was not. His arm was around her shoulders and he brushed his lips against her temple. The movie was *The Bells of Saint Mary's*, the popular film starring Bing Crosby, although Alan wouldn't have been able to summarize the plot if his life depended on it. All he could think of was which maneuvers he could get away with at a public event. Priscilla certainly didn't seem to mind, although she was very engrossed in the film.

Afterwards they walked down the street, on the lookout for a place where they could get a bite to eat. Priscilla playfully reached for Alan's hand. "You should be flattered we went out tonight," she said. "I turned down another invitation to go out."

"Who asked you out?" Alan's voice sounded angry, and he meant it to be.

"Just an old school friend I ran into Thursday night when I went out for a couple of drinks with Janine. I probably wouldn't have gone out with him anyways, even if you hadn't asked me."

Alan dropped Priscilla's hand and stopped in the middle of the sidewalk, unmindful of the people that were forced to walk around them.

"Probably?"

"Okay, I definitely wouldn't have gone out with him. Why do you look so angry?"

"Maybe because I didn't know you were still interested in other guys."

"Look, I didn't ask him out – he asked me. And it's not as if we have any kind of agreement."

"Then we can make one right now." Alan grabbed Priscilla's arm and pulled her underneath a nearby awning. "Look, I know we've only been dating a little over a month, but to be honest, it eats me up inside to think of you dating anybody else. Priscilla, would you go steady with me?"

Alan waited but Priscilla stood silent.

Finally she said, "I have to be honest too, Alan. Believe me, if I wanted to go steady with anybody, it would be you. Maybe it's just too soon."

Alan felt both relieved that he was at the top of her list and upset that she apparently didn't want to rule out other men. He decided then and there that he would have to pull out all the stops when they went out – the best restaurants, the finest wine, bouquets of flowers. If their relationship ended, it wouldn't be for lack of trying.

Chapter Twenty - Nine

"Rebecca cried and cried until exhausted, then dragged herself to bed, hoping that sleep would temporarily provide some relief."

That was one silver lining in her breakup with Alan. With quiet weekends, especially now that the holidays were over, she was making progress. She had just finished the climax and it was much easier to write a heart-wrenching ending when she felt exactly the way her character did. Reluctantly putting down her manuscript, she went to start on dinner.

Elizabeth began peeling potatoes at the kitchen table. She was waiting for Grandpa to arrive home from Fred's, and when she heard a noise at the backdoor she assumed it was him. Before she could rise, in swept Paul, looking fitter and healthier than she'd ever seen him. With a cry, Elizabeth jumped up and threw herself at him, embracing him in a huge hug.

"Wow!" Paul exclaimed with a wide grin. "Now I know how a G.I. must feel when he comes home. I travel on business for a week or so, and look what I get."

"It's just that we didn't expect you this soon. And it's been a rough couple of weeks."

Paul set his bag on the floor and took a seat. "Why don't you tell me about it? I'm all ears."

Elizabeth poured a cup of freshly brewed tea for each of them and took a seat opposite him. "Well," she began hesitantly, "it's Alan. I was a girl who fell in love and made a fool out of herself. The problem is I didn't even realize it until I was hit over the head with it."

Paul rested his tea cup on the saucer. "To be perfectly honest, Elizabeth, I had my doubts about Mr. Alan Bates. From what I'd seen of him in a business setting, he seemed a little too self-centered for my taste. It is my firm opinion that your dear departed ex-boyfriend has lost far more than you have."

Elizabeth smiled weakly.

Paul scratched his jaw. "I know that you were worried at Christmas time about Alan being interested in the boss's daughter – don't look surprised, Elizabeth. Dolly spilled the beans, of course – and I think I'm beginning to see the picture very clearly now. Obviously Mr. Alan Bates foresaw the various business possibilities to be had from dating her and decided to seize a golden opportunity to move up in the corporate world." Paul paused to look at Elizabeth's downcast face. "Somehow I have the feeling that there's more to this. I know this isn't easy for you, but I'm sure you'll feel a lot better if you get it all off your chest."

"Well…" Elizabeth began hesitantly. She hated to keep tugging on Paul's ear, but she did feel better talking about it with someone. "It's just that it's been hard enough getting over Alan, especially when I run into him from time to time at work, but it's even harder when I see Priscilla. I feel like she's always trying to…to…" Elizabeth groped for the right words, "flaunt it in front of me."

"Ah, yes," Paul nodded his head in acknowledgement. "Not uncommon in a romantic triangle when there's a winner and a loser. You know, I've been out of the dating game for quite a long time, but I guess when it comes to love, some things never really change. I think I'll share with you a little gossip which might help you get over Mr. Bates. From what I understand, he was expelled from Brown University his junior year for cheating."

"Are you serious? How could anyone do that?"

"Very easily if you have no scruples. At any rate, he got caught, so he paid the price."

"Then he didn't graduate from college?"

"He transferred to Providence College in Rhode Island, but Alan tells everyone that he graduated from Brown. I just thought I'd tell you so you wouldn't feel like you've lost a man with stellar values. Instead of building a good reputation, he fabricates one. Or uses others to prop up his own. At any rate, do you know what my solution would be?"

"What?"

"Find another job."

"Another job!" Elizabeth's mouth dropped open. "But doesn't

'shunned girlfriend' seem like a rather petty reason for leaving?"

"Not at all. If you go to bed every night dreading the next day, then why continue to put up with that situation? It's not as if you've invested a long period time of time working there. How long have you been there? A year?"

"Just under."

"Then you have nothing to lose and everything to gain. You'll undoubtedly find yourself in a more relaxed atmosphere, probably receive the same amount of vacation time, and maybe even make more money somewhere else."

Elizabeth let the idea sink in. It might be the best solution to a situation that she saw no end to. "But where would I get another job?"

"I've got a few business contacts. Let me make some calls this week. Sound good?"

"I guess I've not much to lose," Elizabeth replied. She studied her uncle for a moment. "You certainly seem to know all about heartache."

"Believe it or not, I've had my share during my forty years on earth. But there are good times in relationships, too. Lots of them."

Elizabeth followed Paul's gaze towards the basket on the counter's edge where several cards from Dolly peeked out. "Oh, really?" Elizabeth gave Paul an inquisitive smile.

Paul batted the air with his hand, ignoring her implication. "Don't worry," he finished. "You may feel nervous about making a change at first, but you'll be happier in the long run. You'll see."

~

The next day after work Paul greeted her at the door. He had good news, he said. He guided her to the kitchen where Grandpa and Fred were sitting. There he explained that he had found several companies that were looking for a good, reliable secretary and one in particular seemed promising. It was a law firm – Phillips & Godfrey – and Paul had frequently used them in some of his business dealings.

"In fact," continued Paul. "Stephen Wright works there. I think you met him at my mother's wake.. He's a great guy. And," he added, "he's single, unless something has changed in the last couple of months."

Elizabeth rolled her eyes. "Please! Right now I'm just trying to get a job, not a date!"

"Sounds like you could get both if you work there," Fred said, and winked at Elizabeth.

Grandpa and Paul laughed, and Elizabeth was forced to break a smile.

~

Elizabeth called Phillips & Godfrey the next day, and, thanks no doubt to Uncle Paul's connections, she was asked without preamble to come in for an interview that week. The open position, she was told, would report directly to one of the lawyers, Mr. Winslow.

When Elizabeth told Betty about the job opportunity, Betty was excited for her but also exhibited plenty of sympathy for herself. "Who will I have lunch with if you leave? Who will I share my gossip with?"

On Wednesday Elizabeth left work a few minutes early and walked the short distance to Phillips & Godfrey. The interview with Mr. Godfrey went well, and she left in good spirits. That night Elizabeth called the Sullivan house, and Mary Francis picked up the phone line. Dolly, in the background, insisted that Mary Francis hold the phone aloft so that she could hear too.

Elizabeth told them about the interview. "If they offer the job, should I take it? I'm rather nervous to start new somewhere, but it would be five dollars more a week and I'm tired of running into Alan and Priscilla."

Dolly was quick to contribute her opinion. "If a company offered me more money, I'd go like a shot. What else is there to think about?"

"What does your grandpa think?" Mary Francis questioned.

"Grandpa and Uncle Paul both think I should take it if it's offered." Elizabeth replied.

Mary Francis commented, "There's also bound to be single, young men working there."

Elizabeth replied. "I know there's at least one. I met him at Grandmother's wake."

"A young, *single* man at a new job with a higher salary?" Dolly's voice squawked. "Now I know you've got some brain cells missing if you even have to think it over."

~

Elizabeth was thrilled to find out on Thursday that she had gotten the job. When Elizabeth told Mr. Summersby her news, he was congratulatory but chagrined. "I think you'll be hard to replace,

Elizabeth. You've been a wonderful secretary."

Later that day Lillian stopped by to announce that everyone at Hodge's was invited to gather at three o'clock in the staff room for cake and ice cream to celebrate the firm's twenty-fifth anniversary. When she heard Elizabeth's news, she was excited. "Good for you! I'm sure you'll love it there. I've heard good things about that firm, although I'll miss you terribly."

Elizabeth had trouble thinking of anything all day except what her new job would be like. She also couldn't help but be curious about Stephen Wright. She remembered being introduced to him at her grandmother's wake, and she remembered him being unassuming but charming. She also remembered his deep brown eyes holding hers, just for a moment. Then she chided herself for being silly. She was starting to think like Dolly! Stephen Wright probably wouldn't even remember her. Or maybe he had a girlfriend. At any rate, she would need to spend her time learning the ropes at the new company.

Shortly before three, Elizabeth made her way to the staff room. On the way she ran into Betty and told her the news.

Betty hugged her. "Sounds like a good reason to jump ship to me. We'll stay in touch all the time, right?"

Elizabeth nodded and then she and Betty joined Lillian in line for a slice of cake. Elizabeth suddenly heard Priscilla and Janine behind her. Their voices rose, and Elizabeth had the impression that their conversation was directed at her.

"Priscilla, how's your dating going with Alan? He's so good to you!"

"I know! We went to *The Ritz Carlton* for dinner last weekend."

"The Ritz Carlton! That's one of the most expensive places in town! I'd say you've got him in the palm of your hand."

"Don't I?" tittered Priscilla.

Elizabeth felt her face burning. She hoped Betty and Lillian didn't notice her embarrassment. Suddenly, Betty spoke loudly. "Elizabeth, it's so exciting about your new job! Lillian, did you hear?"

Lillian spoke clearly. "I did! I'm so happy for you! Phillips and Godfrey is such a prestigious law firm! I know they only hire top-notch people."

Priscilla stepped forward. "A new job? When is your sad departure happening?"

Elizabeth drew in her breath and then raised her chin. "Two weeks from today."

"Congratulations!" Priscilla's voice dripped with sarcasm. "Maybe there are some eligible bachelors there you can pick from. If there is one, you'd better grab him quick before some other girl steals him away from you." Her innuendo was glaringly obvious.

Lillian turned to face Priscilla. "Maybe he'd better grab Elizabeth quick before someone steals *her*!" As she spoke she stared down at the younger woman. Priscilla took a step back and said nothing.

As soon as they were out of earshot, Elizabeth turned to Lillian. "Thank you for sticking up for me."

"That girl has needed to be put in her place for a while," Lillian said, "and I was glad to be the one to do it." She gave Elizabeth a small smile.

She certainly had good friends, Elizabeth thought. She knew they would stay in touch, which was very comforting.

~

On her last day at Hodge's Investments she gathered her few things into a box. It was hard not to be sentimental. After all, she would miss Lillian and Betty, and even Mr. Summersby. And of course she might never see Alan again. In spite of the way he had treated her, she couldn't help but feel pained. He had been her first real boyfriend, even though he had never claimed that title. He had certainly been the first man to lavish attention on her. He was also the first man – and hopefully would be the last – to break her heart.

Her walk kept step with the beating of her heart as she approached the elevator for the last time. She was looking forward to putting the drama and the heartache of Hodge's behind her. She would be learning a new job and make a little more money. She might even find a new romance with someone else. Anyone but Alan Bates.

Part II

Chapter Thirty

The first Monday of February dawned bright and clear. Elizabeth had hardly slept, thinking about the changes in her life. She was glad she had a new job, and relieved that she would no longer have to worry about running into Priscilla and Alan. She only hoped that she wasn't jumping from the pot into an unknown fire. Then she stopped her mind from racing - *she must stop thinking like that*! After all, there would be new people to meet and new things to learn. She was going to like it.

She arrived at Phillips & Godfrey at exactly eight o'clock. The receptionist in the lobby looked up with a smile as Elizabeth approached.

"Miss Keene? I understand you'll be Mr. Winslow's new secretary. I'll show you the way." Elizabeth followed the young woman down a long corridor, at the end of which was an office with lights on. The receptionist knocked quickly and entered without waiting for a response.

"Mr. Winslow? I'd like you to meet Elizabeth Keene. Elizabeth, this is Jonathan Winslow."

The man behind the desk rose to meet them. He was in his late forties, with thick, wavy black hair. He was attired in a double-breasted suit which he filled out completely, but not unflatteringly so.

Mr. Winslow motioned to Elizabeth to sit down and he returned to his own seat. "I'm glad to meet you. Paul had high praise for you, and Tom Godfrey was also very impressed. We're glad to have you on board."

Elizabeth blushed, not quite sure what to say. "That's very nice of them. I do want you to know that even though I wouldn't be here without my Uncle Paul's help, I'm a really good worker and – "

"Don't give it a second thought. We hire people all the time that get referred to us. Now, why don't I fill you in on some of the office routines before everyone else arrives?"

Mr. Winslow gave Elizabeth a quick tour of his inner and outer office, then he showed her to her desk and gave her some company policy forms to review. He assured her that one of the other girls would be in soon to assist her with any questions she might have.

She had been reading for a few minutes when a woman came towards her. She looked to be a few years older than Elizabeth, with short, auburn hair, a spattering of freckles across her nose, and an over-sized pair of glasses perched low on her nose. She stopped at her desk. "Are you Jonathan's secretary? I'm Maura Driscoll. It's nice to meet you."

"It's nice to meet you, too. I'm Elizabeth Keene."

"My boss, Mr. Godfrey, asked me to walk you around and introduce you to everyone." Maura guided Elizabeth toward the other end of the hall. She rattled off information about various employees, and Elizabeth struggled to keep track. After a minute Maura said, "Your boss, Mr. Winslow, is a good guy, as long as he doesn't get 'hot under the collar'."

Elizabeth continued to follow Maura, smoothing her skirt and hair as she went. Maura took Elizabeth office to office, mentioning who worked in each. Finally they reached a darkened end of the hall. "There are a couple of lawyers who work down here but who are away on business." Maura cracked open one of the doors. "This is Stephen Wright's office." Elizabeth's heart skipped a beat. She stole a glance inside. His office was impeccable and his desk accessories were arranged neatly. She wondered if Stephen knew she had been hired. She wondered if he would remember her.

~

When Elizabeth arrived at home, Grandpa was waiting to welcome her. "How was your first day?"

"It was wonderful! Everyone was so friendly and helpful. I'm so glad I changed jobs. Do you mind if I call Dolly and Mary Francis before dinner? I can't wait to tell them about everything."

Grandpa nodded. "I'm going to wash up."

As soon as he was gone, Elizabeth rang up the girls. Dolly answered and summoned Mary Francis to her side. Elizabeth reported on her day. "Mr. Winslow seems very accommodating, and Maura, one of the other secretaries, is so friendly. I think I'm going to like working with her."

"Did you see Stephen Wright?" Dolly blurted.

Elizabeth laughed. "He's out of town, but he's supposed to be back at work by the end of the week or next Monday at the latest."

"You will call when you meet him to tell us how it went, won't you?"

"Dolly, Stephen probably won't even remember me. But I'll call."

Elizabeth hung up just as Grandpa entered the kitchen. She hoped that Grandpa hadn't overheard her mention Stephen Wright. If he had, there would be no end to his teasing.

She decided to pre-empt any questions. "Grandpa, I've decided to send in a few of my short stories to the Saturday Evening Post."

"It's about time you let the world enjoy your literary work!"

"I don't know if they're publish-worthy, but I'll never know if I don't try."

"That's the spirit! If you get the envelopes ready tonight, I can mail them for you tomorrow."

~

On Friday Maura informed Elizabeth that a group of them were going to splurge for lunch at a local café and that she was welcome to join them. Elizabeth happily accepted.

At noon she followed Maura and several others to the Steaming Kettle. It was a comfortable, informal place where, Elizabeth was told, the food was excellent and reasonably priced. They were led to a booth in the rear by a waitress who was obviously familiar with the group, for hearty hellos were exchanged as they sat down. Elizabeth studied the menu then looked up as a tall man with brown eyes appeared at the table. Elizabeth immediately recognized Stephen Wright.

"Steve!" Maura exclaimed and motioned to a vacant chair. "Come sit down. I didn't think you had returned yet." Then she laughed. "You must have timed it to miss Winslow's staff meeting."

"Oh yes, I feel just awful about that," Stephen said with a smile. Before sitting down, he paused to greet the others. When his eyes rested on Elizabeth, she knew that he recognized her.

"Steve," Maura said, "I'd like you to meet Jonathan's new secretary, Elizabeth Keene. Elizabeth, this is Stephen Wright."

Stephen reached out his hand and grasped Elizabeth's firmly. "It's very nice to see you again. I was hoping we'd run into each other sometime. I'll have to thank whoever did your hiring for Phillips & Godfrey."

Everyone looked back and forth between Elizabeth and Stephen.

"You know each other?" Maura asked.

"I had the good fortune to be introduced to Elizabeth five or six months ago. However, it was a difficult time of her life – her grandmother's wake." Stephen sat opposite Elizabeth and leaned toward her. "How are your grandfather and uncle doing?"

Elizabeth cleared her throat. "They're fine. Grandfather Keene is working in Europe and Uncle Paul is staying with my grandpa and me for the time being."

"That's very nice of you to take him in. And what about you? Where were you working before you came to Phillip's?"

"I was at Hodge's Investments for the last year or so."

Maura let out a low whistle. "Hodge's Investments! That's la crème de la crème of accounting offices in town. Why did you ever want to leave?"

Elizabeth was unprepared for the question, and she stumbled over her words. "It's not that I didn't like working there, it's just that – I mean, it was – "

Stephen cut in. "I'm sure Elizabeth had her reasons for wanting to leave. Not every job is for everybody." He gave Elizabeth a small smile then turned to Maura. "How was opening night for the play you're in? I know you've been preparing for it for weeks."

"It was so thrilling!" Maura gushed. "Better than I even imagined!" She launched into a detailed description of the costumes and the entertaining mishaps that went on behind the scenes. Elizabeth listened attentively; she was glad that the attention had turned from her.

They ate while Maura prattled on. At the conclusion of lunch Stephen came to her side and kept step with her while they walked back to the office.

"I think you'll enjoy working at Phillip's," he said. "We're a colorful group, which keeps work interesting."

Elizabeth smiled. Stephen, she noticed, kept stealing surreptitious glances at her. She wondered if he was interested in her or if he had a girlfriend. Thinking back to Alan's wandering eye, Elizabeth knew enough to be cautious. But at least someone new – even a new friend – would keep her from dwelling on Alan, and that alone would be progress.

Chapter Thirty - One

At the edge of the tennis court at the Longwood Cricket Club in Newton, Alan glanced at his watch for the second time in thirty seconds. He wondered when Priscilla was going to finish talking to a group of admirers. Even though she wasn't looking his way, he glared at her from the other side of the court, hoping that she would glance his way and notice how irritated he was. There seemed little chance of that happening, however, for the group of men surrounding her seemed captivated by her conversation. He saw Priscilla put her hand on one young man's forearm while animatedly speaking. Striding quickly to where the group was standing, he pushed through and wrapped his arm around Priscilla's waist.

"Ready for our tennis match, darling?"

"In a moment," Priscilla answered, then turned back to her admirers.

"Now!" Alan ordered, not caring that the men around them gave him startled looks.

The man whom Priscilla had touched jumped back, while Priscilla turned to address the group in a sugary voice. "Excuse us, won't you? Our tennis match beckons, but I'm sure I'll bump into you all again soon."

The group quickly dispersed.

As soon as they were out of earshot, Priscilla hissed, "Don't you ever speak to me like that in front of other people!"

"Then don't give me a reason to!"

"What is that supposed to mean?" Priscilla placed her hands on her hips.

"It means that if you're going to put your hand on another young man's arm, then you should expect the same reaction in the future."

"Just like the party when an old friend gave me an innocent kiss good-bye?"

"Exactly."

Surprisingly, Priscilla began laughing. "I think you're jealous."

"I would call it 'protecting my interests,' but you can call it whatever you want, as long as you don't do it again."

"Just for the record, because you seem to be making a habit of reprimanding me in public, I don't answer to anybody regarding my actions. Now, would you like to serve, or shall I?"

"And let *me* add – just for the record – if you ever start flirting again, you'll know exactly what my reaction is going to be. Now that that's settled, you may serve first."

Alan held out the ball. She hesitated for a moment, then grabbed it, tossed her head, and marched past him towards the opposite side of the net.

Alan was angry about their argument. Clearly, Priscilla was not happy that he had interrupted her socializing. He thought they had settled this issue after the New Year's party, and Alan momentarily wondered if she was the right girl for him. He was no saint, but he expected a girl to at least be dedicated to him while they were on a date. If she couldn't do that, how could he possibly expect her to go steady?

It didn't help that he'd been in a bad mood since yesterday. Mr. Hodge had stopped by his office in the afternoon to discuss a report. Before leaving, he had brought up Brown University. "Your name came up the other day when I was having dinner with an old classmate of mine from Harvard. His son joined us, and he graduated from Brown the same year I believe you did – Class of 1941– but he didn't know your name."

"Really?" Alan shifted in his seat.

"I know. I was surprised myself. I did get it right, didn't I? Graduate of 1941 from Brown?"

"Yes, sir."

"Well, you can't know your whole class, I suppose. Now, back to business. Give that report to my secretary when you finish it."

Mr. Hodge left and Alan sank back into his chair. This was an unexpected wrinkle. If the son of Mr. Hodge's friend pulled out his yearbook, Alan was in trouble. This seemed unlikely, but if he did, how could Alan possibly explain? The fact that a stranger could undo his career at Hodge's was unsettling.

As Alan walked home from work that night he had an idea. If Mr. Hodge found out that he was not in the yearbook, he would tell him that he had forgotten to submit his photo in the midst of finals. It was plausible enough and hopefully after that the subject would never be brought up again. Anyway, the alumnus from Brown – whoever he was – probably had better things to do than investigate old classmates. At least Alan fervently hoped so.

Chapter Thirty - Two

Elizabeth pressed the iron gingerly around the pleats in her dress. She planned to wear the dress to work on Monday. She wanted to make a good impression. Not on Stephen, she told herself, just a good impression on the job. Elizabeth's thoughts were interrupted by the sound of the doorbell. She set the iron down and went to see who could be calling on a Saturday morning. When she opened the door she found Dolly, Mary Francis, Auntie May, and Margaret Sullivan huddled on the doorstep.

"Surprise!" they shouted.

With a cry of gladness, Elizabeth stood aside and urged them to enter. "My goodness, it's freezing out! Come inside quickly!"

As they began taking off their coats, she scolded them, "You should have told us you were coming! We could have made something special to eat when you got here."

Auntie May replied, "One of Father Joe's parishioners was driving down here to Boston today to visit a relative. That's when Margaret decided it might be nice to take the girls to do a little shopping in town. We tried calling you last night to let you know we were coming, but there was no answer. Then we left so early this morning, we didn't want to wake you."

Elizabeth ushered them into the parlor. "Grandpa was at Harry's house last night and Uncle Paul and I went to a movie together. Come in and sit down while I put on some tea. I'm so glad that we don't have ration books anymore! It's nice to have a full canister of sugar."

Mary Francis followed her to the kitchen. "Do you think you'll be able to go shopping with us today, Elizabeth? I hope you didn't have anything else planned…"

"No, I didn't." Elizabeth took five tea bags out of a nearby canister and grabbed a serving tray from an upper shelf. "Actually, this is a perfect day for me. I just finished my chores, and Grandpa went over to Fred's house. Maybe we can even go out for lunch."

Mary Francis returned to the parlor with Elizabeth, carrying the tea tray, in her wake. Elizabeth set the tray down and then realized she had forgotten to grab spoons.

"Dolly can get them," Margaret stated, and motioned Elizabeth to sit down while she gave her younger daughter a lifted eyebrow. Dolly reluctantly headed toward the kitchen.

Seconds later, however, Elizabeth realized she had also forgotten to bring napkins. "I don't know where my head is today." She got up and made her way to the kitchen. "I think I'm just so excited that you're all here."

Just as she entered the kitchen, Paul walked through the back door, stomping his boots on the floor mat. Dolly, meanwhile, stood stock still, staring wide-eyed at Paul. There was a pregnant pause.

Finally Dolly curtseyed and gushed, "It's indeed a wondrous pleasure to see you again, Mr. Keene."

"Hello, Dolly. I meant to tell you before what a pretty name you have. I also like the formal name for Dolly – Dorothy, isn't it?"

"Yes. You can call me Dorothy if you want. I won't complain about it."

"Excuse me?"

Elizabeth answered for Dolly. "Dorothy is Dolly's baptismal name, but she's never cared for it, so ever since she was a young girl, we've called her by her nickname."

"I see. Well, whichever name you prefer is fine with me."

Dolly gazed, enraptured, as Elizabeth changed the conversation.

"Paul, the Sullivans and Auntie May came to town unexpectedly. We're having tea right now in the front parlor, and afterwards we're going to town to do some shopping. Would you like to say hello to everyone?"

"Certainly. After you, ladies."

Paul followed the two girls down the hall.

They bumped into each other when Dolly turned around in order to give Paul a flirtatious glance. When they reached the parlor, Paul exchanged greetings as Paul, Elizabeth, and Dolly took their seats.

After they enjoyed their refreshments, Margaret stood up to say, "I think it's time we get started on our errands. Our ride is leaving at six o'clock today and it'll be time to go before we know it."

Everyone stood up to gather the dirty dishes when Dolly suggested, "Why don't you all go along without me? I was thinking I'd stay here at the house today."

Margaret gave her daughter an incredulous look. "Now, why in heaven's name would you want to do a thing like that? You talked of nothing on the way here but window shopping and being in the city."

"I know, but if I stay behind, I could have bread and tea ready for you when you get back."

Mary Francis whispered to her mother, "She just wants to stay here because she likes Paul."

Margaret looked at Dolly's transfixed face and sighed exasperatedly before replying, "Dorothy Ann Sullivan, I don't want to hear another word of nonsense! We didn't come all the way to Boston to leave you here to daydream all day. Now, let's go."

Dolly had no choice but to accept her fate, but she gave Paul a mournful parting glance as she was propelled out the door.

The girls enjoyed strolling the sidewalk while window shopping. The clothes and accessories were far too expensive to buy, but they ogled the displays of clothing and home goods. At noon they stopped at Woolworth's to grab lunch at the counter. While they ate, Elizabeth brought everyone up to date on her new job. At the end she added, "We went out to lunch yesterday and Stephen Wright showed up."

"Was he glad to see you? Do you think he's interested in you?" Mary Francis asked.

"I certainly couldn't say. He did spend quite a bit of time talking just to me."

Dolly sighed. "I wish someone would be just as interested in me."

Her mother quickly admonished her. "For goodness sake, Dolly! Even if there were someone, it would certainly be nice if you could spend a few moments being happy for someone else."

When they returned home, Dolly was cheered a bit when Paul arrived from his father's house. He explained that he'd spent the afternoon placing dust covers on the furniture and boxing up items. He'd be done in time if they wanted a ride to their friend's house for their ride home, he said.

When he showed up in his Ford Deluxe, Dolly claimed the seat next to him. "Are you going to write me?" she asked in front of the group.

"I've already written you three letters. Actually, it's four, and I do apologize for my rudeness. I'm not much of a writer, but I will have to make an exception or I could be accused of having poor manners."

"I'll be anxiously awaiting your letter every day." Dolly turned to look at Elizabeth, Mary Francis, Aunt May, and her mother squeezed into the seat behind her. She raised her eyebrows in excitement.

Margaret Sullivan gave her a stern look, and Mary Francis rolled her eyes.

~

Back at home, Grandpa, Paul, and Elizabeth shared tea. Elizabeth took the opportunity to tease Paul about Dolly. "She certainly seems smitten with you."

"She is very pretty."

"And?"

"She's a charming girl, but even if we were closer in age, I think she'd be a bit too much to handle."

Elizabeth was intrigued by the fact that her uncle was still single. She set her tea cup down and asked, "Uncle Paul, if you don't mind my asking, did you ever date during all these years?"

Paul had a twinkle in his eye. "Don't you recall that on several occasions when you visited Mother, I wasn't there? I would try to coincide my dates with times when someone was visiting so she wouldn't be alone. I also never mentioned my dates to Mother. She was always worried that if I married she would be left alone."

"You certainly looked out for your mother's welfare," Grandpa put in. "But you're free now to date as you like."

"True. All I have to do now is find someone. Elizabeth, does Dolly have an identical relative that's eighteen years older than she is – and about ten degrees calmer?"

"If she does, it's a family secret."

"I guess we all know why that would be the case," Grandpa chortled.

Paul and Elizabeth laughed.

"So, barring that, I'll take Dolly's school-girlish attention. It's flattering that she seems to be sweet on me. But I'm sure she'll get over it. After all, I could almost be her father." Paul paused and stroked his chin. "Although I look quite youthful for my age, don't you think?" He tilted his head sideways, as if posing.

Elizabeth looked at her grandpa and raised her eyebrows. Grandpa gave Elizabeth a wink and smiled.

Chapter Thirty - Three

It happened in the span of twenty-four hours and was indeed a stroke of good fortune for Alan. While picking up a cup of coffee in the lobby, Alan overheard two managers discussing a proposal that Phil Lawrence planned to unveil at Friday's staff meeting. Apparently, Phil was keeping it 'close to the vest,' but the gist of it had already leaked.

Alan was well aware that because of the war, the economy – and investments in particular – had languished as the bulk of the nation's finances had gone towards weapons and supplies. Since the end of the war, investment firms had begun to see a glimmer of light. People were beginning to invest again and the competition among firms for a 'piece of the pie' had begun.

Alan's pulse raced. He had to find out what the proposal was before Friday's meeting. Being part of an innovative plan would skyrocket anyone's career. Alan would have to resort to unconventional ways of getting in on it. But how?

His plan fell into place on Wednesday. He knew that Phil went to lunch from twelve-fifteen to one o'clock and that his secretary usually took lunch at the same time. Alan surmised that Phil would be actively working on the proposal and would leave the paperwork on his desk while he left for a bite to eat.

At twelve-thirty, Alan strolled casually into the outer office of Phil's suite. It was eerily silent. Alan double-checked the hall before quickly entering Phil's office. As he had hoped, papers were strewn across the desk. Many of the sheets had lists of statistics and numbers, which he rapidly perused. At the top corner of the desk Alan spotted a manila folder. When he opened it, on the top sheet was typed in bold-face, "Proposal for Latin American Investments, Friday, February 15, 1946".

Latin America! Alan quickly read the introduction. It explained that the oil industries were steamrolling into Latin American countries, making significant inroads in the mining of iron and other minerals. Having an international part of the business was like finding a new frontier. Phil's proposal outlined a plan for Hodge's Investments to successfully enter the market. That was all Alan needed to know. His goal now was how to attach his own name to it.

Putting the folder down, he exited the office and came face to face with Betty, who eyed him suspiciously. Betty had become friendly with Phil and was probably wondering why Alan was looking for Phil as the two men were not fond of each other. "Are you looking for Phil?"

"Ah – yes. He must be at lunch."

"He is. In fact I was just talking with him outside the snack bar downstairs. Do you want me to leave a note with his secretary that you were looking for him?"

"That's not necessary. I'll catch up with him later. Excuse me."

Alan brushed by her and strolled down the hall, trying to look nonchalant. By the time he got to his own office, he had broken into a sweat. Betty would probably mention his visit to Phil's office, but there was nothing he could do about it. If he was questioned about being there, his excuse of stopping for a quick chat would have to do, however implausible that would seem. In the meantime, he needed to focus on the rest of his scheme.

~

The next day was Valentine's Day, and Alan couldn't wait to see if his Valentine's Day surprise was a hit. He had arranged for flowers to be delivered to Priscilla at the office. He'd also made a reservation at the Ritz for after work. He was glad this 'lover's holiday' was on a Thursday; it gave him the opportunity to make a very public display of his affection.

Mid-morning he peeked around the corner to see Priscilla, Janine, and two women from the typing pool laughing and admiring the bouquet he had sent. Alan smiled. He could bask in Priscilla's gratitude later.

Next on his agenda was an appointment with Mr. Hodge. When he arrived at the office Lillian Graham greeted him. "Good afternoon, Mr. Bates. Mr. Hodge will see you now."

Alan walked through the door that Lillian held open and briskly approached Mr. Hodge's desk. He shook his hand.

"Thank you for taking the time to see me, Mr. Hodge. I know you are very busy."

"I'm never too busy for one of my favorite employees. What can I do for you?"

"I'm sure you're looking forward to Phil Lawrence's proposal at tomorrow's staff meeting."

"Indeed I am. I was impressed with the outline he gave me a few weeks ago."

Alan was counting on Phil having given Mr. Hodge a heads-up on his idea in order to have it on the agenda. "Yes, it looks promising. I just wanted to make sure he gets all the credit for the idea."

"How do you mean?"

"Phil and I were tossing ideas around a few months ago when I mentioned the potential in Latin America." Alan paused, watching Mr. Hodge's expression. Alan immediately knew that he had struck gold. All he had to do now was fancy it up. "While I was aware of how such an investment would positively impact our firm, it was Phil who formalized the plan. Of course, Phil kept insisting that I share the credit, but because he was the one who did most of the work, I had him swear that he would only put his name on the proposal. I'm just mentioning it to you because I didn't know if you had caught wind of it. You know how office grapevines are. Nothing's ever a secret for long."

Mr. Hodge frowned. "I think if you had any part in the proposal, Alan, you should share in the limelight. Phil's been a great employee, but I would want him to give credit where credit is due."

"Really, Mr. Hodge, Phil was insistent. But because the actual labor involved was his and my contribution was minimal, I wanted to make sure he presented it solo. I would also appreciate it if we kept this conversation to ourselves."

Mr. Hodge seemed to ponder his words. While he did, Alan realized how reckless he was being. If Mr. Hodge decided to discuss the situation with Phil, Alan's scheme would be exposed. Not only his reputation, but his career at Hodge's would be in tatters.

Finally, Mr. Hodge nodded his head. "As you wish; however, in the future, I want to make sure that all my employees receive credit for any contributions they make – no matter how minimal."

"Yes, sir. I understand."

Alan shook Mr. Hodge's outstretched hand before departing. Alan could tell from the expression on Mr. Hodge's face that he was thinking critically of Phil now. Alan had taken a risk, but he was now elated.

He whistled while he walked back to his office. He felt a little sorry for Phil. He really had nothing personal against him. The fact of the matter was that somebody on the business ladder had to look bad in order for Alan to shine.

Chapter Thirty - Four

"Good morning!"

Elizabeth was startled when she heard Stephen Wright. She had noticed someone seated on a bench in front of the entrance to Phillips & Godfrey's, but his features had been hidden by the newspaper he was holding. Now he lowered the paper to look at her. "It's nice to see a pretty face so early in the day."

Elizabeth smiled shyly. "Thank you. I gather you also like to get into work a little early?"

Stephen opened the door for her then fell into step with her once they entered the building. "I do. I feel as if I'm ahead of the game when I get a chance to look over my schedule and grab a cup of coffee before the day starts." Stephen approached the elevator and tucked the paper under his arm. He looked at Elizabeth shyly. "I know I'm belatedly saying it, but 'Happy Valentine's Day'." He shifted his feet. "Did you spend the day with anyone special?"

"I certainly did." Elizabeth watched as the smile left Stephen's face. She gave a small laugh and then added, "My grandfather made a chicken pie for the two of us for dinner and I made a heart-shaped chocolate cake for dessert."

Stephen raised his eyebrows. "So there's no one else that the heart-shape is for except your grandpa?"

"No." Elizabeth glanced at Stephen. She was pleased to see his face light up. They entered the elevator as Elizabeth continued the conversation. "My grandfather and I always wish that Valentine's Day was another time of year. One of his passions is growing roses and he has quite a variety in our yard; however, roses, as you know, don't bloom in February."

"I'll bet your 'rosy' personality gets him through the winter."

Elizabeth gave a small laugh. "Thank you. I'm glad to have him around too."

~

On Saturday afternoon Elizabeth met Betty downtown in front of Jordan Marsh for some shopping. After they had exchanged civilities, Betty said, "Elizabeth, you won't believe this. Phil Lawrence asked me out for a date!"

"Phil Lawrence? Really? I'm guessing that's a good thing by the look on your face, but I didn't know you were interested in him."

"I'll be honest. He's never really stood out to me, but I've interacted with him at work a lot and sometimes I run into him at the newsstand downstairs. He has a really good sense of humor and he's very sweet. On Valentine's Day he asked me out." Betty sighed. "It will be nice to go out with someone I didn't meet at a bar."

"Where's he taking you?"

"He said he's picking a really nice restaurant."

The girls browsed at some of the upscale stores then stopped at a local dinette for a bite to eat. While they were eating, Betty asked, "Have you gotten over Alan yet? Trust me. You're much better without him. I had him pegged from 'Day One' as an unscrupulous man."

"Oh, did you?" Elizabeth smiled as she spoke, but she felt a big lump in her throat. "What if we were still dating? Would you have been willing to let me become serious with such an unsavory character?"

"I really do think I would have warned you, but I was hedging my bets that your relationship wouldn't get that far."

Elizabeth put down her coffee cup and stared at Betty. "Why were you convinced of that?"

"Remember I told you he had too much of a wandering eye? I saw him several times at bars picking up girls – hey, I'm sorry." Betty scavenged in her pocketbook for a tissue in response to the tears that were welling up in Elizabeth's eyes. "I should have realized it's still rather raw for you."

"I'm fine, really." Elizabeth dabbed at her eyes. The revelation that Alan was picking up other girls while they were dating was heartbreaking. "I don't even know why it bothers me after the way he treated me."

"It's always the bad boys that catch our hearts, isn't it? Don't worry though. You'll get swept up someday by a guy who really deserves you. If it makes you feel any better, one day I was talking with Phil at the snack bar and Alan walked by and Phil said under his breath, 'He'll get what's coming to him someday.' So I don't think you've missed out on 'Man of the Year.' Listen, I hate to seem rude, but I've gotta run. I need to stop at our neighborhood butcher shop on the way home before it closes."

After Betty's departure, Elizabeth stopped at Woolworth's to purchase some thread. As she perused the aisles she recalled Betty's last words regarding Alan. Then she recalled the time Paul had informed her that Alan had lied about his college education. He certainly didn't seem to have much character. She knew she was better off without him. If only her heart would believe it.

As she emerged from the store she heard someone from behind calling her name. She turned to see Stephen Wright walking briskly towards her.

"Well, this is a pleasant surprise," he said with a wide grin. "I hoped it was you, but I wasn't sure. Are you out doing your Saturday shopping?"

"Oh – uh, yes, I was. And I met a friend from Hodge's. A girl friend," she added quickly. Elizabeth was flustered by Stephen's attention. He looked so genuinely pleased to see her. "Are you shopping too?"

"I needed to pick up some shoe polish so I stopped in at Woolworth's. Can I give you a lift home?"

"Oh, no! It's quite all right. The trolley stop is just around the corner."

"Now, what kind of gentleman would I be if I didn't insist on giving you a lift?"

Elizabeth found that she could not resist. Besides, Stephen looked so earnest. "Thank you. I would love a lift!"

Stephen placed his hand under her elbow and steered her away from the congested shopping area. After about a block they stopped at a black sedan parked at the curb. He opened the car door for her then walked around to the driver's seat and climbed in. "Where to?" he asked.

Elizabeth told him her address and he started the car. They had exited the downtown area and the accompanying congestion. They drove down Washington Street heading south. In a few minutes they pulled up to the familiar colonial. As Elizabeth stepped out of the car, she thanked him for the ride. Then she turned and, with some hesitation, asked him if he would like to come inside for a few minutes.

"I'd be delighted. I'm not in a hurry, and I'd enjoy seeing your grandpa again, if he's home."

As they stepped into the hall, Elizabeth called out, "Grandpa? I'm home!" She escorted Stephen towards the back of the house. They entered the kitchen just as Grandpa emerged from the cellar. Elizabeth kissed him on the cheek and then motioned to Stephen. She couldn't help blushing as she said, "Grandpa, maybe you remember Stephen Wright. He was at Grandmother's wake."

Elizabeth looked at her grandpa, imploring him with her eyes not to reveal that Stephen had been a topic of conversation in their household. "Stephen," she continued, "is one of the lawyers at work. I bumped into him while I was shopping and he kindly gave me a ride home."

"It's nice to see you again." Grandpa's face was a model of decorum. He reached out to shake Stephen's outstretched hand. "It's very considerate of you to go out of your way for Elizabeth."

"No trouble at all, sir. Your granddaughter's an easy person to go out of my way for. Elizabeth invited me in and I was happy to accept. I hope you don't mind."

"Not at all." Grandpa glanced thoughtfully from Elizabeth to Stephen. "My stomach was just reminding me that it's time to feed it. Mr. Wright, would you care to join us for supper?"

"Please, call me Stephen. And that sounds wonderful. That is, if Elizabeth doesn't mind."

"Oh, yes, please stay! We'd love to have you. I'm afraid it won't be very fancy. We're just having leftover pot roast."

"That sounds better than the food that's in my icebox."

Elizabeth offered to take Stephen's coat and then began preparing supper as Grandpa and Stephen chatted.

"Have you been with Phillips & Godfrey for a long time?" Grandpa inquired as they both sat down at the kitchen table.

"Actually, I've been with them for just over two years. I joined the firm right after I passed the bar exam. I didn't think I would stay too long as it was my first job, but I'm learning so much there. And Mr. Godfrey, the firm's president, has been especially helpful. Although he doesn't take on any cases of his own anymore, he's always taken an interest in the young lawyers just coming out of law school, and he's extremely knowledgeable and skilled when it comes to law." Stephen glanced at Elizabeth. "Of course, I won't be in a rush to leave now, since they just hired the prettiest girl in town."

Elizabeth blushed deeply and Grandpa smiled and laughed.

There was a light knock at the kitchen door and it swung open. Paul entered the room and Elizabeth greeted him by kissing him soundly on the cheek. She then turned to Stephen. "Stephen, I believe you know my uncle, Paul Keene."

Stephen stood to shake Paul's hand. "It's great to see you again Paul. How's your father?"

"Great. I just talked to him a few days ago. He's living in England now." Paul pulled out a chair and motioned for Stephen to sit beside him.

"Has your father mentioned if Europe is beginning to recover from the war yet?"

"I know it's very slow going. At Thanksgiving I was in Europe, but I wasn't in any of the hard-hit areas, but Father has been to a few. There was enormous damage to many of the big cities because they were such easy targets. And of course there was a tremendous loss of lives." Paul paused. "When I was there, the thing that really struck me was the effect the war had on the survivors. There was fear. It was in people's eyes, in their voices when they spoke. Fear can be a terrible thing. It makes people afraid of moving forward, afraid of realizing their hopes and dreams."

Stephen put in, "I wish I'd been part of the war effort, but I've been supporting my mother since I got out of college."

"Don't be apologetic. That's admirable," Paul said.

Grandpa clapped Paul on the back. "You for one should know."

Paul gave Grandpa an appreciative smile then stood to pull silverware out of a drawer. "Elizabeth, have you heard from the Sullivans this week? How's my Dolly doing? Has she been pining away for me?"

"Well, if I answered that, I'd be giving away a dear friend's closely guarded secret, now wouldn't I?"

"Somehow, I don't think it's a secret that's all that closely guarded," Paul replied, his eyes twinkling, "unless you consider everyone east of the Mississippi river as 'just a few people' being in on it. However, in order to avoid you having to compromise your loyalties, I suppose I'll have to wait to find out until I see her again. When I do, will she come charging at me with the force of an eighty mile an hour hurricane, or will she play hard to get – at least for a full twelve seconds?"

Elizabeth and Grandpa laughed merrily. Stephen looked utterly confused. "Who's Dolly? Someone worth meeting, I gather?"

"Oh, she's definitely someone worth meeting," Paul replied, glancing with unconcealed glee at Elizabeth. "Just make sure you have enough stamina when you do."

Elizabeth briefly described Dolly to Stephen and told of some of her more memorable escapades. She also filled him in on the Sullivan family, Aunt May, and their homes in Maine.

Grandpa reached to grab an envelope that was sitting on the counter. "Speaking of Dolly, this came for you today." He handed it to Paul and Elizabeth could see Dolly's return address on the corner of the envelope.

"Dolly sent you a note? Or should I say 'another note'?" Elizabeth teased.

"Apparently so." Paul slid open the top of the envelope with a dinner knife. Slipping a piece of paper out, he read aloud. "It was truly delightful to see you again last weekend. Please consider yourself invited to Maine with Elizabeth and her grandpa on their next sojourn here."

"No moss on that girl," Grandpa mused. "She's got her eye on you."

"She does seem to."

"I'm not sure when we're next going up," Elizabeth said, "but it looks like you are expected to come." She hesitated then turned to Stephen. "We've now told you all about the Sullivans. Would you like to take a ride up with us sometime?"

"Of course. That would be wonderful!" Stephen looked pleased by her invitation.

She hoped she had not seemed too forward. Her thoughts were interrupted by Paul, who asked, "Is anyone interested in going to see *The Bells of Saint Mary's* starring Bing Crosby after dinner? It's the biggest movie out there."

"Sounds good to me," Stephen replied. "Elizabeth? Mr. Burke? Are you interested?" Stephen's gaze lingered on Elizabeth.

"Thank you for asking," Grandpa answered, "but my weekly poker game is tonight instead of last night, so I'm afraid I'll be busy raking all those chips over to my side of the table." Grandpa winked at Elizabeth. "But you three go ahead and have a nice time."

That evening they sat three across at the movies, Elizabeth in the middle. Before the show Stephen and Paul talked about the war and business and Elizabeth noticed that Paul and Stephen got along very well.

When the show was over Paul exclaimed, "There's one of my friends from my old college days! Excuse for a moment, will you?" He rose and Stephen leaned close to Elizabeth. "Let me take advantage of this opportune moment and ask you if you're free next Saturday night. I've heard great things about the Totem Pole Ballroom for dancing. Would you care to join me?"

Elizabeth hesitated, and Stephen, misinterpreting her slow response, added, "Perhaps Maura would like to go too, with a date. We could double."

"Oh, I'd love to go," Elizabeth said. "I've heard so much about it, and I've always wanted to go. But, I'm not exactly an accomplished dancer."

"Neither am I. But we could learn together." He very softly touched Elizabeth's hand.

She smiled.

They stood, and Elizabeth said, "Thank you so much for everything tonight. Not just for the movie, but for giving me a ride home from shopping and – "

Stephen interrupted her. "Don't thank me. I should thank you. I had a wonderful time. If you hadn't invited me to supper, I probably would have roamed around my apartment all night, listening to music or trying to find a good show to listen to on the radio." Stephen paused as Paul approached. Then he added, with a sudden earnestness in his eyes, "So, next Saturday?"

"Yes, I – I'm looking forward to it."

Elizabeth thought about what a nice evening it had been. And how unlike Alan Stephen was.

Chapter Thirty - Five

Alan inched his way towards the bar, feeling penned in on all sides by the crowd. As he drew closer, he twisted his head, hoping that he would spot Neil and that Neil would have managed to save him a seat.

When he finally reached the counter he saw Neil sitting with a beer in front of him. A coveted empty stool was next to him. "Sit down," Neil called. "And hurry up about doing it. I've had to fend people off with my life!"

"I can well imagine. Sorry I'm so late. If I thought I would be so long, I wouldn't even have asked you to go out after work."

"No problem. I'd rather sit on a bar stool with a drink in my hand waiting for you than hear the clicking of needles at my wife's knitting club. Want a beer?"

"Do you even have to ask?"

Neil signaled the bartender, who set a bottle in front of Alan. Alan clinked bottles with Neil. "Cheers! To another work week finished and another weekend just begun."

"Ditto! I'm ready for the weekend after that endless presentation of Phil's. I have to say, though, I admire his business savvy and research skills. He has some great ideas and the numbers to back them up. What was your take on it?"

Alan fingered his beer bottle. "It was okay." He paused. "Tell you what, let's not talk about business." He smiled in what he hoped was a reassuring way.

"Fine. How's everything else going?"

"Can't complain I guess, except for Priscilla and me."

Neil arched an eyebrow. "Things aren't working out as you hoped?"

"Actually, things are great between us."

"That's a complaint?"

Alan laughed. "The problem is that for a while now I've wanted Priscilla to go steady with me and she's not interested. I think she likes feeling uncommitted – especially because she's portrayed as a 'great catch' in the public domain. Does that make sense?"

"I think so. I'm sure she enjoys being the 'single socialite.' But do you think you're her number one guy?"

"From everything I can tell, although she certainly seems to enjoy the attention she gets from other males."

"Why don't you just give her a taste of her own medicine?"

"You mean do a little of my own flirting?"

"Exactly!"

Alan grinned at Neil. "Have I told you before that you're a genius?"

"I think you did once, but it's one of those phrases that never gets old."

"I'll remember that, especially when I'm picking ushers for the wedding."

"I may be too old for that, but I certainly appreciate being considered. One step at a time though, my friend."

"True. Next Thursday we plan to go out, and that might provide a perfect opportunity to get things rolling."

"Somehow I think that flirting with the opposite sex isn't too outside your zone of capability."

"You've sized me up well, my friend. Cheers!" Alan raised his glass before taking a gulp, almost choking in his excitement. Alan couldn't wait to see how Priscilla would react when he did a little socializing of his own.

~

The following Monday afternoon Alan was returning from lunch when he saw Phil head towards him. Phil stopped, blocking Alan's path. When he spoke, he had an unmistakable edge to his voice. "Betty mentioned that you were in my office last Wednesday looking for me. Any particular reason?"

"Oh – yes. I did stop by, but it was nothing important."

"Sure you weren't looking for anything in particular? Some advance information on the proposal I was to present at Friday's meeting, for instance? "

Alan gave Phil a hard glare. "What are you implying?" Alan stepped forward to pass by, but Phil caught his arm.

"The reason I'm asking is that Mr. Hodge had mentioned prior to the presentation that I was in line for a promotion. Then, this morning, he said it wouldn't be happening. Would you happen to know why Mr. Hodge would suddenly change his mind?"

Alan pulled his arm away as he answered carefully. "That's too bad, Phil, but I haven't a clue. Excuse me."

Alan walked to his office and shut the door behind him. Even if Phil thought that Alan had seen his proposal, he probably wouldn't figure out the exact connection between Alan and Mr. Hodge's change-of-mind – as long as Mr. Hodge never leveled with Phil. Alan wished he could count on that.

Chapter Thirty - Six

The remainder of February was a flurry of activity at Phillips & Godfrey. The firm had been aggressively pursuing new accounts, and more and more clients were being added to their roster. Everyone on staff found themselves overloaded with work, and tempers flared with the pressure of last-minute deadlines.

One afternoon when Elizabeth returned from the mailroom she heard a titter of laughter sweep through a small group gathered in the hallway. Elizabeth surmised that something out of the ordinary must have happened while she was gone. By the looks of glee on their faces, they were enjoying an unexpected but welcome interruption from normal duties.

Maura was walking towards Elizabeth as one of the girls in the group called out to her, "Bravo, Maura!"

Maura smiled as she greeted Elizabeth. "Your timing was bad. You missed all the fun a few minutes ago!"

"What happened?"

"I mistakenly gave Mr. Winslow five copies of Romeo and Juliet instead of the January report he requested for his meeting with his client."

Elizabeth's hand flew to her mouth. "What did he say?"

"He said I should consider myself very lucky that he noticed my mistake before he handed them out."

"How did you answer him?"

"I told him that maybe the client would have been lucky if they had gotten to read about the Montagues instead of his boring summaries."

"You certainly know how to stand your ground, Maura."

"I consider it one of my better talents!"

~

When Elizabeth came home from work on Friday, she had some

unexpected good news. Grandpa gave her a letter. The return address was immediately recognizable. Elizabeth opened it with trembling hands. Inside, a letter informed her that the Saturday Evening Post was going to publish one of her stories.

"Grandpa, I can't believe it! I'm going to get published in the Saturday Evening Post!"

Grandpa gave her a big hug. "That's wonderful! I guess that means I finally get to read something you've written."

"I'm sorry, Grandpa. I didn't mean to be so private. I've just always been nervous about sharing my stories – even with you."

"I understand and I want you to know that I am very proud of you. When will it be published?"

"It's going to be in a spring collection in April. Oh, I can't wait to tell everyone in Maine!"

Chapter Thirty - Seven

The evening had fallen into place perfectly. Because both he and Priscilla worked late on that Thursday evening, Alan suggested they grab a bite to eat at Joe & Nemo's. He had chosen the place because he knew that he was likely to find Dee Dee – the girl whose company he'd thoroughly enjoyed while Elizabeth had been out of town last fall – at the joint, and she was just the girl to help implement his plan. Dee Dee had a voluptuous figure, sure to yank Priscilla's jealousy string.

The waitress showed them to a table and left them with menus while she hurried over to another table. The restaurant was already very crowded for a typical Thursday night. He and Priscilla chatted casually while they waited for their waitress to return, while Alan's eyes casually scanned the room to see if Dee Dee was there.

Suddenly, Alan saw Dee Dee standing in line at the bar. He couldn't believe his luck. He immediately visualized in his head how his plan would play out and he began putting it into action. "I'm sure the waitress is busy. I'll go up to the bar and get some drinks."

Priscilla nodded her head, as the room was quite loud. Strolling casually up to the bar, he stood next to Dee Dee, giving her a light kiss on the cheek as he spoke. "Hello, Darling! Fancy seeing you here!"

Dee Dee turned sideways, a look of delight in her eyes. "Hi, Alan! Happy almost weekend!"

"You too!"

The bartender was waiting for Dee Dee's order. While she gave it, Alan stood very close to her. When she was finished, he smiled engagingly at her. "You must be on a date tonight."

"How did you guess?"

"I can't imagine you alone any night. We'll have to get together again soon." Alan continued to stand close to her as he gazed into her eyes.

"You know where to find me."

"Yes, I do."

From the corner of his eye, he could tell that Priscilla was able to watch them from the position of her chair. He leaned into Dee Dee's neck. "I like the perfume you're wearing. What kind is it?"

"I honestly don't remember, but I'm glad you like it, Alan."

"I definitely do."

Meanwhile, Alan saw that Priscilla had risen from her seat and was quickly approaching them. The bartender had returned with Dee Dee's order as Priscilla reached them.

"Are you socializing, Alan?"

"Actually, this is…"Alan paused pointedly, "a friend of mine. Priscilla, this is Dee Dee. Dee, this is Priscilla Hodge."

Dee Dee glanced quickly at the beers in her hands as she spoke. "Nice to meet you. I'd shake hands but they're rather full at the moment."

Priscilla stared coldly at Dee Dee. "Did Alan tell you he was on a date with me?"

"No, but if it's your first date, Alan's a lot of fun. Nice to meet you."

Dee Dee hurried away while Alan turned to give his order. While he talked with the bartender, he could feel Priscilla's eyes glaring at him.

"What was that all about?"

"What do you mean?" Alan feigned innocence.

"I mean flirting with an ex-girlfriend, that's what I mean."

"She's just an 'old friend'."

"Are you getting revenge on me for flirting at the tennis club?"

"Not at all. I just happened to run into her, although I hardly think you can resent me for flirting when you don't seem to mind when you're doing it."

Priscilla's eyes narrowed.

Clearly Alan's words had struck a nerve. The move had been risky, but it seemed a valid point to make. Priscilla opened her mouth and just as quickly closed it. While they waited for their food, they both remained silent. He felt they were at a crossroads and he was not at all sure how it would settle.

As soon as they were finished eating Alan said, "Why don't we get out of here?"

Alan drove to Priscilla's house. When he pulled up to the curb,

Priscilla turned in her seat to face him. "I've been thinking about our dating status."

"Go on."

"I think I want to go steady with you."

Alan flashed a quick look at her but said nothing. He didn't want to seem too eager. He shifted in his seat but continued to look straight ahead.

Priscilla remained silent for a moment then said, "It appears as if I'm too late. You don't seem very interested."

"I'm very interested. The only condition I have if we do go steady is that there is to be no flirting with other men."

"Honestly, Alan, it doesn't mean a thing. It's just my style, but if it's a big deal to you, then I won't flirt anymore."

"Promise?"

There was a moment's hesitation before Priscilla replied, "Promise."

Tipping her head back, he bent down for a long, hard kiss. It would have even bordered on rough. He wanted Priscilla to know in no uncertain terms not only that he wanted her, but that he was in charge.

When they finally broke apart, Priscilla looked at him with shining eyes. Apparently, she didn't mind his aggressiveness. On the contrary, she seemed to appreciate it. He was good for her and she knew it.

Alan breathed an inward sigh of relief. His plan had worked. Priscilla was finally his girl and he could tell other men to back off if the occasion arose.

Chapter Thirty-Eight

When Stephen arrived to pick Elizabeth up to head to the Totem Pole, she was ready. She had chosen a navy-blue satin dress that Mary Francis had passed on to her, and she had been fortunate to find a pair of stockings to purchase. Stockings were still hard to come by. They had been completely unavailable for nearly the past five years, as silk had been used to make parachutes and other war materials. New stockings felt heavenly on her legs. She had curled her hair and pulled it back with a heart-shaped clip. She had even added a hint of blue eye shadow and rose-colored lipstick.

Stephen took one look at her and exclaimed, "You look beautiful! You'll be the best-looking girl there!" He handed her a small, square box, tied with a pink ribbon. "I thought you could wear this tonight. I got white because I didn't know what color you'd be wearing."

Elizabeth opened the box to find a corsage of white lilies accentuated by an arrangement of green leaves and baby's breath.

"Oh, Stephen, they're lovely! I've never gotten a corsage before. I'll put it on right now."

While Elizabeth was pinning it to the top of her bodice, Grandpa came down the stairs. "Good evening, Stephen. What do you think of this fetching young woman? Doesn't she look beautiful?"

"I've just been telling her that, sir."

Elizabeth stood back so the two men could get a clear view of her corsage. "Grandpa, look what Stephen gave me."

"That's very pretty. You can never go wrong with flowers for a woman, Stephen."

Stephen smiled broadly then glanced at his watch. "We'd better get going. We're meeting Maura there with her date, Bill. I don't want to keep them waiting."

"I know she's in good hands with you," Grandpa said, giving Stephen a pat on the back before ushering them down the hall.

~

The Totem Pole Ballroom, in Newton, was about a forty minute drive. Stephen and Elizabeth chatted effortlessly on the way there. When they arrived they saw Maura waiting for them at the door with a sandy-haired man next to her. Maura introduced Bill, whom she'd been seeing for some time. The four of them made their way into the club and headed to one of the ballroom's famed couches.

Elizabeth was mesmerized by the huge dance floor, the stage, and the majestic staircase.

As they sat down, Bill commented, "Last weekend Jimmy Dorsey and his orchestra were here. I heard you could hardly get in the place. I'm not sure who's playing tonight, but I know Harriet Hilliard will be singing as usual, and just hearing her is a good reason to come."

It was still early, but already there was quite a crowd milling about. Elizabeth watched young men and women float by. Many of them were dressed in sequins which sparkled from the lights. Some had lavish fur coats or expensive mink stoles. Even Maura had a racy-looking dress which was off the shoulder and cut low in front. Elizabeth's navy satin dress was far more conservative than the other girls' dresses, but she still felt fashionable.

A waiter approached their table to ask for their drink requests. "What'll it be?" Bill asked everyone. "First round's on me."

Elizabeth hesitated and then said, "A glass of white wine, please." She'd let herself partake tonight if everyone else was.

The others ordered drinks, and as the waiter departed the orchestra began playing. Maura jumped up excitedly.

"Bill, let's dance. Coming guys?"

"I think we'll sit this one out. You two get going," Stephen replied.

The music made it hard to converse so Elizabeth leaned close to Stephen. "I told you all about my family last week. What about you? Do you have any family?"

"I have a mother who lives in New York, along with an older sister and her family, but my father died seven years ago."

"You'd mentioned you'd been caring for your mother. I'm so sorry about your father."

"Thank you. I still miss him terribly. He was quite a man. He was devoted to my mother and a wonderful father to my sister and me. My mother hasn't done very well getting used to living without him, alone. My sister doesn't live far, but I'm always a little worried about Mom."

"I understand. I'd be just as worried about my grandpa if the situation was reversed."

"Yes. I know you would be, Elizabeth. That's one of the things I like about you so much. You're a very caring person.

"I first came to Boston when I attended college at Suffolk Law School. When I graduated, I was offered a job at Phillips & Godfrey, so I decided to stay here. I probably would have tried to get a job in New York and move back home if my sister didn't live in the next town over from Mom. I do get home about once a month, so I feel like I've been able to see my mom pretty consistently."

"I think your mother's very lucky to have you and your sister," Elizabeth offered. She couldn't help comparing Stephen's devotion to family versus Alan's indifference. With the exception of Alan going home for Thanksgiving, he had seemed to ignore his family and rarely mentioned them.

"And I think your grandpa is very lucky to have you."

Elizabeth looked up to see Maura and Bill. "What's all this talk about being lucky?" Maura asked.

"Why, I was just telling Elizabeth how lucky I am that I missed making a spectacle of myself dancing to that last jazz number!"

Maura and Elizabeth laughed. Just then, Elizabeth looked up to see Betty and Phil coming toward them and Elizabeth jumped up. "Betty! Phil! What are you doing here?" Betty linked her arm through Phil's. "When we talked on the phone last week, Elizabeth, and you mentioned you were coming here, I told Phil. He said he's always wanted to see the Totem Pole, so here we are!"

Elizabeth introduced Phil and Betty to Stephen, Maura, and Bill. Stephen and Bill left to scout for chairs. Betty slid in next to Elizabeth and whispered, "Guess who else is here? Don't look now, but Alan and Priscilla are on the dance floor."

Elizabeth's heart began pounding and she struggled to maintain a composed look. After a moment she casually turned her head toward the crowded floor. She couldn't see Alan or Priscilla. The orchestra began playing *Sentimental Journey*.

"Who's ready to dance?" Bill challenged.

Stephen cocked his ear towards the orchestra. "Fine with me. In fact, I think they're playing our song. Elizabeth, shall we?"

Elizabeth would have preferred to remain hidden on their couch, but she didn't want Stephen to think there was anything wrong. She turned her eyes to Stephen. "So, we have a song, do we?" she teased.

Stephen smiled. "I'm hoping so," he replied. She threw Betty a helpless gesture as Stephen escorted her onto the floor. He slipped his arm around Elizabeth's waist and they began to sway to the music.

When the dance ended, Elizabeth spotted Priscilla and Alan. They were standing, entwined, at the edge of the ballroom floor. Her heart began pounding at the sight of them together.

She hadn't seen Alan for nearly a month. She wondered if he missed her but quickly dismissed the notion when she saw how affectionate he was being with Priscilla.

As Elizabeth stood there, Priscilla looked up. Upon meeting Elizabeth's gaze, she wrapped her arms tightly around Alan's neck and kissed him passionately on the lips. Obviously, it was for show but it still hurt that Alan was so responsive.

When Alan finally lifted his head, his gaze drifted in Elizabeth's direction and their eyes locked for a moment. Alan quickly looked away and Elizabeth looked down. There had been only coldness in his eyes.

Stephen touched her arm. "Is everything alright?"

"Oh, uh, yes, everything's fine." She tried to appear calm. She knew that Stephen was too polite to press any further and Elizabeth certainly didn't know Stephen well enough to tell him that her ex-boyfriend was just feet away. Stephen guided her back to their seats where Betty and Phil were sipping drinks. Betty stood and grabbed Elizabeth's arm.

"Your friends Maura and Bill are still on the dance floor. Elizabeth, I'm going to the ladies' room. Would you like to come?"

"Uh, sure."

Grabbing her clutch, Elizabeth got up and began walking towards the restroom; however, Betty grabbed her arm and steered her towards the exit door. "Just before we saw you tonight, Phil and Alan had an altercation. I'm so upset I have to tell someone what happened, but we have to go outside. The ladies' room will be too crowded."

As soon as they left the building, Betty began talking, the words tumbling over each other. "Phil was walking through the crowd and when he saw Alan walking near him, he shoved Alan, which he shouldn't have done, but I think he's just so mad at him. Then Alan made a comment along the lines of 'What are *you two* doing here?' Then Phil said something – I'm not even sure what – and for a moment I thought Alan was going to punch Phil right here in the club. I had to pull Phil away." Betty exhaled. "I didn't get a chance to tell you earlier, but Phil thinks Alan was snooping around in his office the week before last looking for confidential material."

"Why does he think that?"

"I caught Alan in Phil's office one day during lunch when no one was around. I didn't actually see him looking at any papers, but Phil's Latin Proposal for Mr. Hodge was on the desk. According to Phil, Mr. Hodge had been very excited about the proposal up to that time, but when Phil gave the presentation on it the next day, Mr. Hodge was only lukewarm. Before the presentation, Mr. Hodge had told Phil he was in line for a promotion, but then afterwards he recanted. Phil is convinced that Alan has something to do with it."

"Does Phil want to even the score?"

"I think so, and honestly, I'm all for it. But I certainly don't want a fist fight, and I don't want to ruin our evening here. Let's go back in."

Elizabeth thought about how revolted she was by so many of Alan's actions – lying about college, apparently trying to backstab Phil, flirting behind her back while they were dating. In theory, she was glad their romance was over. But emotionally, why did Alan still have the ability to pull her heartstrings every time she ran into him?

~

The rest of the evening flew by. Thankfully, Priscilla and Alan were nowhere to be seen after that first encounter. Maura and Bill and Betty and Phil joined them on the dance floor for song after song. They switched partners several times, but Stephen always reclaimed Elizabeth when a slow dance began.

After the band played their last song, Stephen asked, "Did you have a nice time tonight?"

"It was wonderful! Not just the dancing and the music, but watching all the people and seeing the inside of this grand building."

Stephen nodded. "Would you be interested in going out to dinner next Saturday night? Just the two of us?"

"I'd – I'd like that very much." She couldn't quite meet his eyes when she spoke.

They said their goodbyes to the other two couples and Stephen drove her home. At her doorstep he touched her arm then, suddenly, before she was aware he was going to do it, he gave her a gentle kiss on the mouth.

"I hope that wasn't too forward of me," he said. Then he added, "I'd better let you go. It's late enough as it is. I'll see you Monday."

He departed, leaving her standing on the step with a hundred and one thoughts to keep her company.

Chapter Thirty - Nine

Alan had been excited to bring Priscilla to the Totem Pole. It was the grandest ballroom, by some accounts, in the country. Alan had never been, but Priscilla said she had been numerous times and it was exquisite. When they got there the band was warming up and Alan and Priscilla settled themselves on one of the private couches. Priscilla looked beautiful, with her golden blond hair swept up in a chignon and a burgundy red dress with narrow straps that left her shoulders bared.

Alan was extra attentive, and Priscilla commented on it. "Are you making up for our spat the other week?" She rested her deep blue eyes on him.

"Not at all. I'm just enjoying the most elegant and breathtaking woman I have ever seen."

"Flattery will get you everywhere!"

"You stay right here. I'm going to get us a couple of drinks." Alan made his way toward the back and, as he did, Phil Lawrence, coming from the other direction, bumped in to him hard, knocking Alan back a step. Betty Higgins was one step behind Phil.

"Watch it!" Alan said, straightening his jacket. He looked at Betty, and then back at Phil. "What are you two doing here?" he said. "Out on a date?"

"As a matter of fact we are," Phil replied. "It's no secret, so you can tell whomever you like. Including Mr. Hodge. You seem to have his ear at work."

Alan wanted to slug Phil but kept himself in check. "I'm going to overlook that comment."

"Why? Does the truth hurt?"

Betty stepped in. "Phil, why don't we dance? Excuse us, Alan."

Phil pushed by him, giving Alan a glaring look. Alan walked back to his seat, forgetting about drinks. Phil was beginning to be a thorn in his side. Alan considered his options. He could ignore Phil, and hope for the best, or he could take it to the next level. If he subtly slandered Phil's reputation to Priscilla, she would surely rally to Alan's side. Then if Phil made any attempt to damage Alan's character with Mr. Hodge, Phil would likely have even less credibility. Alan had already made a dent in Phil's armor with Mr. Hodge. Another damaging story reported from his daughter would solidify it. Alan felt better now. He would get to work on it that very night.

"Let's hit the dance floor," he said to Priscilla, helping her up from the couch. He led her to a spot as far away from Phil and Betty as possible. There he leaned close to her, taking in the low cut of her dress and the smell of her perfume. As he lightly brushed her cheek with a kiss, he saw something attract Priscilla's attention.

"I wouldn't believe it if I hadn't seen it with my own eyes: Elizabeth Keene, at a nightclub. With some man!"

Alan followed Priscilla's gaze just in time to see Elizabeth walk onto the dance floor and put her arms around the neck of a man. Alan gritted his teeth. First Phil, and now Elizabeth. Had they come in a group? And who was the man Elizabeth was with?

"I wonder where she met that guy," he mused aloud. "Maybe at her new job?"

"Who cares where they met? Let's go dance near them." Priscilla pulled Alan through the crowd.

"Priscilla, let it go!"

"Why are you defending her?"

"Why are you attacking her? She doesn't bother you."

Softening his tone, he moved close to Priscilla to whisper in her ear, "We're having a wonderful evening. Who cares about anyone else? The only one I can think about is you."

Alan saw Priscilla relent a little. "I guess you're right. To be honest, I don't know why she annoys me so much. She just seems too innocent to be true."

Alan shrugged his shoulders. "She doesn't work at Hodge's anymore, so forget about her."

"Yes, let's." Priscilla planted a long kiss on Alan's lips just as the song ended.

When their kiss finally ended, he raised his head to see Elizabeth Keene looking at him. Their eyes met only for a moment before Alan turned back towards Priscilla. Had Priscilla kissed him in order to show off? He pretended he hadn't noticed Elizabeth and concentrated on dancing. When he ventured a peek in the direction where Elizabeth and her date had been, he was relieved to see that they were no longer on the dance floor. He inwardly breathed a sigh of relief.

He felt bad for Elizabeth - she seemed to fan the flame of Priscilla's jealousy. He never would have thought that someone as beautiful, wealthy, and socially-connected as Priscilla Hodge would feel so threatened by a quiet, humble secretary.

After that Alan kept Priscilla close to him on their two-person couch. He told her he was in the mood to listen to the music, not dance. Priscilla pouted but was appeased with a steady supply of drinks. Finally, when the band was ready to take a break, Alan motioned to Priscilla that they should leave. She turned down the corners of her mouth but followed him. As they walked towards the coatroom, Alan saw Stephen and Elizabeth walking towards the bar. He deftly turned Priscilla in the other direction.

Alan drove to Boston Harbor and parked the car. They strolled by an old pier, watching the twinkling lights along the edge of the harbor and the dim gleam of the moon on the water's surface. As they walked, Alan stayed silent, bending his head low and furrowing his brow. Finally Priscilla noticed his somber mood.

"Everything all right? You look upset."

"It's nothing."

"Obviously it's something. What's wrong?"

Alan gave a loud sigh then spoke hesitantly. "You didn't see him, but Phil Lawrence was at the Totem Pole tonight. He made a point of talking to me in order to toot his own horn about something. It's not the first time he's done it and, to be honest, I'm getting very tired of it."

Priscilla made a puzzled face. "Phil? I never would have thought Phil would be like that. He's such a marshmallow."

"I wouldn't have either, but he's not the person you think he is once you get to know him."

"What was he bragging about?"

"I had given him the idea of going international with our investments – Latin America to be specific – and I didn't mind at all when he put a proposal together. In fact, I insisted that he take full credit for it. However, I didn't think he would flaunt how much your father loves his proposal when he knows I'm letting him have all the limelight."

"The nerve of him! I should tell my father how he's been handling it."

Alan's heart raced faster. "That actually might be a big help, but you know me, I'm not a complainer and I wouldn't want your father to think I am."

"I don't have to mention your name. I can just say I heard it through the grapevine."

"All right, but only as long as your father never knows I said anything. Honestly, I'd be just as happy to keep this to ourselves." Alan smiled as he spoke and kept his tone light.

"Don't worry. I'll take care of it." Priscilla wrapped her arms around his waist.

He knew Priscilla would be good to her word, and, after that, he doubted he would ever have to worry about Phil Lawrence again.

Chapter Forty

The first Saturday morning in March was cold, with skies threatening a freezing rain. Elizabeth found she was still wondering what she would wear to dinner. Although her winter clothes were appropriate for the chilly weather, she was dying to wear something new. She decided to walk down to the corner consignment shop to find something. They were not the finest of clothes, but they were far cheaper than the big department stores and most of the time she found nice items.

Elizabeth was delighted to find a black and white silk skirt that zipped up the side in the current fashion. She could wear with it her frilly white blouse with the pearl buttons that she saved for special occasions.

That night she dressed carefully. She was excited about seeing Stephen again. After washing her hair, she had set it in damp rags, and now she brushed out the long banana curls before securing them back with a silver-plated clip. She pinned a pearl-studded brooch that had been her mother's to her blouse. Grandpa had given it to her on her sixteenth birthday and it was among her most cherished possessions.

She skittered downstairs as soon as she heard the bell ring. Stephen seemed just as pleased to see her as he had been the week before.

"May I say you look even more beautiful than ever, if that is indeed possible?"

"On the grounds of pure modesty, I find myself totally incapable of responding." Elizabeth found that she was getting more comfortable talking with him and could even manage a joke or two.

"Recognizing the fact that you are a true lady who would never compliment herself, I accept your answer, although I need no other affirmation except my own. You do look beautiful. Now, off to our magical evening!"

They dined at Blinstrub's in Dorchester, a large, bustling restaurant that Elizabeth knew was popular. From there, they drove over to the Harbor where they spent the rest of the evening talking and laughing. Elizabeth found Stephen affable and unassuming. When she told him about her story that was to be published in the Saturday Evening Post, he was very excited.

"When does it come out? I'm going to buy a bunch of copies and give them to everyone at work!"

"That's very kind of you, but I don't want to look like a showoff."

"You wouldn't be doing the showing off – I would."

Elizabeth blushed. She changed the subject. "How do you like living in Boston?"

"It's a great city. I love the history of it – the North Church where the colonists hung the lanterns for Paul Revere to see, Boston Harbor where the Tea Party occurred. The only wrinkle is I don't think I'm ever going to be able to root for the Boston Braves instead of the New York Yankees. You can't expect a lifelong Yankees fan to defect anytime soon."

Elizabeth laughed. "Do you miss being near your family?"

"Like crazy. I love my job at Phillips, but I try to get home as much as possible. Family's important!"

Elizabeth smiled. Stephen certainly got points for being family-oriented – Yankees fan or not.

~

March's arrival was accompanied by forsythia, followed by the first buds on Grandpa's rose bushes. Elizabeth went inside to tell Grandpa about the buds, but he held up his finger to his lips as he listened to the radio. Winston Churchill's "Iron Curtain" speech was being broadcast. When the recording finished, he looked at Elizabeth. "Churchill truly is one of the greatest leaders of our day."

Elizabeth nodded her head. She knew how Grandpa felt about the war and the respect he held for the Allied leaders.

"Now," Grandpa continued, "what were you saying?"

Elizabeth excitedly announced her finding and Grandpa nodded his head. "Always good to see that sign of spring popping up."

"Grandpa, do you think sometime soon we could go up to Grandmother Keene's house and prune back the bushes?"

Grandpa gave her a sideways look. "I know you're worried about how those bushes will hold up without consistent care."

"It's not just the roses – it's the house. It looks so lonely and abandoned. Uncle Paul can only do so much. What's going to happen to it?"

"Paul told me that his father will put it up for sale as soon as he has it updated. It needs a new coat of paint on the outside, along with some electrical and plumbing renovations." He put his hand on Elizabeth's. "I know it's hard to let that piece of your life go, but we still have the roses in our own garden, and there will be some new family that will appreciate all those beautiful roses in your grandparents' yard."

Elizabeth nodded. Grandpa was right. Still, she hated to think of those bushes going untended. "Please, Grandpa? It would make the house show better." Her grandpa sighed. "My arthritis won't allow me to do much pruning, but I'll go up with you if it makes you happy."

~

True to his word Grandpa took Elizabeth up to the Keene house on a mild day in early April. While Elizabeth pruned, Grandpa inspected the flower beds, pulling dead leaves and fingering the fresh buds. While they were working Grandpa commented, "Nice fella, that there Steve."

"Yes, he is," agreed Elizabeth. She had been thinking the same thing lately. She knew that people considered them a couple, and while she had to admit that was true, she didn't want to think any further than that. She had been deeply hurt by Alan and was reluctant to get too involved with anyone else. She also could not ignore the fact that in spite of the way Alan had treated her, she still somehow couldn't forget about him.

Grandpa gingerly knelt on one knee to clean out some dead leaves from around one of the bushes. "He appears to have taken quite a likin' to ye."

Elizabeth brought her mind back to Stephen. "Yes, he does seem to have," Elizabeth returned. She couldn't help but be amused over her grandfather's efforts to try to glean information.

"Could do a lot worse," Grandpa continued. He whistled as he slowly straightened up and moved to the next bush.

"Oh, you think so?"

"Aye, I do."

"Well, I'll tell Stephen he has at least one vote."

"You can add Harry to the list." Grandpa made a show of avoiding Elizabeth's gaze. Then he turned and added with a wink, "And Fred Cummings, too." He escaped into the shed, leaving Elizabeth to laugh at his obvious, but light-hearted attempts to persuade her. It warmed her heart to know how much Grandpa thought of Stephen. He was a good judge of character, Elizabeth thought. Perhaps better than she.

~

Elizabeth and Grandpa traveled north for Easter, hitching a ride with Harry, who was spending the holiday at his son's house. They had asked Paul and Stephen to come, but both had reluctantly declined. Stephen had plans to visit his mother and Paul said he had work to do at the office that could not wait.

Elizabeth couldn't help but recall the last person she had asked to accompany them to Maine. She remembered how much she had missed Alan last Thanksgiving and she also realized with a start that she was going to miss Stephen. Since that wintry day in January when Stephen had driven her home from shopping, she had spent part of every weekend with him. Elizabeth laughed at herself. They would only be in Maine for three days, and besides, she would have a nice time seeing the Sullivans and Auntie May again.

On Saturday morning Elizabeth walked over to the Sullivans' to see what everyone was up to. When she entered the front parlor, she found Mary Francis and Dolly helping their mother clean up. Margaret Sullivan welcomed her and then left the three girls to themselves. Dolly and Mary Francis pounced on Elizabeth.

"A new beau, Elizabeth!" shrieked Dolly. "My! It certainly didn't take you long!"

Elizabeth wagged a warning finger at her. "Now, Dolly. I don't want you – or anyone else for that matter – jumping to any conclusions. Stephen is just a nice, young man I'm casually dating and that's all there is to it."

"That's what they all say!"

Mary Francis rolled her eyes at her sister's know-it-all attitude. She addressed Elizabeth. "Never mind that. Tell us what Stephen is like. And what he looks like. Every detail!"

"Well, he's fairly tall – taller than Uncle Paul, in fact, and he has light brown hair with brown eyes."

"Brown eyes," Dolly cried, as if disappointed.

Elizabeth laughed. "Something wrong with that, Dolly? Yes, very nice brown eyes with little flecks of green in them. You'll see when you meet him."

"Will that be soon?" Mary Francis asked.

"I hope so. Actually, we asked him to come with us this weekend, but he's spending the holiday with his mother. We'll be up again soon, if not in June, then by July 4th at the latest. Stephen has promised he'll come then no matter what."

"Maybe you'll have a ring on your finger by then," cooed Dolly.

Mary Francis cast her sister a dismissive glance. "Dolly, don't be ridiculous! Why, I've been dating Robert for over a year and I don't even have a ring yet."

Dolly flung back, "You'll be dating Robert for ten years and you still won't have a ring! He'll never have the nerve to ask you to marry him and, frankly, in my opinion, a man like that isn't worth waiting for."

Mary Francis stared aghast at her sister. Then her face crumpled as she cried, "Dorothy Ann Sullivan! Sometimes I think you're just the meanest, most hateful person I know! You have no consideration for other people's feelings!"

Mary Francis rushed sobbing from the room, leaving Dolly to say defensively, "I'm not hateful! I'm just telling the truth!"

"Dolly, I really think you should apologize to Mary Francis. You know how much she's hoping to get engaged."

"Oh, I guess so. But it's not my fault that Mary Francis is so sensitive!"

Dolly went looking for her sister, and Elizabeth decided that it would be a good time to return to Aunt May's house. She spent the rest of the morning helping Aunt May peel potatoes. They would use them to make potato salad for the family cookout the next day. Grandpa had gone out at the crack of dawn with Charles Sullivan on his fishing boat.

That afternoon Elizabeth decided to venture back to the Sullivans' to see if the girls had patched up their differences.

When she walked in the door she saw Charlie listening to Buck

Rogers on the radio. When she asked him where the girls were, he shrugged his shoulders. Seeing no one else around, Elizabeth ventured upstairs where she found the two sisters in their bedroom.

Apparently, apologies had been given and accepted for Dolly was seated in front of the dressing room mirror while Mary Francis finished the last snips of a haircut.

"There," Mary Francis exclaimed, standing back to survey her work. "Elizabeth, what do you think?"

Elizabeth gazed at Dolly's newly clipped bangs that curled just above her eyebrows. Dolly had always worn her hair pulled back into a braid, leaving her forehead clear. Although it had always looked nice, this new style did look quite becoming.

"I like it very much. It makes you look very stylish, Dolly."

"This is just a trim," Mary Francis said, "but the first time I cut it, she wailed and screamed all kinds of nasty things and vowed she'd get back me back for ruining her hair. But when so many people kept telling her how pretty her hair looked, she decided it didn't look so bad after all. Now for the past week, she's been bugging me to trim it for her."

"Maybe I was a little unhappy when you first gave me bangs," Dolly said as she turned her head from side to side. "But once again, Mary Francis, I think you're greatly exaggerating the story."

Elizabeth couldn't help laughing. In spite of her recent quarrel with her older sister, she was back to her old self again.

"Elizabeth," Mary Francis said, with a look of mock importance on her face, "if you're ever interested in trying a new hairstyle, feel free to make an appointment with me. I'm really good, you know. I took a one-day course at the new beauty parlor, and I can even advise on makeup and skin products. I'm the resident expert." She studied Elizabeth. "You know, you should probably consider a new look now that you're practically a published author."

"Did you publish your novel?" Dolly cried excitedly.

"Hardly, but I do have a short story coming out in the Saturday Evening Post."

"That's fantastic!" Mary Francis exclaimed. She threw her arms around Elizabeth. "Then you definitely need a new look. And I would be happy to help you out."

"Do you really mean it? I would love to get a new hairstyle! I just haven't known what to do."

"That's what I'm here for. In fact," Mary Francis released Elizabeth and flipped through an open calendar book, as if she needed to check her schedule, "I don't happen to have anyone else booked at the moment. If you'd like me to do it now, I could squeeze you in."

Elizabeth sat down on the stool that Dolly had just vacated.

Mary Francis immediately put a towel around her shoulders and began brushing out her wavy, dark hair.

"Now, is there anything in particular you were thinking of?" Mary Francis asked in her most professional voice.

"All I know is that my hair keeps getting in my eyes, and it never seems to stay neat for long."

"I think you have beautiful hair, but it would be nice to go for something really different. Let's look at some magazines."

Mary Francis dragged over a pile from beside the bed and divided them between Elizabeth and herself. Dolly grabbed several from Mary Francis's hands.

"There was one picture in here of Jane Russell," Mary Francis said. "You know, the movie actress? I think she always looks very fashionable. Now, where was it? Here it is! Yes, this is just the one for you. Not too short, mind you, just to your shoulders, and parted on the side. With your natural curl, it would look just adorable on you! Go get your hair wet, and then we'll start."

Elizabeth did as she was told, then reseated herself.

Mary Francis picked up her scissors and began snipping away. As she did so, locks began falling to the ground. Elizabeth couldn't make up her mind whether it was better to close her eyes until it was done or watch every move in order to be poised to stop a possibly fatal mistake. She alternately opened and closed her eyes, accomplishing nothing but a headache in the process.

Three-quarters of an hour later, Mary Francis was finished. Dolly had wandered downstairs and had now returned, munching on an oatmeal cookie. She took one look at Elizabeth and gasped. "Elizabeth! Why, you look absolutely gorgeous! Not that you should let it go to your head, Mary Francis, but I must say I think this is your best do ever! Why, you could even open up your own beauty salon!"

Elizabeth saw a new reflection staring back in the mirror. Mary Francis really had done a wonderful job. Not only was it a good cut, but the shorter, neater style made Elizabeth look more grownup and mature. It also complimented her slender neck and oval-shaped face. She jumped up and kissed Mary Francis on the cheek. "How can I ever thank you? I would have had a new haircut years ago if I'd known it would look so good. Dolly's right! You could own your own beauty salon."

Mary Francis blushed at such lavish praise but continued briskly, "Never mind that. Just sit down. I haven't finished yet. I want to put some makeup on you and see how it looks."

"Oh, I don't think I'm really a makeup person. Occasionally I throw on lipstick and a little eye shadow, but that's all."

"That's just because you haven't known what else looks good. You just let me do a little experimenting."

Mary Francis hummed and whistled to herself as she examined all the various jars and bottles cluttered on top of the dressing table, finally selecting a few. She pulled a cotton ball out of a glass canister and began rubbing some tan liquid over Elizabeth's face. Next she selected rose-tinted powder rouge and spread it across Elizabeth's cheekbones. Then she selected brown-tipped eyeliner and ordered Elizabeth to keep her eyes shut. That was the most difficult part, for it seemed as if Mary Francis kept pressing down on her bottom eyelid. Elizabeth kept leaning away from the pressure until she nearly slid off the chair. Dolly giggled as Elizabeth righted herself. After careful consideration, Mary Francis chose an eyeshadow named Green Moss and brushed it across Elizabeth's eyelid. As a last touch Mary Francis applied a touch of lipstick in a shade called Brandywine Berry.

Elizabeth slowly turned and looked in the mirror to see a stranger staring back at her. The lipstick made her lips fuller, the eye shadow caused her eyes to appear more lustrous, and the rouge gave her cheeks just the right hint of color. She felt like a totally different girl. In fact, she didn't feel like a girl at all. She felt like a woman.

"Gee, too bad you aren't going out on a date tonight," Dolly said wistfully. "It's a shame to see all that effort wasted."

Suddenly they heard the honking of a horn. Dolly ran to the window.

"Who is it, Dolly?" Mary Francis asked.

"I don't know. I don't recognize the car."

The other two peeked out the window and Elizabeth instantly recognized the car. "It's Stephen and Paul!"

"Paul!" Dolly screamed. She squeezed past both girls, then suddenly turned and raced back to the mirror to brush her hair.

Elizabeth was the first one out the door. She ran straight into Stephen's outstretched arms, who responded by kissing her long and hard in front of the others who were gathering outside. Elizabeth turned crimson, but Stephen looked thoroughly pleased, and the Sullivans and Paul were whistling and cheering. Over the noise she asked, "Stephen, I'm so glad to see you, but is everything all right? Is your mother okay?"

"Yes. Everything is fine. She got a last minute invitation to visit her sister for the holiday. That left me free, so I decided to call Paul to see if I could drag him away from work. That didn't take much effort, and here we are. By the way, you look like a million bucks!"

Charlie, who was standing next to them, pulled on his mother's skirt and whispered loudly, "Is that Elizabeth's new boyfriend?"

"I hope it isn't anyone else!"

Everyone laughed and Elizabeth, feeling a little less flushed than she had a moment before, began to make introductions. She came to Dolly last, who had finally appeared in the doorway. "Dolly, I'd like you to meet Stephen Wright."

Dolly offered no response as she stood silently gazing at Paul.

"Dolly!" Charles Sullivan ordered. "Stop making googly eyes and introduce yourself."

Dolly tore her eyes away from Paul long enough to nod vaguely in Stephen's direction and murmur something unintelligible before focusing her attention on Paul again.

"Stephen, you'll have to excuse my daughter. She has a habit of letting her heart overrule good manners." Charles Sullivan smiled, and everyone laughed.

After Steven and Paul had settled in, Elizabeth asked Stephen if he would like to walk up the hill to see the Nubble Lighthouse.

As they strolled through the softly waving grass towards the waterfront, Stephen turned to face Elizabeth. He looked steadily at her and said, "You know, I don't think I will ever forget the look you had on your face when you rushed outside to greet me earlier."

"I'm so glad you came, Stephen. I am so happy to see you."

Bending over her, he gave her a kiss for the second time that day, although this one was long and slow. Then he said, "Now, let's go take a look at that lighthouse. Grand old buildings, aren't they?"

Arm in arm, they walked to the edge of the road leading to the lighthouse and watched the dark, foamy water lapping at the rocks below.

Chapter Forty - One

Alan held the brown paper bag for Priscilla. She grabbed a handful of peanuts and tossed them to the cluster of swans that floated past their swan boat in the Public Garden. The swan boat driver, peddling with ease, moved them closer to the graceful birds. The swans arched their long, slender necks as they grabbed the welcome treats. Alan thought this was the perfect way to spend a cool, sunny afternoon after a long winter.

"This is just lovely, Alan! I haven't done this since I was a little girl."

"I'm glad you like it. I heard the driver say that the Swan Boats have been in operation since 1877."

"Probably. I remember my parents saying they rode these when they were little." Priscilla turned in her seat. "Say, isn't that Phil and Betty?"

Alan leaned back on the wooden bench and shielded his eyes against the sun. He saw two familiar figures strolling across the bridge spanning the middle of the lake. "Looks like them."

Alan watched the couple leave the bridge and turn towards the entrance to the Swan Boat ride. With his luck they would be waiting to enter their boat just as he and Priscilla were getting off.

Priscilla followed his gaze. "They're certainly an odd couple," she said.

"You mean that he's so straight-laced and she's so..."

"If you were hesitating to use the word 'loose,' that's exactly the word I would use."

"Two minds think alike."

"Has Phil still been bothering you? Because if he has been, I'll talk to Daddy again. I told him how Phil has been treating you and he won't tolerate that kind of behavior if he hears of any more problems."

Alan's head shot up. "You spoke to him? How did it go?"

"Fine. Actually, Daddy wasn't too surprised when I told him. He said he had already heard rather unflattering comments about Phil, so you aren't alone in your summation. Originally, Daddy was going to give Phil a promotion, but now he's backed off of that. He said he couldn't reward someone who obviously wasn't a team player."

Alan could hardly hide his delight. His scheme had worked out better than expected. Mr. Hodge had kept his word about not revealing his confidence with Alan to anyone – including Priscilla – and now Phil would not receive the sought after promotion after all his work.

"If Phil is still bothering you, I'll bring it up again."

"He's fine. No need to mention it."

Alan didn't want to pour any more misery on Phil. All that mattered was that Priscilla had addressed the issue with her father. If Mr. Hodge heard of too many problems, he might decide to talk with Phil and that could be a catastrophe for Alan – a situation he was determined would never occur. *You win some, you lose some*, as the saying went, and at Hodge's Investments, Phil wasn't winning much at all.

~

Their boat headed towards the pier. Betty and Phil got in a waiting boat as Alan and Priscilla's boat approached. As the boats passed, the girls gave each other small waves. Phil gave Alan a cold stare. Alan looked away and pretended to study the landscape.

"Did you see that look Phil gave you? He's pretty nervy and he didn't even wave to me. I have a good mind to complain to my father anyways."

"Let it go, Priscilla. He's just a sourpuss." Alan knew the weight Priscilla carried with her father. It seemed foolhardy of Phil to not be civil to Priscilla, but it was his choice. Phil's career trajectory was pretty much doomed at Hodge's. Now that he was no longer a hindrance, Alan was done with him. He didn't need – or want – to destroy him. He also didn't want to 'rock the boat' any more with either Priscilla or Phil. He didn't need either of them to bring up Alan to Mr. Hodge. If that happened Mr. Hodge just might put two and two together and realize that Alan was at the bottom of it all.

Chapter Forty – Two

All week Elizabeth re-lived Stephen's surprise visit to York. He'd loved the coastline as much as she did. He had also fit right in with Aunt May and the Sullivans. She was still trying to process her thoughts when Grandpa informed her they had another opportunity to go to York this coming weekend and Paul had agreed to drive. Two weekends in a row!

When she told Stephen that she was going to York for the weekend, his face looked downcast.

"Would you like to come with us?" she offered. "I know Grandpa and Uncle Paul would be glad to have you."

"How about you? Would you be glad to have me?" Stephen asked.

Elizabeth gave him a coy smile.

"Then it's settled," he said. "I don't know what I would do on my time off otherwise – besides miss you."

It pulled at her heart to know that he would have missed her. And she would have also missed Stephen.

She was also excited about her short story that had come out in the April edition of the Saturday Evening Post. The editor had called her and told her that they had been receiving a lot of positive feedback about her writing. When she shyly showed Steven the edition, he was thrilled. "I didn't know I was dating a famous writer!"

"I don't know if you should use the word 'famous'."

"Of course I should! Don't you know how many people read 'The Saturday Evening Post'?" Stephen encircled Elizabeth in his arms. "Honey, in the world of writing, you've hit the lottery!"

~

It was late when they got to York. Elizabeth, Grandpa, Paul, and Stephen exchanged hugs with Aunt May, updated her on their trip, and headed to their separate rooms.

The next morning after breakfast the men walked down to Charles's boat to see the new fishing rods he had purchased for sport. The men had barely left when there were three raps on the door. Before Elizabeth had time to answer, Mary Francis burst inside, followed by Dolly and Margaret Sullivan. Mary Francis's face was glowing.

"You'll never believe what happened to me last night!"

Aunt May and Elizabeth exchanged expectant looks.

Mary Francis threw out her left hand to reveal a sparkling diamond ring.

Elizabeth jumped up and threw her arms around Mary Francis. "That's wonderful, Mary Francis! Isn't it Aunt May?"

"The best news I've heard in a long time! I thought I heard wedding bells last night."

Elizabeth was happy for Mary Francis. She looked at her glowing face but felt a small stab. Mary Francis knew what she wanted. And Elizabeth had thought she had. But did she? She still had feelings for Alan. At the same time, she was certainly looking forward to where her relationship was headed with Stephen. It was a lot to process.

"I don't think it was wedding bells you heard," put in Margaret. "It was probably Mary Francis waking up the whole household when she came home. I had to double-check to make sure it was Mary Francis and not Dolly making a racket," Margaret laughed.

"And she has me to thank for getting engaged," Dolly piped up, looking very proud.

Mary Francis cast a sardonic glance at her sister. She was apparently too ecstatic over her engagement, however, to be too truly annoyed at Dolly's conceit. Turning to Elizabeth, Mary Francis explained. "Remember last weekend, when Dolly said that Robert would never have the nerve to ask me to marry him? Well, I didn't want to admit it at the time, but I rather felt the same way. So last night when we went out, I informed him that if he didn't have any serious intentions towards me, I was going to start seeing other men. Then right then and there, he pulled a ring out of his pocket. He said he'd had it for a whole month, but that he'd been afraid to ask me."

Mary Francis sighed, looking as if she would lapse into a dream state, but she brought herself back to reality. "Elizabeth, I'm so glad you are here. Now I can ask you in person to be one of my bridesmaids." She clasped her hands to her chest. "You will, won't you? I mean, after all, you've been like a sister to me."

Elizabeth couldn't help laughing at her earnestness. "Of course I'll say yes. That is, if I can manage to get a word in edgewise."

"Good! I've been babbling nonstop, but I've never been engaged before, and it's so exciting! Of course, Dolly's going to be my maid of honor. We're going to get married in June, and Robert's parents are going to give us a piece of land in Kennebunk where we'll have a little house of our own built, and we'll live happily ever after!"

Dolly giggled. "Mary Francis, you're starting to sound like me."

Margaret Sullivan piped in, "And I'll live happily ever after when I get your brother and sister to leave too, married or not!"

~

The Sullivans decided to have an outdoor barbecue that day, inviting some neighbors and friends to share in Mary Francis's good news. Grandpa, Stephen, and Paul had returned with Charles, who had told them about the engagement. Margaret Sullivan and Aunt May pooled available food and Charlie was dispatched to set up chairs and tables with the men on the side lawn.

Grandpa gave Mary Francis a hug. "Congratulations to you and Robert. I'm sure you'll be very happy."

"Thank you! We're very excited."

"How did Dolly handle your news?" Paul asked.

"Surprisingly, very well, although her mood can change at any moment."

A crowd of young people arrived and the girls gathered around Mary Francis to admire her engagement ring. The boys, meanwhile, gave the ring one glance and then began a football game.

After a while it occurred to Elizabeth that Dolly had not been around for quite some time. Finally she appeared at the top of the verandah. It was obvious what had taken her so long. She was attired in her very best dress: a white cotton lawn dress with three tiers of lace on the lower half of an ankle-length skirt and sheer, tapered sleeves that puffed at the shoulders then narrowed to button at the wrist. A tiny, white drawstring bag hung from the belt loop at her waist. Dolly paused a moment, then slowly descended the first porch step and removed a silky white handkerchief from the miniature bag. She gently dabbed her nose with it, then stopped to gaze skyward as if to impart to her audience a memorable picture of femininity, grace, and beauty. She returned the handkerchief to her bag, struggling a bit to stuff it in, before slowly continuing her descent.

All of this, Elizabeth thought, would have been comical enough without the straw-colored hat adorned with an abundance of assorted wildflowers that was perched on Dolly's head. The flowers, Elizabeth was sure, had been snatched from the open field behind the house. Daisies, honeysuckle, and primrose flopped up and down along the brim and threatened to obstruct Dolly's view. In fact, she was forced to stop after every step in order to clear her field of vision.

Dolly strolled past the group of boys who had gathered at the edge of the grass. They had suspended their football game to eye her, and now they stood giggling and whispering. Mary Francis, rushing to the group of boys, tried to shush them. Dolly steadfastly ignored the boys; the only person she took notice of was Paul. She gazed at him, repeatedly batting her lashes in between movements to push the flowers out of her face.

Elizabeth watched Paul stifle a laugh.

The boys, after a stern look from Mary Francis, resumed their game. Seconds later, by design or by accident, Charlie's football toss missed the goal by a wide margin, coming to land in a pool of muddy water near Dolly.

Dolly jumped back, but it was too late. Mud splattered over the front of her dress and deposited several spots on her cheeks and nose. Dolly stared in disbelief at her spoiled dress. She turned to Charlie in an outrage.

"You idiot! Look what you've done to my dress! It's ruined and it's all your fault! And don't think I don't know you did it on purpose!"

Dolly took a few strides towards Charlie and suddenly realized that everyone was staring at her. Her voice quickly changed to a sugary tone.

"Perhaps we can discuss this later, dear, sweet brother. Now that I've finished my afternoon stroll, I think I'll go change into something more appropriate for the cookout."

Holding her head up and pretending to be oblivious to the smothered giggles that followed her, she proceeded up the stairs and disappeared inside.

~

Later that afternoon Elizabeth observed that Dolly's spirits were restored when Paul suggested that everyone take in a movie that night.

"That sounds so romantic," Dolly gushed.

"I don't think that's what Paul had in mind when he suggested it," Robert stated.

Dolly ignored his comment, her gaze fixed on Paul.

Stephen gave Elizabeth a hopeful glance.

She smiled and nodded slightly.

"We'd love to go," Stephen replied.

Dolly continued to gaze at Paul, making her message clear. "I'd love to go too. I never refuse a date from a handsome man."

Robert laughed. "I don't think Paul considers it's a date."

Dolly glared at Robert. "Of course it is. What else would you call a social activity with three men and three women?"

Elizabeth intervened for Dolly. "I'd call it a date."

Dolly linked her arm in Elizabeth's. "Thank you!"

The next morning Elizabeth walked to the Sullivan's and Dolly talked of nothing but her first 'date' with Paul. Since Mary Francis and Elizabeth had paired off with their respective beaus, Dolly and Paul had been left as an unintended couple. "Did you hear Paul ask me if he could buy me popcorn?"

Mary Francis rolled her eyes. "He asked everyone if they wanted popcorn."

"Yes, but he asked me first. He also put his arm around the back of my chair."

"You asked him to."

"He could have said no."

"I give up," declared Mary Francis. "You are so unrealistic! I hope you'll be able to handle it if Paul ever has a girlfriend."

"She'll have to get past me first!"

"That will probably be true," Elizabeth said. "Just like last night."

Mary Francis nodded her head. When they'd been waiting in line to purchase tickets, a woman in front of them was giving Paul a 'come hither' look. Dolly had put her hands on her hips, staring the woman down until the woman looked away. Elizabeth noticed that Paul hadn't seemed to mind. In fact, he seemed rather taken with Dolly and her attention. Given their age difference, was Uncle Paul just humoring her? Or was there something more there? Elizabeth decided, with a smile, that she'd keep an eye on Uncle Paul.

Chapter Forty - Three

On Monday, Alan finished the lunch Janine had picked up for him from the corner diner and perused his figures one more time. He had a meeting with a representative from Phillips & Godfrey and he wanted to make sure that all his ducks were in a row. Mr. Hodge wanted to make sure that all their legal angles were covered before introducing a new investment system, and Alan was the designated spokesman for this end of the project. It was, Alan admitted to himself, outside his comfort zone, but as Mr. Hodge had personally asked him to handle it, he felt it necessary to oblige. And if he played his cards right, he thought, he could let others do most of the implementation work while he came out looking like a hero.

His intercom buzzed and Janine informed him that the representative from Phillips and Godfrey had arrived and had been escorted to the conference room. He collected his materials and headed down the hall. When he entered, he immediately recognized the man as Elizabeth's date from the Totem Pole back in February. Alan hesitated then stepped forward to shake hands.

"Alan Bates, Junior Vice President for Hodge's." He skimmed over the word 'junior' and emphasized 'vice president.'

"I'm Stephen Wright."

Alan appraised Stephen. "How did you like The Totem Pole?" Enjoying Stephen's startled expression, Alan continued. "I saw you and Elizabeth Keene across the dance floor a couple of months ago."

"It's very nice there. I'd like to go again when the Dorsey Band is playing. I assume you know Elizabeth from when she worked here?"

"Actually, we used to date, but she wasn't my type." The moment Alan spoke, he realized his error. Stephen's eyes narrowed at Alan's comment about Elizabeth.

"Well, she's definitely my type," Stephen replied brusquely.

"I certainly didn't mean any slight – she's a great catch for any guy."

"She certainly is."

They got down to business. Alan outlined the legal angles they wanted to cover, and Stephen made suggestions and went over their plan. After making a tentative appointment to meet again, Alan escorted him to the elevator. As he returned to his office, his mind kept returning to Elizabeth Keene and Stephen Wright, together. She had moved on, a fact that surprised him, especially as she had seemed so heartbroken. He had to admit that he preferred to visualize her pining away for him. No matter. He had bigger fish to fry. He had plans to become a fixture in the Hodge family.

~

Alan was meeting Priscilla for an early dinner on Saturday night. She'd had a gallery show that day and would have a second one on Sunday, and Alan had decided not to leave her side all weekend. He wanted to keep tabs on her. While they were eating dinner at the Ritz, Alan told Priscilla about meeting Stephen Wright. He hesitated to bring up Elizabeth, but he thought it would calm Priscilla to know that Elizabeth had moved on.

"I wonder if that's the same man that old war-horse Lillian Graham and Betty Higgins were bragging about in front of Janine and me."

"Makes no difference to me if it was Stephen Wright or not – as long as it's someone else she's hanging on."

"How true, darling." Priscilla closed her lacquered mouth around the cherry from her martini and swallowed it before continuing. "You should thank me for saving you from her. I don't know if you would have known better if I hadn't come along."

"You certainly give yourself a lot of credit. Besides, you make it seem as if I thought Elizabeth Keene was the one for me when she never was."

"And do you consider me 'the one' for you?"

"A man never reveals his innermost thoughts to a girl. It would be like showing your hand at a card game."

Priscilla pouted. "I'm not good at wondering if a man thinks he can do better than me."

"You'll just have to trust me!" Alan smiled.

Chapter Forty - Four

In the weeks following Stephen's unexpected arrival in Maine at Easter, Elizabeth basked in Stephen's attention. And she knew without a doubt that they were very companionable. Why then, she kept asking herself, couldn't she forget about Alan? She never mentioned it to anyone, for she felt to do so would infer that Alan had possessed some desirable quality that Stephen lacked, and that was not true. Stephen was the most wonderful man she had ever met. He was kind, generous, caring, and, perhaps most importantly, honest. Alan possessed none of those traits, nor was he ever likely to. It should be easy to forget about him, yet Elizabeth could not, a fact which frightened her. She had heard of women who pined for years after lost loves, and she did not want to be one of them.

In spite of this, she had deep feelings for Stephen. She didn't think she was head-over-heels in love, but she liked him immensely, and she enjoyed every moment she spent with him. She knew these feelings were reciprocated, for Stephen never seemed to get enough time with her, and a large part of their weekends were spent together, whether just the two of them or with other people. Still, after her experience with Alan, she didn't quite trust her heart.

~

On the weekend in May prior to Decoration Day, Grandpa, Elizabeth, Paul, and Stephen once again traveled to Maine, this time to celebrate Elizabeth's birthday.

On Saturday Father Joe and Paul went to Kennebunk to help Robert work on the new house he and Mary Francis were building. Dolly, not surprisingly, tagged along when she heard that Paul was going. Stephen, declining to see the house site, asked Elizabeth if she would like to go for a walk along the beach.

As usual the ocean water was frigid. They laughed as they dipped their bare toes into the rising surf. They wandered along the edge of the shore hand in hand, watching a few brave souls who dared a quick plunge.

Suddenly, Stephen stopped walking. He turned to Elizabeth. "I know we're going to have a birthday celebration tonight, but I wanted to give you a gift now."

"You didn't have to get me anything. Just the fact that you came this weekend is enough of a treat for me."

He reached into his shirt pocket and withdrew a small wrapped package which he handed to her.

Shaking her head at him, Elizabeth undid the silvery paper. Inside was a velvet covered jewelry box. She pressed the clasp on the cover and the lid flew open to reveal a sparkling diamond ring, flanked on either side by two smaller stones of the same gem. The ring was brilliant and beautiful.

Elizabeth gasped. "Stephen! I – I don't know what to say!"

Stephen responded by wrapping his arms around her and whispering, "Just say yes, and I'll be the happiest man on earth!"

"Stephen, can I think about it?" Elizabeth watched helplessly as the eager anticipation on Stephen's face changed to confusion. "I'm so sorry about this, Stephen. I do care so much for you. I just want to make sure it's love."

"Don't feel bad, Elizabeth," his voice showing disappointment in spite of his weak smile. "I know I caught you off guard. I'm sorry I sprung this on you. I know we've only been dating seriously for three months."

"Don't be sorry. I just need some time."

Stephen scanned Elizabeth's face. "Elizabeth, is there someone else?"

Elizabeth paused. She had never discussed Alan with Stephen, but she didn't want to hide it, either. Turning away, she walked a few steps while she thought, then turned to face him again.

"There used to be someone, but that was before I met you. I thought I was madly in love, and I thought he was too. He never really wanted me, though, and even if he did now, I wouldn't take him back. He could never be half the man you are. I think I just rushed into that relationship so recklessly that I've been a lot slower this time to let myself believe."

Stephen pivoted Elizabeth to face him, looking at her for a moment before speaking. "I want to ask you something, and you don't have to answer me, but I feel as if I have to ask you." Stephen paused. "Is Alan Bates the person you are referring to?"

Elizabeth let out a gasp, so surprised that Stephen had guessed. "How did you know?"

"I put two and two together. I had to go to Hodge's Investments for a joint project. I met with Alan Bates. When he mentioned that he had dated you, I remembered the look on your face the night you saw him when we went to The Totem Pole."

"I didn't think you'd even noticed – "

Stephen interrupted her. "It's all right. I understand. And I'd rather wait and have you come to me with a whole heart than have you give me only half your heart now."

"It's not even that I would want to go out with him again. What I can promise you is that I'll always be honest with you." It seemed such a pathetic thing to say, so little to offer, but she didn't want him to think that she would lead him on needlessly or carelessly. She would not treat him as she had been treated.

He smiled a little. "I know you'll always be honest with me because that's the kind of person you are. And I do know one thing. Any guy who was willing to let you get away couldn't have been that great."

They stood for a moment in silence, watching the roll of the ocean waves breaking on the shore. Finally, Stephen spoke lightly. "It's a little chilly out. Why don't we walk back to the house? Just let me put this ring back in its original resting place until we're ready to bring it out again." Stephen closed the lid to the box and slipped it back into his shirt pocket.

Placing Elizabeth's hand in his, they walked back to the house.

~

That night after eating ice cream and cake, the girls followed Elizabeth upstairs while the men listened to the Braves-Giants game on the radio.

"Elizabeth," Mary Francis said, "you and Stephen seemed rather quiet tonight. Is everything okay?"

"It's fine. Actually, he asked me to marry him when we took a walk on the beach today."

Both girls' eyes opened wide.

Dolly cried, "Did you say yes?"

"I said that I wasn't ready to make that commitment yet."

Mary Francis plopped herself down on the bed. "Do you still have feelings for Alan?"

"I did before, but not anymore. To be honest, I'm not sure why I am holding back."

"Maybe you're afraid of getting hurt again," Dolly offered.

"I've been thinking the same thing. Believe me, I do have strong feelings for Stephen. He's so good to me, and he's caring, and fun to be with."

"He's crazy about you." Mary Francis wagged her finger at Elizabeth. "I think Stephen's the man for you."

Mary Francis seemed so sure. If only Elizabeth were as well.

Chapter Forty - Five

"Come on, let's try the water out," Alan pleaded. It was early June and unseasonably warm. He and Priscilla had decided to enjoy the day at the beach. "Even if it's still cold, I'm hot enough to take a quick swim." As he spoke, he looked to where Priscilla reclined in her beach chair, reading the newspaper.

"In a minute."

Alan dropped to the double beach blanket beside her. He trailed his finger up and down her calf. It amused him that a girl could expose her legs up to the top of her thighs in a bathing suit and still be considered socially correct, but if she wore a skirt or dress that short, it would be considered nothing less than scandalous. Not that he was complaining. Priscilla had the longest legs of any girl he'd ever known, and they were shown to their fullest in the bathing briefs she was wearing. As his finger traveled towards her thigh Priscilla pushed his finger away. "Alan, please! Not in public!"

"Stop reading the Engagement Section – which is the section I'm sure you're preoccupied with – and I'll stop caressing your leg."

"Fine. I'm finished anyways."

He pulled Priscilla to her feet and kept hold of her hand, keeping her close. They strolled down to the water's edge.

Priscilla turned to him. "Alan, why don't we get married?"

Alan stopped in his tracks. Then he laughed. "Hey, wait a minute – isn't the man supposed to ask the woman?"

"Yes, but you've been taking too long, so I thought I would move things along."

Alan arched his eyebrows. "I've been taking too long? Are you sure you haven't got things upside down? Weren't you the girl who took forever to agree to go steady, then finally agreed only three months ago?"

"That was then, this is now. It's just that I've been thinking how wonderful a wedding would be. We could get married at Holy Cross Cathedral, have an elegant reception at the Ritz, and then go someplace really exotic for our honeymoon – like England or France or Africa!"

Alan's eyes lit up at the thought of a honeymoon with Priscilla. "Who cares what country we're in? I just want to get my hands on a 'do not disturb' sign."

"So single-minded!" She smiled.

"Somebody has to think of those small but critical items." Alan's face sobered. "Look, I'm not trying to upset you, but are you sure you just aren't overly excited because you see so many engagement pictures of girls you know?"

"Darling, don't be silly. I just think it would be lovely to be married. Let's do it!"

In response Alan pulled her into the water until they were waist-deep. He held her close. Clusters of adults and children played near them, finding relief from the heat.

"I'll do the asking, if you don't mind, and we won't be in our bathing suits when I do."

Priscilla gave him a pout. She certainly did match him for stubbornness. However, Alan could forgive that trait. *She wanted to marry him!*

Pulling away, Priscilla dove into the frigid water, her slender form sleek and smooth. She swam with rapid strokes.

Alan studied her intently. He wanted her desperately – both physically and as his counterpart in life. Yet a small voice in his head whispered that he would regret his pursuit of her one day. She was self-absorbed and ambitious – in fact, she was so much like him, he suspected big battles would be the norm. A bigger voice, though, pushed him on. He wanted to claim her for his own and become part of the Hodge dominion, whether or not it would be to his peril to do so.

Part III

Chapter Forty - Six

Grandpa and Elizabeth spent the morning trimming and pruning in the backyard. For early June, it was unusually warm. Grandpa reported that he'd heard on the radio that the temperature would reach almost ninety degrees.

Elizabeth finished tying up a cluster of roses that had fallen over from the burden of their own weight. She sat back to view the results and wondered how the roses at her grandfather's house were faring. Since her visit in the spring, she had meant to stop by, but each weekend had been busy, and, besides, it seemed pointless. Even if she took time to care for the roses now, she wouldn't be able to keep it up. Grandpa had comforted her by pointing out that the roses were perennials and were sure to survive, tended or not, until the house was sold. That could be soon, Elizabeth thought. Paul had informed them that he planned on putting the house on the market as soon as the estate was settled.

Elizabeth looked up when she heard a car pull up out front. She stood and rounded the corner leading to the front walk. There was Stephen. He rarely stopped by unannounced, and she couldn't fathom why he would be here on a Saturday morning. She looked down at her garden dungarees, realized how messy she looked, and determined that she was in need of a good bath.

He seemed unaware of that, however, when he came directly to her and clasped her hands in his.

Elizabeth knew immediately that something was wrong.

"Stephen, what is it?"

"It's my mother. She passed away last night."

"Stephen, I'm so sorry! I feel terrible. I know how close you were to her."

"Thank you. I tried calling you this morning and when there was no answer, I thought you might be outside. I just wanted to let you know what happened and that we'll have to reschedule our dinner plans for tonight. I'm leaving from here to drive to New York. We'll probably have the funeral on Monday or Tuesday."

"I completely understand. Grandpa and I will keep you all in our prayers."

~

On Sunday morning Stephen called with updates. According to his mother's wishes, there was to be no wake. Instead, a short Mass with a few friends and relatives was to be held on Tuesday morning before the burial. Stephen planned to return home the following Saturday evening and he told Elizabeth he wanted to stop by, if it wasn't too late.

On Saturday he arrived about eight o'clock, and after Grandpa offered his condolences, he left them alone in the parlor.

Stephen clasped Elizabeth's hand in his as they talked. "You know, when I first found out my mother's health was declining, I prayed with all my heart that she would recover. Then I realized that she didn't want to live. Not that it would be easy for her to leave my sister and me and her grandkids; it's just that she's never been happy since Dad died. I think she saw her passing as an opportunity to be reunited with him. I hope her wish has come true."

Elizabeth placed her hand on top of his hand. "I'm sure it has."

"I do know one thing. It really is true that it helps to have support from family and friends. When my father died, I could find comfort that my mother was still with us. Now it's my mother who's not here anymore, but I have my sister Carol and you to help me through this. I just want you to know how much it's meant to have you."

Elizabeth gazed at the man at her side, so full of thanks and gratitude. She had missed him while he was gone. She was also startled to realize that what she was feeling was more than affection.

Stephen clasped her hand. "Since we haven't had too much time for ourselves lately, I thought if the weather is nice tomorrow, we could take a walk through the Public Garden."

"I'd love that."

He gathered her in a close embrace and she not only welcomed it, she yearned for it. As he leaned down to kiss her, Elizabeth pulled back slightly.

"You look as if you want to tell me something," Stephen prodded.

Elizabeth paused. "Maybe another time. You've just had one of the most difficult weeks of your life and you must be exhausted."

Stephen released her and crossed his arms over his chest. "I'm not leaving until you tell me what's on your mind, and I sincerely hope this doesn't mean that we'll still be standing here when your grandfather gets up tomorrow."

Elizabeth bit her lip. "I just wanted to tell you that I – I love you."

Stephen's jaw dropped. He held her at arm's length. He could not have looked more astounded, Elizabeth thought, than if someone had told him he had won a million dollars.

"You what? You love me?" He grasped her shoulders and squeezed them hard. "You're not just saying it because of my mother's death, are you? What I mean to say is, sometimes a person can confuse sympathy with love and —"

Elizabeth took a big breath. "No, Stephen. I really love you – more than anyone I've ever met in my entire life."

"Then, why were you afraid to tell me? Was it because you weren't sure if you still had feelings for Alan?"

"I've been over him for a while now. At first I didn't realize it, and then I was just waiting because there didn't seem an appropriate time to bring it up, especially with everything that's happened this week. However, I do know that it has nothing whatsoever to do with sympathy. If your mother rose from the dead on Easter Sunday, my feelings wouldn't change."

Stephen tried to pull her close but Elizabeth stepped back so she could talk clearly. She had a feeling that if he started kissing her, she'd never be able to say what she needed to say.

"I mean it, Stephen. I really don't want to talk about Alan, except to tell you that whatever feelings I had for him are gone. They're dead. And I know that it wasn't love I felt at the time. I know that now, but I didn't know it then. You can't love someone who you can't admire." She sighed. "But that's not the only reason I held back. I knew how much you cared for me, but I think I also doubted my own self-worth. I used to wonder how anyone could really love me – just me – above anybody else."

"Elizabeth, you know how I feel about you."

"I know, but please let me finish. I wasn't doubting you, I was doubting myself. I think I always felt that way, and then when Alan deserted me for someone else, I think I became convinced of it. Now I know that what happened with Alan has nothing to do with us. I just wish it hadn't taken me so long to figure that out."

Stephen pulled her towards him and held her firmly in his arms. "Sorry for what? Waiting to come to me with a clear conscience? Honey, look. Do you think you're the first person in the world that had to take time to figure out what they were looking for in a mate or got involved in a bad relationship before they finally found the right person? If everybody stayed with the first person they ever went out with, there'd be a whole lot of mismatched people inhabiting the planet. The only thing I want to be sure of is that you'll really be happy with me."

"Stephen, you're the person I know I'll be happy with, in every way. My Aunt May always says, when you find someone you love more than anybody else, hold on and never let go. That's what I'm prepared to do."

"I think I'll give her a great big box of chocolates the next time I see her. Right now I need to kiss the most wonderful woman in the world."

Chapter Forty - Seven

It was a perfect Saturday for June. The temperature was warm, the day was sunny, and they had both enjoyed watching the competitive tennis games in Newport, Rhode Island. The last match had been a neck-to-neck set that kept the crowd on the edge of their seats.

They stopped for dinner at the Wyndham Bay Voyage Inn, a Victorian-style inn that overlooked Narragansett Harbor. An endless expanse of green lawn surrounded the restaurant; beyond lay the sparkling blue Atlantic waters. The sky was streaked with rosy tones of pink and orange as the sun began its descent. Inside, a trio of musicians greeted them. Alan asked for a secluded table and slipped the maître d' a twenty dollar bill to make sure no other diners would be seated in their vicinity.

Alan took a moment to gaze at Priscilla, sitting at ninety degrees to him. She had never looked so lovely. There was a light flush to her cheeks from being outdoors, and her honey-blond hair was casually tossed around her shoulders. Alan involuntarily reached out to wind a strand of it around his fingers, causing Priscilla to look at him.

She said nothing, seeming to appreciate the intimacy of the moment.

Finally Priscilla relaxed in her chair. "I must say, it's been a delightful day,"

"I was just thinking the same thing."

"I was also thinking how attracted I was to you the moment I met you, Alan."

"Please go on. I never mind my ego being fed."

"That's probably one of the reasons I'm attracted to you. I've dated quite a few men – no comments please – but no one has held my interest as long as you. You always keep our conversations interesting."

"Thank you for the compliment. I must reciprocate by saying that you also hold my attention – both mentally and physically."

"A typical answer a woman would expect from a man, but somehow charming."

After dinner Alan excused himself. He located their waiter and gave him a small wrapped box which he instructed him to discreetly place on the dessert platter.

In a few moments the waiter, without the slightest hint of expectation, brought coffee and presented the dessert plate to Priscilla. The box was wrapped in gold-colored paper and it blended in with the assortment of cookies. The waiter backed away, and Alan fixed his gaze on Priscilla, holding his breath.

In a few seconds, her expression met all his expectations as a look of puzzlement crossed her features and then her eyes opened wide. "Alan! You didn't!"

Grabbing the box, she ripped the paper open, carefully lifting the lid to expose an engagement ring - the exquisite pear-shaped diamond encircled by a band of sapphires. She lifted it from the case, only to have Alan gently take it from her fingers. "I believe this is my cue."

Alan went down on one knee next to Priscilla's seat. "Priscilla Hodge, would you do me the honor of being my wife?"

Priscilla let out a cry as he slipped the ring on her finger. As he stood up, pulling her to her feet, she gushed, "Yes!"

They turned to the sound of applause from the waiters, who'd shed their restrained demeanors and gathered in front of them. The maître d' stepped forward with a bottle of champagne. "This is on the house, in honor of such a special occasion!" He poured the sparkling liquid into two glasses and handed one to each of them.

Clicking their glasses, Alan said, "To the future Mrs. Alan Bates."

"Our compliments to you both on such a happy occasion," the maître d' said. "May you and your future wife be blessed with a long life and many children!"

Priscilla blushed while Alan shook the maître d's hand, thanking him for his thoughtfulness. The trio of musicians whom they'd seen upon their entry appeared and began a romantic love song.

Alan pulled Priscilla toward him and spun slowly with her to the music. "Alan, this is just magical! Did you plan all this?"

"Of course," he glibly fibbed. He had reserved the private table and come up with the idea to have the ring brought out with the desserts. He might as well take credit for the music and the champagne.

"I can't wait to tell our parents and all our friends! And there's so much planning to do! I've had my eye on a wedding dress that I can't wait to try on!"

"I'm sure we'll get to all that. Right now, I want to tell my fiancée how much I love her."

Priscilla looked startled and hesitated for a fraction of a second before she opened her mouth and murmured, "I do too."

It was a small thing, but for a moment Alan wondered why she had hesitated. A small voice inside his head warned him that it was an omen of the future, but another voice told him to let it go. After all, could he hold her accountable for a quality that he had told Elizabeth Keene didn't factor into the equation? Besides, Priscilla had told him tonight that no man had ever held her attention as long as he had. Would she say such a thing if she didn't love him?

Chapter Forty - Eight

 It was an afternoon she would never forget. Stephen picked her up after lunch on Sunday and they drove to the Public Gardens, where they strolled along the flower-lined walkways.

When they reached a secluded corner of the park, Stephen led Elizabeth to a nearby bench. He pulled a box out of his breast pocket.

She recognized it as the same one he had tried to give her on her birthday. It was a gift that she had not been able to accept at the time, but now she could without hesitation.

Popping the lid open, he removed the diamond ring inside and bent down on one knee in front of Elizabeth's seat. He looked earnestly at her.

"Elizabeth, will you do me the honor of marrying me?"

Her voice trembled as Stephen slid the ring on her finger. "Yes! Yes with all my heart!"

He pulled her up from her seat and kissed her long and hard.

Elizabeth stayed in his embrace, then broke apart giggling when a man walking by with his dog cleared his throat loudly. "I guess we should be more discreet."

"Why? I want everyone in the world to know I'm getting married to the most wonderful woman! Now, where should we go for a celebration dinner? How about we paint the town red at the Parker House?"

"This might sound strange, but I've been there quite a few times, and I'd prefer something less fancy."

"Sure. Any ideas?"

"How about Durgin Park?"

"Great! We can walk there."

Hand in hand they sauntered through the gardens and onto Boylston Street, making their way toward Faneuil Hall Marketplace. When they arrived at the restaurant, the waitress led them to a table covered with a red-and-white checkerboard tablecloth. Sawdust was scattered on the wooden floors.

"Is this what you wanted?" Stephen asked.

"It's just right – simple, homey, and down-to-earth."

Stephen ordered a bottle of wine. "To the future Mr. and Mrs. Stephen Wright. Cheers!"

~

It was early evening when Stephen drove Elizabeth home and escorted her up the walk.

Grandpa met them at the door. "I was starting to wonder where the two of you had gone."

Elizabeth held up her hand to show him the sparkling diamond.

The look on Grandpa's face said it all. "Congratulations!" He gave Elizabeth a hug before shaking Stephen's hand. "She couldn't have picked a finer man, Stephen. When's the big day?"

"We'll let you know as soon as we figure it out, although if Elizabeth said we could get married tomorrow, that would be fine with me." Stephen gazed down at his newly betrothed.

While the two men talked, Elizabeth rang up Aunt May to tell her the good news.

"I knew I liked that young man the moment I met him," Aunt May told her.

After their call ended, she rang up Mary Francis and Dolly. Dolly's voice squawked over the line. "Was it romantic? Was the moon out and were there stars in the sky?"

"Actually, it was late afternoon."

Elizabeth could hear Dolly's groan of disappointment.

Mary Francis came to her aid. "I'm sure there were plenty of stars in Elizabeth's and Stephen's eyes."

"That's right," Elizabeth replied.

"Tell Stephen that we said congratulations."

"I will."

~

The next day at work Elizabeth had barely set her purse down when Maura pounced on her. "I don't know what caught my eye first – the sparkle from your finger or the glow on your face! Elizabeth, I'm so happy for you! Stephen must be thrilled!"

As if on cue, the elevator doors squeaked open and out stepped Stephen and Mr. Godfrey, who was slapping Stephen on the back. Stephen was smiling from ear to ear.

"I think I just got the answer to my comment!" Maura said.

The two men spotted the girls and strode to meet them. Without hesitating, Stephen bent his head and, much to Elizabeth's astonishment, deposited a kiss on her lips. "I hope everyone isn't going to think this is all we're going to be doing at work from now on, but I don't think one little kiss is too much out of order."

Mr. Godfrey stepped forward to shake Elizabeth's hand. "I'd have done the same thing if I had just gotten engaged. Congratulations, Elizabeth! You picked a fine, young man for a husband!"

"Thank you, Mr. Godfrey. I think so, too."

Chapter Forty - Nine

 Neil was the first to congratulate Alan. "Marrying the boss's daughter! I think we know who will be getting 'the keys to the kingdom'."

"I'd like to think that my old-fashioned work ethics and nose-to-the-grindstone philosophy had something to do with it."

"I'm sure those qualities might factor into your climbing the corporate ladder at Hodge's."

"I stand on my merits. However, I admit that being son-in-law to the president is sure to have its perks. To be honest, Neil, I couldn't be happier. Priscilla is the girl for me."

Neil leaned back in his chair and motioned Alan to sit down. "You should consider yourself a lucky guy. Priscilla Hodge certainly tried out enough guys before she settled for you."

Alan's head jerked up. "How did you become privy to such information?"

"Don't be alarmed. It's from seeing her picture in the papers with different guys at various events. That's old news, though. The only thing that matters is that you're the guy she said yes to."

Neil was right, Alan thought to himself. He had never pressed Priscilla for details about her previous boyfriends. He had always considered those things unimportant. Besides, he had certainly dated enough girls. Maybe some gender bias was the culprit. It always seemed less reputable for girls to date around.

Yet for the rest of the day Alan couldn't get Neil's comments out of his head. What other boyfriends had Priscilla had, and was she really content with him? Then he chastised himself. Priscilla was an independent, strong-willed girl who didn't do anything she didn't want to. He just hoped she wasn't in the marrying mood as a reaction to seeing so many friends become engaged. He wanted to get married because he thought they were a perfect match. They both loved the finer things in life, they both worked hard to climb the corporate ladder, and they were both aggressive, especially when it came to romance. Alan had to constantly keep himself in check. She was everything a man could want in a woman. He just had to make sure that now that he had her, it would be for keeps.

~

Alan rang the doorbell and waited impatiently for Joseph, the Hodges' butler, to answer the door. Tucked under Alan's arm was the Saturday morning newspaper and he considered it an incredible stroke of luck that the photo and write-up that Priscilla had submitted to announce their engagement was being highlighted on a weekend. He and Priscilla would be able to savor the moment together, and with her parents.

The door swung open and Joseph nodded his head. "Mr. Bates, please come in." Joseph ushered him into the drawing room on the right. Priscilla was waiting for him and he kissed her before he unfolded the newspaper and turned to the social pages. On the front page of the section was a black and white picture of Priscilla and Alan smiling at each other. The headline read, *"Socialite Priscilla Hodge announces her engagement to Alan Bates, Junior Vice President of Hodge's Investments."* The write-up below detailed Priscilla's notoriety, along with a list of education and career accomplishments for each. Alan's eyes rested on the mention of Brown, Class of 1941, and his heart skipped a beat. He wished he'd remembered to ask Priscilla not to include that. Too late now. Oh well, he thought, no one in his former circles read society pages.

"You have no reason to complain today about not seeing your engagement announcement in the newspaper."

Priscilla threw her arms around Alan's neck and kissed him. "This is so exciting!"

They both turned to see Joseph returning with a tray of fruit, muffins, and a sterling silver coffee pot.

"Joseph, you are worth every penny the Hodges pay you." Taking the steaming cup Joseph extended to him, he clinked his cup with Priscilla's. "This will have to suffice for a toast until we can substitute it for champagne."

Mr. and Mrs. Hodge were taking them out to dinner that evening to celebrate their engagement. As Joseph quietly withdrew, Alan and Priscilla reclined on the couch. Alan envisioned thousands of Bostonians enjoying their own morning coffee while reading the newspaper where their picture was front and center of the society page. Priscilla continued to scan the engagement section.

Suddenly she sat up straight, her eyes blazing. "I can't believe it, I can't! Alan, read that!"

Pushing the paper at him, she pressed her finger on one of the engagement pictures. Staring back at him was a small black and white formal photo of Elizabeth Keene. Underneath the photo read:

John J. Burke, of Dorchester, Lower Mills, is pleased to announce the engagement of his granddaughter, Elizabeth Keene to Stephen W. Wright. Miss Keene graduated from the Katherine Gibbs School in 1943 with a secretarial degree and Mr. Wright graduated from Boston College in 1938 with a B.S. in law. Both Miss Keene and Mr. Wright are employed by Phillips & Godfrey in Boston, MA.

"That little upstart! She probably planned it so that her picture was in the paper the same day as mine! She probably pressured him into getting engaged just to compete with me!"

"Priscilla, where do you get these crazy notions? There was no way for her to know we're engaged, and even if she did, people don't run around getting engaged just to pick a certain day to announce it!" He softened his voice, although he was fed up over Pricilla's assaults on Elizabeth's character. "Why don't you just concentrate on our write-up and forget Elizabeth Keene? Nobody's going to notice her tiny little announcement compared to our half-page one."

"That's true. She's such a little nobody."

Alan took Priscilla's hand in his. "Now, let's talk about the reception. There's certainly no better place to rent than the Ritz!"

Chapter Fifty

Stephen and Elizabeth's plans to be married in May of the following year were threatened when Mr. Godfrey announced that Phillips & Godfrey would be merging with another company the following spring and he'd expect all hands on deck at that time. Stephen brought up the subject on the Friday morning before Mary Francis's wedding. They were in Maine, at Aunt May's, and were waiting for Grandpa, Aunt May, and Paul to get ready to walk over to the Sullivans'.

"I was wondering how you'd feel about moving our wedding date up to this summer. I know it might be a rush, but work is going to go into high gear in the fall and next spring, and I think I will have trouble taking time off."

"I understand. The main reason I picked next spring was that I wanted to carry roses from the garden for my bouquet. Both my mother and grandmother did when they walked down the aisle, and I thought it would be a nice tradition to carry on. Grandpa always said that when the roses bloom, it's time for a wedding."

"I think that's a wonderful tradition, and I'm sure it will also mean a lot to your grandfather. Roses are still in bloom in August, right?"

"Yes, they are, and I think that would be perfect!"

~

As soon as the group got to the Sullivans', Elizabeth charged into Mary Francis's and Dolly's bedroom and held out her hand to display the sparkling diamond ring. Mary Francis squealed with excitement and hugged her so tightly that Elizabeth nearly had the wind knocked out of her.

"Elizabeth, I'm so happy for you! I'll have so much fun helping you with your wedding plans! I'm practically an expert now!"

Dolly, not surprisingly, was not as delighted. She groaned and threw her hairbrush on the bed. "Another wedding to plan. I always thought I'd be one of the first to be a bride. Now it looks like I'll be the last. It's not fair! It's just not fair!"

Mary Francis stared at her younger sister. "Dorothy Ann Sullivan! I have seen you act rude and immature on numerous occasions, but I have never seen such childish, selfish behavior in my entire life! One of our dearest, closest friends in the whole world is engaged and all you can do is think of yourself! I am truly appalled!"

Dolly's hands flew to her mouth. "Elizabeth, please forgive me! You know that I'm deliriously happy for you and Stephen, but Mary Francis is right! I'm horribly selfish to be thinking of my own hopeless circumstances. Oh, please find it in your expansive heart to accept me back into your esteemed graces!"

Elizabeth laughed at the girl who had now gone down on bended knee and whose hands were clasped as if in prayer. "Dolly, there's nothing to forgive! I know that you're happy for me, and I also know how much you have your heart set on being married, so please don't give it a moment's thought."

"That's only one of many things I'll never understand about you, Dolly," Mary Francis said. "How can you continually fantasize about being married when you can't even date anybody for more than a month?"

"I'd date for more than a month if a certain someone were involved."

"We've told you a thousand times, Dolly. Not only is Paul too old for you, he's Elizabeth's uncle, which practically makes him family. More importantly, he's not even the least bit interested in you."

"He just hasn't noticed me yet, that's all."

"Not noticed you? Believe me, you are impossible not to notice. Now, enough of this silly argument. I'm getting married tomorrow, and I haven't got time to listen to nonsense. I'm going to pick up my dress. You can both come if you want to."

Elizabeth followed immediately and Dolly dutifully trailed in their wake.

"Come on, Dolly, smile," Elizabeth said. "You and I can help Mary Francis and then take a peek at the other wedding dresses at the shop. I can't afford one and you don't need one yet, but we're both allowed to dream."

Chapter Fifty - One

Alan couldn't put a name to the face of the young man who loitered at the dessert table across the room, and it made him nervous. The man had looked quizzically at Alan several times during the evening and Alan, feeling on edge, made sure that he kept distance between them. He never knew who he would run into – a jilted girlfriend's brother, a bartender from a place where he'd never closed his tab, or even someone from college. That could be ruinous.

He felt someone tap him on the arm and he jumped.

"You seem jittery," Priscilla remarked. "Aren't you having a good time?"

"Yes, it's a great party. I've enjoyed meeting everyone."

The Hodges had invited friends who had belonged to the exclusive Hasting Pudding Club with Mr. Hodge at Harvard, along with several of their grown children whom Priscilla had been friendly with over the years. That guest list made Alan wary, as it brought to mind Mr. Hodge's friend who had been curious about what year Alan had graduated from college.

"I'm going to freshen up. Are you okay until I return?"

"Absolutely." He raised his drink to her as she turned away. He took a swig before realizing that the man across the room was now standing next to him.

"Excuse me. I feel as if I know you, but I've been scratching my head for the last couple of hours trying to figure out how."

"I can't help you. Your face doesn't ring a bell. Sorry."

"Wait a minute – you played tennis in college, didn't you?"

Alan's mind froze, trying to decide how best to sidetrack the question. "In college? Those days seem like a million years ago." Alan felt that back of his neck prickle. He looked around for Priscilla.

"Well, you did, because I remember now. You really stood out because you had a mean back hand. We played so many schools I'm having trouble putting my finger on yours."

"Excuse me." Alan didn't care if it seemed rude. After all, he didn't know the man nor did he plan on getting to know him. His only priority was to end the discussion.

He was a few feet away, heading towards the entrance to the drawing room, when the man shouted, "I know! You played for Providence College!"

Several people turned at the sound of the man's booming voice. Alan's mind raced. He could deny outright that he'd gone to Providence. He could say that this man was confused, he'd played for Brown. He could claim that he'd never played college tennis at all and that this was a case of mistaken identity. What other options were there? He could tell the truth, but that was impossible. And then, suddenly, the moment had passed for Alan to refute it. Alan looked straight into the hostile glare of Mr. Hodge.

"Alan, I'd like to see you in my study. Right now."

"Yes, sir."

Alan followed Mr. Hodge. They entered the spacious office. Mr. Hodge closed the door and turned to face Alan, his eyes penetrating.

"I just want to ask you one question. Did you graduate from Brown University?"

Alan wiped his palms against the edge of his suit coat. "No, sir. I didn't, but I did attend Brown for three years."

Mr. Hodge's expression softened a little. "Why did you leave?"

Alan swallowed, and his face blanched. And then a story, fully formulated, came to him. He lifted his chin and looked Mr. Hodge right in the eye. "I didn't realize that my father was cutting into savings in order to send me. He had just retired. One night I found my mother crying and she told me that the remaining savings was just enough for them to get by on in coming years. She was doubly worried because my father was not particularly well. Right then and there, I decided I couldn't let them pay for my final year."

Mr. Hodge crossed his arms. "Didn't you consider taking out a loan?"

"I would have, but my father, even though he was a banker – or maybe because he was a banker – had never taken out a loan in his life. I knew it would have deeply upset him."

"So you made your own decision to transfer schools."

"Yes, sir."

"Yet Brown University is on your resume. I know. I hired you."

"I admit that was a terrible mistake. I felt such deep resentment that I had not graduated from Brown, and I felt that I deserved recognition for having done most of my college requirements there."

Mr. Hodge said nothing, turning to the cigar box on the corner of his desk. He took one out, tipped the cigar to light it, and puffed on it several times until the tip was glowing.

Alan felt it was a moment of critical importance in their relationship. He had walked in the room a doomed man, and now a glimmer of hope hung in the air.

Finally Mr. Hodge spoke. "Under normal circumstances, I would not be tolerant of such behavior. I think you are well aware that I abhor lying. However, in this situation, I applaud your noble action in transferring to another school in order to put your parents' welfare above your own interests. I also can understand your desire to receive recognition for attending an Ivy League school for most of your college career. I'm willing to forgive the matter as long as you agree to change your record at Hodge's so that it states Providence College instead of Brown. It's always better to be honest, and I think the accomplishments you've made in your brief career will stand out more than the college you graduated from."

"Yes, sir. Thank you for understanding." Alan's voice was barely above a whisper as he spoke.

"I'm glad we've settled this. After all, you're going to be family in a couple of months." Mr. Hodge reached behind him. "Cigar?"

"Thank you, sir. I believe I will." Alan selected one from the box that Mr. Hodge held open for him. He was not a smoker, but in the relief of dodging a bullet, Alan was happy to join in.

When Henry Hodge turned away, Alan wiped his forehead with his handkerchief. Even though he'd been able to pull the 'loyal son' card out this time, next time Mr. Hodge might not be so quick to believe him.

Chapter Fifty - Two

While the day before Mary Francis's wedding had been a swirl of activity, on Saturday morning all traces of hysteria had vanished, and Mary Francis was the picture of tranquility. In fact, Elizabeth thought, she appeared almost ethereal in her filmy, white wedding dress as she floated down the aisle of St. Martha's Church on her father's arm. Father Joe officiated, smiling broadly at his sister, and Robert looked as if he was the happiest man in the world.

The reception was held in the open field beside the Sullivans' house. Tables and chairs had been set up a short distance from the three-piece band. There was a vast assortment of food, donated and served by several ladies from the church. Margaret Sullivan, who was usually one of the ladies to serve at functions, was today on the other side and was thoroughly enjoying her eldest daughter's wedding.

As Elizabeth and Stephen waltzed on the grassy dance floor, Stephen whispered in her ear, "Are you sorry you won't be getting married up here instead of in Boston?"

Elizabeth looked over Stephen's shoulder at the cottages and farmhouses which dotted the landscape below and at the sapphire-blue expanse of ocean beyond. She murmured, "York has always been like a second home to me, but I was born and raised in Boston and so were my parents. I'm looking forward to being married at St. Gregory's, as they were. Actually, I've been meaning to ask you if that would be all right. I had just been waiting until this wedding was over before we went over our own plans."

"Anything you decide will be fine with me." Stephen bent his head and Elizabeth tilted hers back to accept his kiss.

Suddenly her attention was caught by Dolly, who was trying to cajole Paul into dancing with her.

Stephen followed her gaze and chuckled. "You certainly have to give

Dolly an 'A' for effort. She never gives up. I just hope she doesn't get hurt in the end."

"What do you mean?"

"Your uncle may be older, but he's not ancient by any means. It's not inconceivable that he'll want to get married someday. I just hope that when it happens, Dolly won't take it too hard. Of course by the time that happens, Dolly will likely be married herself."

Elizabeth said nothing as they walked to the dessert table. She saw Dolly, plate in hand, feeding Paul a bite of cake.

Robert and Mary Francis were dancing nearby and Robert shouted, "Hey, Sis! Only the bridal couple gets to feed each other cake. Wait your turn!"

Dolly tossed her head and fed Paul another bite as Paul shrugged his shoulders.

At that moment one of Robert's friends approached Dolly. "Could I have this dance?"

Dolly looked mildly annoyed, but Paul stepped back and with a sweeping motion encouraged the young man towards Dolly. Dolly had no choice but to comply. Dolly craned her neck for a last glance at Paul.

Grandpa joined Elizabeth, Stephen, and Paul. "You'd better hurry up and hide, Paul. That dance isn't going to last very long."

"True." Paul, however, lingered, and Elizabeth watched as he kept half an eye on the dancing couple before walking a few feet away to talk with Aunt May and Margaret.

"Perhaps I spoke too soon," Stephen murmured. "Actions speak louder than words."

~

The next morning the Boston group stopped at the Sullivans' to say goodbye. They promised to be back in two weeks for the July Fourth weekend. Dolly looked at Paul, a shadow of a question crossing her face.

"If I'm invited," Paul said, "I might tag along."

"Of course you're invited," Aunt May interjected. "We wouldn't have it any other way."

Dolly clasped her hands together and beamed.

They piled into Paul's car. For a while they drove in silence, and then Paul spoke up. "I have something to tell all of you. I know the timing on this is not ideal, but I've decided to move out at the end of the month. I've been looking around for a while. My father told me I could live in the Adams Street house, but I'm not interested in living in a big empty mansion, and it will be on the market soon anyway. I found an apartment on Willow Street in Louisburg Square. Those are hard to come by, and I don't want to miss this opportunity."

Elizabeth looked at Grandpa. She saw a flicker of concern pass over him, but then he put on a brave face. "With Elizabeth and Stephen getting married, and you moving out, I'll be living alone. I've been fortunate up to now to always have someone around. But naturally you have your own life to live. I'll be fine. Besides, I'll have my card buddies visiting and Elizabeth is sure to stop by often."

Elizabeth and Stephen hadn't yet decided where they would live. In spite of his protests, she knew her grandpa was bound to be lonely. He also wasn't getting any younger, and he'd had some health problems. If anything happened to him, who would be there to help?

Stephen must have noticed her troubled expression. He reached over to squeeze her hand and whispered, "Don't worry. We'll figure something out." He smiled at her and Elizabeth felt relieved. She knew Stephen would come up with a solution. The question begged, what?

Chapter Fifty - Three

"Alan, it's perfect!"

He was standing with Priscilla in the master bedroom of a brownstone on Willow Street, in the middle of Louisburg Square. It was just around the corner from the Hodge residence on Acorn Street, which in Alan's view was the most picturesque – and expensive – street in the square. Willow Street was almost equally picturesque. The Willow Street property was quite a bit smaller than the Hodge residence, but it was still spacious, with a large drawing room to the right of the hallway and a private study on the left. The kitchen and pantry area were in the rear, connected to the formal dining room. There were two bedrooms and a large bath upstairs.

"I would be happy to call this 'home' for the foreseeable future," Alan said, "as long as we have two boys or two girls. Otherwise, we'd need a third bedroom."

Priscilla turned from inspecting the closet and looked at Alan. "Actually, I was thinking that there would be only one child."

Alan was startled at her reply. How like Priscilla to have already made up her mind without even discussing it with him. Not that he'd discussed his ideas with her, but he'd assumed there would be two – or more – children in their future. Wasn't that the norm? He decided to keep his tone even. "I can see how our backgrounds come into play. You're an only child and I grew up with a brother."

Priscilla smiled and softened her voice. "Good point! It's just something we've never talked about."

"Yes, but I do know one thing." Alan stepped forward and encircled Priscilla's with his arms. "There's going to be at least one baby, and we can start working on that on our honeymoon in a few weeks."

He bent to kiss her but Priscilla held him off. "We don't necessarily have to start then. After all, I'd like to enjoy a few years of married life before I'm confined to motherhood."

"I don't know if we need to use that word to describe motherhood, and I am intending on exercising my marital rights." Alan didn't bother this time to keep the hardness out of his tone.

"Of course, darling! I certainly plan on using all that pretty lingerie I've been buying. I guess I'm just getting used to the idea that motherhood could be right around the corner."

Alan relaxed. "I can understand. One day, you're a single carefree woman, and a year or two later you're pushing a baby carriage."

Alan felt Priscilla's body tense up. Clearly, the topic of motherhood was not a subject she was comfortable with. Perhaps it was best if he let Mother Nature take its course; the less said the better. However, he couldn't help teasing her. "What would you say if we had twins?"

To his relief, Priscilla looked at him with a twinkle in her eye. "I'd say, 'Lord, have mercy'!"

~

At work the following day Alan had his office door open a crack and he overheard Betty talking to Lillian Graham.

"I called Elizabeth the other night to thank her for getting engaged. It's been very beneficial to my own love life."

"How so?"

"Ever since Phil heard that they were engaged, he's been paying extra attention to me. And he confides in me. I'm not sure I've ever had a beau who really treated me like an equal. It's nice!"

Alan froze. What was Phil confiding to Betty? Then he shook his head. Betty and Phil were small change. Why should he give a hoot what Phil Lawrence did?

Alan remained motionless, listening. Betty's next words cut him to the core. "Elizabeth also told me that Stephen wants to have kids right away. I wouldn't be surprised if she gets pregnant on the honeymoon. I can see the two of them with a whole tribe someday."

Alan stared out his window. Isn't that the way it was supposed to work? Couples got married and had kids? Maybe after they had one, Priscilla would warm up to the idea of having more. Surely those motherhood instincts would kick in.

Just then Lillian poked her head in the door. "Excuse me, Mr. Bates.

Mr. Hodge would like to meet with you at four o'clock this afternoon. Is that all right?"

"Of course. Tell him I'll be there."

Lillian closed the door, and Alan tried to figure out the reason for the meeting. His next update on the merger was not due for over a week and there was nothing else going on that would bring Mr. Hodge's attention.

~

At exactly four o'clock he stood in front of his future father-in-law. "Have a seat, Alan."

Mr. Hodge leaned forward. "The company has been doing well – especially this last year. Because we are growing so rapidly, I need someone to run the international end of the business. I've been quietly watching both you and Phil Lawrence, but in light of the circumstances surrounding the Latin America venture, I'm offering this position to you. Are you interested?"

"Absolutely, sir! In fact, I'm deeply honored."

"I thought you might be. And aside from the 'indiscretion,' shall we say, regarding Brown, you've been a stellar employee. I think you'll do well with this promotion. There aren't too many young men who achieve such a position so early in their career, although you remind me of myself. I rose through the ranks rather quickly. The only difference was that I switched companies several times in the process, eventually starting my own company."

"That doesn't surprise me, sir. I'm sure you've been ambitious from the very start."

Henry Hodge tapped some papers on his desk. "Your promotion won't go into effect for several months, since we'll need to do a bit of realigning. But there will be, at that time, a pay increase to accompany it. I'll be announcing your upcoming promotion at this week's staff meeting. Congratulations!"

"Thank you!"

Alan let himself out, whistling as he returned to his office. A promotion was not what he had fathomed. Of course, it would be another thorn in Phil's side when it was announced on Friday. How appropriate, Alan thought. On this Fourth of July week there would likely be fireworks inside Boston's financial district as well as on the waterfront.

Chapter Fifty - Four

Their Fourth of July plans changed unexpectedly when Elizabeth came home from work on July second and heard a grunting sound in the hallway.

"Grandpa?" She ran down the hall and found him lying at the bottom of the stairs. He was dazed and had a small cut on his forehead. "Grandpa! Are you all right?"

His voice was thin. "My legs felt shaky and next thing I knew I was at the bottom of the steps."

She tried to help him up but he was too heavy for her to move. "I'm going to call Harry."

Running to the phone, she quickly dialed. She was relieved when she heard Harry's gruff voice. "Grandpa's fallen! Can you come and help me get him on his feet?"

"I'll be right there!" Harry only lived a block away, and he walked through the front door a few minutes later with Fred, who, blessedly, had been visiting Harry at the time. The two men lifted Grandpa up by the arms and helped him walk to a chair in the parlor.

Elizabeth called Dr. Tinsdale. While they waited, Harry brought Grandpa a cup of water while Elizabeth wet a cloth and pressed it to the cut that was still bleeding.

When Dr. Tinsdale arrived, he checked his pupils and his pulse. "He took a bad fall, no doubt due to his heart being weak."

Elizabeth was alarmed. "What do you mean 'his heart being weak'? I haven't heard anything about that!"

Grandpa answered, "I knew if I told you, you'd be worried."

"That's true, but I'd still rather know than not."

"I guess now you know." Grandpa smiled at her.

Dr. Tinsdale interrupted. "John, you'll need to rest up for a few days and, after that, you need to take it easy on a permanent basis. My suggestion would be to quit that job of yours. You're seventy-one years old. You're not doing yourself any favors working long hours."

"I suppose I can agree with you on that. I was thinking of giving my notice in the fall, but I guess I could move up the date."

"Please, Grandpa," Elizabeth pleaded. "I would die if anything happened to you!"

His voice softened. "If it will make you happy, Elizabeth, I'll give my notice next week."

"Thank you." She hugged him close as he lay underneath the coverlet, his weathered hand stroking her hair.

Dr. Tinsdale turned to Harry and Fred. "In the meantime, I don't know if we can get him up the stairs, but if you two could put a bed in the parlor, he could rest there."

Harry and Fred carried the bed from the spare bedroom while Elizabeth gathered blankets and a pillow. Grandpa admonished them to stop hovering. "I'll be fine by tomorrow. I don't need to be looked after like a baby."

Dr. Tinsdale, Harry, and Fred left after assurances from Elizabeth that she would be able to care for Grandpa. She called Stephen, who came over immediately and sat with Grandpa while Elizabeth dialed Aunt May to tell her they would not be driving up to Maine for the holiday.

"A July Fourth without the two of you! It certainly won't seem like a celebration, but maybe it's a blessing in disguise if that brother of mine is finally going to retire. It's time he enjoyed life. I'll tell the Sullivans what happened. Call me in the morning and let me know how he's doing."

~

The next day Grandpa was sitting up and by Thursday, July 4th, he seemed like his old self.

Paul had moved to his new apartment over the weekend and he stopped by to see how Grandpa was doing. At Paul's urging, Elizabeth and Stephen agreed to attend the fireworks at the Boston Esplanade with Betty and Phil. "I can keep an eye on him. I can also pinch hit as a host, since Fred and Harry will be coming by. My culinary skills consist of passing around a plate of cookies and opening bottles of beer."

Stephen voiced his approval. "You're hired!"

As they drove to the concert, Stephen drummed his fingers on the steering wheel and hummed a tune. He glanced over at Elizabeth. "I have a surprise. Yesterday I booked the new VFW Post in South Boston for our reception. It's brand new and very reasonably priced."

"Stephen, that's wonderful! Can we take a peek at it beforehand?"

"Of course! The manager said we can make an appointment with him at our convenience."

They parked on Memorial Drive then hurried to the Hatch Shell. Throngs of people were dressed in red, white, and blue. The lawn by the Charles River was a sea of blankets and picnic baskets. Elizabeth spotted Betty and Phil waving their arms. She and Stephen threaded their way through the crowd to reach them.

Betty hugged Elizabeth. "I'm so glad you could make it! How is your grandfather doing?"

"Much better, thank God."

Stephen added, "He should be, with round-the-clock nursing care from Elizabeth. Hi, Phil. Nice to see you again."

Stephen and Phil shook hands warmly.

Elizabeth and Stephen laid out their provisions and sat down.

"Phil, how's work?" Stephen asked.

"Not bad."

Elizabeth detected a grimace, belying his words.

Betty piped up. "Phil won't tell you, but Alan screwed him at work."

"I can't prove it," Phil said. "Otherwise I would have already done something about it."

"I don't have to know the details to know that if Alan is involved there must be some shenanigans," Elizabeth put in.

Phil answered. "You've got that right. As you probably remember, Alan tried to take credit for my Latin proposal. Par for the course, he's been criticizing the project behind my back and then yesterday he was able to switch my meeting on it from morning to afternoon when most of the upper managers – including Mr. Hodge – were taking off early for the holiday."

Stephen put in, "He's a fool to think he can sabotage your project."

"Yes, but that's only the first part. There was a staff meeting this week, and guess what happened there? Mr. Hodge announced that Alan is being promoted!"

Stephen was aghast. "Do you mean he got a promotion after hoodwinking you?"

"He sure did. He's going to be my direct boss now for international business."

"It's like salt to a wound," Betty said.

Elizabeth was quick to respond, "It seems so unfair!"

Stephen stretched out on the blanket. "My father always said, 'What goes around comes around.' He'll get his due someday, just you watch."

Elizabeth was about to weigh in when she saw Maura and Bill walking through the crowd. She stood up and yelled to them.

Bill and Maura's faces lit up when they spotted Elizabeth. The two of them joined the group, 'Hellos' were exchanged, and everyone squeezed close on the two blankets. The sound of clapping drew their attention to the stage. The Boston Pops Conductor, Arthur Fiedler, was being introduced.

Elizabeth had never heard the Pops in person before. She watched Arthur Fiedler step up to the podium, his salt-and-pepper hair slicked back and his thick mustache clipped and shaped. When he turned to acknowledge the crowd, they erupted in applause. As he bowed, the coattails of his tuxedo flapped in the breeze.

The first song was "Stars and Stripes Forever," with the violins, trombones, and bugles in perfect syncopation.

After each number, the crowd cheered. At intermission, the group stood and stretched. Many folks hurried to nearby pushcarts and vendors for refreshments.

"Should we walk around?" Stephen asked.

"Sure!" Everyone was in agreement. Phil and Betty wanted to purchase soft drinks and Elizabeth and Stephen went with them. Elizabeth stood with Stephen's arm around her shoulder. She glanced to her side and with a sinking heart she saw Priscilla and Alan standing one line over. She hoped that Alan and Priscilla wouldn't look her way. On second thought, she wouldn't mind if Alan saw her with Stephen. She had moved on and she wanted him to know it. Unfortunately, it was Priscilla who turned, her icy blue eyes staring in distain when she recognized Elizabeth.

After a moment Priscilla approached, Alan trailing. "Elizabeth, how lovely to see you," she crooned. "It's been so long. Phil, Betty." She nodded her head towards the couple before turning back to Elizabeth. "Is this the fiancé I've read about?" Priscilla eyes flickered to Stephen.

"Yes, this is Stephen Wright."

"Alan and I are also engaged." Priscilla flung out her hand and Elizabeth looked at the large diamond sparkling on her finger.

"It's beautiful," Elizabeth offered.

"Thank you. So tell me your wedding and reception plans."

Elizabeth was loath to talk to Priscilla Hodge about wedding plans, but she didn't want to make a scene. "We plan to marry at St. Gregory's and we just booked the reception at the VFW Post in South Boston."

"VFW?" Priscilla smirked. "How quaint!" Priscilla linked her arm in Alan's. "Alan and I are getting married at Holy Cross Cathedral and the reception will be at the Ritz." She smiled broadly at Alan. "What's your wedding date?"

"August 3."

The smile instantly dropped from Priscilla's face. "Are you teasing me? That's the date of our wedding. You must have read our date in the paper and copied us!"

Elizabeth was annoyed. She'd had enough of Priscilla's arrogance and she didn't care if she was rude. "I never bother reading the 'Society Pages' so I hadn't the slightest idea when your wedding date was."

Priscilla tossed her head and gave Phil and Betty a cocky look. "I hope we're not putting any pressure on you two with all these wedding plans." Sarcasm dripped from her words.

"Not at all," Betty answered cheerfully. "Our relationship is just fine where it's at."

Priscilla wagged her finger. "Don't take too much time, Phil. Betty doesn't stay with anyone for too long."

Phil stepped forward, apparently ready to say something, but Betty pulled him back. At the same time Alan grabbed Priscilla's arm and pulled her up to the vendor, apparently unconcerned that they had just cut the line.

As soon as they left, Betty exploded. "The nerve of her! The day she gets her due, I want a front row seat. She is the most condescending person I have ever known. I have to hand it to you Elizabeth. You really gave it back to her."

Phil agreed. "Yes, you did, and it was a moment to savor. Priscilla Hodge takes the cake, but Alan runs a close second."

Stephen lifted his hand. "People like them, who try to put others down, only succeed in making themselves look bad. At least you don't have to deal with her every day. My mother – God rest her soul – always told me to 'offer it up' when I had to deal with a difficult person."

Phil said, "I wish I could be more like you, Stephen, because I was just about to tell Alan to get his future wife under control. I've had it with him, and if I ever get a chance to get even, there won't be a prayer in the world that will be able to stop me."

Chapter Fifty - Five

As they left the soft drink stand, Alan glanced back. He did not want to get into it with Phil, and Priscilla had gone a bit far. During the exchange Alan had been discreetly studying Elizabeth. She looked different. She had always been pretty, but now her hair was cut stylishly, and he had detected a hint of makeup. She was a real head-turner. He thought she might have at least looked his way; she had been so smitten with him less than a year ago. But she'd taken no notice of him.

Priscilla slipped her arm through his. "Miss Goody Two-Shoes is getting married on *our* wedding date. Well, who cares! Good luck to them! She's such a square. I bet she's never even had a Bloody Mary!"

"Undoubtedly." Alan knew better, but he decided not to raise the point. He also wanted to ask what being a 'goody two shoes' had to do with getting married, but he decided it was best to let the whole thing drop.

They were standing at the edge of the crowd when Alan heard a man call out Priscilla's name. Turning, he saw one of Priscilla's admirers from the tennis club waving at her.

"Do you want to sit with us?" the man called.

"Yes!" Turning to Alan, she cried, "Look! The whole crowd's here! Come on!"

Alan had little choice, although he was not enamored at the idea. They walked towards the group, stepping on corners of blankets and around folks sprawled on the lawn. As soon as they reached the group, the young man who had invited them over asked, "Are you guys interested in going out for a couple of drinks afterwards?"

Alan noticed that the man's eyes never left Priscilla. He spoke up before Priscilla had a chance to. "It's been a long day. I think we'll go home after this."

"No problem. We go out all the time. You're welcome to join us anytime you like."

Alan put his arm around Priscilla. "We're a little busy for the next few weeks. We're getting married in a month."

The young man lifted his eyebrows. "Hey guys, we're losing a good one from the single crowd. Priscilla and – is it Alvin?"

"Alan."

"Right. Priscilla and Alan are getting married! Cheers!" The man held his can of soda high and the group hooted.

Priscilla yelled above the noise. "Don't think I'm out of the loop! I'll still be around!"

Alan gave Priscilla the eyeball, but she didn't notice. She was too busy talking and laughing. The Pops played a medley of war songs, then reached the final number, "God Bless America." The crowd stood, giving the orchestra thunderous applause. People waved their flags, shouted, and cheered. Priscilla turned and kissed Alan hard on the lips. His anger instantly evaporated. When Priscilla gave him her attention, he was putty in her hands. They would be married soon, and with the victorious knowledge that she had chosen him for a husband, nothing else mattered.

Chapter Fifty - Six

After the Fourth of July holiday, Elizabeth threw herself into wedding plans. Mary Francis had gleefully accepted Elizabeth's request to be her matron of honor, and Dolly would be a bridesmaid. In turn, Stephen asked a cousin to be his best man and Paul would be an usher. Stephen was happily in charge of the honeymoon.

"What would you think of New York City?"

Elizabeth gasped. "Stephen, that would be a dream come true, but wouldn't that be expensive?"

"I don't think so. We can get a reasonable hotel, and a lot of the tourist attractions are inexpensive. And, as you know, I received a small inheritance from my mother, and I think a honeymoon is a worthy occasion to splurge."

The only thing that had not been decided was where they were going to live after the wedding. Elizabeth was concerned about Grandpa living alone since his fall. She and Stephen would be getting their own place, but she would make sure she visited Grandpa frequently. She'd have more time to be with him when she left her job at the end of July. She was loath to leave Phillips and Godfrey, but because of the marriage bar that stated that once a woman was married, she could not hold a job, she had little choice. She would dearly miss the people she worked with.

One evening Elizabeth and Stephen sat in the parlor sipping lemonade. They were going through their guest list, but Stephen's mind was elsewhere. Finally he spoke. "Elizabeth, I've been going over the various options of where we should live after we're married. I think I've reached a conclusion, but I thought I'd walk you through exactly how I arrived at it."

"I'm all ears."

"We can't stay in my apartment because it's barely big enough for me, let alone the two of us. We could always buy a house, but I'm not too keen on that idea right now. I want to be able to have the time to fix a house up when we buy one, and I'm not going to have much time for anything in the near future with this merger taking place. I suppose the most logical solution would be to simply find a big enough apartment for the two of us, but then I started thinking. Since you'll leave Phillip's once we're married, what if we just live here with your grandfather?"

"Here?" Elizabeth was immediately excited, but she didn't want her approval to be based on sentiment. She only wanted to do it if it was logical to do so. She sat back and waited for Stephen to continue.

"It's the perfect solution, if you stop to think about it. During the next year or so, I'm going to be traveling quite a bit and I know that every time I go away I'm going to be worried about you being alone in some dreary apartment. If you lived here, you could keep an eye on your grandfather, and he would love having you around. So what do you think? We can buy a house someday, but for now I think it would be the perfect solution for all of us."

Elizabeth's jumped from her seat, her face lit with happiness. She wrapped her arms around Stephen's neck and bestowed a kiss on his lips. "Stephen, I think it's the most wonderful idea I've ever heard! I didn't want to say anything, but I've been dreading having to move and leave Grandpa all alone. I worry about him. I love your idea."

"Great! Now when I travel, I'll be able to rest easy knowing you two are together. I also thought I would add some improvements to the house, like a new heating system, and a coat of paint for the 'honeymoon suite'."

Standing up, Stephen slipped his arm around Elizabeth's waist and turned her towards the hall. "Before we consider it final, we should probably discuss this with your grandfather."

Elizabeth looked at Stephen, her eyes sparkling. "Somehow I have the feeling he's not going to mind."

Chapter Fifty - Seven

"You may now kiss the bride."

Like any other groom, Alan didn't need to be told twice. Tipping Priscilla's chin up, his lips landed on hers long and languorously. This was his moment, and he wanted the world to know that the most beautiful, sophisticated, and wealthy girl in Boston was now his wife.

A moment later, they turned to face their guests at Holy Cross Cathedral. Immediate family, along with friends and extended relatives of the Hodge's, filled the church.

The Hodges also had a distinguished guest: Mr. Joseph P. Kennedy, the former ambassador to the United Kingdom, who had graduated from Harvard with Mr. Hodge. He sat with his wife Rose and their son Jack, who was favored to win the Democratic seat for the Massachusetts House of Representatives in the fall election. Alan had been introduced to them before the wedding. Their presence confirmed for Alan that he was entering the social elite.

As they left the church, confetti showered the air amidst cries of congratulations. A cluster of photographers and society writers were there to take their picture. Mr. Hodge had provided them with his Packard Clipper Sedan and chauffeur, who whisked them to the reception.

In line, Neil was the first to congratulate them. Giving Priscilla a kiss on the cheek, Neil introduced his wife, Eleanor, to the bridal couple.

Priscilla was called away to pose for pictures with her parents, and Alan headed toward the bar. His brother was already there.

"That's quite a girl you've got, Alan!"

Alan nodded.

His brother continued. "Don't know how you got her to finally settle down, much less with you, the son of a small-town banker."

"What do you mean, 'finally settle down'?" Alan asked. Alan stared at his brother, who had never met Priscilla before.

"Hey, I just overheard that group of guys by the bar talking about the dates they've had with her. Seems like common knowledge. Don't look so surprised."

Alan looked towards the end of bar. There was a group of young men standing there that he did not recognize. Had Priscilla had the nerve to invite ex-boyfriends to their wedding? He had not paid much attention to the guest list, as Priscilla and her parents had several hundred invitees while he had very few. Apparently he should have been more diligent.

"Excuse me. I have something to do."

He headed straight for Priscilla, where she was now amongst a cluster of admiring girlfriends. Placing his hand firmly on her forearm, he excused them, and propelled her onto the dance floor.

Alan swept her immediately into a waltz. "Darling, I need to ask you, did you forget to tell me that you invited some ex-boyfriends to our wedding?"

"Who are you talking about?"

"Oh, that group of fellas standing by the bar. Or there is another group also here? Should I differentiate?"

"Don't be snide, Alan! And I don't see them as ex-boyfriends. They're just some old college friends. I might have had a couple of dates with one or two of them."

"I just wish you would have told me so I could have invited some girls – maybe Elizabeth Keene." Alan knew he was speaking rashly, but he didn't care.

"That's completely different! She was crazy about you!"

"Well, I was never serious about her. Apparently, it's not okay when the shoe is on the other foot."

Priscilla opened her mouth to reply, but Alan immediately planted a kiss on her mouth. People around them had begun to take notice of their conversation, and this kept her from a retort. After that they danced in silence.

Alan was still upset, but at least Priscilla seemed sincere that she didn't feel as if she had done anything wrong. Maybe she just felt the need to have a 'fan club' wherever she was. That was perhaps understandable, considering the public life she led.

Priscilla also seemed to consider the matter settled. She smiled at him and circled her arms around his neck as they swirled to the music. This was their special day and he didn't want to risk marring it any more than he already had. But after the honeymoon, he decided, he would make his expectations crystal clear. And after that, Alan thought with satisfaction, if Priscilla became pregnant, she would be too busy to think about a 'fan club' anymore.

Chapter Fifty - Eight

 The third of August dawned bright and sunny, with only a few fair-weather clouds scuttling across the horizon before fading into a powder-blue sky.

As Elizabeth's room filled with sunshine, she looked to where her satin wedding gown, ironed and encased in plastic, hung from the top of her closet door. Purchased from the dressmaker's shop Mary Francis had worked at until her marriage, it had Juliet sleeves that puffed up at the shoulders and ended in lacy points at the tip of her wrists. The jewel-neck bodice, which flatteringly skimmed her waist, was accented by a double row of cloth-covered buttons from the top of the neckline down the back to her waist. A petite cap was affixed to a rose-point veil which came to her shoulder blades, and a billowing chapel train was beautiful, especially when it flared.

She hopped out of bed and scrambled to the window to see if the rosary beads were still on the ledge. Auntie May had told her that a bride was blessed with good luck and many children if she hung a pair of rosary beads outside her bedroom window the night before her wedding. They were still there and, as she pulled them inside, she noticed that the early morning dew was clinging to its ivory beads.

Elizabeth had also followed the old adage that a bride should have something old, something new, something borrowed, and something blue. For something old, she was using her grandmother's prayer book, which her mother had also used on her wedding day; new was her wedding gown, veil, and shoes; borrowed was a pair of diamond earrings Stephen's sister Carol had lent her, and "something blue" Dolly had insisted on donating – a pale, blue garter that Elizabeth would slip on her left leg last of all.

The Sullivans had arrived the day before on the afternoon train. Paul and Stephen had picked the group up at the station. Charles Sullivan,

Charlie, and Father Joe had been invited to stay at Harry's, while the gals were staying at the house with Grandpa and Elizabeth.

Elizabeth had suggested that Mary Francis and Robert use the second bedroom and Dolly sleep in Elizabeth's room with her. Margaret Sullivan snubbed that idea, though. The probability of Elizabeth getting any sleep, she said, with Dolly in the same room, was highly unlikely. She insisted that her two daughters share a bedroom while Robert sleep on the couch. Consequently, it was Mary Francis who appeared red-eyed and grumpy that morning and not Elizabeth.

By ten o'clock Elizabeth was ready. Her hair, rolled in curlers the night before by Mary Francis, fell in a cascade of soft curls from underneath her wedding cap. The dress fit beautifully. Elizabeth was excited and nervous. The day that she had thought might never happen was now unfolding before her very eyes.

At the church they emerged from Paul's luxury Studebaker that he had insisted they borrow for the day. The bridesmaids and ushers were lined up at the back of the church. Behind them Charlie, designated as ring bearer, was impatiently waiting. Margaret Sullivan was keeping an eye on him and pulled a wad of gum out of his mouth just before the procession began.

After a few moments "Mendelssohn's Wedding March" began and Elizabeth walked down the center aisle on the arm of her grandpa. He took slow, even steps, and she could tell he was positively bursting with pride.

Elizabeth glanced down at her bouquet, a dozen long-stemmed pale pink, fully blooming roses from Grandpa's garden. Her most fervent wishes had all come true.

Stephen, waiting at the front of the church, looked lovingly at her before he shook Grandpa's hand. Father Joe stood between them. At the end they were introduced as the new Mr. and Mrs. Stephen Wright, and they hurried down the aisle to the applause of their guests.

Elizabeth looked around. There was Auntie May and the Sullivans. She also saw many of their neighbors, Grandpa's poker pals, including Fred and Harry, and a few friends Grandpa had worked with at the paper mill. Grandfather Keene was there with his new wife Sophia. Elizabeth had been reluctant to meet her, feeling an allegiance to her grandmother.

However, Sophia had been very cordial, and Elizabeth wanted her to feel welcome. Lillian Graham was there, along with Betty and Phil, and Maura and Bill. On Stephen's side there were his sister and her family plus many cousins, aunts and uncles, plus classmates from college. Everyone they loved, it seemed, had come to celebrate their wedding day with them.

At the reception Elizabeth and Stephen danced their first dance together while everyone watched and applauded. After a few minutes Mary Francis and Robert joined in, along with Charles and Margaret. Grandpa stood at the sidelines, smiling and clapping.

"Your grandfather looks good," Lillian later commented to Elizabeth. "Did you say that he was retiring?"

"Yes. He retired two weeks ago. He doesn't have to get up so early now and he has more energy left at the end of the day."

Charlie barreled by and Elizabeth grabbed his arm. "You did a wonderful job, Charlie! You walked down the aisle like a little soldier. And the ring switch went off without a hitch!"

Charlie gave her a puzzled looked, and Elizabeth laughed. Elizabeth and Stephen had decided it would be wise to place an inexpensive ring on the pillow, given Charlie's penchant for mischievousness. Then the ring would be discreetly swapped out by Uncle Paul after Charlie reached the front of the church. So many people had suggested the idea, including Charlie's own parents, that it was easier to remember the people who hadn't suggested it rather than the ones who had.

When it was time for Elizabeth to throw the bridal bouquet, Betty, Maura, and Dolly clustered together along with several of Stephen's cousins and a few of Elizabeth's neighbors. Dolly precipitously stepped ahead of the other girls and lunged for the thrown bouquet. She scooped it up just before it landed and hurried to where Paul was standing. Elizabeth, Father Joe, and Stephen walked over.

"Did you see that I caught the bridal bouquet?"

"Who didn't see that?" Father Joe said. "You looked like a football player."

Dolly ignored him, still focusing on Paul. "Did you know that means that I'm most likely to get married next?"

"I wonder what the accuracy rate is for that tradition," Paul mused.

"I think it's a very high percentage," Father Joe said, winking as he spoke. "Of course you need someone to marry."

"Yes, I do."

"Just so you know," Father Joe said, "I'm available to officiate every day except Wednesdays and Thursdays. Those are my days off."

Paul nodded his head. "Thank you for that information."

"Anytime. If you'll excuse me, I want to ask my mother to dance. She never refuses me."

Elizabeth and Stephen entered the dance floor behind Joe. Over Stephen's shoulder, Elizabeth could see Dolly talking to Paul. His head was bent to hear her over the music.

Stephen spoke in Elizabeth's ear. "Do you think we'll be hearing more wedding bells soon?"

"I would say yes except for their age difference, which is a tricky thing to get around."

"Really? I thought the hardest part would be keeping up with Dolly – no matter what the man's age is."

"True!"

After dancing for several more songs, they were ready to take a break when Aunt May tapped Elizabeth on the shoulder to inform them that it was time to change into their going away outfits.

When they returned to the reception, their guests had gathered in a circle and they walked around slowly, saying goodbye to each person. It was hardest for Elizabeth to say goodbye to Grandpa, although Paul had said he would stay with him while they were away.

Phil and Betty drove them to South Station, where they were to take the train to New York City. As they drove, Betty gushed about the wedding. "Elizabeth, you looked gorgeous! You were the most beautiful bride I have ever seen!"

"Thank you. I felt like a princess." She looked at Stephen. "I still do."

~

Elizabeth and Steven stayed in downtown Manhattan at the moderately priced but comfortable Hotel Pennsylvania, conveniently located across from Penn Station. Elizabeth could have spent the entire week in their room, enjoying the plush furnishings and adjoining bathroom.

When she told Stephen that, he teased, "I can think of several other reasons why I would enjoy staying in this room all week."

Elizabeth blushed.

During the days they were able to enjoy all the tourist attractions that Elizabeth had heard of but had never dreamed she would ever see. She was awestruck by the soaring sky scrapers, especially the Empire State Building and the bright billboards in Times Square. She was overwhelmed by the innumerable stores and restaurants in Rockefeller Center and charmed by the horse and buggy ride they took in picturesque Central Park. She and Stephen were able to see Ellis Island, where Grandpa had arrived by boat from Ireland as a young man. On Sunday morning they attended Mass at the magnificent Cathedral of Saint Patrick in downtown Manhattan before heading home. She couldn't wait to tell everyone about the city that never seemed to close down.

~

When they returned, rested and eager to begin their new life together, Elizabeth and Stephen settled down easily. They had decided to use the spare bedroom in the rear of the house because it afforded them not only more space, but more privacy. Stephen had spent the month before the wedding scraping and repainting it. He had also installed an oil burner to replace the antiquated coal unit. The new heating system now heated not only the kitchen and the parlor, but the entire upstairs. It was too warm in August to enjoy its benefits, but Stephen assured Elizabeth that on the first cold morning when her feet landed upon a warm, hardwood floor, she would definitely appreciate it.

A month after the honeymoon, Elizabeth woke not feeling well. Even though she'd had a good night's sleep, she felt tired and her stomach felt unsettled.

Since she would still be training the young girl who was to take her position for the next few weeks, she dragged herself to work. By the end of the week she was still not feeling herself, and Stephen ordered her back to bed. As he solicitously tucked the bedcovers around her he announced, "You're not going anywhere today. You're staying right here and I'll make sure your grandfather takes good care of you. You've almost certainly picked up some kind of bug and hopefully if you rest and take it easy, it will go away in a few days."

Elizabeth rolled over to a more comfortable position as she mumbled, "Actually, I was thinking of making a doctor's appointment."

Stephen, seated on the side of the bed, stared at her in alarm. "Do you think it's that serious?"

Elizabeth couldn't help mustering up a smile. "No. I just thought that's what most girls do when they think they're pregnant."

Stephen's jaw dropped, then he grasped Elizabeth by the shoulders. "Pregnant! Honey, this is the best piece of news ever! Do you really think you're pregnant? Are you sure?"

"No, I'm not sure, but I seem to have all the symptoms."

"I just didn't think it would happen so quickly! Not that I know much about these things." Stephen nervously paced the room. "Should we tell your grandfather now? He'll be tickled pink, I'm sure. Do you think it would be all right if we tell my sister too?"

"I'd like to just tell Grandpa it's nothing serious, so he won't worry, but I think it would be wise if I met with Dr. Tinsdale first. Then if he says I am, we'll tell everyone. Okay?"

~

Dr. Tinsdale was available to see Elizabeth that afternoon and that evening Elizabeth greeted Stephen at the door with good news.

Stephen enveloped her in a close embrace. When he lifted his head, there were tears in his eyes. "Honey, I'm so happy for us!"

Just then the back door opened and Grandpa entered the kitchen.

Elizabeth rushed to hug him. "Grandpa! We're going to have a baby!"

Grandpa looked at Elizabeth, affection in his eyes. "That's wonderful! Imagine – me at my stage of life being able to see a great grandchild!" He turned to Stephen and stuck out his hand. "Congratulations, Stephen! There's nothing much better than becoming a father."

Elizabeth said, "We'll want to break the news to Paul, but I want to tell the girls in person when we go to Maine next week for Labor Day."

Stephen and Grandpa both nodded. Then all three of them laughed and threw their arms around each other in a happy embrace.

Chapter Fifty - Nine

"I can take your bags, sir."

"Thank you, Edward." Alan handed the luggage to his new butler, a service that he was not going to have any trouble getting used to. Mr. Hodge had been extremely generous to them for their wedding, paying for them to have both a cook and butler for their first year of marriage. In addition to that, he had paid for their honeymoon at the Newport Beach Hotel, a quaint New England-style Gambrel situated on a strip of land with panoramic views of Easton Lake behind the hotel, Easton's Beach in front.

They had a very relaxing honeymoon, playing tennis in the mornings, shopping or browsing in the afternoon, and dining out at night. Their favorite eating establishment was the historical White Horse Tavern in downtown Newport. They enjoyed the fresh halibut so much they returned on the last night of their honeymoon. They also enjoyed taking walks along Bellevue Avenue where the wealthiest families of Rhode Island spent their summers, including the Vanderbilts' mansion, The Breakers.

As Mr. Hodge had commented to Alan before they left, "When you only have one child, you can be found guilty of showering that child with anything they want."

Alan quickly stepped aside in order to let one of the moving people squeeze by with a leather chair.

When he entered the hall, the brownstone was a beehive of activity. Painters were busy on the landing and in the drawing room, and Priscilla was discussing curtains with a decorator. A heavy set man was directing his crew of movers as a steady stream of furniture, boxes, and personal items were carried in.

Alan spent the rest of the balmy fall afternoon organizing his books, papers, and miscellaneous items in the study. Soon after, Priscilla appeared in the doorway.

"Our new cook is planning on serving soup and sandwiches for dinner, unless you would like her to make a 'sit-down' meal."

"That's nice of her to offer, considering the fact that our new dining room table won't be delivered until Monday."

"I'll tell her the sandwiches will be fine."

As Priscilla stopped to adjust the accessories on the desk, the phone rang.

"That didn't take long for someone to have our new phone number," Alan remarked. "Hello. Who's calling? Todd who? She's right here."

Alan silently handed the phone to Priscilla, but his face registered annoyance. "Hi Todd! You did? I will definitely be there. Okay, Thursday at five o'clock; I'll put it on the calendar. Thanks for letting me know. Bye."

As Priscilla hung up, Alan demanded. "Who the hell is Todd?"

"Alan, there's no need to sound so accusatory. I went to college with him. He was at the New Year's party we went to – and he's not the one who kissed me, if that helps."

"It definitely helps, because if it was that other cad, I'd be changing our phone number. What did *Todd* want?"

"The gang who was at the July 4th concert is going to the Green Dragon Thursday night."

"Does that invitation include husbands or do you plan on going 'stag'?"

"You can go, although I don't think you would want to. They didn't seem your type of people."

"That's true, and even if I did go, I wouldn't get there until at least six-thirty. I've got a four o'clock meeting that's probably going to drag on past the end of the workday. Are there going to be other women there?"

"Of course! The whole gang's invited."

"Then yes, you can go, as long as you miss me terribly the whole time you're there."

"My teardrops will be filling up my wine glass."

Priscilla reached over to kiss him on the cheek, but Alan caught her chin in his hands in order to give her a slower, more passionate kiss.

"That will tide me over until bedtime," he told her.

Priscilla rolled her eyes. "Men! Now I want to oversee putting the linens in the right drawers upstairs. I can't stand when things are out of order. We're going to eat in an hour."

As Alan returned to sorting his tax manuals, he couldn't shake his thoughts on Todd. He shouldn't feel threatened by him, but he was. He might be just an old college friend, but the problem was that Priscilla seemed to have a dozen 'Todds' hovering on the perimeter of her life. He certainly didn't want her 'painting the town' without him, but a casual get-together with friends he supposed he was going to have to get used to. Priscilla was extremely social, and he liked that about her. But once they had a baby or two, the 'Todds' of the world wouldn't be calling their house anymore.

Chapter Sixty

On Labor Day weekend they traveled to Maine with Paul as the driver. Elizabeth could hardly wait to tell everyone the news. The moment they walked into Aunt May's kitchen, Elizabeth cried, "Aunt May, I'm expecting!"

"Glory be! That's the best news I've heard in a long time! John, are you ready for a little one runnin' around?"

"I certainly am! I'm already planning on making a crib."

"Grandpa, that would be wonderful! Is that too much work?"

"Not at all. Now that I'm retired, I have plenty of time for it."

The screened kitchen door flew open and Mary Francis burst through. Her eyes were snapping with excitement.

Aunt May exclaimed, "My goodness, Mary Francis! You look like a balloon that's ready to burst! You must have something awfully important to tell us!"

"I do! I'm pregnant!"

"Me too!" cried Elizabeth.

Mary Francis's eyes opened wide. "You aren't really, are you?"

"You can't make this stuff up," Paul interjected.

Elizabeth nodded her head, her eyes brimming with tears as Mary Francis enveloped her in a close embrace. "When are you due?"

"In June. How about you?"

"April."

"What does Dolly think?" Grandpa asked.

"She's excited, although I think she's a little preoccupied at the moment with her own bit of news."

Passing the back of her hand against her forehead, Auntie May groaned. "More news? I'd better sit down for this."

Stephen obligingly held out a chair for her as Mary Francis rushed on. "Dolly's received a proposal of marriage!"

Elizabeth's eyes opened wide. "I can't believe it! I didn't even know she was dating anyone." She stole a look at Paul, who had a stony look on his face. "When did this happen?"

"Friday night," Mary Francis continued. "She was going to call you but she knew she would see you today."

"I can't imagine that she'll say yes," Grandpa said, stealing a sideways glance at Paul.

Mary Francis replied, "We'll see. She'll have to give Arthur an answer soon." Then she added, "I almost forgot. Mama told me to invite all of you over for dessert tonight. Mama wanted to celebrate my pregnancy – and now Elizabeth's. Can you make it?"

"We'll be there," Aunt May replied.

That evening after dinner Father Joe sat down to play the piano in the parlor just as Dolly and Arthur arrived. Elizabeth and the others waited to see how Dolly would react to Paul's presence.

Dolly gave Paul a courteous kiss on the cheek and a dutiful hello. She stood by Arthur's side while her mother served refreshments, but Elizabeth sensed tension in the air. Even though Dolly and Arthur looked companionable, Dolly didn't gaze at Arthur the way she had at Paul nor did she hang on his every word – in fact she looked distracted.

Paul was polite but quiet. Arthur, meanwhile, was jovial and seemed oblivious to the dynamics in the room. He prattled on about his work at the town's auto repair shop and hummed along to Father Joe's tunes.

Perhaps, Elizabeth thought, he didn't know that Dolly had been enamored with Paul. And how could he? Surely Dolly had not told him.

Elizabeth glanced again at Paul. He met her eyes briefly then quietly slipped out of the room.

Chapter Sixty - One

Alan motioned to his secretary that he would be leaving momentarily for the conference meeting as soon as he finished his phone call with Priscilla. "Honey, I'm sorry, but this merger is top priority right now. I don't have to tell you how important it is to your father."

"It's fine, Alan. I have an art gallery showing tomorrow night, and I have plenty of odds and ends to finish up."

"Well, you could be at least slightly upset that we're spending another Friday night apart." Alan spoke in a teasing tone, but he was serious. Priscilla appeared completely unfazed by the fact that they seemed to have little time together, even on weekends. Alan often worked late and had even been spending quite a bit of time doing work at home on Saturdays and Sundays. Once his promotion was in place, and he wasn't trying to gear up for the new position, he hoped his work week would go back to normal. In the meantime, he wanted to put in the hours.

"Maybe Sunday we can go out for an early dinner. How does that sound?"

"If you like."

He could hear her yawning as she hung up and he realized that she was probably tired too. Right after their honeymoon, Priscilla was not allowed to have a paid position, as dictated by the marriage bar. When she had been offered a volunteer position at the Boston Museum of Art, she had immediately accepted. The opportunity to work where her passion rested was an opportunity she had not been able to resist. She didn't need to work at all, but Alan knew she was happy to be in the art world. However, he would miss lunching with her at Hodge's. He would also miss keeping an eye on her during the day.

Hanging up, Alan gathered his things. Lawyers from Phillips & Godfrey would be arriving momentarily and he wanted to be in the conference room to meet them. He would have preferred not to have to meet again with Stephen Wright, but he had to admit that Stephen was excellent at his job.

After the meeting he overheard several of his coworkers congratulate Stephen on the news that he was going to become a father. He and Elizabeth certainly were settling down quickly. He felt a sting of resentment. He had hoped that Priscilla would become pregnant, but nothing had happened so far. Of course, they had only been married a bit over a month, but Priscilla didn't seem particularly interested. He remembered that when several of his friends had gotten married, they had commented on the fact that their wives were nagging them about wanting to have children right away. That certainly wasn't the case with Priscilla.

That evening when he got home he was pleased to see that Priscilla had also just returned home. The fact that they would both have the evening free was a good omen to Alan. Moving quickly to help her remove her coat, he encircled her waist with his hands and turned her around to kiss her.

"Someone's in a romantic mood," Priscilla murmured.

"Yes, I am, and that's just what I want to talk to you about." He clasped her hand in his and propelled her towards the study.

"You want to talk about romance? Can't this wait until after dinner? I'm starving."

"It will just take a minute." Sitting down on the coach he pulled her down next to him. "I think we should start putting some extra effort into having a baby."

"Alan, we just got married!"

"Most people start trying on their honeymoon or right afterwards."

"How would you know what 'most people' do?"

Alan shrugged, not wishing to irritate Priscilla.

Priscilla peered at him. "Next you're going to tell me that Elizabeth Wright is expecting, so we should be too."

Alan stared at her. How did she know that Elizabeth and Stephen were expecting? Or was it a wild guess? "Honey," he cooed, "even if she is, what happens in her life has nothing to do with us."

"I suppose. But she's written some silly little story that got published, and in the write-up in the newspaper she mentioned her 'new family'."

"We're getting off the subject about your getting pregnant. What do you think?"

"Honestly, I haven't even thought of it, Alan. It's just that I love working at the museum, and I don't know if I'm ready to stay home and take care of a baby."

"I'm sure if it happened we could hire a nanny if you wanted one. I just think we could at least start trying. Sometimes it can take longer than you think."

"And sometimes it can happen right away," Priscilla retorted, her hands on her hips. "With my luck, that would be what would happen with me. Can you stop harping about children?"

"Are you trying to tell me you don't want to have children at all?"

She looked away and he forced her to turn back.

"Priscilla, answer me!"

She crossed her arms and looked deep in thought, as if grappling with the issue. "I think I want to have a child at some point in the future, but when I think about it happening very soon, it makes me feel nervous. I don't know if I'd make a good mother or not."

Alan stepped back, breathing a sigh of relief. He could understand how the prospect could be unsettling. "I'm sure you'll make a wonderful mother, and I'm sure all mothers feel that way at first." Actually Alan had no idea whether all mothers felt that way – in fact he suspected that they didn't – but he wanted Priscilla to feel she was part of the norm.

Priscilla sighed deeply, shrugging her shoulders as if she had admitted defeat. "I suppose you're right. But I can't think about this right now. I've had the longest week and next week will be even busier, right up until the gallery exhibit."

"That's fine. I've got a few deadlines coming up as well."

Priscilla stood. "I'll get changed for dinner."

After she departed, Alan loosened his tie and walked to the mini-bar situated in the corner of the room. He poured himself a glass of scotch. Why did everything have to be such a battle with Priscilla? For a brief moment, Alan wished Priscilla were more like Elizabeth Wright. Elizabeth may not have been a city girl – worldly and sophisticated – but that phase of their lives had already passed, and she was more naturally suited to the role of wife and mother than Priscilla was.

Alan leaned back and swirled the drink in his hands. The fact was that he and Priscilla were married now, and even if she was not over-the-top excited about the idea of motherhood, she had said yes to a baby, which was all he needed to give him hope.

Chapter Sixty - Two

Elizabeth looked at the smiling waitress. "I'll have a glass of white wine."

"Are you sure you want one along with the bottle of champagne I'm about to order?" Paul asked, grinning.

"Uncle Paul! You're being gracious enough to treat Stephen and me to dinner. You don't have to go over the top."

"It's my pleasure! After all, I wanted to celebrate your new life as newlyweds and parents-to-be. Cheers!" Paul clinked his water glass with Stephen's and Elizabeth's in lieu of the forthcoming bottle of bubbly.

As Elizabeth sipped her water, she wished that Grandpa had been able to join them. They had invited him, but he had said he was tired and was going to bed early. She was glad he had retired now. He probably should have retired a few years ago. At least now he could sleep in whenever he wanted and have all day to get chores done.

Paul and Stephen were discussing business. During a pause, Paul turned to her and asked, "Have you talked to Dolly?" His tone sounded casual, but Elizabeth could see intensity in his eyes.

"No. I did call last week, but she wasn't home."

"Is she still mulling over Arthur's proposal?"

"She must be. To be honest, she's been very quiet about it, which is not like Dolly."

"Maybe she's holding out for another offer?" Stephen asked, stealing a sideways glance at Paul.

Paul caught his look. "If that's a veiled suggestion, I'm afraid I don't qualify as a potential candidate."

"And why would that be? From what I could glean, Dolly seemed to think you had potential."

Paul said nothing.

Elizabeth put her water glass down and leaned toward her uncle. "Is it your age difference? It seems to me, Uncle Paul, that maybe you're the only one who thinks that might be an issue. Dolly doesn't. I don't. Margret Sullivan doesn't – she's said as much to me. In fact, I can't think of anyone who doesn't think you two are pretty special together. But what do I know? I'm just your niece."

Paul gave Elizabeth a small smile. "Well, Niece, you seem to know all about this. And you have been known to give good advice – that's happened before as I recall." He gave Stephen a wink then picked up his menu. "Now, what should we order?"

~

On their way out of the restaurant Paul turned to them. "By the way, I forgot to tell you that I have some neighbors that you know."

Elizabeth pressed forward. "Who?"

"The new Mr. and Mrs. Bates."

Stephen laughed. "As the saying goes, there goes the neighborhood!"

"I'm sure they're saying the same thing about me," Paul replied.

Elizabeth grimaced. "Paul, do you mind?"

Paul shrugged. "Personally, it doesn't matter to me. I don't interact with them, although I've got a big chip on my shoulder after the way he treated my niece. He'd better never say something derogatory in front of me."

Stephen said, "You're not the only one who's nursing a grudge. Phil Lawrence feels the same way after Alan tried to take credit for one of his proposals. Alan's a slick guy, but if he ever has a misstep, Phil's going to take full advantage." He turned toward Elizabeth. "Too bad you won't be around for the fireworks, darling."

"Don't worry," Paul said. "If there are any fireworks – at Phillips and Godfrey or in Louisburg Square – you'll be able to see them all the way from Boston to Dorchester, Lower Mills!"

Part IV

Chapter Sixty - Three

Fall was a wonderful season. For the first time, Elizabeth was happy to be retired from work, and she was doubly happy that Grandpa was at home. The two of them had settled into a leisurely routine. Grandpa no longer had to rise at dawn, and after relaxing over the newspaper he usually spent mornings outdoors while Elizabeth did chores. If the weather was good, they ate lunch outside. Afternoons, Grandpa invariably visited some of his retired card-playing cronies while Elizabeth worked on a baby's blanket she was knitting.

She also spent time putting the finishing touches on her novel.

One fall afternoon Stephen walked in and Elizabeth held out a large manuscript. "It's finished," she beamed.

Dropping his briefcase on the floor, Stephen picked her up and whirled her around. "You really finished your book?"

"Yes, and you know what, Stephen? I don't even care if it gets published. I'm just excited that I actually finished it."

"I think it's the best book ever written!"

She laughed. "You haven't even seen the final copy! And while I appreciate your unbiased opinion, I can think of more than a few authors – Dickens right off the top of my head – who are contenders for having written the best book."

"The only advantage Dickens has on you is that he's written more books, but I'm sure you'll catch up soon."

"You just don't give up, do you?"

"Not where my lovely wife is concerned." Stephen leaned down to give her a long kiss. The front doorknob rattled, startling them, and they broke apart. There stood Paul.

He glanced from Elizabeth to Stephen. "Sorry to interrupt."

"No problem, Paul. I was just congratulating my wife on finishing her book."

"Elizabeth, that's wonderful. I'm so proud of you."

"We're glad you showed up, Paul," Stephen said, "because tonight we are celebrating. And on Monday I'm going to get copies printed at work. There's no time to waste!"

Paul lifted his hand in a mock toast. "Here's to the next best-selling author!"

~

Elizabeth mailed copies of her manuscript off to publishers the day before they were to leave for Maine for the Columbus Day holiday. She was glad to travel to York; it was a welcome distraction. They traveled on Saturday morning, and as they drove up they could see figures on the Sullivan's front porch, including Aunt May.

Paul parked in the gravel driveway and they walked over.

Elizabeth noticed Margaret sitting in the corner of the porch. Grandpa approached her. "Everything okay, Margaret?"

Charles Sullivan answered for his wife. "She's fine, but with Mary Francis expecting and Dolly considering a proposal of marriage, it's a little bit much at times."

Margaret stood. "I've said for years that I couldn't wait until the children grew up and were on their own, but now that it's happening, I don't know if I'm too happy about it. Before I know it, they'll be no one left at home."

At that moment Charlie ran up to her and chirped, "Don't worry, Mama. I promise I'll never leave home."

Grandpa chuckled. "If you change your mind and do leave when you grow up, Charlie, I'm sure your mother won't hold it against you."

The group laughed.

Margaret suggested a picnic at Long Sands Beach, since bright sunshine was the order of the day. After gathering provisions, they descended the grassy slope to the shore, shed their shoes, and spread blankets. They set out baskets containing sandwiches and cookies and thermoses of lemonade and iced tea.

Robert, Stephen, and Paul began a football game. Charlie, under the watchful eye of his father, worked on building an intricate castle, complete with moat and gully. Aunt May and Margaret Sullivan settled themselves under umbrellas, and Dolly sat beside them, keenly watching the men and their game. Elizabeth and Mary Francis walked to the water's edge.

The two women chatted amicably then paused to take in the view. After a few minutes Mary Francis turned to face Elizabeth.

"Elizabeth, do you think the fact that we're both married and expecting is putting pressure on Dolly to tie the knot?"

Elizabeth sighed. "Possibly. Dolly's always been so competitive about romance. I think she always thought she'd be the first of us to walk down the aisle. What answer do you think she is going to give to Arthur? It's been weeks, and she's still stringing him along."

"I would have thought that would be an easy question to answer, but I think she's torn. Of course she's crazy about Paul, but he's so adamant that their age is an issue that I think Dolly's thinking it's not meant to be."

Elizabeth nodded. "Arthur seems nice, but somehow I can't imagine Dolly marrying him. He's certainly smitten with her, but I don't think Dolly has the same feelings for Arthur that she has for my uncle."

"True. But she probably thinks that since Paul won't court her, she needs to fall in love with someone else."

"Can't you talk to her?"

"I tried, but she always says she's busy and leaves the room."

"Maybe I'll talk to her if I have a chance."

~

The following afternoon the Boston crowd walked over to the Sullivan's. The entire family was there, including Father Joe, who had come for Sunday dinner. Arthur was also present and stood hand-in-hand with Dolly.

Dolly was welcoming to everyone, and she paid Paul no more attention than the others. Arthur chatted with the group, and when Dolly turned to Paul to ask a question, he abruptly walked away. Dolly looked crestfallen.

If Paul refused to commit, Elizabeth thought, he couldn't blame Dolly for wanting to marry someone else.

When everyone sat down to the mid-day meal, Dolly sat across from Paul, with Arthur to her right. Dolly leaned toward Paul. "How is your new apartment?"

Paul avoided Dolly's eyes. "Fine."

Elizabeth watched Dolly bite her lip and look down at her plate. She picked at her food, but when Arthur addressed her, she turned to him with a bright smile. Clearly, Elizabeth thought, Dolly was torn between getting married to Arthur and waiting for Paul.

After dinner, Stephen suggested a football game, to which all the men agreed.

"I'm going to be the quarterback!" Charlie announced.

"You've got it!" his dad said with a smile.

The men strolled outside while Mary Francis, Elizabeth, and Dolly cleared the table and Margaret and Aunt May departed to the kitchen.

Elizabeth lightly touched Dolly's arm. "Dolly, you know I like to mind my own business, but it's clear to everyone that you're still crazy about my uncle. Why don't you at least tell Arthur that you can't say yes to him right now? That's what I told Stephen last summer when he asked me to marry him."

Dolly's face lit up. "Elizabeth, I'd forgotten about that! You're right. I don't have to say yes or no."

Mary Francis went to her sister's side. "And maybe you should talk to Paul. I know he's been playing it cool, but maybe it's a good thing that he's seeing you with someone else. It's certainly affected him. Maybe he realizes that he could lose you."

Dolly bit her lip. "Arthur is leaving soon. Maybe I could ask Paul if we could go for a walk before all of you leave."

Elizabeth clapped her hands. "Perfect!"

When the dishes were done, the women stood outside and Arthur walked to where Dolly and Elizabeth were standing. He took Dolly's hand. "I have to leave. I told my mother I would go to the family cookout for a while. Would you like to come with me?"

"Thank you for the offer, but I told Mother I would watch Charlie for her."

Clearly it was a fib, but Elizabeth knew that Dolly wouldn't miss her opportunity to talk to Paul.

"Of course! I'll call you later." As Arthur leaned forward to kiss Dolly, she turned her head sideways, receiving his kiss on her cheek. Arthur didn't seem to notice the maneuver and he whistled as he walked out the door.

Elizabeth moved to join Stephen, who was standing with Father Joe and Paul.

Father Joe was watching his younger sister with unconcealed amusement. "Stephen, do you still think Dolly and Arthur aren't going to get hitched?"

"I stand by my statement until I hear wedding bells ring – and that's when they're leaving the church, not when they're going in."

Father Joe winked at Paul. "Oh, ye of little faith."

Stephen grinned. "I'm just a man of reality. However, I will make a deal with you. If I'm wrong, and those two tie the knot, I'll double the largest donation you receive in the church collection the following Sunday."

"That sounds like a worthy deal," Paul added. "What do you say, Father?"

"I never turn down a contribution that's given in the name of the Lord," Father Joe replied formally, but with a hint of glee in his voice.

Father Joe left whistling *I'm Getting Married in the Morning*, while Stephen and Paul shook their heads after him.

Elizabeth smiled.

"What do you think, Paul? Did I make a good bet?" Stephen asked.

"I couldn't say."

"I think you could say, since you just might be able to influence the outcome."

Paul gave Stephen a bemused smile then walked toward the field, snatching the football on his way.

Stephen leaned towards Elizabeth. "Do you mind if we leave a little early? There's no cause for alarm, but I think Grandpa is tired."

Elizabeth looked at Grandpa, who was seated on a lawn chair and was nodding his head. "Of course. I think we're going to serve dessert shortly and then we can pack up."

Elizabeth went to retrieve the jacket she'd left on the lawn. She watched as Paul stood near to where she'd dropped it. At that moment Dolly dashed up and tapped Paul on the arm.

"Paul, could I go for a quick walk with you before you leave?"

Paul turned and glared at Dolly. "Are you asking me to go for a walk without your fiancé present?"

"He's not my fiancé!"

"You mean you said 'no' to his proposal?"

"No, I didn't."

His voice hardened. "Then you said 'yes'?"

"I didn't say anything to him yet." She hesitated. "I was hoping I might receive another offer."

Paul looked at the sky. "You know that's not possible."

"Then why do you seem so upset that someone else is interested?"

"I didn't think you would jump to someone else so easily."

Hands on her hips, Dolly stamped her foot. "I wasn't looking for anyone else. He made the offer and I didn't see anyone else putting in much effort!"

"You could just say 'no'!"

"Or I could just say 'yes'!"

Elizabeth could see tears spring to Dolly's eyes. Dolly turned and ran to the house. Elizabeth followed slowly, keeping her head down so Paul wouldn't think she had been nosy.

When Elizabeth got to the kitchen, Mary Francis walked over and whispered in her ear.

"I don't know what happened, but Dolly flew up the stairs in tears and Paul looks like he wants to explode."

Elizabeth whispered back. "Let's just say that their conversation didn't go well. I'm sorry, but we have to leave. Grandpa needs to get to bed at a decent hour."

"Okay. I'll check on Dolly later and see how she's doing."

Chapter Sixty - Four

"Honey, I'm home!" Alan walked through the entryway of their property in Louisburg Square. The living quarters were everything Alan had ever dreamed of. The brick-front two-bedroom townhouse, accessed by cobblestone sidewalks, was in the oldest and most exclusive neighborhood in Boston. A marble foyer graced the entrance and large bay windows in the expansive front drawing room overlooked the picturesque park in the middle of the square.

"I'm in the study," Priscilla shouted.

Alan walked in and found her looking at curtains with a decorator.

She looked up and gave him a smile. "We won't be much longer, darling. I think I've decided what style would look good in here."

He gave her a quick kiss on the cheek. "Great. While you're finishing up, I think I'll run back out and pick up a newspaper."

He let himself out the front door and turned left on the sidewalk. There he saw a man, three buildings down, checking his mailbox. His features looked familiar and Alan realized with a start that the man was Paul Keene. Alan drew in his breath. Did Elizabeth Wright's uncle live here?

Because he couldn't easily avoid him, Alan put on a smile. "Hello, Paul."

Paul looked at him, his eyes narrowing as he realized who he was. He nodded his head slightly. "Alan." Paul peered at him.

"I didn't realize that we are neighbors. My wife and I just moved in last month. We're in the brownstone on the corner."

"I see." Paul turned abruptly toward his door.

Alan watched him go in, then strode on. He shouldn't have expected anything else from a man whose niece he had unceremoniously dumped.

When he returned home, the decorator was gone.

Priscilla saw Alan and her face brightened. "They can start making the curtains next week and they should be done by the end of the month.

Isn't that wonderful?"

"Indeed it is. By the way, guess who one of our neighbors is?"

Hands on her hips, Priscilla threw him an exasperated look. "How in the world would I know? Just tell me. I hate guessing games."

"Okay. It's Paul Keene, Elizabeth Keene – I mean Elizabeth Wright's – uncle."

For a moment Alan wondered if he should have said anything. After all, Priscilla never reacted well to Elizabeth's name.

She rolled her eyes. "Who cares? From what I've heard he's just a boring old bachelor. Let's just hope his niece never visits. We don't need her kind around here!"

"Her kind? What does that mean?" Alan studied his wife's face.

"Oh, you know." Priscilla flipped her hair from her shoulders. "So...so...middle class."

Alan thought back to his own upbringing. He said nothing.

Priscilla shrugged. "Let's eat."

Alan escorted Priscilla into the dining room. He pulled out her chair for her before he took his own seat. The maid filled up their water glasses and Priscilla placed her napkin neatly on her lap. "Since you brought Paul up, I have a tidbit of gossip Janine had when she called the other day. Paul was at Hodge's the other day and Janine overheard him telling an office manager that he was renovating his parent's 'mansion', although it might be bought by a family member. Do you suppose he was referring to the new Mr. and Mrs. Wright? And, if so, where would they get that kind of money to buy such a place?"

"I also heard that through the work grapevine. I have heard it's rather a stately place on Adams Street. I'm guessing if they do buy it that Paul would sell it to them at a deal."

"True. Well, it may be a mansion, but I certainly wouldn't trade our townhouse in the hub of Boston for some oversized house in the suburbs. I think I'd die of boredom!" Priscilla toyed with her fork. "I should have guessed that she's getting some kind of break from a relative. Although you would never know that any of her relatives came from money, the way she dresses and wears her hair."

"Actually, I thought she looked much better when we saw her at the July Fourth concert."

Priscilla raised her eyebrows. "I didn't think you noticed her."

Alan groaned inwardly. He should have known better than to say anything semi-complimentary about Elizabeth.

"Darling, it was just a casual observation. I've told you before, she couldn't hold a candle to your looks and style."

"I might accuse you of having a wandering eye if she was anything to look at. But she's not. Therefore, I'm willing to accept an apology from you."

Alan didn't think he needed to apologize, especially since Priscilla's flirtations were certainly more egregious than just looking at members of the opposite sex, but he decided to let it go. It would only result in a heated argument.

"I'm sorry, darling," he said and looked away.

"Apology accepted."

Chapter Sixty - Five

Stephen walked in and placed an envelope on the kitchen table. "Did someone forget to check the mail today?"

Elizabeth picked up the envelope and read the return address. *New England Press Company.* "I can't believe I've gotten a reply so quickly," she cried.

"I'll get a letter opener for you," Stephen offered, but he was too late.

Elizabeth was already tearing open the envelope and removing the enclosed stationary.

October 15, 1946
Dear Mrs. Wright,
Thank you for submitting your manuscript to us for review. While your theme was original, and we enjoyed your literary style, we are not looking for books of this genre to print at this time. Thank you for considering our company in your search for a publisher. Good luck in your venture.
Yours Truly,
Richard C. Barrows
New England Press Company

Stephen looked at her somber face. "Disappointed?"

"A little. Oh, all right. More than a little – a lot. But if they had agreed to publish it, I'd probably be the first writer in the history of the literary world to have their book published on the first try. I'm just going to have to develop a thick skin and learn to be patient."

"That book will be published, you'll see. Even if the other two publishing companies don't come through, we'll just keep trying until we find one. And if no one's smart enough to recognize a good book when they read one, then we'll just publish it ourselves!"

Elizabeth smiled. "And how would we do that? Make copies at Phillips and Godfrey and hawk them on the street corner? You're sweet, Stephen, but let's keep our hopes up that a publishing house takes it."

Elizabeth knew she would need to maintain an optimistic viewpoint, but that seemed hard when two days later she received a second rejection. This one was even briefer and more to the point.

She crumpled up the letter and threw it into the wastebasket. "I wouldn't let them publish my book even if they begged me. At least the first company appreciated my 'literary style!'"

"That's the spirit! They'll be kicking themselves when they see your book on the best-seller list because another company was smarter than they were."

~

A week later she was preparing supper when she realized she had forgotten to check the mail. She turned her chicken stock down to low and walked quickly down the walkway.

It looked as if there were only a few pieces of junk mail, but then the return address of one envelope caught her eye: Groton & Leeton. She tore open the envelope. She couldn't believe her eyes. She was staring at an acceptance letter with a check enclosed for an advance. Her book was going to be published!

Stephen and Grandpa were going to be so excited when they heard the good news. She rushed up the walk and yanked open the front door. She felt like the luckiest girl in the world! She was happily married to the most wonderful guy on earth, they were expecting a baby, and now her lifelong dream of publishing a novel was coming true!

She raced through the house, calling for her grandpa. She glanced out the kitchen window and spotted him in the back yard. He was sitting on a rusty lawn chair that he refused to throw out, even though Elizabeth often joked with him that he would wind up sitting on the ground one day because the chair would give way. It was good enough for the few times he used it, he'd say, and there he sat now.

In spite of the uncomfortable chair, he was dozing. As she approached, she noticed that a copy of her manuscript was open on his lap.

Reading had never been one of his strengths, as he had left school at the age of fourteen to work on the family farm in Ireland. However, he expressed determination to read Elizabeth's book.

Elizabeth approached and then stopped short. With a sudden stillness of her heart she realized that he would never find out how the fictional little boy who came from the shores of Ireland had fared in America, for it was not a nap he was enjoying in the middle of a warm October afternoon, but the sleep of eternal peace.

How long she stayed with her head on his lap sobbing, Elizabeth was not sure. She heard Stephen calling and knew that he was home.

She lifted her tear-stained face as he approached and she knew that without saying a word, Stephen knew what had happened.

~

Dr. Tinsdale arrived soon after Stephen called him.

"He must have had a heart attack while reading. It looks like he died instantly." He looked from Elizabeth to Stephen. "I'm very sorry."

Stephen walked with her into the house and sat with her on the couch in the parlor. He dialed Aunt May and handed the phone to Elizabeth.

When she heard Aunt May's cheery voice on the other end, her voice broke. Unable to speak, she handed the phone back to Stephen.

Stephen spoke quietly, then told Elizabeth that Aunt May would arrive on Thursday with the Sullivans.

Harry was home when Stephen called to tell him the news, and he said he would be over immediately. Stephen then called Paul's office, leaving a message with his secretary for Paul to call as soon as possible.

Harry arrived just as the hearse was leaving. Stephen showed him into the parlor. Removing his soft-brimmed hat, he slowly approached her.

"I'm very sorry, Elizabeth. I don't want to bother you. I just came over to offer my condolences and tell you to call me if you need anything. The finest of friends he was, I'll tell ye. I couldn'ta asked for a better one."

"Thank you, Harry," Elizabeth quietly responded through tears.

Putting on his hat, he shuffled out the front door, the loneliness of a long friendship ended undoubtedly beginning to sink in.

Paul finally called, and he was very much grieved at the news. He told Elizabeth he would come over that evening.

"It's a tremendous loss, Elizabeth. He was a mother and a father to you, and I was also blessed to be able to receive a little bit of that myself. I'll never forget everything he did for me."

~

Grandpa was waked in the front parlor on Thursday afternoon and Elizabeth felt comforted by the many friends and relatives who came to pay their respects.

When Aunt May arrived with the Sullivans, Elizabeth fell into her arms.

"I know dear," said Aunt May. "I always hoped I'd go before your grandfather so I wouldn't be the one left to cry, but we have to take comfort in the fact that it was best for him to go that way. You know he wouldn't have been one who would have wanted a long illness or to be bedridden."

Elizabeth nodded, trying to stifle sobs. She had never known what it was like not to have him around every day – looking out for her, caring for her. She looked around. It was heartwarming to see so many people there. Betty and Phil and Maura had come. Even Lillian Graham came. Of course Fred and Harry were present.

It was deeply touching to see the many lives John Burke had touched during his lifetime. He had always had a great love of people and he had been personally responsible for helping many of the families in their neighborhood – Polish, Irish, French, Italian – start their new lives in America by letting them stay in his home when they had first arrived or by helping them find a job.

Some of those her grandparents had helped came, including several who had been children when they immigrated. Most Elizabeth had never met, but they each had a story of how her grandparents had lent them an extra bedroom, shared meals, or given them money in return for a household repair.

Paul stood next to Elizabeth as people stood in a line to offer their condolences. When the Sullivans turn came, Paul gave Dolly a quick peck on the cheek before turning to talk to Mary Francis and Robert.

Elizabeth could see the disappointment on Dolly's face. She tried to cheer her up a bit. "Dolly, I'm so glad you came. And your dress looks lovely."

Dolly's attention was still focused on Paul, but the line was backing up.

For the remainder of the wake, Elizabeth noticed that Paul always seemed to be on the opposite side of the room from Dolly. The tension between the two of them was obvious and she wondered how it would end. She knew that Dolly still hadn't given Arthur an answer.

~

At ten o'clock on Saturday morning the service began for the man who had never missed a Sunday Mass his entire life, regardless of whatever troubles or difficulties prevailed.

They laid John Burke to rest beside his long-departed wife, Rose, in Old Calvary Cemetery in Hyde Park. Dappled sunshine shone through the spreading oak trees, which was a sharp contrast to the mood of the day. Closing prayers were said at the graveside.

After the final prayers at the gravesite, officiated by Father Joe, Elizabeth lingered, kneeling in prayer for a few moments. As she rose, she felt a hand on her shoulder and looked up to see Harry, his eyes brimming with tears.

He held out a bouquet of crème-colored silk roses.

"I wish we could leave some of John's roses with him, but they're long past their bloom. I thought these might do until we can bring some in the spring."

Elizabeth threw her arms around Harry's neck. "Harry, you are the most thoughtful, caring friend. I can't thank you enough."

Harry wiped his eyes and his voice broke as he answered her. "It's the least I could do for my best friend."

Elizabeth gently placed several roses on top of the casket. Then she placed the rest on top of Grandma Rose's grave. Her grandparents' roses. Roses are perfect for funerals, she thought. Or for weddings. Roses were for love.

Chapter Sixty - Six

One evening toward the end of October, Alan arrived home to find Priscilla fashionably dressed and applying makeup.

"Are we having a special dinner tonight?" Alan murmured as he brushed his lips against the side of her neck while she sat at her dressing table.

"I'm sorry, darling. I'm meeting the girls for a bite to eat down the street."

Alan frowned. "You're going out on a weeknight – and without your husband?"

"For goodness sake! I've spent every spare minute since our honeymoon trying to organize this place and I'm going stir crazy! Surely you don't think I'm going to just stay home every night for the rest of my life?"

"No, but I did think we would go out as a couple. We are married, you know."

Priscilla applied mascara, seemingly unperturbed by the fact that Alan was unhappy. "Obviously we'll be doing something on the weekend, but Alan, I just cannot sit around every weeknight while you do office work."

"Every weeknight? Are you trying to tell me that you plan on going out every weeknight?"

Alan could hear his voice rising and he didn't care. He wanted Priscilla to know in no uncertain terms that he was not going to stand for it.

Priscilla turned towards him, her eyes snapping. "I don't think I'll be out every night, but when I do go out with friends, I certainly wasn't planning on asking your permission first!"

"Then maybe I'll start making plans of my own." Alan hoped this would shake up Priscilla, but it seemed to have no effect on her.

"I hardly think that will happen, Alan. You've got a date with your briefcase every night."

Alan leaned closer to Priscilla "Do any of your 'friends' happen to be of the male gender?"

Priscilla stood up and faced Alan, her hands on her hips. "I don't like what you're insinuating, Alan. Janine will be there tonight and you can ask her in the morning if you feel the need to check up on me."

Alan was upset. He had lost the upper hand in their argument. It angered him that Priscilla disregarded his feelings about what kind of lifestyle they should have.

"Can't you ever find something at home to do?"

"Like what? The staff takes care of all the cooking and cleaning!"

"Then find a hobby – like knitting, or reading, or drawing."

Priscilla rolled her eyes. "I don't think I have to point out the fact that those things are not my idea of a good time.

"Look," she said, "I've already promised them I'd go out. I suppose I could just go out for a short time and be home in a couple of hours, but I'm not reading a book!"

"That's fine. Maybe we can turn in early – it's been a while, you know." Alan rose from his chair as he spoke.

Priscilla walked abreast of him, turned, and kissed him lightly on the lips.

"Look, I'll be home early, and I'll put on something more…intimate."

Alan's irritation evaporated. Perhaps he was overreacting. After all, he knew what a social creature she was. Surely there would be no harm if she went out while he worked on business. He couldn't just expect her to sit by his side while he was preoccupied with the merger. And he couldn't blame her for being bored at home when everything was taken care of. Still, something nagged at him.

Was she trying to limit their moments together in order to reduce her chances of becoming pregnant? Half the time when he made advances Priscilla pled a headache or tiredness. Was Priscilla making sure that they would not be intimate during the times of the month that she was fertile? Did her 'headaches' and 'tiredness' coincide with those dates? Well, like it or not, no matter what her physical condition, he was going to start insisting on his marital rights. She was his wife and he planned on taking advantage of opportunity – starting that night.

~

Nine, ten, eleven – the twelfth stroke of midnight chimed as Alan lay in bed, listening to the grandfather clock in the downstairs hall.

He had never been angrier with Priscilla. She had known how reluctant he had been to have her go out; she had promised to be home early, yet here it was after midnight and she had not returned. He rose and walked to the window. There was not a single sign of life on the tree-lined street. Anyone who had half a brain was already in bed on a weeknight.

He sat in the wing-backed chair in the corner. At last he heard a car pull to the curb. He strode to the window and saw Priscilla park her black Lincoln Continental. The front left tire climbed over the curb and the car came to rest diagonally between two other cars. He could only imagine how many glasses of wine she had imbibed.

He grabbed his dressing robe, pushed his arms into it, and tied the belt as he hurried down the staircase. As he fiddled with the front door lock, he decided that no matter how drunk she was, he was going to give her a piece of his mind.

Throwing open the door, he stepped outside. To his horror, he saw Paul Keene helping Priscilla, as she swayed next to her car. Damn! Of all people, why did Paul Keene have to appear at just that moment?

He stifled the words that were on his lips and descended the stairs. "Hey, Paul. Hello, darling!"

Priscilla slurred, "Alan, what are you doing up? You're never up this late."

"Just waiting for you, dear." He took hold of the arm that Paul was not holding and addressed Paul. "Those girls' nights out can be really lively."

"Todd was there too," Priscilla giggled, "so I guess it wasn't only girls!"

Alan clenched his teeth. He should have realized that Todd would somehow be part of the evening. They were going to have a serious discussion about Priscilla's social life, but for now it was crucial to put up a good appearance.

"That Todd, what a great guy. How nice of him to stop by. Watch your step, Priscilla."

Priscilla would have fallen if not for the two men propping her up. She reeked of alcohol. He was embarrassed to have Paul see her in such a condition. When they reached the doorway, Alan swallowed his pride. "Thanks for your help, Paul."

"You're welcome. Goodnight."

Alan imagined the smirk that must have crossed Paul's face as soon as he turned away. In spite of that Alan was probably fortunate that someone else hadn't seen Priscilla drunk, like Betty or Phil. At least Paul didn't seem like a gossip. He was certain, however, that Elizabeth and Stephen would hear about this. He cringed.

As soon as the door closed, Priscilla said, "I don't think I feel well, Alan."

"That's hardly a surprise, considering you've spent the whole evening drinking." He steered her towards the bathroom just in time for her to empty the contents of her stomach. He helped her up the stairs and to their bedroom and plopped her on the bed, putting the coverlet over her. She was asleep in moments. The conversation he wanted to have with her would have to wait.

~

At lunch the next day he called home. Her voice sounded weak when she answered. "Hello, Alan."

"Feeling better?"

"Almost. I can't believe how much I drank last night."

"At least you know you went a bit overboard."

"I don't think I would have drunk so much if it hadn't been so long since I'd been out."

Alan was incredulous. "Are you trying to say that you need to go out more often?"

"If I knew I was going out at least once or twice a week, I wouldn't have so much when I do go out."

Alan groaned. Why was Priscilla so difficult? Every situation was an argument with her.

"Fine. Go out once a week then, but you're going to have a curfew, a limit to the number of drinks you have, and no more having Todd stop by."

"Alan, I didn't even know he would be there. One of the other girls invited him."

"Maybe so, but you are probably the reason he showed up."

"Alan, Todd is not interested in me."

"Maybe that's what you think, but I'm a man and I know what makes a man tick – and believe me, a blonde, pretty socialite will make a man's night anytime."

"You're being ridiculous!"

"And you're being irresponsible!"

Priscilla slammed down the phone.

Alan put the phone down on his end and rubbed his ear. He would have to remember to hold the phone at a distance if they were having a disagreement. It would save not only his eardrum, but his mood.

Chapter Sixty - Seven

Elizabeth and Stephen settled into life without the familiar presence of Grandpa. One night in mid-November they were sitting in the parlor, performing the painstaking task of sorting through the sympathy cards that had been sent, when the telephone rang.

Elizabeth got up. When she picked up, she heard Mary Francis's voice. "Elizabeth, I promised Dolly I wouldn't tell you, but I just have to. She's accepted Arthur's proposal."

"What? How could she?" Elizabeth lowered her voice. "Clearly, she doesn't have the same feelings for Arthur as she does for Paul."

"I know, but I guess she's thinking that since Paul won't budge, she might as well choose Arthur. Maybe you can say something to her. Dolly said she was going to call and tell you the news, but I thought I'd give you the background on it first. I'm going to tell her that you called and I'll put her on the phone..."

Elizabeth could hear Mary Francis calling Dolly.

In a minute, she heard Dolly's voice. "Elizabeth, I'm so excited you called! I have some big news. I've accepted Arthur's proposal."

Elizabeth tried to sound happy. "Congratulations. You sound very happy." Elizabeth paused. "Are you sure it's the right decision?"

Dolly groaned. "For goodness sake! I'm so tired of everyone asking me that. I wouldn't have said yes if I didn't want to. Arthur is the same age as I am and we get along really well."

"Do you love him?"

Dolly seemed to swallow and then plowed on. "Of course. By the way, Mary Francis will be a matron of honor, but I want you in the wedding too. Would you be a second matron of honor?"

"I would love to."

"Good. I was sure you'd say yes. I have to go now. I'm going out with Arthur. Bye."

Elizabeth returned to the living room where Stephen was still seated. "Who was on the phone?" he asked.

"Dolly. She's accepted Arthur's marriage proposal."

"Wow. Is she sure that's what she wants?"

"She may think it's what she wants, but 'happily ever after' may not be what follows. Do you think I should tell Paul?"

"Probably. Actually, he's coming here next Saturday for some legal advice regarding his parents' house. You can talk to him then. Meanwhile, there's a topic I'd like to discuss with you. I thought that since we'll be starting a new phase of our life with the baby, it might be worth thinking about finding a place of our own to live."

"But this is our own place."

"You're right, but we did always say we'd choose our own house someday. I think it might be a good time to think about moving, especially before the baby comes." He paused. "I also came across an opportunity that is too good to pass up."

Elizabeth couldn't disguise her disappointment. "What's wrong with this place? I know it needs some work, but it could look nice when we're done."

Stephen moved closer to Elizabeth and took her hand in his. "Darling, I know that not only is this the only home you've ever had, it was both your mother's and your grandparents' home. Moving would be a big change for you, but in the long run, I think it will be for the best. It's time to start a new life, just as your mother did when she married your father and as your grandfather did when he moved to another country. Does that make sense?"

Elizabeth looked at Stephen, seeing the love in his eyes. "Maybe. It's just so hard to let go."

"It is, and it will take time, but in the long run, I think you'll be happier."

"Where is this 'opportunity' you have in mind?"

"I think it would be better if I showed you instead of told you. It's too late tonight, but I can leave work a little early tomorrow, and I'll drive you over to have a look. What do you think?"

"I suppose so. But can't you tell me where it is?"

He shook his head. "Nope. I think it would be better as a surprise."

~

Stephen picked Elizabeth up at the house before dark. They rumbled up Adams Street, past Baker's Chocolate Factory, and drove by the Ashmont train station, where the afternoon throng of people appeared.

Apparently, Elizabeth thought, the house was in Milton.

As they reached the crest of the hill and the road flattened out, Elizabeth looked ahead to her grandparents' house on the left. Had Steven found a spot near her grandparent's house? She hadn't been by in ages. She knew Paul had been struggling to maintain it. The house appeared forlorn and deserted in the fading light. The barren shrubbery on the front lawn was unkempt and only added to the air of desolation.

Elizabeth was astounded when they turned into the driveway.

Stephen alighted from the car. As he walked around to open her door, she looked up at him with an expression of shock. "Stephen, do you think it would be possible?" Her mind churned. "If we did, I could care for the rose bushes here, but would Grandfather sell it to us?"

Stephen laughed. "The first thing you think of is the rose bushes?" He planted a kiss on the top of her head. "Actually, it's Paul's house now. If you recall, your grandfather gave it to him after your grandmother died. And he's more than willing to sell it to us."

Stephen walked toward the front door and then turned around. Elizabeth stood by the car, taking in the peeling paint, the cracked asphalt, and the lopsided shutters. "Stephen, I would love to have a house like this, but it needs so much work. Even more than our current home!"

Stephen placed his hands on her shoulders. "I know, but I think we could do it. The design and detail of the house is truly exquisite and they certainly don't build 'em like this anymore. When it's renovated, it will be a magnificent mansion – which it surely must have been when it was new." He reached down to grasp her hand and pulled her behind him. "Why don't we just take a look inside before it gets dark?"

He turned the key in the lock and pushed the creaking door open. They stepped into the shadowy hall that had a damp, musty smell. Even at a quick glance, Elizabeth could see that everything appeared as she remembered it. All the furniture, wall hangings, and rugs were in the same places. The furniture was now shrouded in dust covers, but that seemed the only change. She shivered, whether it was from the cold or from the memories the house evoked, she was not sure.

Stephen swept a hand towards the rear of the hall. "Just look at that staircase! You can't find a house with something like that today! Once that mahogany is refinished and the marble on the hallway floor is refurbished, that alone will be a showcase." He pointed upwards. "Have you ever noticed the curios and cupids along the edges? And look at the scrolls on the ceiling. They're especially noticeable in the dining room."

He grabbed Elizabeth's hand. They crossed the hall and entered the dining room to the right. It was too dim to make out more than some darkened shapes, and Elizabeth found it almost spooky. Then Stephen led her to the drawing room on the left side of the house, a room which Elizabeth remembered all too clearly.

There were the stiff horse-hair chairs, opposite her grandmother's parlor chair, where she had been required to sit. There was the familiar butler's cart on which tea and cookies had been served. She half expected her grandmother to come marching in to admonish Fred about some detail that had been overlooked, but the only sound she heard was the cold November wind rattling the windows.

Stephen was pointing out the elaborate carvings. Their crevices were caked with dirt and cobwebs. Their state did not dampen his enthusiasm, however. "Once we have them refurbished, they'll look like new. So will the hardwood floors, once they're redone."

She followed his eyes to the floor. The scraped and worn floorboards were partially covered by her grandmother's worn and dusty Oriental rugs.

Stephen looked amused at her dismayed expression. Turning her around, he walked her across the room to pause at the double doors leading to the study. "I didn't think that having a look around was going to endear you to the place, so I decided that I'd have to rely on more than just your vivid imagination to sell you."

With the tip of his shoe, he brushed aside a small pile of sawdust that was mysteriously lying on the threshold. Pulling down the two long-handled knobs on the double doors, he pushed and stood aside to allow Elizabeth to enter first.

Elizabeth walked a few steps into the room and stopped. The entire room had been restored, its mahogany woodwork varnished and then polished until it gleamed, the walls and ceiling were sanded down and repainted a warm shade of ivory, and the curios and cupids that graced the ceiling had been cleaned and retouched.

All the furniture had been moved out in order to have the floor refinished. The room sparkled. Even the fireplace had been renovated, the Spanish tiles bordering it and the surrounding brick-work scrubbed of soot and ashes until they shone. Stephen flicked a switch on the wall and two polished brass sconces on either side of the fireplace flickered on, flooding the room with light.

"Stephen!" Elizabeth gasped, catching her breath at the transformation. "When did you possibly do all this? How?"

Stephen grinned at her reaction. "Actually, your Uncle Paul was responsible for handling most of it. I've been up to my neck at work. I'm afraid I was only able to contribute my opinion. But I don't want you to think I'm pushing you into a corner just because this room is redone. I made a deal with Paul. If we decide to buy the house, we would of course absorb the cost of renovating this room, but if we don't, Paul is more than willing to pay for it because he can use the room as a sample for potential buyers."

Stephen led Elizabeth to gaze out the French-paned windows. Their woodwork was repainted a soft, ivory tone and the windows were sparkling clean. The sun was rapidly disappearing into the skyline, leaving streaks of orange and red that stretched across the horizon. They stood silently for a moment and gazed beyond the partially hidden yard to the twinkling lights of Boston's skyline.

"Isn't it breathtaking? And this is probably at its worst. Imagine how it looks with a blanket of snow covering it, or in spring with all the roses in bloom."

Elizabeth looked back at the remodeled room, resting her eyes on the new paint and shining floorboards. "I know if we moved in the way it is, I would always have the old memories surrounding me, but having it remodeled would bring new life to it." She looked back into her husband's face that was so full of animation and hope. "Together we'll erase the old memories and start with new ones."

"Oh, darling, I'm so glad you like it!" Stephen wrapped his arms around her waist and kissed her cheek. "I figured we could move in after the holidays. That would give us enough time to have the master bedroom and the baby's room renovated." He looked at Elizabeth and she nodded in approval.

This would be the beginning of their new life together and would be the house that their child – or children – would call home.

Chapter Sixty - Eight

Whether it was divine intervention or pure luck, Alan thanked his lucky stars that the museum's escalated schedule for the holiday season kept Priscilla extremely busy, giving both of them a break from battling. He did worry, though, that when her schedule lightened up, the problem would once again occur. In the meantime, when she came home too tired to do no more than eat and relax with him in the drawing room, he enjoyed their quiet companionship.

They planned on taking the week after Christmas off to stay at the ski lodge that the Hodges owned in Vermont. It seemed as if it would be the climax to their camaraderie they were enjoying and he was looking forward to it.

He was also looking forward to a break from work. Just that morning, Phil had again proved to be a thorn in his side when he made a smart business suggestion.

"All in favor of creating a subcommittee to review individual investment accounts, please raise your hand."

Every staff manager had raised his hand with the exception of Phil. If it had been Alan's idea to vote on increasing their salaries, Phil would still not have voted for it, just out of spite, Alan thought. It had been over a year since Alan had taken credit for the Latin America proposal. For a mild-mannered man, Phil was certainly holding on to his grudge.

After the meeting had adjourned, everyone had quickly dispersed. As Neil and Alan reached Alan's office, Neil let out a whistle.

"That was certainly a cold blast of air in there."

"I take it you're referring to Phil's cold shoulder towards me, and his adamant refusal to support anything I suggest."

"I am." Neil stood aside for Alan to enter the office. He closed the door before speaking. "Alan, it's none of my business, but there's word through the office grapevine that you've somehow slandered Phil's reputation. I'm hoping that's not the case."

Alan shifted his feet. "What have you heard?"

"That you're trying to take some credit for Phil's 'Latin America' idea. Look, I'd rather not be involved, as I happen to like both of you, but if there's anything you need to fix, you should probably do so. Phil's a good guy."

"That's what I like about you, Neil. You always see the good side of people."

"That's what I tell the other guys when they complain about you."

Neil grinned, taking the sting out of it, but Alan could well imagine the truth in his statement.

"I know you like Phil, but he happens to have a different approach from me. However, I appreciate your 'heads up'."

Neil walked out, leaving Alan to his thoughts. For a moment he had felt embarrassed that his actions had reached Neil's ears. He almost regretted his maneuvering of the prior year. Neil, he knew, would never have slandered another employee's character in order to get ahead. But it was too late now. He could not own up to his deceit with Mr. Hodge; his career would be in ruins if he did. The best he could do was not to add any more fuel to the fire. He would leave Phil alone, and that was the best he could do.

Chapter Sixty - Nine

Stephen stood at the kitchen door and gave Elizabeth a nod. She nervously smoothed down her dress and walked out to the hall.

Stephen's nod had meant that he was finished discussing business with Paul and she could tell him about Dolly.

She walked into the parlor. "Paul, could I talk to you for a few minutes?"

"Sure!"

Elizabeth sat down next to him and spoke, her voice soft and gentle. "Dolly called me the other day to tell me she's accepted Arthur's marriage proposal."

Paul's expression hardened. "I see." He rose from his chair, snapped the locks of his briefcase and turned to leave.

Elizabeth jumped up. "Is that all you're going to say?"

Paul turned in her direction. "What else is there to say? Dolly has made her decision."

"Well, I have something to say. I think if you had given her a marriage proposal, it wouldn't have taken her all this time to make up her mind. That should tell you something."

Paul shook his head. "How could I have? It would never work!"

"Says who? You know Dolly has believed with every ounce of her being that the two of you could make it work, and I think you know down deep in your heart that she's right. What else matters?"

Paul sank into the upholstered chair. His voice was tense with emotion. "Do you really think we'd have a chance?"

"I do! I think you're the one who needs to have a little faith."

"What should I do?" he asked, giving a small shrug.

Elizabeth looked him in the eye. "Tell her right now how you feel. Ask her the same question Arthur did. I think you know what Dolly's response will be."

Paul took a deep breath. With some hesitation he said, "I suppose I could go up to York today."

"That's the spirit!"

"Elizabeth, would you go with me?"

"Me? I think in these situations, two's company and three's a crowd."

"I didn't mean that you'd be there when I talk to her. But could you ride up with me for moral support?"

"Of course I'll go. Let me just tell Stephen."

Elizabeth rounded the doorway and bumped into Stephen, who looked suspiciously guilty.

"Sorry. I couldn't help overhearing you two. Of course you can go. I've got a lot of errands to do today anyways."

After grabbing sandwiches, Paul and Elizabeth left for Maine. By mid-afternoon the car was climbing the hilly slope to the Sullivans' drive. The car swung into the dirt driveway by the side of the house. There appeared to be no one around. They walked towards the back of the house and saw Charlie standing in front of the barn. He was working on a contraption that had a rope and a slingshot attached.

Paul asked, "Charlie, where's Dolly?"

Charlie stopped what he was doing and looked up at Paul, registering surprise that they were there. Then he scrunched up his face as he thought about the question. He threw his thumb back over his shoulder, words apparently too much of an effort, probably due to the huge wad of gum in his mouth.

"In the barn?" Elizabeth prompted.

Charlie shook his head and pointed back over his shoulder again. The hill. Of course! Set back behind the barn a little ways, the hill had been a favorite spot of the Sullivan children for sledding or rolling down. In later years, Dolly was still inclined to go there, for beyond the short, steep incline was a small, flat meadow and Dolly could act out her plays there to her heart's content without fear of being interrupted.

"Uncle Paul, she's at the top of the hill behind the house," Elizabeth offered.

"Will you come with me – just until I find her?"

Elizabeth nodded. She trudged up the hill and was out of breath by the time they reached the crest. She looked around and saw Dolly sitting on a tree stump with her back to them. She wore a straw hat with a single blue ribbon around its brim. The ends of the ribbon mingled with the braid that hung down her back.

Paul strode quickly past Elizabeth, his feet silent on the grass. He stood a few feet behind Dolly.

Elizabeth retreated to a nearby tree, hoping that Dolly would not notice her.

"Hello, Dolly."

Dolly started at the sound of Paul's voice, but she remained seated.

Elizabeth watched Paul nervously roll a pebble back and forth beneath the toe of his foot.

"You must be surprised I'm here, especially as our last talk was, well, a disaster. But there's something I need to get off my mind." Paul cleared his throat but Dolly didn't turn around. "I think my rudeness goaded you into saying 'yes' to Arthur. But I want you to understand that I figured that if you were settling for someone else so quickly, then maybe I was just a passing fancy."

Dolly jumped up and turned to face him. "Paul, that was never the case."

Paul moved to her and put his finger to her lips. "Please let me finish. I learned only this morning from Elizabeth that you said 'yes' to Arthur."

At this Paul turned to Elizabeth, seated behind a nearby tree. Elizabeth bowed her head and fingered blades of grass, pretending to be oblivious.

Paul turned back to Dolly. "I was convinced until that moment that things could never work between us. But then my dear niece made me realize that maybe it's not too late. I guess what I'm trying to say is, I love you, Dolly. I think I've loved you from the moment you came waltzing out in your Sunday best with that ridiculous hat on. I just didn't recognize it as love. I thought it was just my male ego responding to the attentions of a young girl. But it's more than that. It's your exuberance for life, the way I feel when I'm around you. I realize now that it's too late, but I'm glad that I was at least able to tell you my true feelings."

He took a step back. "I'm sorry if I've overstepped my bounds."

"Oh, no, no! Please don't think that! Why, those were the most wonderful words ever said to me! It's just that – Oh, Paul! I've been such a fool!"

"Now, Dolly. Whatever it is, I'm sure it can't be as bad as all that."

Elizabeth peeked out from around the tree to see Paul hand Dolly a handkerchief from his breast pocket. "Here. Blow your nose and then tell me all about it."

Paul sat down on the grass and pulled Dolly down next to him. She obediently blew her nose. They both sat a moment. Finally Dolly spoke. "I broke off my engagement with Arthur this morning."

Elizabeth saw Paul's face light up for a moment before discouragement set in. "Maybe it's just a lover's spat. It's only natural when there's so much to do before a wedding."

"No, no. You don't understand! We haven't had a quarrel or an argument. In fact, we haven't had any kind of disagreement at all." Dolly rose and began pacing back and forth. "The fact is, I'm not in love with Arthur and I never have been. But I don't want you or anyone else to think that getting engaged was just another childish prank or game on my part. You see, all my life I've been a hopeless romantic. I've always dreamed of that special person who would make my heart beat faster the moment he walked in a room – someone who would make me feel like the sun was always shining overhead. But everyone kept telling me that I didn't know what I was talking about, that I was too young and immature to understand what love really was.

"And then I made a very big mistake. I started thinking people were right, that what I needed to do was find someone who would make a good companion. So I started seeing Arthur. I figured we had the same interests, the same lifestyle, and we got along well. When he asked me to marry him, I needed time to think, but finally I figured this must be love, so I said 'yes.' But I was just fooling myself. Yesterday I realized that it wouldn't be fair to Arthur or me if we went through with it. I told him earlier today that it was over and I told him why. I told him I had made the awful mistake of confusing love with affection and settling for less than I wanted instead of waiting for the real thing."

She clenched her fist. "I've decided I'll never marry until I blush all the way from my head to my toes when that special someone glances at me or when I feel weak at the knees if he asks me to dance." She lowered her eyes. "I know you think our age difference matters. And that's something I can't change." Then she whispered, "You'd better be going.

I just want to thank you for being honest with me. Even though you can't get past the age difference, it will bring some comfort to me in the days ahead to know that you said you love me."

She sat with her chin up and a gallant look about her, like a soldier who had lost a great battle.

Paul grabbed her shoulders. "I'm not going anywhere and you're not going to say another word until you hear me out! You love me and I love you. I came to tell you that I don't care anymore if I'm over twenty years older than you. You'll keep me young, and I'll try to keep you from getting into too much trouble."

Paul's voice softened as he slipped his hands around her waist. "Honey, look. If this is the only obstacle we have, then we should be deliriously happy for the rest of our lives. Now, hurry up and say you'll marry me so I can kiss you. Or maybe I won't wait for an answer."

Dolly looked stunned but Paul made good on his word and bent down for a long, hard kiss.

Elizabeth decided it was a good time to slip back to the house.

~

Elizabeth grabbed Charlie on her way past the barn and they joined Margaret and Charles on the porch. Father Joe was there as well, having come down to see his parents for the day. Elizabeth gave them quick hugs then ran to her aunt's house to collect her before filling all of them in on why she and Paul were there.

She tried not to give too much away, feeling that Dolly would want to give the details. And of course only Dolly would know if there was an announcement to be made.

It was quite some time before the couple descended the hill, arm in arm. Their faces were beaming so the group knew what the outcome had been.

Margaret Sullivan threw her arms up in the air. "Dorothy Ann Sullivan, I don't know how my heart will survive your life adventures, but you certainly couldn't have picked someone from a finer family. Congratulations!" She rushed over to give Paul a giant hug.

Chapter Seventy

"Happy Thanksgiving, darling!"

Priscilla stirred in bed, her eyes opening in response to Alan's accompanying kiss. "Take your time getting up. I'm leaving now to meet your father and his pals at Harvard Stadium for 'The Game.' I'll meet you at your parents' house for dinner."

Priscilla mumbled a reply.

Alan knew she was tired. They had gone to bed exhausted after each had stayed up finishing work. Alan wouldn't have minded more sleep too, but he wouldn't have missed attending the prestigious Harvard-Yale game for the world. Besides the usual alumni, elected officials and well-known Boston businessmen were sure to be in attendance.

At the stadium Alan sat with Mr. Hodge and a group of his alumni friends. Some were renowned businessmen, not only in the Boston area, but throughout New England. He was more than happy to sit between Mr. Hodge and a staff member who worked for Mayor Michael Curley.

As usual, the competition was fierce between the two teams. The game was hard fought by the home team, but unfortunately Yale rode to victory at 27-14.

"At least they didn't get slaughtered, like last year," Alan commented as they rose from their seats. He'd done his homework.

Mr. Hodge laughed. "Yes, 28 to 0! I can still feel the pain."

In spite of the loss, the gathering afterward at the Hodges' home proved festive. While they ate, Mrs. Hodge turned to Alan.

"How are your parents doing? They must miss you today."

Alan winced. He did feel guilty that he rarely went to Connecticut to see his family. But it just never seemed a good use of time.

"Yes," he said, "I was sorry it didn't work out to go home, but I was able to wish them a 'Happy Thanksgiving' by phone."

"That's nice. It's always good to remember family during the holidays."

Alan changed the conversation before Mr. Hodge had a chance to chime in.

"By the way, as tomorrow is Priscilla's birthday, I thought you might like to come to our house for dinner."

Mrs. Hodge smiled. "We would love to!" She turned towards her daughter. "Could I bring the birthday cake?"

"Surely you aren't offering to bake?" Priscilla asked.

Her mother made a face to convey how preposterous that idea was.

~

The next morning, Priscilla was still asleep when Alan got up. He was surprised to see that it was hours beyond the time they normally rose. He walked to the Boston Commons to purchase a bouquet of flowers for her.

When he returned, he saw that other bouquets of flowers had been delivered in his absence. Alan read the cards. One was from the museum and one was from her parents. He heard the sound of footsteps and looked up to see Priscilla walking down the stairs. He handed her his bouquet while waving towards the others. "Apparently, my idea wasn't too original. You seem to be a popular girl today."

"Alan, they're lovely. Thank you!"

"You are very welcome! The cook is making a light brunch for us. Would you like a mimosa while we wait?"

"Certainly."

Alan glanced at the hall table again and noticed several cards. On top was one with Janine's return address. He passed it to Priscilla.

"How sweet!" Priscilla sat down and ripped the envelope open while Alan looked through the rest of the cards. One in particular caught his attention. In the upper left-hand corner was the name Todd Ellerton.

His anger rose. "What's this? A birthday card from your 'casual friend'?" He tossed the card in her lap and folded his arms, waiting.

Priscilla looked at him angrily. "Yes, it is a birthday card! We've exchanged them for years!"

"Exchanged? I'm glad to hear you don't forget about his special day."

"Stop being so childish! It's just a silly card. Don't you have any old friends you send birthday cards to?"

"No. I don't have any female friends whose birthdays are on my calendar."

"Well, if you did, I certainly wouldn't be giving you a hard time about it."

"Perhaps then I should consider acknowledging their special day another way – maybe I'll take some old flames out for a drink or two – maybe even dinner!"

Priscilla stood up. "I'm not going to engage in this ridiculous conversation any longer."

She turned but Alan strode ahead to turn and face her. "You can leave as soon as you promise that there will be no birthday card exchanges with Todd or any other male friends. Understood?"

Priscilla's face tensed and she hesitated before answering. "Fine!"

"Good!"

She brushed by him, the door banging behind her.

He was sorry that they were arguing on her birthday, especially after they'd gotten along so well the previous day. It couldn't be helped, however. They would have to get on the same page if their marriage was going to work, and he'd be dammed if Todd – or anyone else – was going to get in the way.

Chapter Seventy - One

With mixed emotions, Stephen and Elizabeth put the weather-beaten colonial in Dorchester, Lower Mills on the market after Thanksgiving. It sold almost immediately to a young family with several children. Elizabeth was saddened to move from the house that had been home to three generations of her family, but a small part of her was relieved that she did not have memories of Grandpa everywhere she looked. His woodworking table down cellar, the kitchen table where he always had tea before bedtime, the creak of the front door when he used to walk out to pick up the mail, all reminded her of him. It was time to move on, and she had memories to cherish for the rest of her life. She was, however, thrilled that the buyers had loved the house from the moment they saw it and had expressed plans to fix it up.

On the morning of Christmas Eve, Elizabeth, Stephen, and Paul traveled to Maine. Almost as soon as they arrived at Aunt May's, Paul excused himself. Elizabeth assumed he was going next door, although when they walked over to the Sullivans' later, both he and Dolly were absent.

Mary Francis, Robert, and Father Joe, there for the holiday, said they'd seen neither of them since Paul's arrival. Their whereabouts were answered when the couple walked in the door just as Elizabeth, Stephen, and Aunt May were about to head back to Aunt May's.

Dolly threw out her hand, showing off a sparkling diamond.

Mary Francis rushed to hug her sister. "Dolly! It's gorgeous!"

Stephen shook Paul's hand. "Looks like you picked a good one!"

Paul laughed. "Do you mean 'picked a good wife' or 'picked a good ring'?"

Charles put in, "Both, if he knows how to live happily ever after."

Dolly clasped her hands to her chest. "Paul and I just walked up the hill to the spot where he first told me he loved me. We sat in the same spot and we reenacted the scene when we both revealed our everlasting love for each other. Except that this time he had a ring!"

"Dolly, that is so romantic," Elizabeth cried.

"Isn't it? When he told me he was going to officially propose, I knew immediately how he had to do it."

Margaret hugged both Dolly and Paul. "It sounds like it was perfect."

May nodded her head. "And very 'Dollyish', if I do say!"

Dolly announced that they were getting married in January, even though there was likely to be snow on the ground.

Elizabeth wondered if such a quick wedding was more Dolly's wish than Paul's. Or was it the other way around? Her question was answered when Paul spoke up.

"I suggested waiting until spring. The weather will be warm, the flowers will be out, and you won't have to worry about the train of your gown getting dirty."

Dolly tossed her head. "If a person is really in love, then I cannot understand how someone could possibly wait an insurmountable number of days and nights to be united. The only reason I have tolerated waiting until the end of January is because my dress won't be ready until then."

Dolly looked at Paul with such a hurt look that he immediately acquiesced.

"January it is! But it would be nice if at least I had enough time to get a haircut!"

Mary Francis intervened. "What about Valentine's Day weekend? That would be a good compromise. And that should appeal to your sense of romance, Dolly."

Dolly looked at Paul, then to her mother. "I hate to give my sister credit for an idea, but that one's not bad. Valentine's Day?" She raised her eyebrows at Paul.

He smiled broadly and nodded.

~

After celebrating Christmas with the Sullivans the following day, Stephen, Elizabeth, and Paul gathered to leave for Boston. They wished everyone a Happy New Year.

Dolly clung to Paul at the door. "Call me when you get home tonight, and I'll write you tomorrow too!"

Father Joe stood behind them. "You're going to talk to Paul tonight and write him a letter too?"

Dolly whirled around. "Of course! It's an intrinsic part of courting, and we don't have much time left."

"My sister's view of the world!"

~

Stephen had taken time off in order to sign the papers and prepare for their move. At the same time Elizabeth was busy shopping for items for the house and the baby, and her schedule included appointments at Groton & Leeton Publishers regarding her book. It was scheduled to hit the bookstands in the summer, shortly after the baby was due.

The people at Groton were excited about the book. Her editor had told her that it was one of the most refreshing new books he'd published in a long time and he had high expectations for it.

Elizabeth had been walking on cloud nine since their conversation.

On the day of the move a light snow dusted the front walkway, but it was brushed aside as Elizabeth and Stephen scurried back and forth moving boxes, crates, pieces of furniture, and personal items. After a long day Stephen uncorked a bottle of champagne and pulled two glasses that had belonged to Elizabeth's grandmother from the dining room pantry.

"To a new baby, a new house, your first book, and a new year! Cheers!" He raised his glass to Elizabeth's and leaned down to kiss her.

"I hope every year we don't have so many new things – my head is spinning," she replied with a smile.

"As long as all my 'new things' happen with you, I don't care how many there are."

They walked through their new house, arms linked, sipping champagne. They'd had the master bedroom repainted a soft green, and Elizabeth had decorated it with print curtains and a matching coverlet on the bed. Paul had informed her that the room had been used as her grandfather's bedroom. Her grandparents, Elizabeth learned, had used separate bedrooms for years.

The small room next door to Elizabeth's and Stephen's room that had belonged to her father when he was young would now be for the baby. It was painted light yellow. In the center stood the crib Grandpa had built before he died.

Elizabeth sighed. She felt very much at home.

Chapter Seventy - Two

Priscilla snuggled in the oversized couch in the private suite of the ski chalet they were staying at in Vermont. "I must say, Alan, skiing, eating out, shopping – this has been one of THE most relaxing vacations ever!"

Alan stopped stoking the fire and turned to look at his wife. She looked very feminine, in spite of the fact that she sported a pair of woolen pants and a heavy ski sweater.

"I think you are right, Priscilla. I'm glad your parents let us borrow their place. It was a good idea to take off the week of New Year's, and if you aren't pregnant after an entire week of being together, I don't think there's any hope for us."

Alan smiled at his wife then reached for his martini. He was in a festive mood. Priscilla had been as romantic as she had been when they were first dating. In fact, there had been no disharmony between them since the blowup on her birthday. She had been relaxed, happy, and seemingly content.

He raised his martini glass. "What should we celebrate?"

"I have a nice surprise. My supervisor at the museum told me on the sly that the department chairman wants to talk to me about a part-time job as Assistant to the Curator. This would be in addition to volunteering," she added quickly.

"Excellent, darling! Guess the museum is willing to ignore the marriage bar?"

"It will only be a few hours a week for salary, and it would be 'under the table'."

"Excellent! Can't hurt to make a little spending money."

"Exactly. If I couldn't, I wouldn't take the position. I'm not my father's daughter for nothing you know."

"How true!" He lifted his glass high in a toast. "To Priscilla's new job opportunity!"

"And to your new position as Vice President! Cheers!" She raised her glass towards him.

"Alan, you never told me how Phil reacted now that you're in your new position. Was he upset?"

"Didn't I tell you? I thought steam was going to come out of his ears! For the past several weeks he's given me nothing but deadly looks."

"That seems a bit threatening, darling. You should be careful."

"He wouldn't do anything foolish. He's not the type that would risk his career for revenge."

"I hope he learned his lesson not to steal ideas. He got what was coming to him."

Alan avoided looking at Priscilla. "Hopefully."

They were quiet for a moment. Priscilla swirled her brandy in her glass, looking reflective.

"Alan, on the off chance that I never get pregnant, would that bother you too much?"

Alan quickly set his drink down and narrowed his eyes. He had thought they were finally on the same page when it came to having children. Now all his old suspicions came flooding back. She had mentioned the likelihood so calmly, as if she was more concerned with how he would accept such a possibility than with it being an actual problem. Had she been responsive to his advances earlier this week because she knew that her likelihood of conceiving at this particular time were very small or nonexistent?

Alan replied in a clipped tone. "If you want my opinion on the topic, I would have to say that I would be very disappointed if I knew I would never be a father. However, it seems very preliminary in our marriage to consider that conclusion. Are you trying to tell me something?"

Priscilla avoided his gaze and shrugged her shoulders. "No, I just thought that as it hadn't happened yet, maybe there was some kind of biological problem."

"Perhaps you should see a doctor then. Or perhaps," Alan continued, "just to make sure we've covered all our bases, maybe we should try every single night for several months and see if that helps."

Priscilla's head jerked up. "I don't think we have to be extreme about it. I'm sure it will happen eventually."

Alan pressed Priscilla into the back of the couch. "Perhaps, but wouldn't it be fun trying every night?"

He kissed her roughly, running his lips on her throat and neck, not caring if he bruised her. He was very angry. There was no doubt in his mind now that she had been playing a game of cat and mouse with him, stringing him along to keep him happy, yet never having any intention of conceiving if she could help it.

Priscilla looked nervous. "Alan, we have a long drive home tomorrow and then we're back to work. Maybe we should just turn in early."

He saw the worried expression in her eyes. That confirmed his theory.

Pulling her close to him, he tipped her head back and looked closely at her. "Priscilla, believe me, this is one night you'll never forget!"

He scooped her legs out from under her, carried her up the stairs, and pushed the door open with his shoulder.

Priscilla hung her head. She knew it was useless to protest.

Alan deposited her on the bed, and with one swift movement slid down next to her. He would not put up with her games any longer.

Chapter Seventy - Three

 "May I present to you Mr. and Mrs. Paul Keene!"

Dolly and Paul turned to face the congregation that was applauding and cheering the newly married couple.

Elizabeth, standing up front with Mary Francis, caught Dolly's eye and beamed at her. Dolly looked beautiful in a long-sleeved fitted gown complemented by a veil whose crown was edged with artificial miniature roses. On anyone else it would have appeared tacky, but using flowers as an accessory had always been Dolly's style and she wore them well. She also carried a dozen pink artificial roses as her bridal bouquet. They would never pass for real ones, but Dolly held them close to her chest and even raised them to her nose several times so that it looked as if she was enjoying their delicate scent.

As Dolly pretended to sniff her roses, Elizabeth saw Father Joe stifle a laugh and Charles Sullivan gave him an elbow. Apparently, one was never too old to be disciplined – priest or not.

Since Valentine's Day had been the day before, Dolly had gone all out with a Valentine's theme. She had bemoaned the fact that the holiday did not fall exactly on her wedding day, but she proclaimed that there was no reason they couldn't celebrate a day later.

"And why not?" said Mary Francis. "Every day is Valentine's Day in Dolly's world."

Elizabeth thought back to the previous day. Stephen had taken the day off work and the two of them had arrived in York in the morning. Almost as soon as they had arrived Dolly had pulled Elizabeth aside.

"Elizabeth, come with me. I have so much shopping to do. I need an extra pair of stockings and I'm always losing my hair ribbons."

"Some things never change," Margaret said as she walked onto the porch. "You've been losing hair ribbons since you were a toddler. I suppose you'll be buying ribbons for your own girls before we know it."

~

The reception was held in the church hall. When everyone was seated, Stephen stood up to offer a toast.

"To Paul and Dolly, whose slight difference in age –" Stephen paused while the guests laughed, "becomes irrelevant by the perfect union of their two hearts for all eternity. Cheers!"

Stephen raised his glass towards the bridal couple and the guests quickly followed suit.

Charles, seated next to Elizabeth, shook his head. "I guess we won't see her flying around the house any longer. We'll only have Charlie to keep us busy."

Elizabeth laughed. "That's probably enough!"

Elizabeth excused herself when she saw Grandfather Keene, in town for the wedding, approach the newlyweds.

Dolly curtseyed before her new father-in-law. "It's a pleasure to meet you again, Mr. Keene."

George Keene put out his hand to help Dolly up. "The pleasure is mine, my dear." He turned to Paul. "You've got yourself a very pretty wife, son – and she's certainly young enough."

There was an awkward silence until Dolly cupped her hand around Paul's upper arm and said, "I'm old enough for Paul."

Aunt May, standing behind Elizabeth, rushed to her defense. "I think it was love at first sight for the both of them."

George Keene nodded. "I suppose if you have that, you're bound to have a long, happy marriage." Her grandfather looked reminiscent as he spoke.

Elizabeth wondered if he were thinking of his unhappy first marriage. Had her father's parents ever felt that rush of true love?

Elizabeth felt awkward around her grandfather, but she was glad he was there. Maybe, after all these years, there was still room for their relationship to grow.

Charles Sullivan, approaching from behind, touched Paul's arm. "Dolly's certainly excited about moving to Boston."

Paul nodded. "You've got that right! It's like frosting on the cake for her."

Dolly smiled broadly. "That's right! Me – Dolly Ann Keene – living in the heart of a major shopping metropolis." She linked arms with Elizabeth. "And one of my dearest friends will be living only a few miles away!"

Stephen said, "Don't forget who will be living a few doors down from you." Elizabeth glared at him. "Oops – never mind."

Dolly pressed. "Who?"

"Sorry! I didn't mean to mention it. It just slipped out."

Dolly put her hands on her hips. "You might as well tell us who it is. I'm going to find out soon enough."

Stephen looked resigned. "Alan and Priscilla Bates."

Dolly folded her arms. "They'd better hope they never run into me. If they do, I'll give them both a piece of my mind!"

"Let's not get into that on such a special day," Elizabeth said.

"Again, my apologies. Besides, you'll probably never see them."

Paul gave Stephen a 'thanks a lot' look, then pulled at Dolly's arm. "Shall we dance?"

As the couple turned towards the dance floor, Father Joe approached and clapped his hand on Stephen's shoulder. "I guess you won the bet that Dolly wouldn't marry Arthur. Too bad, since now our church donations won't benefit."

Margaret Sullivan raised her eyebrows. "Not so loud. Dolly might not like to hear that."

It was too late. Dolly whirled around, her eyes blazing. "You two were betting on my love life?"

Stephen looked abashed. "Don't be mad at me. My odds were on you and Paul. Your brother's the one in the hot seat!"

"I'm not surprised!" Tossing her head, she returned to dancing with Paul.

Father Joe turned to Aunt May. "May I have the pleasure of this dance with the prettiest single woman at this wedding?"

"Yes, you may, although I think I am the oldest single woman at this wedding."

Elizabeth looked up to see her grandfather standing in front of her. "May I have this dance?"

Elizabeth tried to stifle her surprise. "Of course!"

As they joined the dance crowd, Grandpa Keene spoke. "You're pretty close to those girls."

"Yes, they're like sisters to me."

"I'm glad you were able to have that, not having had any siblings, and your grandmother and me not being around a lot."

"I visited you."

"I know, but I was usually traveling, and your grandmother didn't know much what to do with a grandchild." He paused. "Your grandpa did a wonderful job raising you."

Elizabeth had a catch in her throat when she replied. "I thought the world of him."

"As well you should have!"

After the dance ended, Dolly and Paul cut the cake. Before long it was time for them to say good-bye. The couple walked through the doors. Charlie and Father Joe led the way for the crowd that followed.

Paul's car was parked outside the hall and a sign was taped to the back window. It read, 'Finaly Marreed.'

The crowd laughed and even Dolly didn't mind. Obviously, her ten-year old brother was the instigator.

She hugged Charlie as George Keene walked over to shake Paul's hand. "Have a wonderful trip! I only wish your mother were alive to see you get married. But I do believe she would have agreed with me that Dolly was worth the wait."

"Thank you, sir."

Dolly beamed and leaned forward to kiss her father-in-law on the cheek before turning to Elizabeth and Mary Francis, a tear in her eye.

"Thank you for being part of my wedding, both of you! I'll miss you so much!"

Elizabeth gave her a hug. "We'll miss you too. Call us as soon as you get home and tell us all about your honeymoon."

Paul helped Dolly into the passenger's seat before sliding behind the wheel.

As they drove off, Charles Sullivan put his arm around his wife. "Dolly finally found Prince Charming."

Margaret looked lovingly at her husband. "We Sullivan women always do!"

Chapter Seventy - Four

Alan let himself in the front door, startling the housekeeper in the hallway. She hurried to take his coat from him.

"Is Mrs. Bates home?"

"Yes, sir. She's changing for dinner."

"Good."

Since their return from Vermont, Alan had made it crystal clear that Priscilla would have no more evenings out unless he accompanied her. In order to show that he was willing to compromise, he was trying to leave the office earlier than before. He knew that it was not in Priscilla's nature to take orders from anyone, but Alan had no choice.

He had to give her credit; she seemed accepting of their quieter lifestyle. From time to time he studied her, looking for any sign of anger or sarcasm. He found none, but he also didn't find enthusiasm or excitement. He was hopeful that any day she would give him the news he was eagerly anticipating – that they were finally going to become parents. If that didn't bring him and Priscilla together, heaven only knew what would.

He walked into the drawing room and poured a drink from the mini-bar. He looked up when he heard a sound at the doorway.

Priscilla appeared, looking pretty in a pink cashmere sweater and wine-colored wool skirt.

His passion rose when he studied the curves of her sweater. He wondered if she minded spending the night at home instead of hitting the town with friends. For his part, he would enjoy an intimate evening.

Alan gave her a small box that the jewelers had gift-wrapped. He wanted Priscilla to know that he, too, was making an effort.

Her eyes widened. She flipped opened the smaller box to reveal heart-shaped earrings covered with diamonds.

"Thank you, Alan." She gave him a quick kiss, then set the box down to remove the earrings and put them on. After that she was silent.

He lifted her head to gaze into her deep blue eyes. "As always, you look beautiful tonight!"

"Thank you."

Inwardly, he sighed.

She seemed resigned, as if she had no expectations. She had been accepting of his advances since Vermont – almost obediently.

Alan was used to getting his way in situations, uncaring whether the other person involved liked it or not. With Priscilla, however, it was surprisingly different. He wanted her to be happy that they could be starting a family, happy that they were married and had their own home.

When he asked her if anything was bothering her, she always smiled and said everything was fine.

He planted a small kiss on her lips. "What would you think of going out tomorrow night with some friends?"

"If you like."

"I actually thought it would be something you would enjoy. That's why I suggested it."

"That's very nice of you. Thank you."

He held her chin and forced her to look at him. "Priscilla, are you glad that you're married?"

Priscilla blinked twice. "Of course, Alan. It's what I've always wanted."

Alan went upstairs to change. He was frustrated. She seemed so resigned at times, as if her married state was a prison sentence.

When he returned to the study, she was waiting to accompany him to dinner.

They talked little while they ate, and as soon as they had finished Priscilla rose.

"I have some work to do for the museum and I'm sure you also have work to do."

She turned to leave and Alan reached for her, drawing her close. "It's Friday night. Is it work that can wait? Perhaps we could take a walk and stop somewhere for a drink?"

Priscilla stepped away, forcing Alan to let his arms drop.

"It's cold out and we're already going out tomorrow night. Besides,

I really should get this work finished."

He watched her leave and felt helpless. Happiness in her seemed absent since he put his foot down regarding her social life. Should he let her go out whenever she wanted? Should he let her send birthday cards to male friends? He knew in his heart he would be miserable if he did, but, this way, Pricilla was the miserable one. All he could do was hope that she would eventually come to terms with married life.

~

The following morning Alan left the house before Priscilla was awake. He slipped out the front door and eased his car toward the Common. For nearly an hour he cruised around Back Bay, watching the city awaken. Finally, he turned south, toward Milton. He had no plan, he told himself.

By the time his car rounded the corner of Dorchester, Lower Mills and ascended Adams Street, snow flurries were in the air and a cold wind howled.

He drove slowly, looking from house to house. At last he spotted a mailbox that prompted him to stop. "Wright." He let the car idle in front of the stately grey mansion. A circular stone driveway graced the front of the house. The house looked magnificent, warm, and friendly. It was a stark contrast to the worn-looking colonial Elizabeth had grown up in, with peeling paint and a dilapidated picket fence.

Alan looked for signs of movement within but saw none. If Elizabeth or Stephen were home, though, what would he say if they saw him there? What reason could he possibly give? He studied the house for a moment more, then eased the car forward.

When he reached the bottom of the hill, he skirted the edge of East Milton Square and turned towards Boston. He considered looping around and driving past the house one more time, but it would be painful to do so. It was a home that would soon hear the gurgles of a newborn and a mother lulling her baby to sleep. All the money in the world, all the success one could obtain, could not buy that kind of happiness.

Chapter Seventy - Five

It was a wintry March evening and Elizabeth was preparing supper in the kitchen. The doorbell rang.

Elizabeth reached the hallway as the front door opened and Paul and Dolly tumbled in.

Paul spoke. "Oops! I can't believe I just walked in after I rang the bell. Old habits die hard."

Elizabeth laughed as she greeted them. "They certainly do! But that's fine, you can walk into our home anytime. I'm so glad to see both of you. I hardly got to talk to you on the phone about the honeymoon."

She grabbed Paul's coat. "Stephen's in the study if you want to tell him you're here. He just got home from work."

Dolly planted a kiss on Paul's cheek. "Goodbye, darling!"

Paul laughed. "I'm only going to be across the hall."

"That's far enough!"

Elizabeth smiled at Paul. "You should be used to Dolly clinging to you by now, Paul."

"I didn't say I don't enjoy it!"

When Paul left, Dolly turned to Elizabeth. "Look at you! You're really showing."

Elizabeth ran the palm of her hand over the swell of her stomach. "I know. The baby's really kicking now. How's Mary Francis?"

"She feels well, although Robert told her she looks like she's having twins. But she doesn't think so."

Paul appeared in the doorway. "Stephen wasn't in the study."

"That's funny. I could have sworn he was there. I'll get him. Make yourselves comfortable. I'll be right back."

As she climbed the stairs to the second floor landing, she thought fleetingly of how dreary the hall and surrounding bedrooms had been when they had first moved in. She had not anticipated the transformation that would occur with freshly-painted walls and gleaming mahogany wood, stripped and stained.

A brightly-colored scatter rug on the floor and light and airy curtains on the windows replaced the thick, heavy drapes that had hung there.

Her content thoughts instantly disappeared, however, when she saw Stephen lying on their bed looking flush and glassy-eyed.

She hurried to the bedside and gently pressed her hand on his forehead to see if it was warm. "What's the matter, darling? Do you think you might have the flu?"

"I don't know," he murmured as he licked his tongue over his dry lips. "I don't have a cold, but my head feels heavy and my legs ache."

"You must be coming down with a cold. I'll bring you some juice. I'll be right back."

When she returned downstairs, Elizabeth told Dolly and Paul about Stephen.

"He must be getting a cold. I'm just going to bring him up something to drink and then we can eat."

Dolly intervened. "We'd rather not be in your way, Elizabeth. We can get going."

"Oh, don't go! I know Stephen isn't up for coming downstairs and he's going to take a nap, so, I would love the company for dinner. Besides, I have plenty of food."

"Sure, if you insist," Paul replied.

~

In the morning, Stephen was awake but his eyes remained glassy.

Elizabeth felt his forehead. "You seem warm. I'm going to take your temperature."

It registered at 103.2.

"I'm going to call Dr. Tinsdale."

Luckily, she reached him at his office, even though it was a Saturday. He said he would be there in a few minutes.

When the doctor arrived, she escorted him upstairs.

While she waited just beyond the bedroom door, the doorbell rang. She hurried down the stairs. It was Paul.

"I'm sorry to bother you Elizabeth. Dolly thinks she left her scarf here last night. I was doing errands so I told her I would stop by. How's Stephen?"

"Actually, the doctor is examining him right now."

Elizabeth turned to see Doctor Tinsdale walking down the stairs. He came forward to shake Paul's hand, then turned towards Elizabeth. "Would you prefer if we discuss Stephen's condition alone?"

"Condition?" Elizabeth asked.

"Yes."

Elizabeth's heart skipped a beat. "Do you mind if my uncle stays?"

"Of course not. I just wanted to make sure you didn't mind."

Elizabeth led the way into the study.

After shutting the door, Dr. Tinsdale looked carefully at Elizabeth before finally speaking.

"I suspect that Stephen has polio."

Elizabeth gasped. Tears sprang to her eyes. "That's impossible! Stephen's always been so healthy. You must have made a mistake! It must be something else!"

Paul gently held both her hands in his then said to the doctor in a low, but slightly uneven voice, "Go on."

The doctor removed his glasses and set them on the desk. "I don't know how familiar you are with the disease, so I'll give you a brief description. It's a disabling disease that attacks the nervous system. Usually, but not always, it causes partial to complete paralysis of the muscles of the body."

He paused a moment before continuing. "I'm only saying what I have to say next because it's necessary that I tell people the worst-case scenario, but the possibility of not surviving cannot be ruled out. However, very many people have survived, and the medical profession has begun to make great advances in helping people regain the use of damaged muscles. There's a vaccine they're working on, but that's not something that will be ready for Stephen."

"How bad is Stephen's case, Doctor?" Paul asked.

"It's tough to tell right now since it's still early. Every case is different and you can't compare one person to another. We'll just have to let it run its course.

"As Elizabeth mentioned, he's always been in the best of health and that can only help. I'm going to send a nurse over to help you take care of him, and I'm ordering you to use her. I know you want to care for him, Elizabeth, but you have to remember that you're pregnant, and it's a highly contagious disease."

"I'm not leaving my husband's side. Besides, I've already been in contact with him, so if I contracted it, it's already too late."

Paul stepped forward. "I'll help the nurse with whatever she needs and try to keep Elizabeth in the background, although I can't promise I'll be successful."

Elizabeth smiled. "I can't tell you what your help means to us, Uncle Paul."

"Consider it 'thanks' for all you've done for me."

The doctor snapped his bag shut and stood up to leave. "I have more patients to see today, but I'll be back first thing tomorrow to check on him. Try to make him as comfortable as possible. If he's hungry, you can give him some clear broth or soup."

The doctor picked up his bag and headed towards the door, stopping at the threshold.

"I'm sorry I can't do more. It's very difficult as a practitioner to stand by helplessly and do nothing."

Elizabeth watched as Paul escorted the doctor out. As soon as the door shut behind them, her tears poured freely.

It wasn't fair! It just wasn't! Why had this happened when they were just beginning their life together? How would she be able to go on if Stephen didn't make it?

She couldn't consider that outcome. He was going to be okay and that's all there was to it. One thing she decided, however. Stephen needed her to be there for him. She wanted to make sure that Stephen knew that she would be at his side every step of the way.

When she walked upstairs, she took a minute to compose herself before she quietly turned the knob and poked her head in the room.

Stephen turned his head at the sound of her entrance and looked questioningly at her.

Elizabeth spoke gently to him.

"Stephen, I just talked to Dr. Tinsdale. He says that you have polio, but fortunately we caught it in its early stage which gives us a much better chance of fighting it."

"Polio, eh? And here I thought I just had a common cold."

"Stephen, I just want you to know one thing. No matter what happens, we're in this together. For better or worse, as we said in our marriage vows. I meant it."

Stephen gazed back at his wife. "There's nothing I can't deal with when you're by my side."

"I feel the same way. I wish I could be more hands-on, but because of my pregnancy, Paul and the nurse will be doing all your caregiving. Don't think that I won't be the background rooting for you every minute," Elizabeth rejoined lightly, even though the tears threatened to spill over again. "Now, why don't you rest while I make you something to eat?"

"I guess I know who's in charge around here." Stephen gave a half smile.

As Elizabeth turned to leave, Stephen's voice stalled her.

"Elizabeth?"

"Yes?"

"I love you."

"I love you too!"

When she went downstairs, Paul already had a tray for Steven. "It's not a fancy meal – just canned soup and a sandwich. I guess being a bachelor for a while has benefits."

"Uncle Paul, I feel awful that you are being exposed to such a contagious disease. The last thing I want is for you to get sick."

Paul pulled her into a bear hug. "Now, no tears around here. That husband of yours is going to pull through just fine. I'll bring this tray up to him, and there's a tray in the kitchen for you. I'll be back in a few minutes. Now, get going!"

~

Elizabeth woke early the next morning after falling asleep in the guest room after midnight. When she peeked in, Stephen was still asleep, but he was restless, pushing off the blankets, and tossing and turning.

Elizabeth heard a noise behind her and saw Paul walking up the stairs.

"The nurse just checked on him. He has a high fever. I called Doctor Tinsdale. He's coming right over."

As if on cue, they heard a knock on the front door.

She rushed downstairs to let Dr. Tinsdale in.

"He seems so restless. Is a fever usual with polio?"

"Yes. Even in the best of cases, it's not a comfortable disease. I know the fever is causing him to want to throw off the bedcovers, but try at least to keep a light blanket on him and also keep giving him liquids. If he has any pain in any of his limbs, let me know and I can give him some pain medicine to help him along. Other than that, all we can do is wait."

When Stephen woke, he sipped some juice and had a few bites of toast. After he had eaten, Paul stayed to talk with him while Elizabeth took a few minutes to call Aunt May.

"Don't you fret, Elizabeth. We'll get him through this with prayers and well wishes. The Sullivans send their regards too. They know Dolly wanted to help, but I think Paul is wise not to let her come in your house. There is no reason to have another person exposed."

Three days passed and there was no change in Stephen, but then, on the fourth day, Stephen began complaining of tingling in both his legs.

The nurse examined him and then pulled Elizabeth and Paul aside. She spoke in a low voice. "Paralysis may be setting in on the left side of his body. Dr. Tinsdale hadn't planned on coming by until dinner time, but I think I'll call him and see if he can come sooner."

Dr. Tinsdale came as soon as he was summoned. He verified what the nurse had surmised. "It's affected the left side of his body. Whether or not it will spread to any other muscles, we'll just have to wait and see. I'll be back tomorrow to see how he's doing."

"Doctor, will Stephen lose the use of his legs?" Elizabeth asked.

"I'm afraid that's the least of Stephen's worries. He's fighting for his life."

Father Joe arrived in the afternoon to give him the Sacrament of the Sick. It touched Elizabeth that he had driven down from Maine. He would be staying at Paul and Dolly's, at least overnight, and promised he would be available at a moment's notice should they need him to return.

As the day passed into evening, Elizabeth and Paul kept a constant vigil, Paul relaying to Elizabeth any slight change in his condition.

Neither of them bothered to eat.

Stephen was so ill that he could barely open his eyes to respond.

Paul tried to sound optimistic, but Elizabeth knew that the situation was dire.

That night Stephen's fever was the same, and he refused to eat, only taking tiny sips of water out of necessity.

Dr. Tinsdale returned to see how he was doing. After taking the stethoscope out of his ears he said, "It should be anytime now, one way or the other."

It was late when Paul finally persuaded Elizabeth to rest. "You've got to get a little sleep. I'll come and get you immediately if anything happens."

That night, Elizabeth prayed harder than she ever had her entire life. She couldn't lose Stephen! She just couldn't! He was such a good person, so loving and caring, and he had brought such joy and fulfillment to her life and everyone he knew. He had so much life to live. Surely God, in His mercy, would spare him and allow him to live.

Chapter Seventy - Six

Alan looked up as he neared the conference room. Several of the managers were gathered around Phil, shaking his hand and congratulating him. The rumor he had overheard at the water cooler a few days ago must have been true. Phil and Betty were engaged.

He stopped short, pretending that he had forgotten something. He turned and walked back to his office. He wanted to avoid a 'no-win' situation.

If he avoided Phil, he would look rude by not also offering his congratulations. If he did offer his hand, Phil was sure to rebuff him. He grabbed an extra pen and shelved a couple of manuals he had left on his desk before leaving his office a second time.

When he neared the conference room, there was no one at the entrance. He walked through the door and slipped into the only vacant seat. It was diagonally across from Phil.

Mr. Hodge cleared his throat. "Good morning, gentlemen. Before we begin our meeting, I would like to congratulate Phil. In case any of you have not heard yet, Phil and Betty Higgins became engaged this past weekend. On behalf of Hodge's Investments, we wish you both the very best!"

Alan smirked.

Half the men in the Boston bars had also thought she was a nice girl before she had taken up with Phil. Alan realized that Phil had noticed the expression on his face. He openly glared at him. Alan looked down at his papers.

When the meeting adjourned, the managers casually made their way towards the door, talking with each other as the line slowly moved.

Alan hoped to escape without any interaction. Unfortunately, he got caught behind one of the managers who turned to shake Phil's hand. "Congratulations! We should all take you out for a drink. What about

Friday night?"

"Perfect! Betty will be doing some shopping after work that evening."

"Great! Hey guys! We'll meet right after work on Friday at Harvard Gardens Bar on Cambridge Street."

Alan tried to slide by the manager, but he turned his head just as Alan brushed by him. "Coming, Alan?"

The other managers turned towards him and the room grew quiet. "I wish I could, but Mr. and Mrs. Hodge are coming over for dinner."

Mr. Hodge verified his statement. "We are, but we don't mind if you want to stop by for a drink beforehand. Priscilla can keep us company."

Alan groaned inwardly.

Mr. Hodge was the type who would put personal differences aside in order to support someone, and no doubt he expected Alan to do so also.

"I'll see if it works out, but no promises. Congratulations, Phil." He nodded towards Phil, who was standing a few feet way.

Phil was silent, and Alan averted his eyes as he reached the doorway.

He hadn't the slightest intention in joining the group, but at least his reply got the manager off his back. He would come up with an excuse to tell Mr. Hodge. He'd been able to con his father-in-law before. A little white lie now should be no problem at all.

~

Alan slouched on the couch, half-listening to Priscilla talk about new arrivals at the museum. The maid appeared in the doorway, interrupting.

"Excuse me, Mr. and Mrs. Hodge have arrived."

As Priscilla's parents entered, Priscilla jumped up to greet them and kissed each on the cheek. "Mother, Father. I'm so glad you could come for dinner."

"We're always glad to have an invitation, dear," Mrs. Hodge gushed.

Alan rose and kissed his mother-in-law on the cheek and shook Mr. Hodge's hand. "Please sit down. The usual scotch, Henry? Mrs. Hodge?"

As Alan poured drinks, Mr. Hodge turned to him. "I didn't expect you'd be here. Not in the mood for a drink with the staff?"

"Believe me, I would have been happy to stop in, but I finished up work a little late and, to be honest, I figured I'd never get out of there if

I made an appearance."

"That's happened to me more than once. I'm sure there'll be another time."

"Exactly!"

Mr. Hodge put his drink down. "I don't know if you've heard about Stephen Wright, Alan."

Alan scratched his head. "I'm not sure I know what you're referring to. Something to do with work?"

"No. He probably wishes it was only that. He's contracted polio and, from what I hear, it's very touch and go."

Mrs. Hodge turned towards her husband, "Who is Stephen Wright, dear?"

"He's a lawyer for Godfrey & Phillips – a very successful law firm in town that helped out with our company's merger. He's a fine young man. His wife, Elizabeth, used to work for us as a secretary. Apparently about a week ago he was stricken with polio."

Mr. Hodge leaned forward, drink in hand. "From what I hear, he might not make it."

Alan was stunned. "I hadn't heard at all, sir. I certainly hope he pulls through."

Priscilla sighed loudly. "Oh, don't we all. It would be so devastating for her if he didn't – especially as she's expecting."

Alan looked at Priscilla, taking note of the gleam in her eye and the smile that tugged at the corner of her lips. He would have thought that in light of such tragic news, Priscilla would have at least a little kindness and concern. He felt repulsed by her insensitivity.

"Perhaps the firm could send a flower arrangement, sir."

"That's a wonderful idea, Alan. I'll have Lillian order it on Monday."

Priscilla had looked sharply at Alan as he spoke, but he didn't care. In fact, he was glad he had gotten under her skin. If she was angry about his suggestion, so be it. He was starting to care less and less about what Priscilla wanted from him.

Chapter Seventy - Seven

The first thing Elizabeth noticed when she awoke was how chilly it was. At some point during the evening someone had placed a blanket over her, but neither that nor the bright morning sun that sprawled across the carpet could compensate for the absence of the once-roaring fire that was now reduced to ashes.

Elizabeth glanced at the clock on the mantel and gasped. Eight o'clock. Why, she'd been asleep for almost seven hours! There must be some news of Stephen, although Paul had sworn he would wake her if there was. Even so, she was irritated with herself, and with Paul too, for sleeping in so long.

Pushing the hair out of her eyes, she swung her feet to the floor and suddenly realized that she was not alone.

Paul stood leaning against the parlor doors, his head resting against his arm.

Elizabeth opened her mouth to speak and just as quickly closed it.

He was so still and silent.

She instinctively felt that something had happened while she had slept. She was afraid to ask what that was.

Suddenly, Paul straightened up and she saw the tears in his eyes, the look of tiredness, and pain that he wore.

She jumped up from the couch and approached him slowly.

"It's all over, isn't it? I know what you're going to tell me." Tears began to stream down her face as she struggled to speak. "You're going to tell me that Stephen's not in pain anymore. You're going to say that we won't have to worry about him because he's – he's…"

Elizabeth could not go on. It was too much for her, and she bent her head in her hands and wept.

Paul rushed towards her and grasped her shoulders. "Elizabeth! It's not what you think! Stephen's going to be all right! He's going to live!"

With a sob, Elizabeth stared up at Paul.

"Stephen's going to be all right? But you looked so – so –," she sought to find the right word. "Defeated. And you have tears in your eyes."

"I know. I didn't mean to frighten you. I'm just so tired. It's been such a hard fight. But that doesn't matter! Stephen's pulled through. He's won!"

He pulled Elizabeth close in a long hug and together they cried out of relief and sheer happiness.

Then Paul explained what had happened.

"I was so exhausted I fell asleep beside Stephen's bed. Then about five o'clock this morning, I woke up when I heard him moaning. He seemed so feverish and I was so worried that I came out to the hall to call Dr. Tinsdale.

"He came right away, but by the time he arrived, the fever had broken, and Stephen was sleeping peacefully. Dr. Tinsdale said the worst was over. He's going to make it. I was so excited that I tried to wake you up, but you wouldn't even stir. I've been waiting to tell you the good news."

"Oh, Uncle Paul! How can I – how can we ever thank you?" She gazed at him, her eyes brimming. "Can we go see him now?"

"Of course. Dr. Tinsdale is still here. He should be down in a minute."

The doctor appeared in the doorway just as Paul finished speaking.

"It was really touch-and-go there for a while last night," the doctor stated. "I must tell you that Paul was really there for your husband. You've got quite an uncle, Elizabeth."

"I certainly do!"

"Now, about Stephen's long-term condition," Dr. Tinsdale began, but Elizabeth interrupted him.

"I know what you're going to say. You're going to tell me that Stephen has lost the use of the left side of his body. I don't care. I'm just so happy and relieved that he's going to be okay."

"He'll definitely be able to navigate on his own, and other patients of mine with the same paralysis have done very well. We should also be more than grateful that it was his left arm he lost use of instead of his right. He'll still be able to write, plus a million other things you do in the course of any day."

The three of them walked upstairs. When they entered Stephen's room, his eyes fluttered open and he smiled.

"Hi guys," he whispered, still too weak to do more than slowly turn his head in their direction. "Dr. Tinsdale says I'm going to be okay. Right, Doc?"

Elizabeth rushed forward to throw her arms around him. She struggled to ward off the oncoming tears.

"We're very proud of you!" Paul reached down to take Stephen's hand that was lying on the coverlet. You pulled through like a champion!"

Stephen nodded. "I think you're right. I probably won't be able to run a road race, but I think those days were behind me anyways. I'm just thankful that I can still use my right arm."

Elizabeth held Stephen's hand as the men continued to talk. She knew then that Stephen had been on the brink of death and Elizabeth could only offer eternal thanks that Stephen, the love of her life and the father of their unborn child, had miraculously pulled through against all odds.

Chapter Seventy - Eight

Alan gave Priscilla a kiss on the cheek before hurrying out the door. He was leaving early for work, although he felt he had hardly been home. He had worked late into the evening with many of the staff the previous night, preparing for the merger that was imminent. He felt bad that he had left Priscilla home alone the night before. However, he had promised her that he would be home on time that night and they would be able to spend the entire weekend together.

After the merger was finished, he wanted Priscilla to be able to count on his walking through the door at exactly the same time every day.

~

Alan had just settled at his desk, deeply entrenched in getting his materials ready for a long day of meetings and presentations, when an incessant rap on his door caught his attention. He looked up to see Janine in the doorway.

"Excuse me, Mr. Bates. I know you said you were busy, but Mr. Summersby would like to see you for a moment."

"Send him in."

He knew Neil must have something important to tell him; Neil was every bit as busy as he was. Neil entered his office and quickly approached Alan's desk.

"Sorry to interrupt, Alan, but this is very important."

"Sure, Neil, have a seat." He waved him to a chair, but Neil ignored him.

"I take it from your congenial mood that you haven't seen the papers yet."

Alan's head shot up. "Is it Stephen Wright? Is his obituary in the paper?"

"No, in fact, I heard he pulled through and he's going to be okay, although not without some permanent issues. I should have said 'Have you seen the tabloids'?"

"I try to stay away from those publications. Why, what's going on?"

"I wish I wasn't the one to have to tell you, but Phil Lawrence brought today's paper to the meeting this morning. But don't be too hard on him. Mr. Hodge would have seen it anyways. Here."

Dropping the newspaper on top of the desk pad, Neil pointed to a picture that was prominently displayed.

Alan felt a terrible sense of trepidation in his heart. His eyes dropped downward to see a picture of Priscilla reclining in a chair, a drink in her hand, seated next to a man he didn't recognize. The man's arm was draped around Priscilla's shoulder and her head was tipped back against the back of his arm. She appeared to be laughing gaily at whatever the man was saying.

Above the photo was the headline, *"Newlywed shares flirtatious moment with unknown man."* Underneath the photo the caption read, *Socialite Priscilla Bates was once again seen out on the town. Her husband, Vice President Alan Bates, was suspiciously absent.*

Alan sat still, a cacophony of thoughts whirling through his brain. All the excuses, the cover-ups, the pretenses she had told him all came together into one big lie.

Through the fog of his mind he heard Neil softly speaking.

"Alan, I'm sorry I had to be the one to bring it to your attention, but I figured it was better that you heard it from a friend before the press was camped on your doorstep."

Alan rose up from his chair and grabbed his coat. "I've got to go home right away and settle this."

Neil grabbed Alan's arm and forced him to look at him. "Alan, don't do anything stupid."

Alan stopped. "Believe me," he laughed. "I'm about to do one of the smartest things I've ever done in my whole life."

~

Alan slammed the door, not even bothering to hand his coat to the surprised butler. He headed for the center hall stairs. He took the steps two at a time, then suddenly wondered if Priscilla was even home. Perhaps she was already at the museum.

There she was, though, sitting at her dressing table.

She was examining her face for wrinkles – a daily ritual on her part.

At that moment he found her constant preoccupation with her physical appearance repulsive. He had formerly been proud to have a wife who kept her up appearances so well. Now he realized that her beautiful exterior covered up a selfish interior. Inside she was conceited, self-centered, and unfaithful.

He flung the folded newspaper onto the dressing table top, sending various jars of make-up everywhere. A perfume bottle spilled over, leaking its contents down the front of the table.

Priscilla jumped up just in time to avoid the seeping liquid from spilling onto the lap of her dress. "Look what you've done! You've knocked over my Q'Irresistance perfume! That's $20 an ounce! I expect you to replace it immediately, and all of my other cosmetics that you've ruined! You're only lucky that I didn't get any on my dress! What's the matter with you?"

"You know damn well what's the matter!"

Grabbing the newspaper, he thrust it in Priscilla's face.

"Is this good enough for you? Scandal in the newspaper? Are you happy now?"

"What – what are you talking about?"

Priscilla's face blanched as she stared at the picture of herself and read the write-up beneath it. She slowly looked up at him with frightened eyes.

"By God, Priscilla! I thought you were home last night! I took you for your word that you were staying home. Not only did you sneak out behind my back, you wound up in the newspaper!"

Alan could not remember having been more infuriated in his entire life. At that moment he felt an over-whelming desire to hit Priscilla, to knock her senseless, and he had to physically hold his right arm with his left hand.

As soon as he gained control, however, he spun her around and forced her to face him.

"It was nothing, Alan! I only went out for a little while to meet some friends. I don't even know who he is! He just came over to our table. You've got to believe me!"

For once in her life, Priscilla looked scared, as if she knew she had gone too far. The consequences of her actions meant public humiliation for both of them, but more so for him. His self-respect demanded that he be able to hold his head up at work and in public and not have people think that he allowed such behavior from his wife.

Alan spoke, his voice low and firm. "I've had enough of your 'get-togethers' that you insist are nothing. You also apparently aren't the slightest bit ready to settle down and start a family anytime soon."

Priscilla opened up her mouth to speak, but Alan raised his hand to silence her.

"I meant it when I said before that I would crack down on your 'painting the town red'! I will now be hiring a chauffeur. He will drive you to and from any social events that involve the public, and he will instruct the bartender what your drink limit is. We will spend our weekends together whether you like it or not. You are my wife and you will abide by my rules."

Priscilla's face hardened. "I'm not going to live like I'm under house arrest! I didn't get married so someone could boss me around! Maybe I'll just file for a divorce. After all, you're married to your briefcase."

"Neither of us is filing for a divorce for the simple reason that I have no intention of compromising my career and my social place in life just to satisfy your self-serving whims. Besides, you and I both know that your parents would never condone that decision."

He had barely finished speaking when Priscilla picked up a Waterford vase and threw it at Alan.

He had to duck in order to avoid the vase hitting his head. Instead it narrowly missed his left shoulder. It crashed against the wall and shattered into a thousand pieces.

Alan walked two steps towards her. "I'll let that pass, as you obviously have never had to deal with any restrictions in your life, but I strongly suggest that you not have a repeat performance."

Priscilla stepped back. She had a look of fear on her face.

If that was the way he had to control her, so be it.

"Also, I expect that we eat our main meal together, and that I be able to exercise my marital rights. We wouldn't want the staff to spread rumors, you know. Because of the merger workload I'll have to miss dinner tonight, but that will give you plenty of time to change into something attractive for later."

As he turned, Priscilla spoke.

"What a pity divorce isn't more acceptable. There are so many eager young bachelors who would love to have a chance with me."

Alan knew she had spoken out of the need to cut him to the core, but the sad reality was that she had unwittingly revealed the source of her problem – how could she ever reconcile herself to being with one man when a hundred others would always beckon?

Alan turned to face her, saying the words that had hardly crossed his mind, nor would he have even dared to say them had he not been eager for retaliation. "And it's too bad I won't have the opportunity to be with a girl who would embrace marriage and motherhood the way Elizabeth Wright does."

Alan saw the look of shock and hurt on Priscilla's face.

She opened her mouth to speak and then quickly closed it.

Their eyes locked for a moment.

Alan knew that they had both fought for the upper hand in their marriage and he had won.

Their altercation was over. As he shut the bedroom door, the memory of Elizabeth's confrontation in his office after the Christmas party more than a year ago came to mind. When she had stated that she believed that people married for love, he had scoffed at her and asserted his belief that it was wealth, power, or prestige that people sought.

How ironic that they had both found the kind of marriage they had believed in. But Elizabeth's was blossoming and Alan's had withered before it had even had a chance to grow.

Chapter Seventy - Nine

"Time for a snack," Elizabeth called out as she entered their bedroom with a tray with hot chicken soup and apple slices. She placed it beside the bouquet of early May flowers and get-well card that had been sent from Betty Higgins and Lillian Graham. Fred and Harry had called to send their best wishes to Stephen, and the Sullivans were planning on visiting as soon as Stephen was feeling up to company. Even Charlie had sent a card, drawing a picture of Stephen lying in bed eating ice cream.

Stephen struggled to sit up upon her entrance, leaning on his right side in order to push himself up in bed.

Elizabeth hurriedly set the tray on the side bureau and propped his pillows behind him. He smiled at her in gratitude.

"I'm going to have to learn to do this on my own, but I have to say, I don't mind being catered to by my lovely wife."

He was still very weak, but Dr. Tinsdale had promised that in another month or so he would regain his stamina and be able to return to work.

"I need to be back to normal soon so I can take care of you in a few months." He squeezed her hand. "I have the love of my life, there's a little Wright on the way, and I will still be able to perform my job and provide for my family. I think I won the fight over polio hands down."

"I think you're right, darling.

"Oh, Mary Francis called to see how you are doing."

Stephen smiled "Her phone calls must be short with the new baby. What did they name her again?"

"Hannah. I hope we can see her soon... Now eat up before your soup gets cold. I'll be back soon to see how you're doing."

When she returned in a few minutes, Stephen was reading a tabloid newspaper.

"Where did you get that?" Elizabeth asked.

"Dr. Tinsdale brought me papers from his office waiting room; thought it might give me something to do."

He motioned Elizabeth to sit by his bedside.

"You're not going to believe what I just read!"

"I'm not?"

Turning a page, he read the headline, "*Newlywed Socialite Priscilla Bates shares flirtatious moment with unknown man.*"

Elizabeth gasped. "What? That can't be right! Let me see!"

Grabbing the paper, her eyes traveled down to the paragraph underneath his finger. She read the write-up and sighed.

"That's so sad. Believe me, you certainly know that I am not a fan of either one of them, but I wouldn't wish that on anyone."

"Exactly. Alan was never on my list of reputable people either, but I'm sure he wasn't happy that his wife was out having a good time behind his back. I wonder why she even got married."

"I know why Alan got married. When Alan broke up with me in order to date Priscilla, I asked him if he was in love with her. He laughed and said that love had nothing to do with it – that people got married to become richer, or wealthier, or be more socially connected."

"That certainly answers that question. Maybe he now knows that love has everything to do with it. If you don't have love, it's like building a house on sand. The first bad storm is going to knock your house over. I should probably be grateful to Alan, however."

"Why?"

"If he hadn't broken up with you, you wouldn't have been available for me to date."

Elizabeth smiled and handed Stephen his soup.

He took a sip and then looked sideways out the window at the bare branches. "I do wish it was warmer. It would be nice to be able to sit outside."

"Yes. But this summer we'll be able to take the baby out in the yard and enjoy Grandfather's rose bushes."

"Yes. You know, I was just thinking that our lives are just like a rose – we have our winter months, when the darkness of life pricks us with its thorns. But we persevere until finally spring comes, and when we see the rose blooming, we realize we've overcome the tough times and the good days are back."

"Just like you overcame polio. In fact, Harry told me once that was the reason why Grandpa loved roses so much. When the roses started to bloom, it always reminded him that hope never goes away. When he first came to this country, and he and my grandmother didn't know a single soul, he planted them. Then when my grandmother and my parents died, he knew the roses were still going to bloom in the spring, and it always gave him hope when he needed it." Elizabeth paused.

"Stephen, how would you feel if we named the baby 'Rose' if it's a girl? It was my grandmother's name, another one of the reasons why Grandpa planted rose bushes."

"I think it's perfect! And we'll name the baby John after Grandpa if it's a boy. Either, way, it will feel like a part of him still lives on."

Elizabeth looked at Stephen with shining eyes. "That would make me so happy. His love for his family and his rose bushes are legacies we can pass on to our children."

Stephen agreed. "A legacy begun with love is a legacy that will always endure."

Chapter Eighty

"Have a seat, Alan."

"Thank you."

Alan tried to look calm, but on the inside he was a bundle of nerves. His secretary Janine had informed him the previous afternoon that Mr. Hodge wanted to see him at nine o'clock that morning and he could only surmise the reason was that Mr. Hodge had seen Priscilla's picture in the paper.

He felt a bit sick; he had no desire to discuss his marriage with his boss who was also his father-in-law.

Mr. Hodge jumped right in. "First, my wife and I were very distressed to hear that Priscilla not only made a bad decision on a personal level, but that her behavior became so public."

Alan relaxed a little. Mr. Hodge undoubtedly wanted to clear the air. Alan had to be careful, however, not to condemn Priscilla. No matter what her actions had been, she was still her father's flesh and blood.

Alan glanced around the room as he spoke, avoiding Mr. Hodge's gaze. "It was unfortunate, but I think Priscilla was unaware how her innocent evening was taken the wrong way."

"I think you may be right, Alan. That was one of the reasons why I scheduled this meeting. We wanted to express our sorrow for this situation. We think you've handled it the best you can with Priscilla."

"Thank you, sir. I try my best."

Alan was relieved but he had a feeling that Mr. Hodge had more to discuss. He waited for Mr. Hodge to continue.

"That wasn't the only reason I arranged this meeting. There was something else I wanted to ask you."

"Certainly."

Mr. Hodge paused a moment, then looked penetratingly at Alan.

Alan got an ominous feeling.

"As you know, it has been kept confidential what product we decided to invest in in South America, but you would know which one it was if you were involved in the 'idea' stage."

"Excuse me?"

"I'm asking you what commodity we were initially deciding to consider investing in."

Alan was paralyzed. He frantically tried to recall words from the pages of the proposal he had flipped through, but nothing came to mind. He was caught in his own trap.

"I'm sorry, Mr. Hodge, I'm embarrassed to say that I'm drawing a blank on the specifics. I had only thought about expansion to Latin America. Phil, as I mentioned, had done the groundwork. It was over a year ago."

Mr. Hodge leaned forward. "Are you sure? I think it's one of those ideas that a person would never forget – even if you were only on the team in the initial stages."

Mr. Hodge lowered his voice. "I was also disappointed when Priscilla told me the other day that you had asked her to talk to me about Phil. The only conclusion I can now reach is that if you don't know the commodity, and you wanted my daughter to damage Phil in my eyes, that you were trying to sabotage Phil's project."

"I think there is some misunderstanding," Alan stammered. "I can explain."

Mr. Hodge waited, but Alan could find nothing to say.

Mr. Hodge sighed heavily. "The commodity is oil. If you weren't my son-in-law, I would fire you."

"Yes, sir."

Alan's voice was barely a whisper as he spoke. He considered putting out his hand for a shake as a professional gesture, but Mr. Hodge had turned away. The meeting was over.

Alan left the office. The end of their meeting had not been what he had expected – he had never seen it coming. Priscilla had clearly sought revenge for the marriage she was now locked into 'for better or worse'. He should have known that she would want the last word.

It didn't matter. He was in no position now to find the answer. He may still have a job, but he knew he would never be promoted again, never have the boss's ear for important decisions in the company.

He had failed Mr. Hodge – a man of impeccable character, a man who had become successful without compromising his values, a man who would not tolerate a lie from anyone.

As he walked through the secretarial area, he saw Phil enter.

"Mr. Hodge will see you in a moment, Mr. Lawrence," Lillian said.

Alan lowered his eyes in order to avoid Phil's stare.

Was is just a coincidence that Phil had an appointment to see Mr. Hodge, or was it fate that they had crossed paths at the lowest moment of Alan's career?

Chapter Eighty - One

The hallway clock struck eight o'clock and Elizabeth decided to awaken Stephen.

She had gotten up at six-thirty, when the first pangs of labor had woken her. The doctor had forewarned her that until the contractions were twenty minutes apart there was no need for action. For the last hour and a half the contractions had gradually grown closer, from forty-five minutes to the magic number of twenty. It was time to wake Steven.

Elizabeth rose carefully from the living room sofa, where she had been trying to get comfortable. She was not due for another three weeks, but the doctor had said that after thirty-six weeks, be prepared.

Walking upstairs to their bedroom, she gently turned the doorknob and peeked in.

Stephen's eyes flew open. "You're up early! I thought you said you wanted to sleep in this morning."

"I wanted to, but it's hard to sleep when labor contractions keep waking you up."

"Contractions? You mean you're in labor? But you're not due for another three weeks."

"I know, but apparently this baby has his or her own plans. Do you think it's too early to call Uncle Paul and Dolly?"

Stephen grinned as he spoke. "Like hell it isn't! We're having a baby and they're our taxi to the hospital!"

Steven was very much on the mend, but driving a car was not to be in the cards for a while.

Elizabeth reached for the phone but Stephen waved her away. "I can call while you get dressed."

Stephen pulled the phone onto the bed with his right hand.

Elizabeth thanked God time and again that Stephen's paralysis was not on his right side, his dominant side.

"Good morning! Do you and Paul have a busy day planned on this lazy Saturday?"

Elizabeth could hear Dolly's voice on the other end. "Not really – just some errands, maybe go to lunch later. Why?"

Stephen threw a wink at Elizabeth. "You wouldn't want to drop Elizabeth and me by the hospital on the way to lunch, would you?"

"Elizabeth's in labor? She's going to have the baby *today*?"

"She is, although if you two don't get over here, she might just have to have the baby at home – like in the old days."

Dolly screeched and Elizabeth and Stephen laughed.

Stephen hung up and reached for Elizabeth's hand.

"Are you nervous?"

"A little – okay, a lot, but everyone has told me that as soon as the baby is born, I'll feel wonderful and it will be all worth it."

"That's a good thought to hold. Whether it's a boy or girl, I'm going to love that infant as much as I love their mother."

The next few hours were a whirlwind. Dolly and Paul were at the door in twenty minutes and they helped both Elizabeth and Stephen into Paul's Studebaker.

"I feel like we're an elderly couple," Stephen teased.

Only hours later, at St. Margaret's Hospital in Dorchester, the doctor removed his scrub mask and announced to Elizabeth with a wide grin, "It's a girl!"

The pink-faced infant was swaddled and placed in Elizabeth's arms. Elizabeth was mesmerized by the dark eyes that stared back at her. Her little arms were pressed close to her chest as she let out a squall.

The nurse laughed. "Haven't seen an infant who greeted their mother any other way!"

Another nurse stood at the door to Elizabeth's hospital room. "Is it all right if Mr. Wright comes in now?"

"Please!"

She could hear the squeak of Steven's wheelchair as he approached. When he entered the room, his face lit up.

Steven bent to kiss her and then peered into the bundle she held in his arms. "She's as beautiful as her mother!"

A knock at the door interrupted their conversation. "Hey there, do you mind if we take a look?"

Stephen answered. "Of course not! Forgive us our bad manners. It's not every day you have a baby."

Dolly leaned over to give Elizabeth a hug, then Elizabeth propped up the baby in order to give them a better look.

Dolly bent down to give the infant a kiss on the cheek and tousled her baby-soft hair. "Have you decided what you're going to name her?"

Stephen spoke softly. "Yes. She will be named Rose in honor of Elizabeth's Grandma, and in honor of Grandpa's beloved roses, and Catherine will be her middle name, which was my mother's name."

Dolly clapped her hands. "It's perfect! What else could you have possibly have named her? We're so happy for you!" Turning to Paul she clasped her hand in his. "I guess we'll have to start thinking about some baby names."

Elizabeth squealed. "What? You're expecting? Uncle Paul! Dolly! I'm so happy for both of you!"

Stephen stuck out his hand to shake Paul's. "It sure didn't take you long! Congratulations!" He kissed Dolly on the cheek as Elizabeth waved Paul towards her for a hug.

Paul grinned. "Thank you, although I feel as if I could be old enough to be the grandfather."

Dolly protested. "We'll have none of that. You may have the wisdom of a grandfather, but you'll still have the dashing good looks of a new father for years to come."

"Wow…" Stephen said. "Your baby will be Elizabeth's cousin! And what will your baby be to Rose…a first cousin once removed? A second cousin?"

"Best friends," said Dolly.

Rose gurgled.

"Well look at that," Stephen said. "Rose seems to agree."

Elizabeth was overwhelmed with joy. Rose would have Hannah and now Dolly and Paul's little one to grow up with. Their own little Rose would surely grow and bloom. Grandpa would have been so proud.

Epilogue
May, 1952 – five years later

 "Strike two," the umpire roared.

The crowd leaned forward in their seats, anticipating the next throw.

"Strike three! Yer out," came the call.

With a sigh of relief, the crowd sank back into their seats. It was the end of the first inning between the Boston Braves and the New York Giants at The Beehive, the nickname used for the Braves' Field in South Boston.

Two men sitting a dozen rows behind home plate sat casually observing it all. Alan had appreciated Neil's invitation to see the Braves' doubleheader. Alan had no right to such a good friend, he thought. Neil Summersby was cut from the same cloth as Mr. Hodge.

"At least we're off to a good start," Neil said. "The Braves had a win and a loss with the Giants in their double header back in April, so we'll see what happens today."

Neil and Alan turned when they heard the balding, portly man seated next to them say to no one in particular, "Say! Isn't that the famous Boston novelist?"

Alan and Neil followed his gaze to the pretty, dark-haired woman making her way towards an empty cluster of seats about six rows in front of them. Following her was a large group of people. Alan immediately recognized Elizabeth and Stephen, Paul Keene and his wife Dolly, and Phil and Betty. All of them had young children with them.

Elizabeth held the hand of a little girl and a little boy in each hand. Both had dark brown hair and they resembled their parents. He also noticed that Elizabeth was expecting again. Apparently, Stephen's illness had not inhibited them from enlarging their family.

Alan recognized Paul and Dolly's little girl, Amanda. He often saw her zooming up and down the sidewalk in front of their brownstone apartments, with one or both parents close behind. Amanda was the spitting image of her mother, with curly blond hair. In front of him the little girl was ordering everyone where to sit.

He could hear Dolly's voice above the crowd. "Amanda, stop being so bossy! People can decide which seat they want without your help!"

Phil and Betty had a young boy with them. Betty had left the company shortly before she and Phil were married, and Phil had left Hodge's shortly after that.

Alan knew that Mr. Hodge had tried to persuade Phil to stay, but Phil had been wooed by a larger investment firm where, Alan knew from office talk, he'd moved up quickly.

Alan, on the other hand, was in the same position he'd been in for the past five years. He'd considered looking for a job elsewhere, but knew he could not count on a good recommendation from Mr. Hodge or anyone else at the firm.

With the group was also another couple that Alan did not recognize. They had a girl who looked to be the same age as Amanda.

Amanda pulled on the woman's sleeve. "Aunt Mary Francis, can Hannah sit next to me?"

The tall, slender woman looked affectionately at the girl. "Of course, Amanda!"

Stephen was the last to be seated because he walked with crutches. His right leg looked pretty steady, but his left leg dragged behind him. His little boy climbed up on his lap, wound his arms around his neck, and kissed him on the cheek.

Alan was riveted. A moment like that could have been his life if he and Priscilla had a child.

A few years earlier, Priscilla had been 'late.' She had been very angry until she found out it had been a false alarm.

Alan had known, then, that there was no mistake regarding how she truly felt about being a mother.

After that, Alan let the subject drop, considering it a blessing in disguise. He couldn't fathom how she could have transformed into a loving, nurturing mother.

Witnessing such a tender moment now, between Stephen Wright and his son, caused him grief.

The man next to Neil repositioned himself more comfortably as he talked. "My wife is disappointed that she won't be reading any more new books by her unless she changes her mind. My wife said this author is giving up writing for now to take care of her growing family."

Alan felt Neil look sideways at him to see how he was reacting to the man's comments.

The balding man laughed. "She sure has a big enough group with her – must be all family! I don't remember her name – it's just that pretty face that's on the jacket cover that caught my eye."

Neil Summersby supplied the answer. "Elizabeth Wright."

"Oh, yeah! 'Petals in the Sand.' Everyone's talking about her newest book."

Alan knew that Elizabeth's latest book had done well. It had just hit the best seller list.

"Hot dogs," called the vendor who passed by them, hawking his wares. "Peanuts! Hot dogs," he repeated. "Get yer hot dogs here!"

"Want a hotdog?" Neil asked.

"No thanks."

Alan's eyes were still fixated on Elizabeth and Stephen, who had his right arm resting along the back of her chair. "I'm not hungry."

It was true that he was not hungry. He thought back on Elizabeth's words to him all those years ago and her quest for love.

Alan had always been up front about his quest for status. And he'd gotten that with Priscilla, along with plenty of unwanted notoriety.

In the meantime, Stephen Wright had received what Alan had not: a loving wife and now children who adored him.

In spite of the fact that he was sitting in a baseball park, surrounded by thousands of people, he felt very alone.